Trevaylor

"Margaret Ryding has created in Rona a heroine as spirited and feisty as the times in which she lived. Elizabethan Cornwall springs to life in the pages of a novel which weaves fact and fiction so surely that we never see the join. The author has clearly done her research so skilfully that we ask ourselves whether Rona's astonishing story might really be true? It is a story rich in adventure and excitement but it also tells of a love which defied all odds and prevailed against all adversity: a love story set against the magical landscape of West Cornwall which Margaret Ryding describes with the sensitivity and sureness of touch it deserves."
Melville Jones, playwright

Margaret Ryding started to tell stories in the time-honoured way of word of mouth - bedtime stories, car stories, wet day stories -until, the family grown up, there was time to write them down. Then came *Trevaylor* written during a long summer spent staying at the Manor of Trevaylor and in Marazion. It is the result of many years' research which the author completed while she was living in Cornwall.

For Joseph and Anna

Trevaylor

by

Margaret Ryding

HILO

A CIP catalogue record for this book is available
from the British Library

ISBN 0 9531221 0 7

Typeset by Amolibros, Watchet, Somerset

Printed and bound by Professional Book Supplies,
Oxford

BOOK I

CHAPTER I

The girl was tossed like a winter leaf, hither and thither, in her flight across the moor. For hours she had struggled forward, regardless of tracks and direction, only keeping the wind at her back as she struck south and away from her pursuers.

Only to get away...away. At first she had headed for Madron, but the storm had blotted out daylight early and she had lost sight of paths and trails. She had lost, too, the little bundle of possessions seized up as she escaped; now, she had only the clothes she wore and the cross that hung on a fine gold chain around her neck. Through long hours she had clung to the cross with one hand, reaching forward in the dark, with the other. But now she was down, imprisoned in pain and fear—sobbing.

It was not until the rain came that Rona wept. The rain joined the darkness: blinding drops, driven like hailstones by the rising gale, dashed against her, chilling her to the bone. The skirts that had blown before her as she fled, were suddenly heavy, clinging. She stumbled. Many times she had staggered and tripped, but now she crashed to the ground and lay, finished. The rain beat down upon her back and the sobs, wrenched out of her throat, were snatched unheard by the savage gusts that leapt over the cliffs and scoured the lonely moor.

Since the horror of the afternoon, her heart had been paralysed, her mind occupied only with flight. Now she saw with dreadful clarity the moment of her father's death—killed by Tranthem's sword; felt again the shock that had propelled her feet through heather and furze, over wet ditches and stony banks; long after they were exhausted...long after she was lost.

1

Even so, benighted, orphaned and alone, her tears were not of mourning—not yet. As she lay gasping, it was furious anger that saved her reason; and, perhaps, her life: anger, the only emotion one dares to feel when all else holds too much grief. So it was the heather root that tripped her that was the object of her dismay; and the battering gale—and Tranthem.

The Vernal Equinox was blowing out of the North and across the backbone of rock—ancient granite, killas and quartz—that probes into the sea like a sword in defence of England's softer pastures. Cornwall was at its most stark on the night of March the Twentieth in 1576.

Cornwall—Kernow—the Frontier was still in the grip of a long winter. Perhaps there was a prick of green, here and there, in sheltered hedgerows; new growth had given promise of winter's end in one mild week in February, but the cold had closed in again and folk could not remember so late a Spring. On the spine of Land's End, the bare stalks of heather were blackened by the salty winds that streamed in from the sea; the gorse was late and few of last year's leaves were left lodged in last year's hollows. And, like a leaf, Rona was caught and, with her face to the ground, wept.

Rona Laity was seventeen. Born in the first year of the reign of Queen Elizabeth, she had lived all her life in the parish of Morvah—writ on the maps as Mornath. The Laity land lay above and to the west of Porthmeor Cove; the low built farmhouse scarcely higher than the rim of the cliff. The land sloped down, inland, before rising steeply to the moor. The pastures, some two furlongs wide, extended east and west for about a mile. It was bound by the sea to the north, by the moor to the south, by a tenant of the Crown to the west and by Squire Tranthem to the east.

Until her sixteenth birthday, her life had been undisturbed by any crisis or disaster. The troubled times of old King Henry's reign, which set England and the Vatican by the ears, had few echoes in the Penwith Hundred and none at all on Laity's farm. Her Uncle Jacques, a Benedictine Brother, occasionally appeared suddenly and, as suddenly, disappeared; but, latterly, even these unexplained visits ended and only the natural events of growing up and the change of seasons marked her years.

Then, on that day, her birthday, in the bright sunlight of a September afternoon, she went with her mother to gather blackberries. The soft, silken wind still had the warmth of the summer, yet it was unmistakably autumn. The air was loaded with scents, the ripe scents of fruit and heather honey, stubble baked by the sun, the cider press and all the natural yeasts of autumn days. Mother and daughter wandered along the lane in search of the abundant fruits. They called it the lane: it was really no more than a rough track that linked the farms and villages of the north coast. Where it bounded Samuel Laity's land, he had lined it with dry stone walling—to prevent his stock from straying and loose stones from the moor from washing down and into his yard. The brambles were well established in these walls, thriving on the reflected warmth and lifting their arched fronds over the supporting stonework.

Marie Laity saw some large and glossy berries on the far side just out of reach. Instead of walking back, going through the gate and approaching from the other side, she climbed part way up the wall and leaned over. Ill balanced and at full stretch, she lost her toe-hold and slithered down to the ground, deeply grazing her ankle as she went.

"Sacré coeur d'Dieu." She swore in French—and then crossed herself in silent apology.

They wrapped a kerchief around the wound and went on picking. Many times, Rona straightened up to stare at the familiar scene, to breathe in the pure air and feel the careless heat of the sun upon her cheeks; and when, with full baskets, and purple fingers, they returned to the farmhouse, it was with deep content. They spent the evening together, making pies and jellies and setting the remainder of their harvest for wine. When Samuel came in from the fields, he sniffed the air: "'Tis better'n incense. Better to God's nose as well, I reckon." He gave his daughter a roll of silk cloth, for a gown, with a piece of lace, extra, for a collar; and sixteen groats—one for each year of her life. It was a happy birthday.

But Marie Laity had hurt herself more than she knew. An infection had entered into her cut and within twenty four hours her wound flamed;. Saint Anthony's fire flowed up her leg like a red tide and no amount of poulticing with hot bread stayed the poison. She died in sweating, shivering surprise and the little family went about in stunned disbelief.

Samuel, dogged and unsmiling, performed the essential duties of a farmer; and, in silence, Rona slipped into the role of managing the household. They moved as puppets—as if holding their breath, waiting for something to pass; and the small community who worked for them, missed the gentle French lady who had been their Mistress. There was none to comfort them and Rona hid her distress in a flurry of work; as if she expected her mother to reappear and must not disappoint her. She worked with a fierce energy that served to exhaust her and to leave little time for tears.

And she did well enough. Marie had been a talented woman and a good teacher. She had taught her daughter more than most girls knew in those years of grace.

CHAPTER II

It had been a strange match: sturdy Cornish Samuel, a Protestant and scarce able to write his name; and Marie Benhault.

Marie was the daughter of a French sea captain who had once himself wooed a Cornish maid and carried her back to Brittany. The Benhaults had three children: two boys, Jacques and André, with Marie in between. They would have been brought up in the tiny port of Pontaubault had not their sailor father disappeared.

He sailed away on a routine voyage, and was never seen again. Though this was commonplace in fishing and trading communities, where relatives closed ranks to help the bereaved, it was particularly difficult for the young foreign widow—for widow surely she was: there had been storms enough to sink their boat three times over—Cornish Anne was all alone. After a struggle, she gladly accepted the intervention of her father-in-law Grandpère Benhault. He was a lay associate of the brothers of Mont St Michel; boatman, ferryman, lobster catcher, he was caretaker of the boathouse and had daily contact with the Brothers. Promising the boys to the Order, he had little difficulty in persuading the monks to give all three children lessons in reading, writing and scripture. "If you do not," he said gruffly to the Abbé, "the girl too, they will all go to the godless country across the water, where the king is killing all the faithful. And," he added grimly, "you will have to catch your own 'homards.'" Appealing thus to their spiritual consciences and physical well-being, he craftily achieved a good education for his grandchildren and got them out from under his wife's feet.

Thus it was that Marie learned to read and to speak in Latin as well as in her father's tongue and her mother's English. Only Jacques became a Brother and, because of his understanding of English, he was sent to discover the plight of the Brothers who had been driven out of their Monastery on St. Michael's Mount in the Bay of Marazion. Marie begged him to take her with him—"to find our English relations"—and to escape from the stifling piety of her grandparents in a village dominated by monks. On one of his visits to the Mount, Brother Jacques found cousins in Paul, up on the hill behind the Bay; and on his third trip he took his sister with him, with messages from their mother to the friends of her childhood.

Marie did not stay long in Paul. Another cousin, married to a potter in Gulval, invited her to lodge with them. They were nearer the Mount and could see it from their cottage window. Although the old king was dead and the boy, Edward, was weak upon the throne, there were still no Brethren returned to the Mount.

They were scattered: some working as labourers; some begging—mendicant as Augustinians; some in plain graves. With Catholic Mary threatening the throne the Benedictines thought to establish another, more secret, House inland. Brother Jacques tried to rally the remnants of the Order and to get the work started. But before Marie's visit ended, the sickly boy king died; Protestants did not know what would befall them, and the ship that should have taken Marie back to France was overcharged: full of frightened passengers withdrawing to the Continent until they could see what the new Queen would do. "Don'ee fret, my lover; Betsy'll look arter 'ee; for the sake o' sweet Annie. 'Twill be like having a darter o' my own, and the Lord knows I've dreamed o' that long nuff."

Marie stayed. She helped the Potter as well as Betsy—travelling with him to market and minding the stall. On a trip to Marazion, she met with Samuel Laity.

6

He was coming to find a calf and she, with ribbons in her hair, was selling pots with Cousin Betsy. He wanted a new cooler and some shallow bowls for his cream. With his eyes lowered, counting his money, he approached the stall. When he looked up, he found himself looking into the brightest, merriest, prettiest face he had ever imagined. The girl's eyes sparkled, her curls danced, and, when she spoke, her voice enchanted him.

"Sam'l Laity, be 'ee struck dumb? What do 'ee want?" Betsy chuckled. "An' if it be Marie, ee'd best take the soft look off 'ee face. Er don' want a dolt. But speak slow, mind. Er be more French'n Cornish yet."

But Samuel never lost that soft look. He swept Marie into his life on a tide of love that never ebbed. On a flood tide of incredulous devotion, he carried her into the farmhouse that crouched behind the cliffs in the north of the county; where the summer sunsets were like the gates of heaven.

It was completely different from anything she had known before She loved the wildness and the raging sea that swirled and foamed at the foot of the cliffs. She loved the freedom, so different from the restrictions imposed by the monks—so many monks. They had seemed to lurk around every corner with their commands and demands and admonitions. "Always," she said to Samuel, "I 'ave to confess somsing. Often I do not know what to confess. Zen zay say: 'impure—'ow you say?—pensées. Impure pensées, you cannot live wizout impure pensées, zay say. Eh bien, perhaps ze monks cannot; but I can—I can live very well wizout zinkings I do not know about. Then it is Saint Zis and Saint Zat! Oh, Samuel, I say my prayers straight to the Bon Dieu. Wizout the Saints to say for me. Le Bon Dieu—Il est partout."

Most of all she loved Samuel for his fierce

protectiveness. Of her father, she had no recollection; her grandfather was generations away and the monks—they were "absent-minded". Monks, she said, were all soul and body. A quarter of the time they were embracing matters spirituelles; three quarters of the time they were rejecting matters physical. "Ze mind— l'intelligence—'as no part. Jacques, I love, but 'e 'as forgotten how to zink."

They were married at Christmas: a little over a month after the death of Queen Mary: and Rona, their first born, was safely delivered in September of the following year. She was baptised, according to Protestant rites, in Morvah Parish Church. And Brother Jacques did it again, in Latin, on his next visit—just to be sure. There were two more children: but one died in childbirth and the other lived only to his third year. Then there were no more and Rona was the apple of their eyes.

She grew up in the farm on the clifftop, protected by the love of her parents; and by the warm thick walled house built by her forefathers and added to by generations of Laitys. It was built of stone, stone roofed, and well windowed. It soaked up all the sun God sent; and, with Marie as Mistress, seemed to hold it there. She brought a lightness and a sheen to the age-old and uncompromising simplicity of the place; and with her skill as a needlewoman, she curtained the windows and the beds with a brightness they had never known before. She made candles, of beeswax and tallow; and soap; and, beside her, Rona learned the arts and crafts of husbandry and housekeeping. By the time she was sixteen, she could milk the cows and make the cheese and butter; she could bake loaves and saffron cake; could salt down beef and make preserves. Her stitchery was nearly as good as Marie's and, best of all, she

8

enjoyed all these pursuits with a pride that quite took away the drudgery. She shared her lessons and her childhood play with Dorothy Bugel, the widowed cowman's daughter. The two little girls worked and played together, and when all their toil was done, Marie read to them in the parlour by the cliff. She was an artist too, and cut quills and mixed dyes and made pictures.

There was little to read in the country districts, and nothing for children. So Marie and the girls made up stories and wrote them down. There was one about a gull that carried a pearl in its beak. The pearl could only be dropped when the gull found a flawless maiden. "Et le pauvre oiseau...il est presqu' mort du faim." Another told of a gypsy lad who wanted to go to France. A French trader promised to take him if he would first learn to bake—his village lacked a baker—when he had learned to bake, the trader said he must also know how to fish; then to turn wood; to make pots...and so on. So the crafts and the language of those crafts were woven into the tale, and, by telling it in English and in French, the children got a working knowledge of both languages. Clem Bugel looked on in amazement; "'Tis all a great mystery," said he, vowing that there was nothing he would not do for his Master and the lady who was like a mother to his girl.

Bugel's cottage was built alongside the farmhouse, with but a small space between. Behind it and reaching back towards the cliff edge, was a vast barn; along the edge was the long low cowshed; windowless to the north and clay-lined, it extended the whole width of the farmstead and was designed to break the force of the wind. The fourth side was stabling, pigsties and fowl

9

houses, all enclosing the yard that lay in the lee of these shelters. There was one gap, wide as a field gate, to give access to the pastures; and even this gap was shielded by a curtain wall. The whole was like a fortified camp—the enemy, the wind.

The Laity land yielded good grass, enough for grazing and for hay. In the mild wet climate, it often gave two crops and Samuel was able to winter more beasts than many of his neighbours. Their main livelihood was in their dairy herd—as their name implied—but it was under the ground that their true wealth lay. Wealth with all its treachery.

Samuel knew about the mineral deposits under his feet; he could see the crystals sparkling on the cellar floor and in the walls of the well; but he was a farmer, first and last, as his fathers were before him; he was not interested in chewing up his land in search of copper or tin.

"I be no mole," he would say. "We do well 'nuff wi God's good grass."

CHAPTER III

Squire Tranthem, to the east, had no time for God, nor for His good grass. He was after minerals and he coveted Laity's land. He even crossed his neighbour's boundary by burrowing underground "to see with his own eyes". It became an obsession with him and he tried every ruse and bribe to secure Laity's strip of coast for himself.

Pretending to Protestantism in Henry's reign, he got himself appointed Constable, hoping thereby, to trick Laity on some point of law. During Queen Mary's time, there was no Catholic more ardent and devout. In that role, he tried to discredit Samuel for his Protestant beliefs. But Samuel and Marie were untroubled, kept their counsel and prospered as the years went by. Rona was taught to worship God in her own way: "Partout.Wi Kings and Queens at odds wi' God and the Pope, 'tis best to believe in private."

Brother Jacques was a frequent visitor during Queen Mary's five years, but with Elizabeth in power, he returned to Mont St Michel. His visits were infrequent, quick and secret. He brought solace to the Brothers, administered Mass here and there, and withdrew discreetly before, as he believed, his presence would be noticed. He reckoned without Tranthem. In fact, his comings and goings were duly noted; and Tranthem laid his plans.

One day, early in March 1576, the news came for which he had been waiting: Brother Jacques was in the Penwith Hundred. Quoting the Act of Uniformity, as if it were a call to arms, he summoned his troop and ordered them to locate the recusant monk and then to raise a hue and cry. This was to be done in such a way and from such a quarter that he would be driven to the north coast. "For he will surely go to ground in his brother-in-law's house, with all other pathways blocked." Tranthem spat on his hands. "Then we shall have them—Priest and Farmer—both. I care not for the Holy Brother; Archbishop Parker can have him for his sport; but Laity—ha!—he shall be committed to Bodmin for harbouring the Queen's enemy." He ran his tongue round his teeth, savouring the very idea. "Don'ee catch up wi' him, mind; it be the farmer I be arter." He sent them off, like beaters in the chase, his son at their head. "There's few come out of Bodmin jail alive, so there's an arrangement easy made. In my great good-heartedness I'll marry the girl to my son. And then—then there'll be none to stand between me and Laity's ores."

The plan worked well. The hue and cry was just loud enough to reach Jacques' ears and cut him off from his port of entry. He determined to go to Samuel for help. He meant to go, anyway, for he had not seen them since getting word of his sister's death. It did not occur to the gentle man of God that he would be leading his pursuers to the farm. He believed himself to be invisible, wrapped in a mantle of God's will. It was fortunate for him that Samuel was not so credulous.

But, for all he was cautious, Samuel made his brother-in-law welcome, for Marie's sake. "She would have folded him in safety," he muttered; but lost no time in shouting for Bugel. "Get the boat out and to the foot of the cliff, below the path." Then to Jacques, "Come thee in and greet thy niece—but don'ee linger over't. They be hard on your heels."

"Here? Mon Dieu. Surely you are among friends? Non?"

"Ah, Jacques, thee be mad to come. If all who serve the lord be such fools as 'ee, heaven help them—for heaven 'lone will help the Lord."

"Tell me of Marie's passing."

"She be gone—that's enough. An' ee'll be gone along o' she, if 'ee don' make haste. Take food—put bread in a cloth, Rona—and into the cellar wi' thee."

Rona put some of the food together for her uncle: bread, cheese, a pasty: and opened up the flagstone in the kitchen floor, that he might slip into the cellar at the first sound of the strangers.

From the cellars, hewn out of the bed rock, a passage led to the cliff-face. It widened out to form a shallow cave, unseen from below, and opened onto a ledge beneath an overhang; there Samuel kept a quantity of dry furze. On stormy nights, when the north was a lee shore, he and Bugel would light the furze for a warning. On such nights, men and furze would likely be blown off the top of the cliff; the ledge was better.

12

For ten years the two men had performed this rite; ever since a tempest that had wrecked a good ship on their own cove. On the morning after, they had found men, women and little children lying like rag dolls smashed and dead upon the rocks. Pathetic belongings littered the tideline; there had been not one survivor.

Quickly, Rona told Jacques of the passage and of the path that twisted down from the ledge. But her uncle was silent, inattentive, deep in thought—as if he were making up his mind about something quite else...He stared at the plate of meat that she set before him; then he stared at her, searchingly. "My niece," he said in a whisper, "I must trust you. I am charged with carrying one of our treasures to safety. See."

From under his habit, he brought a marvellous wrought cross—a pectoral cross on a fine gold chain. "We call it the Cross of Cornwall. It is fashioned from Cornish gold and Cornish amethyst; it is as old as the first Chapel on the Mount. Take it." He thrust it into her hands. "Guard it—and if I get safe away, I will return for it. It must go to the Father House where it will be out of reach of Matthew Parker's greedy hands. If I am caught...remember it belongs to God and to Cornwall—not to the Queen's Archbishop."

The girl looked with wonder and amazement at the lovely thing. "But uncle J...shh, listen."

"What's that?"

"Horsemen—quick."

He snatched up his bundle and scrambled, undignified into the hole that yawned in the kitchen floor. Rona dragged the stone across, thankful she had lit the lamp below, before preparing the food. "Dust—dry dust," she muttered, running outside for a handful from the eaves, where the rain did not reach. She strewed the pale earth over and around the stone and pulled the table over it. She sat down in front of the meal as if it were her own. The cross lay beside the plate. At the sound of approaching footsteps, she slipped it round her neck and under her bodice; and waited—trembling.

It was but a solitary rider on private business. He begged water for his horse and soon pressed on. All unknowing—just by being there—the stranger saved the life of the fleeing priest—and cost another.

For Tranthem's troop were very close; had had to bide their time until the coast was clear; and waiting, they were angered.

Rona could not sit still, nor compose herself enough to stay alone in the house. She went out in search of her father.

CHAPTER IV

As she lay exhausted on the moor, it seemed unbelievable that only a few hours had passed since she went to the back door to look for Samuel.

There she had found Dorothy Bugel, milking stool in hand and fresh scrubbed pails beside, waiting for the cows. And, beyond the gate, she saw her father, ho-ing and hupp-ing as he drove them in for milking.

The sun had been a red ball in the sky, already lowering into the band of mist on the horizon and tracking a red-gold path across the sea. Recollection of that livid sunset, with black clouds gathering in the north—harbingers of the storm—stuck in her mind like claws. Black and red—Tranthem's cloak had been black—and his sword red.

A moment after waving to Samuel, she caught sight of the Squire. He was riding hell for leather with his rugged troop behind; and he was making for their gate. Quickly she prayed for the safety of Jacques and, taking a pail from Dorothy, to make the scene seem calm and natural, she stood by the door, quietly prepared for the evening chores.

The cows, heavy with milk and eager for the shelter of the yard, were jostling each other through the gate. Tranthem and his men were confused by the herd. They had to rein the horses in, check them, wheel around. One was thrown and Tranthem, ever concerned for himself, took care to keep at least one of his men between his horse and the thronging beasts.

Dorothy gave a nervous high pitched laugh when she saw that the Squire was afraid. "'Tis a fine farmer that's afeared o' cows." Rona hushed her; but he had heard and was infuriated. Without a word to Laity, he ordered his men to enter by the front of the house; to search it and the barns without delay nor any respect for property, and to meet him in the yard,

Samuel looked across at his daughter and she smiled: "Le Colomb s'envoi," she said, briefly shifting her gaze to the cliff. Her father nodded and went on driving the cows. He packed them into the gateway so tight that Tranthem had to dismount and climb the wall.

It did his temper no good; he waited, fuming, slashing at his riding boots with a short whip. He took no notice of the girls but stared at the house impatiently. Inside, they could hear the men scurrying from room to room; and from the barns, heard other men charging about with drawn swords. One by one they appeared in the yard, breathlessly, to declare that they had found nothing—no one. No amount of thumping at panelling, nor pulling at hangings had revealed Brother Jacques. Like a shadow, he had vanished—from under their very noses.

In fact, he had lost no time in clambering down the tortuous path that descended steeply, ledge by ledge, to the cove beneath the cliff. There met by Hal Bugel, brother to the stockman, he had embarked into a small fishing boat and made off with all speed to the shelter of the next headland. Then, hid from view, they waited for the light to fade, and with the ebb under them, made good time, west by south, to Sennen, where Jacques transhipped into an Irish frigate bound for Ireland and thence to France.

But all that the party at the farm knew was that the bird had flown. The Laitys thanked God and the Squire cursed the Devil.

Angered by his failure and loss of dignity, he turned furiously upon the two girls. Rona wore a secret smile, and Dorothy half afraid, was still giggling stupidly.

"I'll wipe the grins off your faces, you country fools," he snorted. "Perhaps your traitor father will have something to tell rather than see my sword mar you beauty."

Dorothy shrank behind Rona, but she retorted, "Nay, Sir, for what should he have to tell, who is no traitor? We have no quarrel with you, nor with the law, I b'lieve."

"Mistress Innocence," he spat, drawing his sword so that the blade glinted red in the sunset.

Samuel and Clem Bugel were thrusting through the cattle and Bugel, reaching his mistress first, interposed himself between her and the Squire's threat. "Don'ee touch un, Bully Constable. We be no traitors 'ere."

Tranthem had not thought to touch the girls, but Clem's insolence was the final straw to break his temper. He struck with the flat of his blade.

Laity, coming up fast, saw the blood spurting from the cowman's cheek. "Stay!" he cried. "Stop this. State your business, and hands off my man. I'll have the law on you for this."

He was near enough to grasp Tranthem's arm, which was his intent, when with a roar of rage, Tranthem spun round—and ran through the body of Samuel Laity.

Rona, holding her linen apron to Clem's cheek had heard the swish of the sword, heard the grunt, a groan, a gurgle; all masked by the horrified gasps of the bystanders. She whirled around and, again, saw Tranthem's sword—this time red with her father's blood; blood that dripped from the point onto the fallen figure. Samuel Laity was down.

She flew to him, dropping to her knees. He was clutching his tunic and his face wore a look of agony and dismay. Life was ebbing away and Samuel knew it. He tried to speak and his mouth emitted a croak and pink froth. The sword had punctured stomach and lung when Tranthem had turned to confront him. If anyone had looked at Tranthem's face they would have seen that fear had replaced anger; but all eyes were upon the dying man.

"Father." Rona clasped his hands as if she would hold him to life.

"Fly, my bird...my soul...fly to Abraham's Bosom...to the haven where I would be..." the whispered message faded. Rona nodded dumbly. She understood that this was an instruction—to go to her Uncle Nathaniel, Samuel's brother, who dwelt on the Helford River, on a creek named Abraham's Bosom: it was a haven for boats and Samuel saw it as her only safety. But she did not move. She looked fearfully at the Squire to see if he had recognised the whispers as a message; but he was thinking fast; cunning was following hard on the heels of fear.

Bugel took in the sinister scene. "I'll see Mistress Rona safe, Maaster." He knelt beside her, his bleeding cheek forgotten.

"Don' go, father, don'ee leave me. Stay...stay..." But Bugel shook his head and, supporting her, took her blooded hands from her father's coat to hold them in his own. She held onto his arm.

Then she was near torn in half: Tranthem, pulling himself together, seized the other arm, determined that she would go with him. He had not planned so drastic an action, but spilt blood cannot be un-spilt; he would make the most of it. He would bribe or silence the onlookers; and continue to press his accusations against Laity as a Papist's man. He would get rid of the cowman and carry off Rona. He would marry her off to his son and secure the land—by law. It had worked out excellently...yes, excellently.

"Let go, dolt; I have her," he commanded.

Dolt? Dolt? Bugel's subtle Cornish brain worked quickly. Dolt, was he? That might suit very well. He dropped Rona's arm and gaped foolishly. "Yaas, Maaster," he muttered thickly. "The man's a simpleton," growled Tranthem, "I'll deal with him later." He looked at Rona with a mixture of wariness and lust: "Thou shalt come with me."

"I shall not. Let me be. I must go to father. See what you have done."

"'Twas accident. I shall take you home. You shall be safe with me."

She wrenched her arm free and knelt again beside Samuel: "Father...Father..." But his eyes stared.

Bugel bent over her: "Gather some things quick...I shall help 'ee get away. 'Tain't safe...I shall see to the Master, never fear. An' I shall act stupid until they be gone. Come now Missy, 'tis supper time...Clem wants 'is paasty."

"You—girl," Tranthem pointed at the terrified Dorothy. "See to this man's cheek. Get ye to the pump." Then, turning to Rona, he said with false courtesy, "Fear not, Lady, you will be welcome in my house."

Sick and bewildered, she stumbled to her feet. "I'll get some things: night attire and my Bible."

"Ye'll do as ye are."

"I'm cold."

"Ye'll not be cold at the Manor."

"Never," shouted Clem. "Never let I catch 'ee letting the cows go unmilked. What be 'ee doing, Dolly? Leave I 'lone. Get 'ee into 'em. Tedden no time t'stan 'bout. What'd Maaster say?"

"Sure nuff," said Dorothy, catching on. "Master'll be arter I."

She was touched too, noted Tranthem with satisfaction.

Rona was swaying and trembling, wondering if all the world were mad. "I'm cold," she said again.

"Fetch a cloak. Get 'ee in with her." Tranthem nodded to one of his troop. "Five minutes by the clock."

Rona turned into the kitchen.

CHAPTER V

In the brief period since she had left it, the place had changed. Now it was just a house—any house—home had gone. The sweet familiarity of things well-loved had been replaced by the indifference of uncaring things. She stood in the darkening kitchen as if she were in a strange place, and the sense of loss was so sharp that it shook her out of her daze and into a realisation of her own danger. The flight began.

Tranthem's man came through the door and banged his head on the lintel. He cursed. "Make haste ye. Squire said five minutes."

She went through the house and up the wooden stair. The man followed and would have turned into the room with her, but by now her mind was working again—and with icy clarity. "In Christ's name," she said angrily, "cannot a maid change her clothes privily? Wait there." She pointed to the room across the landing.

"'Tis too dark—I'll stand by your door."

"Please yourself; I can hardly creep past you wherever ye are." She closed the door and bolted it. She flung a few possessions into her cloak and tied it into a bundle. Then she went to the window. Beside it lay a coiled rope. Her father had one in every upper chamber. After a fire scare some years before, Samuel had ridden to St. Ives, to the rope-walk, and bought enough for each window, with ring bolts for the walls. Rona opened the window noiselessly and threw the rope out. Her room faced the west and looked out along the lane, past Bugel's cottage. It was deserted; all Tranthem's men were in the yard.

The last of the colour left the sky and she threw out her bundle and let herself down. Hand over hand, her skirts in the way and fear in her heart. Her hands were very white in the grey twilight, and she tried not to remember the pallor in her father's face, as he gazed sightlessly in the darkening sky. Determination to avenge his death lent courage to her spirit and cunning to her movements. Escape she would.

Below the window was a strip of grass and then a low wall that separated the garden from Bugel's yard. There stood a large manger. With a quick look to the left and the right, Rona darted over the wall and into the shadow of the manger.

The five minutes was up, she could hear the man above banging and thumping on her door. He raised such a hullabaloo that she did not hear Clem snaking along in the grass to her side.

"Get 'ee to Madron—to my sister Nell. I'll get word to your Uncle Nat someways. Know 'ee the road?"

She nodded: "'Bout a mile 'long the lane, then left across the moor."

"Be 'ee afeared?"

"More afeared of staying." She tried to sound brave. "Take care of yourself, Clem—and Dorothy."

"And o' the farm, if un allows it. Make haste, my lady, God go wi' 'ee."

Her guard thundered down the stairs and burst into the yard.

"Go now. Leave that varmint to I."

Bugel wriggled off and reappeared from behind the pigsties. Waving a stick and roaring like a bull he charged across the yard. "Where be un? Where be bully bastard who slashed I? I'll get un." The troop gathered around Tranthem—and Rona slipped like a shadow, from the manger to the wall that bordered the lane. She threw her bundle over and scrambled after it. Dropping onto her hands and knees she paused to listen, just for a second; then she ran.

She was young, strong, and full of alarm; she ran, without stopping, until half a mile was put between her and the horror. She ran into the gathering dusk; away from her home and all she knew, until cramp and breathlessness sent her reeling against a boulder. She took in great shuddering breaths, with her back to the wind, watching her hair and her skirts blowing out in front of her. In spite of the pain in her chest and her aching legs, she had a curious feeling of detachment: she felt as if she were watching some drama or hearing a story: a girl was being chased; was fleeing for her life; the girl must listen for pursuers...

So Rona listened. It was a nightmare—soon she would wake; and, in the meantime, she must listen. Her breathing became regular again, some of the sweat dried on her brow...then she heard them.

Horsemen. Their hoofbeats approaching fast, were borne to her ears on the rising gale. She looked round wildly and leapt off the lane into the shelter of a rocky outcrop. There, crouching low, she heard them thunder by; heard the snorting breath of the horses; and smelled the smell of their passing.

Would they stay on the lane or take the track to Madron? She dared not risk either way. All that was left for her was to strike off across the moor—the lonely wild moor—forbidden to her by her parents, avoided by all sane men, except in bright day.

With every step she took, the wind grew stronger, noisier. Black clouds hurried before it, banking and jostling, blotting out the light. Rona undid her bundle and put on the cloak. Fastening the clasp at her neck, she touched the chain and remembered the precious cross; and it comforted her. But there was no other comfort. It was cold and there was the smell of rain. She knew roughly the direction in which the village of St Madron lay; she had been there before; but only by the familiar track. Although she had known the moor all her life and it had been her playground, she had never left the acknowledged paths, trodden by the feet of centuries.

They were paths that criss-crossed the heather, finding dry land and easy gradients; worn thin by countless generations; by men and women as far back as the ancient Stone Ages: they led to and fro, linking the tiny settlements that crowned the heights with quoits and henges; where the little people worshipped the Gods of weather and seasons. These tracks were more than just paths from place to place; following proven ground, in a terrain pitted with bogs and crevices, they were credited with magical powers. Bocca-dhu—the Black Spirit—kept away from the paths; he waited to snatch the traveller who strayed from the true ways.

Now Rona was straying and the daylight was nearly gone. She remembered her parents' warnings and the stories told by peddlers and old wives, and she was afraid. She could not see the rank tufts of grass that marked the bogs, nor the moss-slimed stones that lined

22

the water-courses. The only certainty was that the wind was blowing out of the north and she must keep it at her back.

She struggled forward: lurching, tripping, staggering; driven by rising panic and the equinoxial gale. Once, blundering into a rabbit hole, she fell and her bundle rolled away. Frantically she felt for it, but her hands encountered only harsh earth. "Oh God, God, God," she cried savagely. "Why so dark? Is not death enough without this dark? Mama, father, help me."

That they would never help her again; that they were not waiting for her return with warm milk and a bright fire; with ointment for her bruises and gentle admonitions for going late onto the moor, hit her like a blow. The nightmare stopped being a terrible imagining and her soul was filled with black despair, far darker than the night. She abandoned her bundle and groped her way forward, bending, feeling for gaps in the heather. And then the rain came. Some cloud, lower than the rest, emptied itself down her neck; her clothes were saturated; cloak and skirts wound about her legs in heavy folds; her toe caught at something in the dark and she fell—full length and winded.

How long she lay sobbing she knew not; but, at last, the burning tears of frustration turned into a dull hopeless keening. The dream gone, shattered by reality, she no longer saw—she simply existed. She was wet, chilled and lost; and she had the night before her. If she had been older and better able to assess the situation, she might have given up all hope; but at seventeen, the likelihood of her own death had no place in her thoughts. She lived in the moment. The intensity of her despair was only exceeded by the cold fury that grew with every new wave of memory.

It was difficult to think with the rain hammering at her head and the wind shrieking in her ears, but she stopped crying and dragged herself into a huddled kneeling position. She pulled the cloak over her head and, thus tented, rocked to and fro—to and fro. Presently she dozed; only to wake abruptly when the rain stopped and the sudden silence roused her. It was a cruel awakening: memory flooded back, her shivering body ached and her surroundings were invisible.

"God where be I?" she whispered; then, "Nay, a proper prayer." She grasped the Cross and cried aloud, "Mother of Heaven, in Thy mercy, tell me the way."

Brilliant moonlight momentarily lit up the moor; then racing clouds blotted it out again. But in that wild sweeping of the sky she had seen something that checked her breath. She saw figures that leaned towards her and wavered in her sight. She pressed herself, whimpering, onto the ground, her fingers gripping the dead winter grass.

Grass? Grass? With her hands she scrabbled the earth and felt grass all around her. Not heather. Not furze. Not the wiry heath plants that covered most of the moor. Taking a trembling breath, she opened her eyes again. The clouds were thinning and even as she watched, light and shadow chased across the land. Again the figures sprang into view. Again they seemed to weave and writhe in the shifting light. Then a hole in the cloud cover released full moonlight…and the figures stood still.

She was staring at the Nine Maidens: the ancient ring of standing stones where, as a child, she had played hide and seek.

The first time she had seen them, she and her mother had brought bread and cheese in a cloth, and told tales, leaning against the mysterious monoliths and watching a kestrel hovering and swooping in the summer air.

Now she could hear Marie's voice saying, "When the Maidens dance, 'tis an end—and a beginning."

"How can they dance, Mama? They are just old stones."

"I do not know my lamb, but 'tis a saying I got from my mother and she from hers."

Rona thought: "I have seen them dance tonight...and, oh Maidens, there's been an end, right 'nuff...but what will be the beginning?"

She crawled into the lee of one of the great blocks and rested against it. If not exactly amongst friends, she knew where she was. She would wait for the cloud wrack to disperse before setting off again; and when she did, she would head for the south, and would know the track to follow.

The remainder of the night was to be just a blurred memory. The track took her for several miles and then petered out. She knew she was lost again when she came up against a wall of stone and turf. As there was no gate to be seen, she climbed over the barrier, only to roll and fall into a muddy lane. It was a deep lane and darker than out on the moor, but the banks on each side were guidelines and the ground, though rough and rutted, was free from undergrowth. She turned right and went blindly forward.

The going was easier and, for the most part, downhill. The lane twisted and turned and twice she cannoned into the hedge. Too exhausted to curse, or even to care, she reeled on. Vaguely she knew she was no longer heading for Madron, but the lane must lead somewhere...somewhere. She was almost asleep on her feet.

Suddenly she stopped, blinking. Ahead she saw a light. She took a few more steps and, rubbing her eyes, blinked again. Yes...yes...there it was—a tiny wavering light. A glow worm? It was not the season for glow worms. Will o'the wisp? He did not dance on stony ground.

She began to run.

Soon she could see that it was a candle-lantern; and forgetting that such a thing would not be in the middle of a lane, she made straight for it.

She tripped. A searing pain tore through her leg and she fell senselessly across a flagged path.

CHAPTER VI

William Vaylor sat in the privy. The shawl about his shoulders did little to warm him and the fury of the storm whistled coldly round his legs. He cursed the gripes in his belly that forced him out on such a night. He cursed his own lack of providence in failing to rebuild the privy in the lee of the barn. He cursed the onset of old age: the creeping frailties that tempted him into putting off any new undertakings "until there was time". He cursed the speed at which time was hurrying by, unwilling to believe that it was he that was going more slowly. Above all, he cursed his sons.

If they had not left home when they should have been taking the heavy end of the stick, he and Elizabeth would not be feeling the weight of their years. But John and Philip had gone: and God only knew to what questionable trade.

He rose as quickly as he could, his warm bed beckoning; and, in his flapping night-shirt, he nearly fell over Rona. "God in heaven. What be this?"

He raised the lantern and moved towards her head. She lay face down and all he could see was a tangle of wet black hair. With a grunt he turned her over.

"A maid. A young maid. Elizabeth." He hurried to the cottage door; "Elizabeth," he shouted. The latch crashed up and he flung it open, letting in the chilling wind.

"Wife, wake up. There be a young 'oman on the path. 'Er may be dead. She be wet through. Light up"

His wife, warm with sleep, turned heavily in the wall bed. "Do 'ee hear I? Get 'ee up." He shook her and ran out into the night.

For all his years, William was still a powerful man. In his youth he had been a wrestler, travelling the fairs; taking on all comers for a purse. He had returned to the farm when his father died and the tenancy was at risk. He had done, alone, all the jobs that had to be done: building, ploughing, stacking, calving, felling and cutting timber: so he gathered up the prostrate girl as if she were a baby. He carried her into the cottage, kicking the door shut behind him, and laid her down on the rag rug before the hearth.

Elizabeth, with frightened eyes, lighted the candle and, together, they stared at the stranger.

"Oh my dear soul, 'tis but a child. Quick, stir up the fire."

The old woman prodded the embers with new dry sticks to make a blaze; then, lowering herself on her creaking knees, she felt for the girl's pulse.

"Wet through she be; but she lives." She fumbled at the soaking garments "Sweet Jesus, blood." She uncovered the gash in Rona's leg.

"Sweet Jesus, did 'ee say? Look at this." William held up the beautiful cross in his gnarled fingers and they gazed at it, both of them speechless. They had never seen such a treasure, let alone touched one. Almost without thought, they crossed themselves, as if against an evil eye—then stooped to kiss it.

"Maybe the Lord has directed the child's feet here— and put the pains in my gut to find her out."

They stripped her and wrapped her cold body in a warm blanket. Even when Elizabeth tended the cut, Rona never stirred.

"Put her in the bed wi' thee, warm up the poor littl'un. I will watch." William poked the fire anew and settled in a chair.

All night he watched, puzzling in his mind what turn of fortune had brought so fine a maid to his gate. Her clothes were good and the cross was worth a bishop's ransom. It was like a dream and William shook himself. But there she was, lying beside Elizabeth, still as death.

With his rough hand, he felt her brow over and over, fearing to find it cold. What if she should die? What should he do? Who to tell?

He had sat up with a cow many times, praying for safe delivery and that the calf should not die. "Don' die. Don' die. Let the young life prosper," had been his prayer. Here was no calf and William needed a special prayer. "Not to die," he crooned softly. "Angels keep 'ee. Not to die."

Dawn light filtered through the shutters and William stretched stiffly and pinched out the candle. Doors and shutters still rattled in the remnants of the gale, but the wind had blown the sky clear and soon brilliant sunlight flooded the scene. Branches were down and the thatch was torn off the end of the barn. The old man stumped out to see the damage, sighed and went to milk the cows. With his head pressed to the warm flank of his best milker, he reflected upon the extraordinary happenings of the night.

The girl who had almost blown in on them, was still asleep and still as pale as death. Presently he returned to the cottage and heated up a panikin of new milk for his wife. While it warmed, he picked up Rona's clothes and pegged them onto a line outside. Then he stirred a spoonful of honey into the milk and some ground oats, to make a brose and, when all was ready, he woke Elizabeth.

They broke their fast in silence, staring at Rona. "Where be she from? Where be she going? I never saw her like before—not in these parts."

"She mun tell us—presently."

CHAPTER VII

It was four days before Rona was able to tell them anything. She drifted between consciousness and unconsciousness; dimly aware of the warmth, of soft Cornish voices, and the taste of new milk. Mazed with shock and pain, she babbled incoherently and called for her father; but William and Elizabeth could make out none of it.

Late on the fourth day, the mists diminished and pain asserted itself to drag her into full awareness. It was evening and she opened her eyes to see firelight and rushlight and flickering shadows. They made the unfamiliar even more strange; it was impossible to see into the corners or to guess at the shape of the room. She must have made some questioning sound, for, upon the instant, an old body detached itself from the shadows and stood beside her.

"Well, my lover," said Elizabeth gently, "rest easy. 'Ee be safe now. Will and I be taking care o' thee."

"Who—who—where be I? Be this Madron?" Rona struggled to sit up. "What be I doing here?"

"'Ee blew in wi' the storm. William, my man, found 'ee on the path."

"The storm—oh God, I remember...I saw the Maidens dance...I saw..." She broke off and covered her face with her hands, rocking to and fro as memory hit her like a shock-wave.

"'Tis over. 'Tis calm now. 'Ee be safe and soon will be mended. Where do 'ee belong, me dear? Tell

Elizabeth…" She waited. "Come child, William can get word to your father. What be his name? Poor soul, he will be sick wi' worry—ye out in that weather. We mun tell un all's well."

"My father," sobbed Rona. "All well?" She shook her head; "All gone. All gone." She wept bitterly.

Tentatively, Elizabeth sat on the edge of the bed and put her arm about the girl's shoulders. "There, there, my pet. Hush. Hush…" She drew the child close and stroked her hair gently. She knew better than to try to stop such weeping. And, presently Rona sank into another exhausted sleep.

Mistress Vaylor stole out to look for William. He was bedding down the stock and shutting in the fowls.

"The child's more'n lost; she be in some other trouble. She spoke to me for a minute…"

"And? 'Ow be she? Her name? What's her name?"

"I told her who us was…but when I bade her tell her father's name—why, the heavens might 'ave fallen, she took on so. I b'lieve he mun be dead."

William shook his grey head; to hide an unaccountable lifting of his heart. Could he be glad? Great God. What sort of man was he, to be pleased to hear such a thing? "Then," said he, stumbling over the words, "we mun look arter she."

Through the long vigils, through the nights when they had thought she might die, William's thoughts had strayed constantly to earlier days—and nights— when he had sat beside his own small sons when sickness had given them caused for fear. For, with all his great strength, he was a gentle and protective man who rejoiced in the knowledge that his little family depended on him. He dreamed fine dreams for his sons, picturing that in their combined strength, they would increase the holding and turn it into a proper farm; and build, maybe, a house of stone. A place to bring peace and comfort to their mother in her old age.

The dreams had died long since.

Watching Rona, he had wondered what it would have been like to have a little maid to care for: a child who would not break away nor take the law into her own hands. Time and again he had wished she were his own. Her fragile beauty touched him and his strong instinct to protect flowered and reached out to her. He took good care of Elizabeth; but, with the onset of age, she had grown to resent it. "Don'ee fuss and fret so…think 'ee I be breaking up?"

They had both hoped for grandchildren, but John and Philip were unlikely to do their parents that honour. William did not doubt that his sons had a scattering of bastards all around the coasts, but he would never know.

He had spent, wasted, a thousand hours puzzling his untutored brain, trying to understand the reason for the boys' waywardness. They were not merely errant, rebellious young men breaking free from the old established patterns—as all youth does; John and Philip Vaylor were outlaws, criminals, ruffians; and William knew it.

"'Tis an evil mixture—laziness and greed together," Elizabeth had sighed; "Philip was ever lazy and John greedy. P'raps John would have worked for gain if Philip had not tempted him into easier ways."

"What did we do wrong, old Wife? We bain't idle nor be we greedy."

Elizabeth shook her head, crying within herself; "I b'lieve 'ee never spent an idle hour in all 'ee days— keeping the land going."

William looked back over his long life. He had been born in the same cottage and worked, beside his father, on the same land. Except for the few seasons when he went for a wrestler, to earn a marriage purse, he had not left the wooded valley of his birth. Working the fairs had got the restlessness out of his system. Sometimes he won, sometimes he slept under the roof, more often under a hedge; sometimes he ate meat, and sometimes was glad of the church's charity or a bag of windfall apples. He learned to pity the many homeless men who lived thus all their lives and died, unmourned, by some lonely roadside. He was thankful that he could return to the certainties and continuities of the land, and to the tiny cottage above Gulval.

There had been Vaylors there for hundreds of years: fathers and sons, tenants of the Crown. And now—what? When he were gone—dead and down to Gulval churchyard—he could not see John or Philip taking up the tenancy. To whom would the holding go then? Who then would pay the rent and tithe of the land enriched with the blood and sweat of his forefathers?

A daughter would have married and brought a good yeoman into the family. A man who would give his toil a continuing meaning and pass it on to grandsons. But Elizabeth never did have another child; it was as if the twins had cast a blight upon her womb.

Had he, unthinkingly, wished upon Rona this role of daughter? Enough to give his heart a lift when Elizabeth said that the child was "more'n lost"? "You old fule," he said to himself savagely; then picking up a shovel, he went to attack the stable floor.

CHAPTER VIII

Rona woke to full consciousness while the cottage was empty. She saw herself to be in a humble place, sparsely furnished and cleanly swept. She wore a linen shift, homespun and of her clothes was no sign. Her hand flew to her neck to find the cross. It was there. She lay, forcing her mind to recall and marshall the events that had brought her to this pass. She realised, with thankfulness, that she had fallen into the hands of good people, and honest ones. She held the cross tightly while a formless prayer thanked God for His protection—and asked for more. She was still very frightened and near to tears.

She was composed when Elizabeth came creeping in. "Awake? How be 'ee, my lover? How be the leg?"

"Better I think. Have I—been here long? Have you told me where I am? I forget. I be sorry. I fear I have been a trouble."

"No trouble, little one. William an' I be glad to look arter 'ee."

"Where is this place? I was bound for Madron. I think."

"I bain't never been to Madron: it be 'bout five mile away. 'Tis to Gulval we b'long. It be two mile distant."

"We're not in the village?" Rona asked anxiously. "Who knows I be here?"

"Only my William. Be it—secret, then?" Rona nodded vigorously; searching her mind for what she could safely tell them.

Before she could decide, William came stumping into the cottage, stinking of the muck that clung to his boots. Elizabeth shrieked: "Get out o' here, you ole' goat. Take 'ee boots off and get 'ee under the pump."

Rona laughed.

They stood transfixed by the sound. "Poor Master William. Why, you smell sweet as a rose."

"'Ee be better my maid. Ah, 'tis good to hear 'ee laugh."

Rona leaned back against the pillow, her face solemn again. "I should be dead but for 'ee," she said at last. "I b'lieve I have not thanked 'ee."

"'Tis no thanks we want, 'tis to see the wound healed and 'ee brought to safety."

She did not break into hysterical weeping anymore, but said gently: "There is no safety for I, Mistress. My

33

father's enemies will stop at nothing to have me dead—or gone. And where can I go? I have no money and my inheritance is in their hands. I have an uncle—Helford way—but Tranthem will surely look first to find me there."

"Tranthem." The old couple looked sharply at each other in sudden alarm. They had heard that name when John and Philip had last visited them. And anything from those two boded no good.

"Aye, Tranthem—Squire and Constable—his land bordered the Laity land—my father's. And now—I s'pose, has it for himself." She paused, looking at them intently. "If I tell all, 'ee will keep silence? 'Twere best for 'ee as well as for I, that 'ee do."

"Tell us nothing unless 'ee be so minded. Whatever it be, it will stay wi' us and go no further."

So she told them everything she knew: of Tranthem's long siege upon their land and of her father's resistance to it; of the minerals that sparkled in the cellar; of her mother's death. And then, at last, of her father's death. It was only of Uncle Jacques and the Cross that she did not speak.

"As I fled, Clem Bugel, my father's man, told me to find his sister in Madron. If he has been there and found me not arrived, he will think me dead. Dead on the moor. No-one will know…"

"Never fear, littl'un, us'll take care o' 'ee; and find the sister. Know 'ee her name? Is she wed?"

"Her name? No. She be wed, sure 'nuff."

"Then William shall ride to Bosigran and find out the cowman himself—and tell him."

"No. No. Anyone going there will be followed back here."

William looked startled. "Be it so? Be it so important to this Tranthem?"

"He killed my father. I saw him do it. He will stake

34

all to have me quiet and to secure his hold on Laity's land. There be only Clem Bugel and Dorothy to see it happen: p'raps he has already rid himself of they..." She was lost again and near to tears.

"There now...there now...first things first...we mun get your leg healed and then decide. Sleep now. All will be well, you'll see." William sniffed noisily and went out into the yard.

The cottage had two rooms, one above the other, with an outhouse alongside that served as wash-house and larder.

When they were first wed, William and Elizabeth had slept in the upper chamber; that was until the boys were too big and four were too many together. Then they came down to the bed built into the corner of the living room. Even when John and Philip had gone, the old couple had stayed below to save their ageing knee joints on the steep ladder. Since Rona's arrival, William had gone into the top room to let the two women share the wall bed. Later, they said, later, when her leg allowed, she would go aloft. If only she would stay.

One day, sometime during the following week, the sun shone warmly and Rona sat in a chair by the open door. She looked across the yard and into the distance where the sea glistened blue on the far horizon. It was the southern sea, quieter and bluer than the deep turbulence on her own north coast. The land fell away in woods and green fields to an open and uninterrupted view of the sea; framed by near trees and distant coastlines, the bay was dominated by the mysterious Mount of Saint Michael. With its Monastery and crowning fortifications, it rose like a fairy castle out of the swirling mists and twinkling seas—the stuff of ballads and legends. Rona stared at it—drinking in the beauty, drawing peace from the ancient scene. The grandeur of Mount's Bay and the delicate beauty of a nearby primrose soothed her bruised heart.

Even the immediate surroundings were reassuring. The yard was like any other yard: trodden earth, wisps of straw, hen feathers, their scratchings and droppings; there was the well with a circular wall, lovingly built out of small shaped stones, each one an hour's work; and down the flagged path, the privy that had been her salvation. A barn, built beside the cottage and in line with it, faced the sun—something east of south. And behind the buildings, rising ground, steep and tree clad, gave shelter from the wild westerlies and the wind from the north that blew bleakly across the moor. This little idyllic upland was the western side of a shallow valley, bordering a stream that bubbled and hurried from the moor to the bay. Between the Vaylors' land and the stream, following the line of it, was a lane—a deep lane— edged with stone hedges and turf; it passed close by, and went on, in both directions, to the moor at one end, and the bay at the other. It was this lane that she had found in the dark and the fury of the storm.

And from this lane she suddenly heard horses approaching. At the same moment William hurried up the field, his old legs going like pistons: "Get 'ee into bed quick," he panted. "'Tis the Constable." He picked her up and called for Elizabeth. "Pull up the quilt— make haste. Nay, don' look afeared. They can sniff fear, like as not. They'll pass by. I'll make myself scarce; they'll not trouble an ole 'oman and a sick child." He left quietly and vanished round the back of the barn and up into the trees. Elizabeth closed the door.

They heard the horses stop and the click of the gate. Rona froze with fear and slid down the bed.

The Constable's knock was enough to wake the dead; there was no way to feign sleep, but she shrank into the shadow close to the wall and watched with frightened eyes as Elizabeth opened the door. A tall young man ducked his head under the lintel and came in out of the spring morning. It was not Tranthem.

"Good day to 'ee Sir," Elizabeth greeted him, returning stiffly to her chair.

"Good morrow, Mistress; we search for a runaway—and for a Priest—a thieving Priest."

"A Priest? Thieving? A man of God stealing from the poor? Never."

"Not the poor; this Priest robs the Church, no less. He steals from God. He carries The Cross of Cornwall: a treasure you poor folks are never like to see. This Priest robs Her Majesty of it."

"You said 'twas God he robbed."

"'Tis the Queen who punishes first."

"Well," grumbled Elizabeth. "'Ee be wasting 'ee time wi' us. Do we look as if we have treasures an' Priests?"

"Aye, aye 'tis nought that you are like to have truck with," answered the Constable. "But maybe there have been strangers around; a Frenchie Brother? Or a young woman, well favoured, in a dark gown?"

"Strangers? Nay. Daughter, have 'ee seen strangers?"

"Not I," she whispered. "But I bain't been 'bout."

"My girl is sick—as 'ee can see."

The Officer drew away. "What sickness?"

"'Tis but a poisoned leg, Sir; she fell in the storm and cut it badly on the garden path."

"Garden? You call that a garden?"

"There will be flowers presently," Elizabeth retorted tartly.

"Your pardon, ma'am; my thoughts were on this other girl—she went missing in the storm."

"Missing? Missing from where?"

"From Bosigran."

"Where be that?"

"The other side of the moor."

"Other side? Why bless me…she bain't this side then. A body couldn't cross the road that night, let alone the moor. Why…Ro—Rose couldn't even get to the privy wi'out mishap. She fell so hard, father had to carry her in. We thought the bone was broke."

"Who else is here? Your man? Your daughter? Who else?"

"None else. An' he's away somewheres."

"Let me see the leg—there's a man outside that has some skill: with animals at least."

Rona retreated even further into the bed, but Elizabeth exclaimed, "Oh thank 'ee Sir. If you please, Sir. If he do know of any herbs or ought else I should use…" She rolled back the cover from the bottom of the bed and made to remove the bandage.

"An ugly wound. Clem. Clem Bugel." Rona flinched. "Nay, I'll not touch; do not flinch, child."

Clem Bugel! "Oh God, let him not show he knows me in front of the Constable."

Clem came in, out of the sunlight, blinking and seeing nothing. The Constable went on: "Who sleeps above?"

"William, my man—while the girl be ill."

"And in the barn?"

"The cows."

He went outside "Search the barn, I will search within. I must look through every dwelling, whether 'ee will or no."

He went up the ladder and stuck his head through the trap in the floor. The bedchamber was poor and would not have hid a cat, let alone a Priest. It took him but a minute but that was time enough for Rona to gesture to Bugel and put her finger to her lips.

Her father's servant gaped, emotions of fear and relief chasing across his face. Elizabeth took him firmly by the arm. "See here," she said. "Does it heal clean, think 'ee?"

38

"Aye. Clean." He stared.

"Nothing in the barn—nor down the well," called a voice from outside.

The Constable backed down the ladder. "Nor inside," he muttered impatiently. "Where's the man of the house? He may have seen something…"

"Taking the sow to the boar. Mos'like sitting on a gate an' hoping for the best." The old woman chuckled richly. Rona wondered how she did it.

"We must be on our way—to the Mill, up the lane."

"Take a drink afore you go—the men and the horses."

"My thanks. Water from the well."

"Nay, better than that—there be home brew in the larder. How many be there?"

"Four. Two of my troop and this man Bugel—he can recognise the renegade; that is, if he can get his wits together."

Clem shuffled his feet and grinned, gap-toothed and innocent.

"I'll fetch pipkins and bring them into the yard. Master Bugel shall help me. Go tell your men to get hold their thirst a moment longer. The horse trough is by the gate." She watched them move out of earshot.

"Clem, Clem, are you all right? You and Dorothy?"

"Us? Aye, Mistress, us be well 'nuff—jus' so long as they take me for a fule. But Mistress Rona, how be 'ee? Us thought 'ee be lost. Praise be to God."

"Praise God later," said Elizabeth, thrusting two pipkins of ale into his hands. "Take these out and come 'ee back for the rest."

"Be 'ee still at home?" Rona asked when he ambled in again. "I be caretakin' for Tranthem, at present. He be searching every cranny round 'bout; quartering the moor. Then he sent for this Constable—Vanner, he be called—and set 'im to find 'ee this side; 'The girl or

the Priest—one or t'other, best both,' he said."
Elizabeth came out of the larder, but Bugel went on:
"The one is in the Scillies safe. And 'ee," he looked at
her lovingly, "'ee be lost, lady." He took the drink and
hesitated. "Go on—out," hissed Elizabeth. Rona could
not bear to see him go.

"Mother," she called plaintively, "may I sit up? Ask
Master Bugel to help me." Elizabeth went out and
patted the man's arm.

"What's amiss, Mistress?" Vanner looked over his
pot of ale.

"Nought's amiss. I do but ask a strong arm to
support my girl in her weakness. She asks to sit up."

Bugel followed her into the cottage and went to
the bed "Get word to Nathaniel Laity, if you can," Rona
said quickly. "Tell him…tell him…what happened. I
can stay here till he may come. Give my love to Dolly.
Here, help me up."

"A shadow fell across the threshold and Constable
Vanner set his pot on the table. He gave Rona a long
look and she went pale with fright.

"Rose? There should be roses in those sweet cheeks.
I should like to see them there." Then he turned and
said shortly: "Come we have spent long enough here.
It is some miles to Madron and supper with Bugel's
sister."

They rode away. In a little while the sound of their
footfalls was replaced by soft silence, and by the
buzzing of an early bee.

It was a little while longer before Rona and Elizabeth
let go their breath in deep sighs. Then in reaction,
Elizabeth started flapping and fussing over small things;
and said, at last; "That man…can us trust un? Will 'ee
tell 'em 'ee are not—what I said?"

40

"Never. In all the world he is my best hope."

"Hope?"

"Hope for—Oh I know not what. Justice. For my home. For a chance to repay you, dear Mistress Vaylor. Dear God—it was to his sister I was travelling..." She shut her eyes against the disaster that would have been. "Perhaps he may get word to Uncle Laity. And you—and Master Vaylor—will be relieved of your burden."

"No burden."

"My thanks. I...I b'lieve I have three friends now: you and Master Vaylor and Clem. Thank God Clem is not slain."

The old woman nodded doubtfully.

"What? Do you still doubt him?"

"I d'say your Clem is true; but this Uncle—I know not. As for us—me and Will—I doubt thee will remember we when 'ee be come into your own."

Rona was too astonished to speak. The intensity of her fierce inward denial of such a thing surprised her. At last she said slowly: "It was easy to call you Mother." She looked at Elizabeth steadily. "You have made me b'lieve that I belong here—and to you."

"Oh my dear child...my dear child. It be a joy 'ee bring, never doubt it: never hurry away."

The old lady had embraced her close and Rona felt her body tremble. "Why...what be...? Dear Mother, don'ee cry."

They clung together until she was quiet.

"'Tis when they go...'ee miss 'em."

"They? When they go?" Rona did not understand.

"Children...babbies."

"Ye never said..."

"'Bout my boys? Twins they be. Us never knew how happy it was when they were littl'uns. Never knew...till they was gone."

"Where did they go? Was it so far?"

"Went off. Off on their own ways. Bad ways...bringing shame to I." Elizabeth rocked in her chair, holding in her misery.

Rona tried to imagine what manner of men could turn away from such loving folk and such a place.

The two of them lost in the quagmires of their own confusions, did not hear William's return. They jumped, startled.

"I were behind the barn—listening—watching."

"I tole 'em 'ee were off wi' the pig."

"Then I'd best go. Bin talking 'bout it all week." He went off whistling, as if nothing had happened to upset the tranquillity of the morning. He scratched the old sow's ear; "Come on my 'andsome, time 'ee had some merrymaking."

Elizabeth watched him go and thanked God she married a calm man.

CHAPTER IX

March blew itself out and April passed; the primroses had come and gone and the sow's piglets, pink as rosebuds, rooted around the tiny orchard ablaze with blossom. Rona pushed open the upper window and leaned on the sill.

She breathed in the lovely scents of early day and felt the silken breeze of a May morning caressing her cheek. She was rested and safe and her cuts and bruises were forgotten. She could now go— to Helford and Nathaniel Laity. For weeks the three of them had known that she was able to go; but always something cropped up to delay her setting out. The need to spring clean the cottage, dusty and untidy after Elizabeth's preoccupation with nursing her. Then the sow farrowed and the cow calved and there was seed to be sown. After all their kindnesses Rona was glad to be needed. Besides, she had no idea of her welcome at Uncle Nathaniel's—

she a hunted and penniless relation.

Then one day a ragged gypsy boy rode up on a donkey with a message William did not understand. "Abraham knows and is gone to Truro to catch the ram by the horns. Stay until he calls."

"Who gave 'ee this message?"

"A man t'other side o' the moor."

"Who were 'ee to tell?"

"A man wi' an orchard and a well and a maid dark as she is fair."

William shouted for Rona. When she heard the message she nodded and clapped her hands. "And the man? The man who gave you this news...how does he fare? What does he do?"

"Minding cows for 'is Maaster, on a cliff top. He does well 'nuff."

They gave him milk and cheese and a saffron cake and told him not to go back to the man on the cliff who minded the cows for his Master. They gave him a penny to go the other way. And Rona sat on the wall of the well and stretched her arms to the blue sky, relieved, excited, as if her life had taken a sudden leap forward. William was not so relieved.

"This Nathaniel—your kinsman—think 'ee he will get back your birthright? Be he a match for Tranthem?"

"He will try. I am sure he will try; and he has the wit to go to Truro—not to try and take him on his own ground."

"Aye—he will try. For if aught should happen to 'ee, it would rightly be his, would it not?"

Rona shivered; could Uncle Laity also wish her dead? She would sooner he had it than be wishing her dead and out of the way. As if he had heard her, William said, "He could give 'ee a dowry and work it himself. 'Tis no job for a maid. What do he do, your Uncle?"

"He's a boat builder; on the creek called Abraham's

Bosom. It bain't really Laity business. It were Aunt Martha's. Her father's, but he had no sons. Uncle Nat managed it, then owned it. Samuel, my father, was the eldest—he had the real Laity land."

"Then we can expect good Master Nathaniel to jump to its rescue. But, my girl I think you should give him the chance of it—for a proper dowry—and if he do not come soon to 'ee, then 'ee mun be sent to him. It should not be left to chance."

But still Rona stayed. And still William and Elizabeth rejoiced in her presence.

The girl was happier too. She loved the old couple and was building up some sort of stability within herself, after the shocks of death and uprooting. The time-honoured routines of their humble rural life—milking, churning, washing, cooking, digging and sowing—worked their magic; and to repay the Vaylors, there was nothing she would not do—and in the doing of it was soothed. She wept less easily and did not start up in the night, gripped by a nightmare that turned out to be true.

"'Tis like having a proper daughter 'bout the place," Elizabeth said wistfully.

"Dear Mistress Vaylor, 'tis like being a daughter. And my own Mother would not think it amiss if she found me thinking of you so."

Elizabeth dropped her distaff and struggled up from the rocking chair to give her pet a hug.

Rona thought idly of these things as she leaned upon the sill and scanned the countryside. She watched the waves breaking against the distant fortress rock of Saint Michael and remembered that Uncle Jacques had said that there were monks to be found in the market town at its foot across the causeway. If she could find one, perhaps she could hand over the cross.

44

Suddenly, something much nearer caught her attention: the grating crunch of wheels in the lane. She narrowed her eyes against the piercing sun and peered down. The track was deep in shadow with some tall trees and the Vaylors' boundary hedge interrupting her view. "Someone is up betimes," she thought. She had not heard anything pass that way so early before. Watching, she saw a heavy white horse pulling what seemed to be a white cart. On one of the shafts, his head and brown smock showing darkly against the horse's flank, sat a young man. There was something strange about him; he did not seem quite to belong to the equipage; flopping beside it like a doll. They were quite close before she realised that the driver was asleep. Even as she saw it, one of the cart wheels bucked against a stone and the young man fell off.

She leaned further out of the window to shout some jest expecting him to scramble up. But he did not scramble up he did not stir at all. He lay inert on the stony track as the horse plodded onwards.

"Holy Saints. Is he dead?" She withdrew from the window and descended the ladder at full speed, dashing past the sleeping couple and out through the door. She left it swinging and sped barefoot across the yard. "Whoah…hold still," she shouted at the horse. The horse obediently stopped and nibbled at the verge. She saw the whiteness of the cart was a film of flour. "Hey. Wake up. Did 'ee hit 'ee head? Heavens. Blood." There was a bloody bruise on one temple. "Silly boy," she said softly, kneeling beside him and taking his head onto her knee.

William, wakened by the sun streaming through the door and perplexed by a shouted command by his gate, arose and came blinking into the sunlight.

"God's Grace. Another. Be all the wounded angels falling on my doorstep?"

"He fell off the cart: he was asleep. I saw it." She leaned over him to feel for the beat of his heart. "It's all right. He's only banged his head."

"Here let me see. Why, 'tis Matthew, the Miller's boy. Passes here ofttimes." He squinted up at the sun; "Be a bit early today; been out all night, shoont wonder. I'll fetch a pail of water to him."

"Master Vaylor, you'll not soak him to the skin, just to wake him up, poor soul. He'll have headache 'nuff to plague him all day wi'out a chill as well."

The old man grunted and went to the pump to douse his own head: and Rona gazed down at the young bronzed face, so strong and yet so dependent. His hair, chestnut brown, was springy with curls, his dark lashes curled against his cheek; "and soon there will be a curly beard," she thought. She found herself holding him tightly and whispering; "Ye be all right, my 'andsome, all right. This be a loving place."

It was this that Matthew heard as his mind cleared. He opened one blue eye and then, quickly, the other; and he saw Rona's face, oval and beautiful, bending over him, with her dark hair falling like a veil about her shoulders. He stared. He was sure he was dead. Then he felt the rough stones under his body and, turning his eyes, saw the track close to his head. Yet his cheek was cushioned and gathered gently on to the knee of a beautiful stranger.

The stranger smiled. "Hello, Miller's boy. Were 'ee dreaming when 'ee fell?"

"Be I dreaming now?" He closed his eyes; "'Tis a good dream, I think I will stay. Ouch!" William started to drip icy water onto his face.

Rona sat back on her heels and laughed; and Matthew sat up, shaking his head sorrowfully: "I know not what be happening but 'twere too good to last. What be this place?"

"Vaylors'," said Rona.

"That's right," interrupted William, offering the boy his jug to drink from. "'Ee bain't far to go; but Elizabeth, or Rona here, best tend that head o' yourn. He hauled Matthew up and turned into the gate. "Come 'ee in now."

Rona was suddenly aware that she wore only her night shift—an old one of Elizabeth's and fitting where it touched. "I'll follow…" she stammered.

"I'll take the young fellow to the pump. You slip in and tell th'ole lady." He chuckled into his beard; "I be turnin' into a nursemaid in my ole age."

Rona dressed swiftly, regretting that she had no other gown: none but the old stuff one that still bore the scars of the great storm. She combed her hair, wishing that the Vaylors had a looking glass.

Elizabeth set bread and milk before them. "Set to," she said, "break your fast. And if 'ee are a bit mazy, Matthew, Rona shall drive you to the Mill."

"I shall drive," said the youth quickly, "'Ee can imagine what Master'll say if a young woman was to drive his wagon in."

"Oh let me—or let me come with 'ee. I've never seen the new mill—though I must have passed close when…" She stopped short, then continued breathlessly, "Be it far? Too far to walk back? Can 'ee spare me, Mistress?"

"Go to," smiled Elizabeth. "Don' get into such a fever. The trip will do 'ee good, and the walk back, too."

"Aye, and there's a sack of grain still to be milled—take it with the rest."

"Oh no," Matthew said. "The wagon be quite full up. Let me call for it tomorrow." He looked shyly at Rona; "And then, if 'ee likes the ride, 'ee can come again."

William and his wife exchanged a glance of great

amusement: it took no time at all for young people to take to each other nowadays.

The lane went up over a rise and down the other side, following on at higher contour the line of the stream that flowed along the valley bottom.

They drove along, each full of questions and neither saying a word. And each believing the other to be the most beautiful creature in the world.

"That be the stream that drives the Mill, I s'pose," ventured Rona hesitantly.

"Aye."

"And these side-tracks, are they to other farms, other homesteads?"

"Aye."

"What be they called?"

"That's Ninni's. That's to Tredinneck." He pointed with his whip.

It wasn't very encouraging, but Rona persisted. "What's the Miller's name?"

"Miller. Henry Miller."

"So 'ee be Matthew Miller."

"No."

"No?"

The boy coloured and jerked the reins to ginger up the horses. Stonily he faced front. Not knowing what to say, Rona said nothing: and presently he flicked his eyes sideways, to check her goodwill, and said: "I was took in. Found. Mistress Miller found me one Sabbath, on the Church steps—in Madron." There was a long silence, then taking a sighing breath, he finished: "It was Saint Matthew's day. So I be called Matthew Madron."

"A foundling. Why, I be a foundling too! William Vaylor found me o' his doorstep. I…" her voice faltered; she had not thought of herself as a foundling: she had said it to put Matthew at ease: she now realised it to be the very truth.

48

"My father and mother are dead and...and..." Matthew was looking at her curiously; he was sure he had not heard of a girl at Vaylors'. A new foundling? Well, one did not have to be an infant to be cast upon the mercy of a stranger. He hoped the Vaylors were kinder than the Millers.

There was a silence as they jogged along; then Rona said, "I was lucky...I might have been left to die...might have been killed..."

"Then I was lucky too. I s'pose I might 'a' been left to die there on the Church steps. And then we would not be here, driving 'long in the light and shadow of a spring morning."

Impulsively she laid a hand on his arm. "You be a poet, Matthew Madron," she said.

"It must be the crack on the head. I've been called a few things afore but never a poet." And a minute later: "What be a poet?"

They rode through the early morning and the silence between them was easier and pleasant. Their destitution was a bond. Recognising that life had been preserved where it could so easily been lost, they were acutely aware of it in all its forms: the newness of springing wheat, the feathering of tiny leaves, the hedgerows starred with daisies and scented by bluebells and the sun glinting on the ancient granite that was the bedrock of their land. These minutes held the magic and the mystery of light and time and eternity: of expectancy and the optimism of youth. Always to be remembered. And, what was more, they knew that these were memorable moments—unlike so many that are not recognised at the time.

They heard the clack-clack of the water wheel before they turned the final corner. And they saw the

49

fine white mist of milling flour rising in little eddies, like dust devils on the breeze. They could taste it on their tongues well before they actually saw the mill. The Miller could not hear them for the noise of the millstones, but Mistress Miller came bustling out of the house.

"Matthew, Matthew, don'ee know how late it is, and out all night? Could ee not finish the orders in time? Know 'ee what the Miller will say? He...Oh my dear soul. What has happened to 'ee head?" She saw Rona. "Who's this? Who's this?"

Matthew sprang off the cart and Rona answered: "Good day Mistress. Matthew was thrown off the cart a few mile back. We patched him up. My name is Rona L—" She hesitated. "I be lodging with Mistress Vaylor. It was there that the accident happened." She smiled. "Poor Matthew—it was a fearful knock."

"Thenk 'ee kindly young lady. Matt, you'd better persuade your friend to give that smile to the Miller. He'll forgive all then, I'll be bound."

Matthew had let down the tailboard and was leaning back to drag a sack of grain onto his shoulders. "Will you?" he grinned.

"I'll try." She looked even prettier when she blushed.

But if the Miller was charmed by his youthful visitor, he gave no sign of it. His glance was more of a leer than one of greeting. His eyes were on the bandage on Matthew's head, which convinced him that the boy had been fighting.

"Late. Late. And no wonder—fighting and wenching—an' in my time. My time, d'ye hear? And where, may I ask, did you spend the night?" he looked at Rona archly. "No need to ask..."

"In the wagon—back o' Gulval. It were dark and the horse were weary, Sithny's a long way."

"Back answering? Get to work. An' take that rag off; it don' deceive me."

"No." Rona cut in sharply. "No. Matthew fell off the cart, because the wheel jerked over a stone and slid into a rut. Master Vaylor sends his regrets and has made the lane smooth again. I saw it happen. He was knocked into a faint. You must leave the bandage."

The Miller rounded on her, red with indignation, but she looked him coldly in the eye and said, "Master Vaylor says to call for a bushel of grain for milling in a day or two. Good day, Master Madron."

"Master Madron is it? Ho. Ho. So that's it...putting on airs are we? Well, get on wi' those sacks; bring 'em in and look sharp. Lost time is time lost. It cannot be found again." He stalked away, iron-faced, to check the water levels and the number of sacks on the wagon.

Matthew shrugged apologetically and the Miller's wife flapped at him with her hands to get on with the unloading.

Rona was perplexed; her upbringing had been so sheltered, so remote and empty of strangers that she had no skill in weighing up new acquaintances. She just knew that she hated the Miller and pitied poor Matthew from her heart.

A puff of wind covered her dark dress with a powdering of flouring; Margery Miller took her arm and drew her away. "Come away in, from the dust, m'dear, and take some apple cider, do." She led the way into the millhouse that stood with closed windows, a little way from the mill.

Inside, Rona saw many signs of prosperity, though none of love. The house was handsomely furnished, panelled and glazed but uncomfortably tidy.

The wooden floor was smooth and polished— something Rona had never before seen at ground level. Pewter, surely never used, gleamed on the mantel, and

51

the smell of beeswax pervaded the house. Despite the polish, or maybe because of it, a fine film of white dust was to be seen on every surface.

"Oh dearie me," exclaimed Margery, "there's no end to it." She flapped her apron over an oaken chair. "Sit'ee down. Sit'ee down. Do." She fussed around, surreptitiously dusting and straightening things. She wiped the table and filled two tankards with sweet apple cider. The she sat down and regarded Rona with unblinking owlish eyes. "And who do 'ee say 'ee be?" — curiosity overcoming all.

"Oh you make lace, Mistress." Rona espied the cushion and bobbins. "I like to make it too. That is—I used to..." She had not thought of lace since the day she had fled.

"Used to? Are you prevented? What...?"

"I am visiting the Vaylors. Elizabeth is a—relative. She had been a little unwell. I be helping wi' the spring clean."

"Unwell?" The Miller's wife leaned forward expectantly.

"She has hurt her back, a little. 'Tis nothing important."

"A relative? What be 'ee called? Where from?"

"My family are in the Helford Valley."

"What do I call 'ee?"

Rona hesitated. "I be R-Rose."

But what other name? There must be no association with the Laity girl. Matthew said he was called after the place where he was found. Rona racked her brains for a place name far enough away. Father once took beasts as far away as the market in Hayle. "Rose Hayle." Then firmly changing the subject: "Let me see your lace. Do 'ee take it to market?"

"I do."

Their heads bent together over samples of Mistress Miller's lace. It was very fine and Rona wanted some for a collar. She was immediately aware that she had no money—no money anywhere, no bargaining counter, nothing. "Something must be done," she thought bleakly. "I cannot mark time forever with naught but one old gown and a borrowed shift."

She sat a little longer, listening with half an ear to Margery's prattle; casting glances through the window in the hope of a further glimpse of Matthew. She wanted to ask the Miller's wife all about him but was unaccountably shy. Instead she said, "I must go back to my duties, thank 'ee for your hospitality."

"Nay, m'dear, do 'ee stay a while. I do dearly enjoy a chat. Our visitors are very few—frit by Master Miller, I dare say. He do have a wicked temper."

"Poor lady," thought the girl. "She would be better suited in a town." She rose to go as her hostess twittered away like a sparrow, and stood by the door until the lady was in duty bound to open it.

"Good day then. Henry, Husband, our visitor is leaving; bid her God speed." But the Miller did not hear—or did not choose to hear—and of Matthew there was no sign.

CHAPTER X

Rona stepped out briskly and turned south. Following the millstream, she proceeded along the valley to her foster home. It was a lovely walk to a lovely place. She thought of it with deep satisfaction: of the tall trees and the gently stream, the green fields sloping away to seaward and in the distance, the broad expanse of the Bay.

As she walked, she thought of it, picturing the long view, and the near; the glitter of the sea twinkling through the blossom of the Vaylor orchard. Only the cottage was insufficient. It was the first time that Rona had considered it objectively; loyalty prevented her from seeing the modest homestead for the poor thing it was. But, without a doubt, it was small; this much was undeniable; and built of humble materials; and rugged. Rona began to dream of the house that would do justice to the delectable spot—the gentle valley with the dramatic view.

She had seen one once; on that visit to Hayle. The Masons were putting finishing touches to it and the doors were wide open. They had peered in. "Faith! It must be the house of a very rich man," Marie had said. "Not for us, mon enfant; not for us this grandeur—how ridiculous it would look on the edge of our cliff—that would be too dreadful even to think. Jamais. Jamais."

The house with the many paned windows was three storeys high. It had tall chimneys and the symmetry of a child's drawing. A square house of hewn granite that twinkled in the sun, with a roof of local Cornish slate, called scantle. Through the door they had seen a wonderful wide staircase with shallow steps and heavy balusters; quite unlike the steep stair in their own farmhouse home. Laitys' was a low rambling building, added to through the centuries by earlier Samuels who had extended it sideways, until grandfather had dared to put on one upper storey: greatly daring, for it exposed the roof to the wind and he had been forced to replace the old thatch with stone. The windows were glazed and shuttered to resist the ferocious weather, and they were small so that, in winter, the farmstead was dark; and it was smoky with backpuffs that hurtled down the chimneys. Even so, thinking upon these things as she made her way back to the Vaylors, Rona was overwhelmed by homesickness. It was a longing beyond tears and her gratitude to William and Elizabeth and the tiny grey cottage that made her welcome, made her run towards it, even though she might cry when she got there.

She arrived breathless to find Elizabeth sitting on the doorstep spinning, a pot on the fire and an atmosphere of gentle good humour better than all Margery Miller's polish and all her dreams of great houses. Cry she did, but not for long.

"Well now that's better. And how did you find them at New Mill? Were they angry with poor Matthew?"

"They would have been, I think, if they had not been so busy trying to impress a stranger. I said I was a relative—is that all right?"

"Better so," the old lady nodded. "Best of all, if it were true."

Rona recalled Margery's fussy efforts to win her praise. "Mistress Miller, she do make very fine lace." She paused: "And I—Mistress Vaylor, how can I get some money? I wanted to buy some lace: a piece for you and one for me, but…"

"Money? My dear soul, that be the least of things."

"Maybe, but I owe you so much and…I can make lace myself, but my cushions and patterns and bobbins are all at—home."

"'Tis hard for thee. I said as much to William, only yesterday. But don't think 'ee owe us aught. We would keep 'ee and gladly, even if 'ee didn't do a hand's turn; as it is, why, 'ee never stop…Anyway, William has an idea."

"An idea? What idea? Oh, not that I should go?"

"Go? What nonsense! But he shall tell you himself?"

"Where be he?"

"In the bottom field, tending the neaps. He'll be back presently, for his dinner. Let us set the table."

When William came in, he was more concerned with appeasing his thirst and then his hunger, than with any talk. Rona became more and more curious and gazed beseechingly at Elizabeth to broach the matter of William's idea. "Do'ee need for something, Rona?"

She has forgotten, thought the poor girl.

"You said—you mentioned—that is, Master Vaylor had an idea."

"What's that?" William asked, his mouth full. Elizabeth whispered something in his ear; Rona caught the word "market". William shook his head vigorously, as if to expel chicken stew from his ear. "Kindly feed me through my mouth, 'oman," he said, inserting his little finger into his ear to rake out imaginary fragments. Then, roguishly to Rona: "So your outing today has given you a taste for more?"

"I—I don't know," stammered Rona; "Mistress Vaylor said you might have a plan for me..."

"How did you get on with Matthew?" he asked abruptly.

"I? Very well," she answered, surprised.

"He took no liberties with you?"

"Liberties? What liberties?"

"I thought as much—not had much in the way of temptation, that one; probably a mite shy." William wiped his platter and munched the bread.

"Willum, Willum. Ye are the very soul of exasperation," cried Elizabeth. She looked at Rona's face. "See the torment of living with a man, be warned."

"Peace, 'oman. Now then," he pushed his chair back, "there was a time when Mistress Elizabeth and I went every month to market. Now it pains her to sit too long in the wagon, and the hustling and jostling all the day tires her half to death. I don' like leaving her 'lone here the live-long day; so...what do'ee say, Rona, to going 'long in my stead—with the eggs and cheese and butter and 'lizabeth's yarn? To Marazion? That is, if the Miller will 'llow 'ee to go with Matt."

Delight and doubt chased around in Rona's mind at the prospect of a whole day out with Matthew. Could she do it? Could she take the responsibility of selling the Vaylor produce? Making the Vaylor purchases?

"I—I Do'ee think I could? Without mistake? Mistaking the right money?"

"You can write, child; I have to carry all in my head. Yes, I b'lieve it will be plain sailing. Besides, Matthew has been taking the flour to market for many seasons— he knows the market ways. And perhaps Mistress Miller will be there wi' thee, if she finds it convenient; she goes sometimes, with her laces and that."

Rona found herself wishing fiercely that Mistress Miller would not find it convenient to accompany them.

"I think I can manage," she said, surprised by the firmness in her voice. "I should like to try." Then she went on eagerly, "I went to the market in St Ives, with my father; and to Hayle once. But we sold pigs and honey—it was not the same…"

"I have decided," cut in William, "that as you make the butter these days, you should have for your wages, half the butter money—for your own spending."

"Half? No. No. It is far too much. I owe you more than all the butter and all the cheese and everything."

"You owe us nothing," said William with a finality that would have made any argument impertinent. "It is settled. Rise early and watch for Matthew's passing. Then we will ask him to make it right with the Miller; to get his consent for the next market day: the Thursday market in Marazion."

It was so arranged.

CHAPTER XI

The day dawned clear with a pearly light reflecting off the sea. It was going to be hot by noon and Rona knew that she must accept William's butter money to buy herself a length of stuff for a summer gown: linen or muslinet with enough for a sunbonnet. The wagon stopped at their gate. It was already stacked high with milled grain. They topped it up with the Vaylor cheese, butter, some salted pork and eggs. Rona climbed up beside Matthew with spools of Elizabeth's spun wool on her knee. In her hand was a slate with a list of their own requirements. This was a great marvel to Matthew.

"What do it say?" asked he in wonderment.

"Salt; barley for malting; a pancheon; fish; yeast and linen; that's for me, with needles and thread besides."

William and Elizabeth were also excited by the thought of a written list and had wanted Rona to write and write; but it was still a bad time of year for shopping lists; the fresh vegetables were not yet ready and last year's nearly spent. Bread and small beer were staples of early summer.

"Can 'ee write the things I have to buy?" asked Matthew; "Then I need not fear forgetting."

She turned the slate.

"Stone chisel; salt; beeswax; fish sufficient for two days; a new whetstone. Us do have our own eggs and a cow." It was but a short list so he added: "Can the goods I have to sell be writ? The prices I get for each one later?" This possibility of accounting was indeed a marvel for Matthew. He enjoyed his visits to market but the reckoning at the day's end was a nightmare. How could his beautiful companion be so clever too?

The wagon wheels ground and crunched under the heavy load; small stones danced from under the horse's hooves and clouds of midges sought the patches of warm air as they wended their way through the slanting rays of the golden morning. They went through Gulval and round the back of the marshy stretch that once had been a forest. Chunks of petrified wood occasionally poked up among the reeds and rushes of the wet land. Skirting Crowlas, they joined a procession of carts all making their way to the little town of Marazion—so called because of the Thursday market. The busy scene began to take shape. It was still early in the day but already the stalls were overflowing onto the shore: penned animals, potters, brewing booths were scattered along the beach, thus leaving the market square for provisions that needed shelter.

Matthew had to wait his turn and finally backed his precious cargo into a covered place for which the Miller paid rent every Quarter Day. He did not unload the flour but used the wagon as his stall, but he did bear Rona's butter and cheese to the stone shelter reserved for dairy produce. And because it was her first experience of marketing, he struck a good bargain for her with another dairyman; that he should take the whole consignment and re-sell the golden produce of the Vaylors' pastures as well he might. For the first time for many months, the girl held money in her hand.

"Make your purchases quickly," said Matthew, "and hide away whatever you may have left: there be many a pickpocket hereabouts."

"Oh Matthew, do 'ee take care of my purse. Please." She looked round anxiously, fearing eyes might already be assessing her frailty.

The young man took it and hid it in his shirt. "Have 'ee any jewel about 'ee?" Rona thought of the Cross that Elizabeth had made her leave behind; she shook her head. "Good." He looked at her ringless hands and plain dress." You have no need," he said; and she blushed.

Then she set out. She found the salt and ran back to Matthew for the right money. Similarly, she found and bought all the other things on her list, leaving until the end her own purchase of cloth. She would wait until there was the maximum choice. She sat with Matthew on the tailboard of the wagon and shared some bread and cold bacon with him, a thumbpiece provided by good Mistress Vaylor.

Then, taking from him her share of the butter money, she wandered off in search of woven stuff.

She walked barefoot down the cobbled street: cobbles interlaced with blown sand: and saw, for the first time, the magnificence of the great rock set in its shallow sea. The tide was out and a causeway, shining with wet seaweed was crowded with folk coming and going with food and provender. She saw no monks in that year of Grace, 1576, but doubtless they were there, clad in homespun and looking like everyone else. Where was Uncle Jacques? She gazed at the Monastery. How many markets had it seen? How many fairs? Brooding like a protector or a judge over the antics of man and beast upon the shore. She sat on the sand and watched squat ships sailing across the bay, or tugging at their anchor chains in deeper water. Some local fishing smacks were homing into Newlyn and, soon, their catches would be spread out for sale. She would wait for the freshest fish before she bought for Elizabeth.

After a while, she moved on. Stall holders were crying their wares and she heard "Fine linen. Strong hessian. Silks and satins." Making for the source of what she heard, she passed between peddlers and tinkers, packmen and a fortune teller; someone was cooking shellfish that made her think of the pasty that waited to be eaten in the Miller's wagon. "Home brew. Cakes and ale. Sweet milk." She succumbed and bought a saffron bun.

The stall she sought was loaded with every sort of cloth. The dyed stuffs were expensive so, after much thought and fingering, and missing her mother's advice, she chose a length of unbleached linen, with a small amount of apple green to trim it. She was pleased and went back to the peddler, with his tray for needles and thread. After that, she had but one groat left.

The peddler patrolled the sands and was, at that moment beside a potter's stall. Pots of all shapes and sizes were stacked on the trestle and on the sand beneath. Unglazed bowls and jugs, pancheons for bread and saucers for cats. And, in the middle, another—a different pot: a bright blue shining pot, a pot for flowers. She saw it, at once, lighting up the cottage windowsill full of buttercups or honeysuckle. It was the perfect gift for Elizabeth.

"Oh how lovely," she cried. "May I touch?"

"Pick it up," the Potter smiled through his beard.

"It's so bright—so shining bright—so smooth. And I have but one groat." She put it down. "I wish I had seen it before buying my stuff."

"'Tis more than one groat, little lady," the old man said.

"I could save up—work for it; but then it would be sold. Could you make another, the same, when I have enough? How much is enough, Master Potter?"

"For you, a shilling—three groats more."

She stood back putting it precisely in the middle of the stall and bit her lip.

"'Ee could earn a penny minding the stall while I have a bite. Would that help?"

"I'll mind your stall, gladly, and never mind the penny," she clapped her hands. "To be a real stall holder—that would be something to tell. But you will tell me how much everything is—and not go too far away, in case I should forget. And what shall I call 'ee? And..."

"Steady. 'Ee will break the pots with your chatter. My name is Potter Jane and I'll not be far away. Call if a customer comes, I don' want a little lass handling money and getting herself robbed for her pains." He heaved himself up and reached for a stick to lean on. He wore a smock smeared with clay and she saw a trace of the blue glaze. His eyes were blue and kindly and he patted her as he limped to the booth that sold the brewed ale and splits filled with broiled fish and chitterlings.

Rona put her roll of cloth under the stall beside some shallow dishes—those used to separate the cream for scalding; and she sat down on the Potter's stool and watched him limp off to his friends in the brewer's booth. He dragged one leg and someone fetched a seat for him. Her eyes kept straying to the blue pot. It was faintly ridged where Potter Jane's fingers had formed the shape of it; she traced the ridges with her own fingers. It would be good to have a skill like that. A number of shoppers lingered at the stall, counted their money and passed on. She smiled at them encouragingly, holding up first one thing, then another. She wanted to sell something to celebrate her day out and this, her first, responsibility. Sailors passed, and women with children clinging close; she heard the sounds of laughter, the stall holders' shouts, the mewing of the gulls, boldly landing and scrapping in their search for morsels to eat. Then, added to this mixture of sounds, she heard a piper and a fiddler. They were behind and coming near. Perhaps they belonged to the Punch and Judy show; perhaps they were playing for pennies. The jingle sounded jolly.

A man picked up a jug and turned it around in his hand. He proffered a groat and she was about to call "Potter Jane", when the music stopped and a voice grated in her ear; "Drop your purse onto the sand behind you, my lady, and you will come to no harm." She couldn't take it in; it could not possibly be meant for her, but the customer for the jug had dropped it and run; and another voice growled: "Drop your takings—now—unless you want your stall toppled and all your wares broke. That will cost a deal more."

An arm came around her shoulders and a hand fumbled her neck. Her body froze under the horror of those searching fingers and she forgot everything except her need for protection. She forgot where she was, the clamour of the market, the Potter, even the thieves. She saw only a blood red sunset and felt

Tranthem's hands upon her. "Father!" she screamed. "Father!" And finding the stall barring her flight she turned straight into the two thieves, her arms flailing.

The ruffians, thinking they had a easy victim, were taken off guard. One took a blow in the face from Rona's fist, the other grunted as her elbow caught him on the solar plexus. Furiously they set upon her: but the alarm had been raised. "Hold. Take them." A voice rapped out. The men were wrenched off her by willing hands. Shaking, she found herself facing an Officer; the very same Constable who had searched for her at the cottage and had examined her leg as she lay abed. "You fought them off bravely, Lady," he said, looking at her curiously. "But another time choose adversaries nearer your own weight." She nodded dumbly with lowered eyes; it was, after all, only her eyes that he had seen above the quilt.

"Your father—he is here?"

"No—I forgot—I wanted him…"

"I stand in for her father." Potter Jane hobbled up; "This is my stall. The young lady was minding it for a moment, while I wet my whistle. Sit 'ee down my dear; 'ee had a fright; I am sorry."

"Get her a drink old friend, while I dispose of these vagabonds. Then I will return for that blue pot."

"Nay Constable, the blue pot is spoken for—it's not for sale."

"Oh but…"

"It is promised. Come next market and I will have one for 'ee."

Rona shivered violently, crouched on the sand and began to sob silently. Another arm came about her: a very different arm from the thief; It was strong, steadying and it raised her up. She leaned against it owner, expecting to feel the coarse cloth of the Potter's smock on her cheek. Instead the cool leather of the Constable's tunic pressed against her.

"Thank 'ee Sir."

Grey eyes regarded her shrewdly. "Have we not met before?"

"I think not. I may have been here once but that when I was a little child." So much was true. Uncle Jacques had brought her on one of his visits, when he could walk free.

"Well, well. I must lock up these rogues. Potter Jane will look after 'ee...and better in the future, I hope."

Potter Jane brought her buttermilk with something stirred in it that tasted strange. "Drink up...every drop." He settled himself on his stool and bade her sit at his feet. "Roger Vanner is keeping the peace. When I was a lad, there was no law officer in the market. Many's the riot these old eyes have seen. Did he ask your name?"

"Y-yes"

"Did 'ee tell him?"

"No."

"Hm...good." They settled down into a companionable silence.

"Potter Jane."

"Yes, my lover?"

"You've been here a long time..."

"'Bove semty years m'dear. I were born at St Bartholomew's Day when the ole King came to rule."

"Are you of the old faith? Or a Protestant?"

"Depends who's looking. My mother was the one and my father the other."

"So were mine. So were mine. And we got on very well."

"Got on? Do 'ee not get on still?"

"They are dead, Master Potter. Both. And my father was the Protestant and yet was killed by one of the same. And all to find a Priest 'In the name of God.' Why? Why?"

The old man eyed her: the child had had a fright and it had loosened her tongue; she was telling him that she was an orphan. Perhaps, if he kept quiet, she would tell him more. More of what he had guessed already. He'd seen black curls and merry eyes like hers before.

Rona picked up the little pebbles, yellow and white, and found some shells, pink as a baby's finger nails. She laid them in a row. And she kept silent too.

"They'm been at each other's throats as long as I can remember—Catholic Christians and Protestant Christians."

"But Jesus said—"

"They don' think on Jesus—never. It's the power and the land—the Church has a lot of land. And land, my lass, is wealth." He looked into the distance of the years: "My father and mother were both Catholics when they were wed. Not strongly, 'ee understand, there was not anything else to be. When King Henry knocked the monks off the Mount and declared himself to be next to God, it did not make much of a dent in Cornish ways. The gentry, maybe, but us of the villages, half of us had never heard of him. We heard more from across the water. Still do. There be always Frenchies, fishermen and traders, in an' out o' our bits of harbours. Sometimes we gets to know what goes on in London long before the news comes over the landways. My father kept his ears to the ground an' he hears of a man, name of Martin Luther, setting the Continent by the ears—on account of selling Pardons. Can you beat it? It set him thinking. Then he hears of Jesuits burning and torturing folk who dared to question them—fearful for their power, see?—heretics they called them—an' all in the name of gentle Jesus. Father, he was a miner; close to the earth and under it. He never did hide from danger and the cruelties of natural life. 'Tis hard 'nuff without men ripping into one another, for Christ's sake. And he would say, 'Tell 'em I can't see the Saviour sitting by His lake with a pair of red hot pincers in His hand—to force his teaching.' If that makes me a Protestor, then so be it."

Rona listened amazed. Such lessons as this she had not known. Her mother had taught her about herbs and simples, nostrums and enough Latin for the Mass. Her priestly Uncle gave her stories from the gospels. She had learnt to count and read. But of the doings of men, and men of other lands, she knew nothing. She sat transfixed.

"There was many a Cornishman who woon't give up the Mass and kept it in secret. Priests scurried 'bout in the shadows, flitting here and there, never in one place long nuff to leave a scent. But Thomas Jane— my father that was—riding round 'bout, he knew— helped 'em, shoont wonder—but he thought th'ole Church greatly at fault. He left it and he left us children to choose for usselves. Mother, she saw no need to change. She said God don' look at externals and wouldn't give an armourer's curse for a change of name. You shake your head; don't you believe me?" The old Potter smiled.

"It—I—'tis hard to understand how 'ee know so much." He chuckled: "'Ee think me an ignorant peasant man fit only for pots, eh?"

"I ask pardon. I only met one Potter before, in Morvah. He made all our pots, clay and wood, but he hardly knew who lived down the lane."

"Down the lane in Morvah? Ole Jem Leitch. I know him. He didn't have a father like mine."

Morvah, she had said Morvah without thinking. Had he noticed? "Tell me about your father, Master Jane; was he a potter too?"

He did not wait for her to answer. "Thomas Jane. You've never heard of Thomas Jane? It's a name known to every tinner. There was two of them, both Thomas

Jane, my father and his father. They both streamed for tin all over the county. Lamorna valley, in the south; Kenedjack, in the west; Camborne Red River—all over. There wasn't a stream in West Kernow that the two Janes didn't know like their own backyards. My father wanted to dig, wanted to chase the lodes under the ground; but the old man wouldn't hear of it. "Men bain't rodents to burrow and scratch—there's plenty for all in the water." But when he was laid to rest, father changed his vanning shovel for a pick and wouldn't be denied. 'Jose,' he said to me 'I have a nose for tin.' Have 'ee heard of Diviners? Dowsers for water, young maid?"

She nodded.

"Well, it seemed Thomas could smell out metals the same way. No bent twigs, mind—just a feeling. 'A knocking' in the joints,' he called it. He said the knackers were his friends, tole 'im where to go."

"Knackers?"

"Where you been, girl? Not heard of knackers? They be the pixies below ground—souls of ole miners. Greatly to be feared." Jose Jane lowered his voice and shook his beard at her: "Greatly to be feared."

Rona shrieked in mock dismay and realised that listening to the Potter had quite taken way her real fear and the affront and horror she had felt in the hands of the thieves. She understood why Samuel and Marie never let her go out alone, had never let her out of their sight.

"Go on about the knackers."

"Aye, well Thomas feared no knackers; and with, or without their help, he chose good sets. And many's the knock on our door; some miner coming to ask advice. 'Thomas, what do 'ee know of this land, or that?'"

"Did he tell them?"

"Oh my dear life, o' course he did. He said, 'There's

a limit to what I can carry—let the rest find their share. We never went short and there was no lack of men who wanted to join him, to make a team. When Grandfather died and father went underground, he had to have a team. Many teams. When he got older he rode between them, from Weal to Weal. A great man— Thomas Jane."

"Were you in a team?"

"Never, my girl. I was tooken wi' the paralysis when I was but six years old. It left me wi' one leg that don' obey me. My mother bought me a potter's wheel to play with. I couldn't play with the other boys." He sighed. "Perhaps it was as well; I'm the last o' them— the lame one—all the rest are dead. All those boys— some in the wars—some in the mines—some in the sea. All gone. Except for Jose Jane."

He stared out to sea muttering, "All gone. All gone. And Betsy too."

They were stirred into action when a woman, dragging a large basket, staggered to the stall to buy the biggest pancheon. She argued and haggled over the price and made a great palaver emptying the basket to put the bowl in the bottom. "Pay for it before you load up, Mistress. You, gal, gather her things together safely and help her pack them when she has paid." The woman glared and spat on the money before parting with it.

"The last one broke," she said angrily.

"You shouldn't have dropped it." Potter Jane was unruffled.

"Are they all like that?" asked Rona.

" Some. Some will try anything. They know I can't run after them."

They settled down when the customer had gone, and Rona hoped for another history lesson.

"Betsy baked wonderful bread," he mused.

"Betsy?" Why did the name sound familiar to her?

"My wife. Oh yes. A man can go courting, though he has but one good leg. Betsy lived here, in Marazion; but we met up on the moor; 'twas the day the Frenchies attacked and fired the town."

"Then you must have been little children. That is old history."

"Not so little. I was fifteen and Betsy a year younger. Whole families went onto the moor to watch. The man went down to help—where they could—or help themselves. A lot of stuff was 'rescued'. But I was too lame to go down and Betsy was too nervous. How the fires did leap up as the night fell. We could see the flames reflecting in the sea. Betsy and her friend Elizabeth sat huddled together in fear—all bedewed and cold. I had a bite of food, I remember, and sought to comfort them. I little dreamed I would be supporting one of them for the rest of my life."

"What was she like—your wife—your Betsy?"

His eyes rested on the horizon. "She was small and neat. Dark like you. She looked fragile but she was strong and quick. She could have married any of a hundred suitors."

"And she chose you."

He laughed, "It could not have been for the beauty of my form. Shall I tell you why she chose me?"

"Because you had a blue pot."

"Because I could read. I couldn't run but I could read. Life keeps its balances. The Priest was sorry for the cripple boy and taught me. Betsy could read too; she had no time for a man who didn't share her delight in it."

"And is it this reading that makes you know so much?"

"Aye. And being stuck in one place, more or less; it forced me into journeying into books. That, in its turn, gave me a great curiosity. I questioned people. Betsy said I should have been a teacher. As it was, we di'nt even have a child of our own."

"I'm sorry. What a pity. What a waste."

"You never know. The other girl—on the moor—she had two sons." He paused. "They have brought her and her good man more sorrow than ever our empty cradle brought Betsy and me."

"Sorrow? They were sickly?"

"Not sickly. Wicked." He broke off to watch a couple of fishing boats come out from behind St Clement's Isle: one with a white sail and one with a ruddy brown sail: they seemed to be racing. "See the brown sail? That will be a Frenchman. Yes wicked. A better pair of parents I s'pose 'ee could not find in a lifetime; nor a worser pair of sons. They thieve and lie and swindle and kill." He spat out the words his eyes burning. "When they was boys, they was always fighting. Thrash 'em, I said to Will. But Will bain't the thrashing kind."

"And now? Are they fighting now? Who's side do they fight on?"

"Where the pickings are richest. Philip and John are on their own side."

Elizabeth? Will? Philip? John? Could it be? Were these two terrible men—Vaylors? Was this why Elizabeth shied away from any mention of her children? She couldn't ask. She couldn't give away her hiding place, not even to this good old man.

A young couple, chasing along the sand, stopped in front of the stall. "Seen something, my lover?"

"Oh Peter, the blue pot. Look 'ee at it. It be pretty."

"I'll buy it for 'ee. If it cost the earth, I'll buy it. A pretty thing for a pretty maid."

"Ye won't, young Master," said Jose. "The blue pot be sold."

The girl pouted with disappointment. Rona felt for her, she loved the blue pot too. "Is it sold?" she whispered. "I thought…"

"Ye thought I wanted a shilling. I changed my mind.

70

'Tis yours for standing guard."

"Oh no. I will earn it. Keep it for a catch penny, meantime; it brings people to the stall. But thank 'ee, thank 'ee Master Jane. For the gift."

"And thank 'ee little one, for saving my goods. I owe for it all, for all of it would have been broke if they had pushed the table over. I am in your debt and I don't even know your name."

"It's—Rona."

"Have you no other name?"

"Marie."

"Rona Marie…a pretty name." Again he looked at her shrewdly, searchingly. "I knew a Marie once; my Betsy's cousin from across the sea. Married a farmer on the north coast. It was a love-match a true love-match. I heard it said that she was dead—of a fever." He watched her closely, lacing and unlacing her fingers. "See Rona Marie, the red sail is leading. Soon the white one will turn back and the other will go on to France. I think you should go to France, Rona Marie."

CHAPTER XII

Rona sat absolutely still. What did this old man know? What would he believe? Who…?

"Roger Vanner—who does he answer to?" she asked.

"The Constable? To the Sheriff."

"In Truro?"

"That's so—or to one of the Sheriff's wardens."

"What are they?"

"I can't zactly say. There be one in Helston and one in Falmouth."

"One in Hayle?"

"Mos'like. Why? Rona child, you be trembling; what's the matter?" Why didn't she speak? Surely she could trust him.

"I'm afeared," she whispered.

"Of Roger? He's a good lad. Tell me, who brought 'ee to the Market? 'Ee never came 'lone. Come lass, tell an ole friend."

"An old friend?"

"Well I be ole and a friend." He leaned forward and patted her shoulder. "Try to b'lieve that."

"Joseph Jane—aren't 'ee a bit old for that?" cried a derisive voice from behind. "Who be the beauty, old man?"

They turned and Rona saw a huge swarthy rogue, standing legs apart, earrings lost in his beard, his beard lost in his hairy chest, leering down on them.

"Christ alive—not another. Here pull me up," Jose commanded. "Which be 'ee?"

"Phil."

"An' where be t'other?"

"Round 'bout. Heave ho—up the anchors!" He seized the Potter under his arms and hoisted him onto his feet. Then he lifted up Rona and dusted her down with a large rough hand. "Who's the beauty?" he repeated with relish.

"How be your mother?" responded Jose calmly; "Or haven't 'ee troubled to find out?"

"'Ee do have good taste, I'll 'low. But thee," he gripped Rona by the shoulders and held her at arms' length, "thee could do better than his bag of old bones."

Rona tried in vain, to shake herself free; he laughed at her and wagged his beard in her face It smelled of beer and fish. She glared at him, cold anger replacing her alarm.

"Unless you let me go this instant, I shall scream."

"Unless I let you go this instant..." he mimicked.

"I can scream. And my friend Roger Vanner will come at once. I am waiting for him." She summoned up her best grammar and most disdainful manner. "And I warn you, he will not be alone."

"She means it. Don'ee be a fule, Philip. She be waiting for Vanner and he is no friend of thine. Make yourself scarce."

"Not till I know who she be with her ragged dress and high and mighty airs."

"I be come from Helford. I be just visiting."

"Oho! An' where is your horse, Mistress? Or do 'ee walk barefoot to Helford?"

"The Constable will put me up before him when he rides that way." She stared at him haughtily, eye to eye, until he dropped his. "I do see John," he mumbled.

"Then do 'ee join him. Find a trollop and leave honest young women in peace."

Rona saw, in amongst the booths along the beach, another such man, fooling with a gypsy girl and drinking heavily. Philip slouched angrily away and Potter Jane let out a great sigh of relief. "That could have been ugly. 'Ee have guessed, no doubt, that beauty be one o' they bad men I spoke of. And there's the other."

They watched the brothers reunite. John pushed the girl away and they put their heads together, arguing. Then one drew a picture in the sand with a stick and they clapped each other on the back moving off on some determined errand.

"There's bad, bad blood in them—though no-one knows where it comes from. Will's mother, the boys' Grandmother, was furrin: French-Irish: 'tis said they met at a Fair and she left at a Fair; leaving a babby, young William, to be brought up as a farmer. Maybe it was a touch of her wild blood as made him turn to wrestling for a while. Who knows what mysteries we carry?"

"What became of her?"

"'Tis said she ran off with a sailor and drownded in the sea. Ole history—water under the bridge. It's the here and now as matters. 'Tis well 'ee said Helford—

73

that will keep 'em off the scent." Jose Jane limped back to his stool "Now 'ee listen to me, Rona girl. If that man—or any rogue—guessed who you are, he'd stop at nothing to get a ransom."

"I—I don't understand. Who would want to hold me for ransom? Penniless in this ragged gown?"

"Tranthem." The name snapped out. "Would not Squire Tranthem give gold—much gold—to have you safe away?"

Rona's face went white and the world seemed to turn turtle. She dropped onto her knees under the blow of his words. The sand was warm to the touch but ice seemed to have taken possession of her spine.

"There now, take heart. I did not want to frighten you—too much. There's been enough of that. But if I can guess that you are Laity's girl, then others can too. Ye are Samuel's daughter, are 'ee not?"

She nodded dumbly, staring at the sand, seeing the minute grains falling under influences that were invisible. She felt herself falling…falling. "How did you guess? What did I say?" She managed a whisper.

"Well, your gown made me wonder; so much wear and tear was ill-assorted with your voice—and the words and phrases. 'Ee speaks like one who reads books. The number o' girls who can read are not found on every tree. Ye tol' me 'ee was an orphan and that mother was a Catholic, and your name was Marie. This is a small kingdom, this claw into the sea; Sam Laity's death was soon known abroad and the disappearance of his only child. Besides, my lover, I knew your sweet mother: was she not the cousin of my Betsy? Did she not speak of Cousin Jane?"

"Of Cousin Jane—oh, I see—Betsy Jane."

"Ye have been careful, I'll 'low, and your secret is safe wi' me."

74

"You—you and Mistress Jane—took my mother in when she came from France? You are that Potter? Oh, I be glad, Sir, glad."

"Call me Cousin, child. And as your cousin, I say again, if I can recognise 'ee, so can others. And why are 'ee here, alone in the market? 'Tis a crazy way to hide. Where are 'ee lodging? Do they know who they have under their roof? And the danger?"

"I think they thought it would make a pleasant change. They live a simple life and they are old. They have been very kind."

"Kindness bain't 'nuff. 'Tis by cunning and the law that we must beat Tranthem."

"We?"

"The folk about; we are all on your side. There's none o' us common folk wants to see a man killed and his child robbed of her inheritance. Do 'ee not know that? But we thought 'ee dead on the moor, or in a ditch or over a cliff. There has been nor sight nor whisper o' 'ee. Where have 'ee been? Who is so mad as to let 'ee roam the market?"

"Mad? They are the dearest most careful folk. I would indeed be dead but for them." She began to cry, unaware of the curious glances from many passers by.

"This must stop." Jose Jane looked round for some means to comfort her. What he saw was the blue pot— which was a foolish inadequacy—and the approach of Roger Vanner. For some reason that he couldn't fathom, she was afraid of Roger.

"Rona," he said urgently. "Raise yourself up and listen to me. Things will get better. They couldn't be worse. Take heart, take heart. D'ye hear me? Roger Vanner is on his way back—tell him everything." She shook her head violently, wild-eyed.

"Then I will."

"No! No!" She stumbled to her feet, intent upon

75

running away. He held her with a strong arm. "Why not? Come now…" He shook her none too gently. "Tell me why not. Quickly , or I will call him."

"He be one of them."

"One of who?"

"A Constable—like Tranthem. Tranthem has set him on to find me; I know it."

"How do you know it?"

"Because he found me—only Eliz…only someone told a lie: said I was someone else."

"Roger? He be on the side of the law. I've known him all his life."

"So said Tranthem. See what sort of law is Tranthem's law."

"My dear, Samuel's death was an accident. One of Tranthem's troop was clumsy."

"Who says that?" she interrupted swiftly. "It was Tranthem's sword. He ran him through. I saw it. I was but six feet away. Bugel—our cowman, and his daughter, we three. Bugel is playing the nincompoop—pretending he saw nothing; that way he hopes to keep the farm under his eye—and to save his skin."

"God's blood." Jose searched her face for evidence of hysteria. But her face was like a stone; she was stating hard facts.

She looked suddenly old. "I'd best go my way. Keep my secret Master Potter—Cousin." She stood a moment, looking at him, and finding that she had several pretty pebbles in her hand, she held them out to him like a child. Then she turned and was running, running, in and out between the stalls and booths: in and out of his view, and he too old and to slow to follow.

She ran past the place where the Vaylor brothers had been fooling with a stick, drawing on the sand. Pausing for breath, she saw a strange outline—that was not entirely strange. It was like a map with places marked where one had stabbed with the point of the stick. She ran on and dodged up an alley into the town.

She found the streets more crowded; people were going about their business with hard and worried faces; heartless faces. It was with great thankfulness that she saw Matthew. He hailed her with a friendly wave.

"I be nearly done. Why Rona, what's amiss? Be 'ee ill? Here, sit; no better still up wi' 'ee into the wagon. There's still a sack to lean on. Did 'ee get stuff for the new dress?"

"Oh, Matthew. I've left it behind. I left it under the Potter's stall. I was so frightened."

"Frightened? Show me who frightened 'ee and I'll break his head."

"First, two men—a fiddler and a piper—tried to rob me and the stall; then a dreadful pirate fellow…he tried to make play with me. Then the Potter—Potter Jane— guessed who I be and was going to tell the Constable. Take me home, Matthew. Take me home."

"I will," he said stoutly. "But 'ee shall not lose your stuff. I will not be above five minutes. Stay where 'ee are."

"Don' go, Matthew. Don' leave me."

But he strode off and she shrank down among the goods they had bought and hid her face against the remaining sack of flour.

CHAPTER XIII

"Good day to 'ee, Master Potter, I am come for Mistress Rona's roll of cloth. Be that it?"

Jose Jane was sitting weary and mazed at the sorrow and wickedness around him. He had not noticed the linen under his stall. "What's that? Rona's cloth? Well, it's not mine; perhaps she did leave it. Take it lad." Then waking to the situation: "Who be 'ee? What's she to 'ee?"

"I brought her to market to buy and sell for..."

"Where do she lodge? Know 'ee that?"

Matthew was instantly on his guard. "I can't say, Sir, we met on the road."

"Met on the road? What road? God in heaven how can I help the child if I know not where to find her?" He looked Matthew over; "Find where she lives, boy and come and tell me. I live above Gulval. I know her father. My good wife was cousin to her mother. The girl is in need of friends."

"I don't know if..."

"Don' know if you can find out? Or don' know if she would want 'ee to tell? I know. I know. 'Ee do well to be discreet. But, Miller's boy, use your head. What chance do a young 'oman stand all alone in a world such as this? I be no rogue—that is something else 'ee can find out. Find me here any Thursday or else at my pottery above Gulval. I've lived there so long it's called Joseph's Lane. Go now—don' leave her 'lone and don' bring her to market again." He shaded his eyes, the better to see him, but the sun was low and in the dazzle he could not make out the features of the boy.

Matthew regarded the man; here, his instinct told him, was someone he could trust; and it was an instinct highly developed in one in Matthew's situation. "I'll take care; and if I can find aught, I'll tell 'ee."

"Good lad. Here, wrap this in the stuff. Tell her I be sorry she ran off." He handed Matthew the blue pot; "Let her find it when she gets off the wagon—well away from here."

At the end of the day, the flour all gone and the market broken up, they joined the procession of carts that left Marazion to climb the hill behind the swamp ground. Once past it, the traffic divided; some turned south again to follow the road to Penzance and the coast beyond; some turned inland to strike north to St Ives. The Miller's equipage turned north, then west, seeking the lane that followed the Vaylors stream, reached the mill and eventually petered out on the wild moor. There was no sign of the Constable, or any horseman. There were just tired farmers, turned merchant for the day, driving tired horses with no other thought but of home.

Views of the sea receded on their left hand, deep blue and smooth as silk, and wild roses scented the air. Rona, still in the back, drowsed and fell asleep. Leaving the reins slack, Matthew leaned back to look upon her sleeping face, which was shadowed with exhaustion and the tell-tale streak of tears.

A great anger rose within his heart.

CHAPTER XIV

"Where's the girl?" Roger Vanner strolled up to the Potter's stall.

"She went," muttered the old man, stacking his unsold wares onto a handcart.

"Here, I'll give a hand with those." The Constable pushed the cart through the soft sand and onto hard ground, then returned for more. "Tough work—who be taking 'ee home?"

"Trefidden. He passes by my place."

Roger knew them both. "Where did she go?"

Joseph shrugged; "Di'nt say—scared off by that swine Philip Vaylor. She tole him she came from Helford; and she said that ye would be taking her back—that sent him packing."

"She did, did she? Was she coming from, or going to…"

"What do that mean?"

79

"What exactly did she say?"

Jane eyed him warily. "I don' recall; maybe it were more general—I b'long Helford way."

"Seen her before?"

"Not that I recall—why so?"

Roger circled the stall, Kicking at the small stones that abound on Marazion beach. He stooped to pick up a pure white one, translucent as alabaster, and another glowing yellow. "Add these to your collection."

"My...? Oh aye." He put them in a bowl with Rona's pathetic offering. How could he protect Marie Benhault's child? How? "Are ye going to tell me why ye are interested in the girl?"

"She's pretty enough for any man to be interested. But—ye be right—there's more to it: we, the Sheriff's men are still looking for a Priest called Brother Jacques..."

"For God's sake man, can't 'ee leave the poor fellow in peace?"

"It's not the man we want: he can go where he pleases; but it's believed he carries with him a jewel—a Church treasure, the Cross of Cornwall; the Bishop wants it."

"I'll be bound he does. So ye think the girl is a Priest in disguise?"

Roger laughed. "No Priest, be he ever so holy, is beautiful as that. No, but this runaway Priest has a runaway niece. Remember that miserable affair when a farmer called Laity had a brush with one of Tranthem's men—and was killed?"

"I remember."

"His daughter took flight. Frightened and foolish. 'Tis thought she meant to get to her Uncle Laity in Helford. She never got there. God knows what became of her—it was the night of the equinox."

"And if you find her, you'll help her to Uncle Laity?"

"Tranthem bade me look for her. He was in charge of the troop that ran amok. Some fool killed Laity—too hasty—unskilled with the sword. Tranthem's willing to take the girl into his own household; to make amends."

"Yes, I'll wager he is," said old Jose softly.

"What do that mean?"

The Potter chose his words carefully: "I've known that family for many years—Betsy, my wife and Mistress Laity were cousins—I've know too that Squire Tranthem has wanted that land ever since he come into his own. He has a son and has tried to marry him to the Laity girl. He's tried every trick he can think of and more besides: getting hold of strangers and bribing them to buy Laity out: discrediting him for marrying a Catholic. But Laity would have none of it. 'It's the tin Tranthem's after,' Laity used to say. 'Well, it's my tin and I shan't dig until I'm too old to farm: meanwhiles let Tranthem play at soldiers. Maybe he be better at it than he is at farming.' Hm. Then, all of a sudden, there's a runaway Priest. Oho! He might be hiding at Laity's. After him, boys. Then in rides Tranthem with a search warrant."

Jose Jane looked at Vanner and weighed him up: "Constable it wasn't one of the troop who was a fool—it is you. You are the fool."

"What the hell are ye saying?"

"I'm saying that Tranthem killed Laity, as quickly and neatly as ye say his men are clumsy. The girl fled because she was going to be the next—as a witness. But there were two other witnesses: the cowman and his daughter. They are playing it simple, they saw nothing; and they go in fear of their lives, but they are determined to preserve their Master's business. Besides, where can they go? That girl, today…"

81

"Jesus Christ. It fits. I wondered why the chase was handed over to me—why Tranthem did not keep up the pursuit—wants to make himself scarce: and his troop too. He sent the cowman to ride with me to identify priest or girl. But he is simple, I assure you."

"Clem Bugel? He bain't simple—best shepherd and cowman in the Penwith Hundred. I've known him since he were a boy. He's playing his own game; and he's out to get justice."

Vanner marched up and down, turning and turning about until his feet made tracks in the sand. Then he stopped. "How is it you know all this and have never spoke?"

"I only put two and two together today. I tole 'ee, there was three witnesses: The daughter, Bugel and his daughter."

"Bugel's daughter."

"You mus' leave her 'lone, Roger. If Tranthem was to know what she saw, her life would not be worth a moment's purchase. No, ye mus' go to Helford for Nathaniel Laity; better still, get ye both to Truro, to the Sheriff. And be quick 'bout it"

"Ye mus' be very sure 'bout this. The whole district b'lieves it were an accident."

"Why then did Rona Laity run? If ye don' b'lieve me, seek out Bugel first. But do't by stealth; send someone else for him. Tell him to come to me. Between us we'll get at the truth. But do 'ee leave the girl's evidence till the end. She's had nuff."

"My thanks to 'ee, Master Jane."

"Dear Lord God, I pray I be right to tell 'ee this. Please God, take Roger Vanner's tongue into Thy charge."

The young Constable was startled by the old man's intensity. "Amen to that," he said at last.

He gathered his horse from a tethering post and with a long backward look at the Potter he rode into the town. He searched briefly among the folk milling about, waiting for the fair that followed in the wake of the Market; looking for the girl he now believed to be Dorothy Bugel. He found his troop in the square and detailed them to control the fair, as he, he told them, had to go to Helston. He went east about a mile then took a road to the north and thence west. He was not about delegating the interview with Bugel to anyone else. Galloping at full stretch, he skirted the swampy ground and crossed two streams in a fine flurry of splashing hooves. At Ludgvan he had to decide whether to go due north to St Ives and take the better coast road to Bosigran, or to make his westering through Badger's Cross. He did not want to encounter any of Tranthem's troop, and they, he reckoned, would stay by the coast. At Badger's Cross the light began to fade. He had intended to go by the ancient settlement of Chyauster, then left onto the track to Treen, beyond New Mill, but the light worried him. He was as superstitious as any Cornishman and he preferred to avoid the old Rings and Quoits and Settlements at twilight. "I'll get across the valleys while I can see," he said to his horse, and turning its head, made for the first of the two streams that converged to meet at Mills. He picked his way through the first, but the second had steep banks and he had to follow it, nearly as far as New Mill, before finding a fordable stretch. The sun had set behind the Galvers and the red-gold glow was into his eyes and suffusing the moor with brief glory as he headed for the Mill.

At the Mill he could water his horse and take refreshment. And the Miller could give him the best tracks across the moor to the north coast. He would not mention Laity's place.

All this time, Matthew drove the Miller's horse along the familiar road home. Except that it was no home for him. He had neither home nor name. Thanks to the girl behind him, he was newly and acutely aware of this and bitterly resentful of his condition. What mother—what father—would abandon their child on the cold steps of a strange church? As it was, he was bound, by common law and tradition, to stay in servitude with his rescuers: an unpaid servant working off an endless debt. If he could go elsewhere— anywhere—he could earn wages, gain prospects, make his own way. But if he ran away, he could be brought back to the lash of the Miller's whip.

He would go, one day…one day. For the moment, he was glad that he had not; looking at Rona's defenceless face, he would not have wanted anyone else to stand guard. In the past few days, since he had pitched off the shaft of the cart at her feet, he had been drawn closer and closer to the waif at the Vaylors.

At first, their similar misfortunes had been a bond, but now, after their day at the fair, they had found many small delights and mutual joys. They were friends. He longed for the means to give her pleasure. And now, with the sense of danger heightened by their visit to the Market, he longed fiercely to give her protection. But bastard that he was, he could work the soles off his feet, and be in no better position to give her anything.

He drove carefully, choosing the smoothest parts of the track; and Rona slept. They rumbled through Gulval and into Mills then turned to the right up the Try valley and into the home lane. There the track was rougher and it was getting dark. He could not avoid the ruts and potholes. The cart jolted and before many yards were covered, the girl stretched and yawned and sat up. Seeing where she was, she was reassured and gazed fondly at Matthew's back. "May I come up beside 'ee, please?" He extended his arm backwards to steady her and continued to hold her close as she scrambled onto the box.

They sat together warmly, Rona resting her head on his shoulder. "Dear Matthew," she said softly, "what would I have done without 'ee? Whatever may become of me, I will..." Matthew's heart leapt as he waited for her to finish her sentence; but the sentence was never finished. A figure burst out of the hedge and came hurrying towards them, waving his arms.

It was William Vaylor. He was out of breath and in an unusual state of agitation. "Oh my dear life," he gasped. "Thank God I caught 'ee in time."

"What's up?" Matthew jumped down to hold the horse's head.

"The worst possible. My sons. They'm come. They be up to something and mean to stay. There be nought else in the world would make me turn 'ee away; but I fear for anyone who gets in the way of Philip and John. If they find out 'ee be here and who 'ee be, they'll be after you and the property, quick as the thought strikes them. Stay on the wagon, my love, and act the stranger. Ask Mistress Miller to gi' thee a bed for a day or two. Tell her Elizabeth is ill. Tell her I will pay for 'ee. Gi' me time now...time to get back. Then do 'ee unload at the gate as quick as 'ee can; then drive on." He turned and dived into his bottom field, disappearing over the hedge.

"Oh Matthew, Matthew, will this day ever stop dealing out troubles? Thank God I have one new friend at my side. Will Mistress Miller object, think 'ee?"

"Never," said Matthew stoutly—hoping he was right.

Presently, he flapped the reins and the wagon wheels lurched into motion. Ahead was the pink glow of a distant sunset, but they could not enjoy the ride any longer. "Stop!" cried Rona suddenly. "Philip Vaylor has seen me this day. He started to tease me and was mightily displeased when the Potter chased him off. If he sees me on this road he will cause trouble. I must get off now."

"But…"

"I will stay in the shadows and watch until you are passed. I can creep by and catch you up."

"I would sooner have 'ee wi' me."

"No. Help me down."

She struggled of the cart and Matthew, looked down at the pale oval face. "Ye be brave," he said. "Here, take the rug." He fished out an old knee rug and threw it down. "Put it round your shoulders like a shawl as 'ee pass."

Reluctantly, he left her, turning frequently to wave until he came to the place where the hedge thinned and the Vaylors' cottage could be seen from the lane.

Leaning over the gate were two enormous bearded men. They regarded Matthew with interest. "Miller's boy?"

He nodded.

"Mm—looks a likely lad. Ever thought of going to sea?"

Matthew kept silent.

"Ho, lost 'ee wits, eh? If 'ee's got wits to lose."

"Maybe 'e bain't."

"Oh aye, Maaster, I bain't got no wits to lose."

"What have 'ee got then?"

"I got Master Vaylor's salt. Master Vaylor…" he shouted. He wanted Master Vaylor there before these two decided to relieve him of the Miller's gold—a fair sum from the sale of the flour. Vaylor's money too. He had nothing to defend himself with—not even a stick. William Vaylor would have a stick. He resisted the temptation to feel into his tunic for the moneybags— two leather bags drawn tight with a string containing the market takings. They lay within his shirt but he wondered how long they would remain there. Thank God Rona was not there to be taunted and dragged down. He leapt off the cart himself before the two giants decided the matter for him; and, as he jumped, the thought struck him that he should ditch the money himself. He ran along the far side of the wagon to pull down the tailboard, and, while the bulk of the wagon was between them, he threw the purses into the hedge on the far side. There were plants in plenty growing there: Jack-by-the-hedge and goosegrass and dandelions; and the light was bad.

"Here be the salt." He started to man-handle a small tub.

"Flog the salt," said the one called John. "Gold first, salt second."

"Gold?" Matthew grinned foolishly.

"Money. Cash. Coin o' the realm. Come on, hand it over."

"Hand it over," echoed Matthew.

A huge hand with a ring flashed across the boy's face, cutting it open. The gate creaked and William and Elizabeth panted through. "Where be she...?" Elizabeth began.

"Mistress Miller? She stayed home—abed—wi' the pox." Then he added: "It started just arter 'ee left, Mistress; two days since."

"The pox?" shrieked Elizabeth. And the ruffians recoiled. The she saw Matthew's face streaming with blood and started to scream. William under cover of the noise, approached Matthew.

"Oh don' 'it me, Maaster. Don' 'it me."

"Get the money off him, father and let un go."

Matthew whimpered and muttered and William bent close. "Purse in the hedge. Rona back there," he whispered. "Let me go Maaster. I be late." He started to bellow, "Oh my cheek. Oh. Aagh…keep 'em off!"

"Get on wi' thee. Leave 'im be, John. Think 'ee I be trusting my purse wi' such a baby? The Constable will bring it in the morn."

Matthew climbed up, waiting like a coiled spring for either one to come near. With the advantage of height he rather hoped they would. Philip did. As he placed his foot on the shaft, Matthew butted him with his head and sent him sprawling. He caught John with the whip as he shouted to the horse to walk on. The horse strained and the cart moved forward.

"'Tis never a good idea to torment an idiot. They be strong when they're crossed," said William. "Bring the salt into the house."

"But Mother…"

"What about Mother?"

"If that idiot spoke right, Mother was with the Miller's wife just before she sickened."

"Then 'ee'd best be on the road to somewhere else. Put the salt in the barn."

They stood at the barn door, looking in, while William, looking into the lane, saw a shrouded figure slip past to follow the wagon.

"Aye, we'd best find a billet in Penzance."

"We need to be here. Us'll sleep i' the barn; leave us some supper on the sill."

William snorted with anger and looked at his sons with disgust. "What's afoot?"

John laughed: it was an unpleasant sound. "'Ee'll grant us no gold—we mun find us our own. An' 'ee will say us was here—all night long. Understand? Understand, old man?" He glanced up at the sunset, wet his finger and held it up into the wind.

88

Rona caught up with the wagon beyond the rise and round the first bend. A crescent moon with one bright star hung low in the southern sky, just above the bands of pink that were sinking into the horizon. In the gathering dark, Matthew's wound cut blackly across his face.

"Matthew. Oh Matthew, what did they do to 'ee?"

"One of the holy twins was wearing a ring: I got in its way. I'm glad 'ee was safe out if it. Come beside me again." He tucked the rug round her as the dew was falling. In spite of the pain, he grinned: "I told 'em Mistress Miller had a pox; 'ee should have seen them back off."

"Oh Matthew, it be 'ee who's brave."

His face was burning but he felt heroic and unconquerable when Rona called him brave. His young heart beat with proud vigour, his young soul surged towards her, and he knew himself to be a man. A giant.

CHAPTER XV

When Roger Vanner crossed the Try, the stream that fed the new Mill, he was half an hour ahead of the wagon and his horse was sweating and beginning to stumble. The new moon, with its attendant star was beautiful, but it shed little light. The young officer was glad to see the glimmer of a lantern ahead: the Miller was standing on the lane awaiting his wagon. When he realised the hoofbeats were those of a single horse, he turned away, angry and worried. He was halted by a shouted greeting: "Halloo there. Stay, friend."

He hesitated. "Who be there?"

Roger reined in beside him and dismounted stiffly. Henry Miller raised his lantern; "The Sheriff's Constable. What be 'ee here for? My wagon—my goods—have they come to harm?"

"No. No. 'Tis nought to do with thee, Master, I be

on the country's business. I have to get to the coast up north, aye, and back again by morning. I crave your help."

"Did you pass my cart on the road?" cut in Henry.

"Your what? I passed nothing—but then I was not on the road; I travelled the east bank. Now..."

"Did 'ee hear it?"

"I wasn't listening." Roger's temper was getting short. "Please rest my horse. Where is your trough?"

The Miller reluctantly put aside the matter of his property; "I'll take 'ee to the stable." They rubbed down the tired animal, gave it water and a warm stall.

"Margery, Margery," the Miller shouted, "we have a visitor?"

"A visitor, what visitor?" shrieked Margery from within. "What visitor?"

"The Constable."

"The C—, oh my dear life, I must dress!"

The house stood dark—country people saved themselves the cost of candles by going to bed at dusk.

"Pray, do not disturb your wife. I can rest in the stable. It will not be for long."

"She will be more distressed if I don't present 'ee to her. We get few visitors—thanks be—and Margery is houseproud."

They ducked their heads and entered the house. Mistress Miller talking nineteen to the dozen, came fluttering downstairs, a mob cap on her head and a lace tablecloth round her shoulders for a shawl.

"Oh my—the officer—oh my—oh dear. Sit 'ee down—here—no, here is better—or what about the rocker?—the rocker is best—take the rocker. I will blow up the fire. Husband, light candles. No, not one— light more—light more candles. How shall he see our fine panels in the black of the night? Come now. Sir, are they not fine?"

"Very fine." Roger looked round obediently. "Exceeding fine."

They were, indeed, an unusual embellishment for an artisan's dwelling in so remote a spot.

The cold stone walls of the house were screened by wooden panelling, and the new oak caught the candlelight to fill the room with golden light. The floor was also light oak; the table too. "I bought a tree too many when the mill was built. The joiner used it up in the house. I fear 'twill darken with the years—what with the smoke and my woman's beeswax."

Mistress Miller, her house duly praised, set bread and cheese before him on a wooden platter. She reached to the mantle for their one pewter mug and surreptitiously blew the dust off it before filling it with small beer. She talked all the time, of this and that; then, passing close to her husband who stood by the door, she asked; "What's he here for? Where's Matthew?"

"Dunno."

A moth fizzled to its death in a candle flame and Margery swished to the window. "I mus' shut it, they foolish creatures will all come in else. My, it looks like we have a score more candles the way your buttons and buckles twinkle. We have not received so fine a gentleman here before now, have we, my love? No, we have not. Can I press 'ee to occupy the guest chamber till the morrow. Whatever is it that brings 'ee to our lonely mill? It is a great honour, is it not, Master Miller?"

She hoped he would not object to her direct question, hidden as it was in a veil of flattery. But he did not answer it. He said instead: "Madam, your house is beautiful and your hospitality warms my heart—and my feet. But I cannot stay."

Before Margery could pursue her enquiry the Miller, straining his ears heard the sound of wheels. "The wagon," he snorted and grabbing the lantern, advanced angrily into the dark.

Matthew in his new found manhood, decided not to make any apology. "We was held up," he said briefly, adding, "by thieves."

"Held up? Highway men? Here? What 'bout the money?"

"I threw it clear; Master Vaylor's too. I know where it is and will get it at first light."

"They didn't see?"

"O' course they didn't see. I bain't a fool. It were the Vaylor twins laying in wait."

"An' I s'pose 'ee was expecting 'em?"

"Aye, Master William came runnin' down the lane to warn us."

"Us? Who else is there?" He raised the lamp.

"'Tis the Vaylors' guest—remember, she called the other day. Mistress Vaylor asks if ye can give her lodging for the night. She'll pay, she says."

"Here, why here?"

"I'm sorry, Master Miller," said Rona, in a small voice from the box. "I will not be any trouble."

"I don' understand. I don' understand anything," muttered Henry; "come into the light." Rona climbed down.

"Sir," she said timidly, "may I do something 'bout Matthew's face?—the blackguards laid it open—it needs attention."

"Matthew's face? By all the Saints, what's been going on? Never rains but it pours. Margery!"

Margery excused herself, and to Roger's great relief, took herself out.

"Yes, husband?"

"Come 'ee here. We have no money—only a visitor and a wound."

Margery who had spent the last half hour, giving

little shrieks, gave another, at twice the volume. "Matthew! Your cheek! What have 'ee done? Oh my dear soul, help the Master unload while I get soap and water."

"I'll help unload—Matthew ought to rest."

"Matthew rest? He can rest when he's done. Who are you?—what be?—you're the Vaylor girl."

"Mistress, Matthew was waylaid by bad men. He was very brave and saved the money and the goods. He is hurt and I—I was afraid to leave him alone in case he fell off the cart in a faint."

"In a faint? Oh dear, in a faint."

"So, please can I stay here tonight. I am afeared to go back in the dark."

"Stay? Here? Of course 'ee shall stay. What a chance."

She bustled off and Rona returned to Matthew. "It's all right—I can stay."

"Good. Best gi' a helping hand; take the beeswax into the house."

Rona carried it into the house and laid it on the dresser. The Miller's wife was filling a warming pan with glowing embers. "Please Ma'am, Matthew's face is more important than…"

"In a minute. In a minute." She stumped upstairs, the warming pan in one hand, her nightdress lifted with the other. She looked so absurd with her mob cap over one ear, that Rona laughed softly as she drew near the fire.

The rocking chair was between her and the hearth, and she did not see the figure in it until she was abreast of it.

They saw each other in the same second.

"Master Vanner."

"Dorothy." They spoke together, jumbling the sounds. He stared at her, standing motionless, still as a stone, in the candlelight. She looked braced for flight.

"Sit down please. Take this chair—it is very restful."
Without taking her eyes from his face she sat down.

"That warming pan for you?"

She nodded.

"Ye come here often?"

"Never before."

"But it's on the way home—or half way, I should say."

How, in God's name, did he know where her home
was?

"Does your father often let his daughter go to the
market alone?"

"My F—I was not alone."

"Ah no, 'ee were with the Potter. May I ask what
'ee talked about with the Potter?"

"Talked? About his pots…and the men you arrested
and Queen Elizabeth…"

"And the death of Samuel Laity?"

She flinched.

"Ye deny it?"

What was the point of denying, she thought
hopelessly; the old man had broken his promise.

"The Potter talked of it?"

Sounds overhead caught their attention. "Come
outside. I would speak privily." He held out his hand.
"There is nothing to fear from me. Help me, girl, and I
will help your Mistress."

"My Mistress?" She was completely at a loss and
could only repeat his words foolishly.

"Come now, tell me what 'ee told Master Jane. He
was not too clear about it."

What had the old man said? He had seemed
perfectly clear about everything. Too clear.

"You want to help your Mistress?"

"I have no Mistress." She was mystified. She could
not believe that Jose Jane, who had claimed her

friendship and kinship, would betray her identity within the hour. "I have no Mistress," she repeated.

"Do not give her up for dead. Not until it be proved."

Rona jumped and her backbone contracted within her.

"See here." Roger took her further under the stars and out of earshot. "The folk hereabout want to be sure that justice is done; justice for Laity's daughter. And, as old Jose put it, justice for the villain Tranthem."

She shuddered and he felt it through his own body.

"Did ye know that Tranthem wanted Mistress Rona to dwell with him? Jose was very sure that she would not care to share his wish. He was so sure that I asked his reason—then he told me what you had seen; you and your father, Clem Bugel. Whose sword you had seen with blood on't."

"Oh I see…"

"It is necessary for this knowledge to be in the hands of the law. Justice cannot depend upon secrets. Potter Jane's story has sent me scurrying across the moor to find your father—or you—and hear your witness at first hand."

"My father…" Sweet Jesus, he thought she was Dorothy; the Potter had not given her away. She wanted more: "And when ye have it at first hand, what then?"

"Then to the nearest Sheriff's office and the Judge; and Master Tranthem's tricks are brought to book and himself apprehended."

"And the Laity land?"

"It will pass unopposed to the daughter—if she be found alive. Poor child, what fears drove her to run like that?"

"D-did 'ee ever see her?"

"Never."

95

"Yet 'ee defend her affairs."

"The protection of orphans should be the first duty of the law," he said curtly, as if reciting a lesson.

"Tell me, Constable, how did the likes of Squire Tranthem ever come to represent the law?"

Roger looked at her sharply; it was not the question of an unlettered servant.

"Who have 'ee been talking to?"

"To Farmer Laity—and my lady. My lady taught us two girls as if we were equals."

"Hm. The Queen has need of many Agents. The law is far and wide. She has to trust as best she may. Understand?"

Rona was sure that Dorothy would not so she shook her head. "She asks landowners who are not at the wars—not too rich and not too poor, to do her work for her."

"Are you a landowner like that?"

"No my girl, I have to earn my bread. I chose to do it defending the law. I fancy friend Tranthem was not of that kind—not interested in the law save as it might serve him."

"He is no friend." She spat out the words.

"We'd better go in." He took her arm and steered her towards the house; unaware that Matthew, coming from the barn saw them with a stab of jealous fear.

As they approached the glow that lighted up the path to the Miller's door, Rona stole a glance at her companion. He was handsome, no doubt of it; and honest, she was increasingly sure of that. In the intensity of her relief, she turned to him impulsively, to tell him of her own true identity. But, at that instant, Mistress Miller burst out and cannoned into them. "Where be they? My guests? Just as soon as the nest is ready, the birds fly away."

"We are not flown, good Mistress. But, I prithee,

do not make this bird too comfortable. I am tired and yet must keep awake. As soon as my horse can carry me, I must take the road to the moor." He sighed, wondering whether a statement from the girl would suffice.

"Whither are 'ee bound?" asked Rona.

"Can it not wait till the morrow?" pressed Margery.

Roger had no intention of telling the talkative Margery of his errand. But "Dorothy" might already have guessed. Looking at her warningly, he said, "I have to go close to Bosigran to meet with one of Tranthem's agents, regarding some missing sheep."

Rona's heart leaped. He was going home—to her home. "Let me come too," she whispered.

He looked at her with narrow eyes. "Hm." It would be safer for her to ride under his protection; safer for him to ride with someone who knew the way. "No. It is too late for a maid to be abroad. I will take your statement here. Ye can make your mark."

Margery looked from one to the other in astonishment, for once bereft of speech. Then the words gushed out in a torrent "Ye know each other? Ye are mixed up with the law? What's amiss? To think I be warming a bed for a..."

"Mistress, Mistress. Be easy. This young lady has done no wrong; but she may be able to help me find a miscreant. Have 'ee a pen, ma'am? And a piece of parchment?"

He sat at the table and drew the candlestick towards him. Presently the scritch scratch of the quill filled the silence. Roger wrote carefully: "I, the undersigned, do affirm that on the twentieth day of March I did see with my own eyes, the arrival, at the farm of Samuel Laity, near Bosigran in the Parish of Morvah, of one Simon Tranthem, and that the said Tranthem did assault and put to the sword the said Samuel Laity until he were dead. This I swear by God the Father, God the Son and God the Holy Ghost. And that this is the sign of…"

"Stop! I will sign. There is no need for a mark."

He handed her the pen; so she could write…

Rona smiled. While he was writing, she had thought: "He is not one with Tranthem and has naught to gain in this matter. I must have faith in him. Besides, at any minute, the Miller or Matthew, even Margery might say my name aloud." Dipping the pen into the inkpot, she wrote with a flourish—Rona Marie Laity.

He leapt to her side: "You." She nodded, rather scared by so violent a reaction.

"Sweet Jesus. What were 'ee doing in the market?"

She had not expected this. "The Market?"

"Ye are wise to keep your true name a secret, wise to hide and keep your counsel; but in the name of all that's holy, why risk the market—the open beach? An' with no-one to defend 'ee but a crippled old man?"

She huddled into the rocking chair. "I needed cloth for a gown. See; I have only this in the world. It is near to being rags. But I know now: I know that the bad men are everywhere. I know why my father would never let me abroad without him. It irked me, but now I understand. Today was to be a break from waiting and waiting."

"Waiting for what?"

"For my Uncle Nathaniel to fetch me."

"Does he know where 'ee are?" Dammit, he did not know himself where she has been hiding.

"I b'lieve so. Clem Bugel got a message to him."

"And Clem Bugel? How did he know?"

"Why, he found me," she laughed merrily; "when he was out with thee, Sir."

"With me? Ye say, with me?" He chewed his lip and stared at her skirts. Without raising his head he looked up at her under his eyebrows.

"My leg has quite recovered," she said faintly.

"Master Vaylor...Mistress Vaylor...Rose...Hm."

"Ye will not reproach them, Sir. They be the souls of goodness; without them I would be dead."

Margery Miller was so completely at a loss that she ran out of the house. "They be mad...as hares in March. Husband. Henry, where are 'ee? Come within."

Roger stood in front of the rocking chair and, bending, put his hands upon her shoulders. "I be glad 'ee are not dead."

She looked up at him and their eyes locked. "Thank 'ee. And thanks be to Bugel, and the Nine Maidens and William and Elizabeth, and Matthew...Matthew." She sprang up; "I had forgot...Where be Matthew?—he be injured. Come and find him."

"What is this?"

"Matthew. He drove me back and, in the lane by Vaylors' we was waylaid and his face was laid open."

She ran out if the house and into the yard, calling, "Matthew, Matthew."

The Miller was laying up his stores and locking the grain store. The building was set high on straddle stones with the dogs' kennel underneath. They were chained, but free enough to pounce on any rat intrepid enough to venture near. When Roger and Rona came out they set up a barking loud enough to wake the whole valley. When the Miller saw the Constable following closely upon the girl, he kicked the dogs into silence.

"Where be Matthew?"

"Gone to rest." He jerked his thumb towards the Mill.

"To rest? In the mill?"

"That's right—better'n any watchdog."

Roger pressed her arm before she could say more. "And is the mill locked, Master?"

"Course it be locked."

"And do 'ee have the key?"

"Course I do."

"And do Matthew have a key?" The Officer's voice was icy.

The Miller was silent but Rona choked with indignation; "He be injured."

"Give me the key, Miller. I wish to question the boy—it is the Queen's business; a matter of robbery."

"Nought was robbed." The Miller was surly.

"Only because Matthew used his head," Rona burst in, "and saved your rotten money. And suffered for't. I warrant 'ee have done nothing for his cut."

"Hush, remember 'ee are both guest and neighbour. We will see the boy is tended."

The "boy"? Yes, beside Roger he did seem to be a boy. She shook the thought away and urged them across the yard to the stout door of the mill.

As the Miller took the heavy key from his belt, Roger said: "The windows are very small—how could he get out if there was a fire?"

"It couldn't catch fire there be no heat within."

"Nor light?"

"What would he want wi' light?"

"I want a light, if you please."

The Miller's mean little eyes glinted, but he went for a lantern.

"Oh Master Vanner, what a terrible way to live. Locked in the mill, cold and dark, like a dog. Poor Matthew. He never told me."

"It is better that 'ee do no know."

"But I do know."

"Keep the knowledge to yourself—it would only humiliate him. Get 'ee into the house, I'll fetch him out."

A little puzzled for she knew nothing of male pride, she went into the millhouse kitchen.

CHAPTER XVI

Matthew was lying exhausted, on a pile of sacks—one cheek chalk white, the other aflame. Although the night was mild he was shivering.

"Into the house wi' thee," Roger said crisply. "That is where 'ee'll spend this night." He glared at the Miller. "Come, we will support 'ee."

Margery, though nervous and foolish, had a kind heart and had nursed Matthew through his infancy. When she saw him, her hands flew to her face and she turned on her husband in bitter condemnation. Her fear of him forgotten, she railed and stormed. "The she viper strikes," muttered Roger in Matthew's ear. He smiled crookedly.

The two women bathed his wound with herbal water and were about to bind it up when Roger stepped into the pool of light. "Miller, bring out your brandy."

"Brandy? Me? How can a poor Miller have Brandy?"

"How can a poor Miller have a panelled house and a riding horse? Only if he does a packet of free trading. I dare swear there be a cellar full of brandy beneath. Shall I take the lantern and look?"

Henry Miller clenched his fists and opened his mouth to speak. The he shut it again, growling a denial.

"Come, Sir, do 'ee bring it or do I?"

"Go, husband. It has been there long 'nuff, God knows."

The Miller disappeared like a rabbit into a rabbit hole. They heard a scuffling underfoot and he emerged with a bottle from which he dusted the familiar film of white dust.

"Wait with the bandage," commanded Roger. He poured out two measures. "Drink this," he said to Matthew. "Toss it back and never mind the taste."

"Never mind the taste? Best French Brandy—wasted on a slavey?"

"We will wait a minute." They waited for the officer to drink the other measure. But he did not. Instead, he said gently to Matthew, "Close your eyes tight." He gestured to Rona and repeated, "Close your eyes tight and take Rona's hand."

As soon as his eyes were closed, Roger dashed the contents of the cup into the cut so that it streamed down stinging cruelly.

Matthew yelled with shock and pain, but managed to cut it short as Roger said: "Sorry, lad. Better a moment's pain and a wound that heals clean. It should be stitched up, but…"

"I will stitch it. Maman, my mother, had to do it for Jacques—once. If you have fine thread, Mistress, and a needle we will put it in the brandy and…"

"And we will put some more brandy into Matthew."

"Bite on this chicken bone, it will keep your teeth from chattering." Margery found a drumstick.

"Keep one for yourself," growled her husband, "if it will keep you from chattering."

When the job was done Rona whispered, "Mistress Miller please let him have the bed you warmed for me."

The good wife looked anxiously at Henry.

"Pray, do not tell anyone. Let me take him up and I will sit with him in a chair," begged Rona.

"Ye be a kind girl, but this is my place. I have sat up with him before—when he was little—and my baby."

They got him to bed and one of the dogs was locked into the mill. Henry sulked but could not gainsay the Constable, so instead he sidled into the cellar to rearrange his brandy store.

Roger waited with his back to the fire until Rona came down the stair. "Sit now. Tell me how did this happen?"

Rona told him. Starting with the appearance of William Vaylor in the dusk, waving his arms in warning, to the time when she regained the wagon in the lane. She had seen and heard the whole episode and repeated it faithfully. It distressed her to tell Roger about the terrible Vaylor twins, but he assured her that they were not unknown to him.

"What I need to know now is 'why'? What game are they playing hereabouts? If threat of the pox did not drive them away, then they want to be known to be here. Matthew was a heaven sent opportunity for them to make a splash. Something has happened and they do not want to be linked with it."

"Or going to happen," chipped in Rona.

He looked at her with respect. Then suddenly, a thought struck him: "Has Master Vaylor a riding horse?"

"Oh no."

"They might have brought one with them—and stolen mos'like. I must go and see."

"Take me—I know the lie of the land and which is barn and which is stable."

Fatigue forgotten, they ran to saddle Roger's mount. He leapt up in a single leap and extending his arm, lifted her to ride in front of him.

"Leave the boy where he is, I shall be back shortly," he called over his shoulder, as they galloped to the gate.

They had two miles to go and covered the ground fast. A few hundred yards short of the Vaylors' land, they dismounted and walked the horse along the verge.

"Master Vanner, your sword is jangling."

He unsheathed it and discarded the scabbard. It gleamed dully in the dark; and they noticed that the moon had set.

"There's a field gate behind the cottage; we can leave the lane and tether the horse off the track."

They left the horse invisible beside some trees and crept forward cautiously, Rona leading the way. She took his hand and they descended the pasture to arrive at the back of the cottage. There was neither sound nor light.

"They mus' be in the barn."

"Is the barn also the stable?"

"The barn is the byre; the stables are between."

"The stables first."

They felt their way along the back wall and turned the corner. Between the cottage and the stable was a gap and through this they squeezed.

Stable and barn opened onto the yard and under the barn door they could see a light.

"They are still there. Wait for me." Roger lifted a shutter-bar and slid into the stable. A minute later he was back again. "Two beauties," he breathed. "I've untethered one, but I can't lead him out without noise. I want you out of the way and back with my horse; then I will ride the other out—noise or no noise—and be off up the hill."

"Let us ride them both out."

"No, they must have one if they are to lead us to— to wherever they mean to go. With two up on a single mount, it will slow them down."

She thought for a minute: "If I go to William and get him to make a clatter—then 'ee could lead the one and they might think it made its own way out."

"Don' risk…"

But she was off like a shadow and tapped on the cottage door with her finger nail.

A bolt was drawn and William's face peered through a crack. "Let me come in—it's Rona—quick!"

Seconds later, William, lantern in hand and two buckets in the other, stamped across the yard and banged on the barn door with the flat of his hand. They were wooden buckets, but iron bound, and made a fine racket.

Two voices swore at him and then one said, "Is't time?"

"Not yet. I forgot to fill the trough, for the cows." He bashed the buckets against the edge of the stone and prodded the cows so that they shifted their feet. Then, for good measure, he bade the cows goodnight, one at a time.

"Shut you mouth, you ole fule. I tole 'ee we wanted three hours' sleep. Pipe down and get back to bed."

"What have I done to get devils for sons? What can I...?"

But Roger and Rona did not catch the end of his lament, as they rode the fine black mare swiftly up the hill. There they remounted—each to a horse. "Now 'ee mus' get back to the mill and..."

"The mill? Never. I will follow, or lead. See I am already changed."

He peered at her through the dark and saw that she wore breeches.

"William's!" she said delightedly; "Elizabeth cut off 'bout ten inches and found a shirt. Don'ee look so doubtful—I've ridden astride since I were six. See." She was up in the saddle and laughing down at him.

Roger was in difficulty: he could not let the girl find her own way back alone; he must lie in wait for the lawbreakers; and she had a new determination to see her home again. He looked up at the slight form on the Vaylors' mare and shook his head doubtfully. Then he leaned back and fished from the saddlebag a flat cap that he carried for rough weather. "Here, pile your hair into this and let me see if 'ee look less of a woman."

He was still weighing the alternatives when a roar

of anger reached their ears. John had discovered the loss of the horse.

"Quick, into the trees. Can 'ee manage both? Keep them quiet. I am going to hear what I can. My guess is that they will he heading south, for Betsy Cove or Mousell. There's been a lot o' stuff coming in down there."

He flung a cloak over his uniform, to hide the polished leather and accoutrements, and went in a crouching run along the hedge, back to the Vaylors' gate. The he crossed the path and hid behind the hedge where the two purses of gold lay. He heard William come out of the cottage.

"In the name of God be quiet. Let your mother sleep. Do 'ee want to wake the whole county and bring the Constable for a breach of the peace?"

"It's gone. The black mare's gone."

"Gone? Can't be gone. 'Twere there when I watered the cows. I give 'em both a drink; two on 'em."

"'Ee be sure?"

"I can count. Do 'ee look down the field; I'll look up the back pasture—though they coont get up there—the gate be shut."

"Look up the lane," shouted John's voice.

Not too far up, Roger hoped devoutly.

"I tell 'ee the gate's shut. Which one is it?"

"Mine—the mare. The black mare."

"In this dark, a black horse won't find it hard to hide."

"Don' be a fule, father; horses don' want to hide."

"The way ye ride 'em, I should think they'd be glad to."

He shambled to the gate and rattled the bolt; then leaned over and stared up the lane. Where the devil were they? Well away, he hoped, and muttered a silent prayer.

Hidden in the clump of trees above the cottage and out of earshot, or so she hoped, Rona sat the black mare. She held the reins with just enough firmness to keep control without tempting the horse to shake her head. With her other hand, she tried to control the Constable's horse; so far, they had stood still as statues.

She thought, with bitter regret, that this new turn of events meant that the journey across the moor would be abandoned. Her heart had leapt when she thought of returning to her home with a safe escort. If only for an hour, she could have could have collected clothes and trinkets; and to see and touch the place of her belonging. Now she supposed, they would be haring off to the south—to one of the many coves where free traders landed their illicit trophies. She shifted in the saddle and sighed. Surely she had troubles enough without taking on the Constable's. It hadn't occurred to her not to help him; but now she wondered why.

Why was she sitting in the dark, in William's trousers, her ears strained, and scared stiff that the harness might creak or jingle? She listened for any signals that Roger might send, and prayed that he might not be discovered. What was it about him that brought her to this pass?

The young man had had a magnetic effect on her, ever since she had given him her trust. It seemed that she had needed to inspire in him the same trust for her. A hooting owl startled her and the horses too. She struggled to control them and wished the Vaylors would give up their search and start what they intended to do. The halloo'ings stopped, even as she entertained the thought. The bolt of the gate shot back in an explosion of sound and the stamping of hooves heralded the departure of the second horse—with both brothers astride.

She craned forward the better to hear and nearly took a pace or two forward, when the Vaylors turned left to thunder up the hill. They passed within feet of her and she buried her pale face in the black mane under her hand.

Under the weight of the two men, the horse was labouring; it was possible to hear the oaths and burst of speech between the riders. "…never get to Jake in time… see to the watch…meet at the cracks…altogether…" Then their words were lost in the clatter of hoofbeats.

Frowning into the darkness, Rona led the horses slowly into the lane; something was tugging at her mind—nagging at her memory. "Quickly. Quickly," Roger panted towards her.

She paid no heed.

"Come on—after them."

"No—wait."

"We'll lose them."

"Not if we know where they be going. I b'lieve I do know—I jus' can't quite…"

"Maybe riding will jog it up," he said without humour. "I know I mus' go with or without thee. Stay with the father and mother. The only sure way to find out where they're going is to follow."

"They've going to the cracks…They said: 'The cracks…' THE CARRACKS! Of course. The sand—on the sand—it were a map. A map of the Carracks. Oh Mon Dieu."

"What are 'ee babbling about? What map?"

"This afternoon, on the beach, the Vaylors were plotting something; one drew a pattern on the sand. Now I recognise it; it was a plan of the coastline up by Gurnards Head; you know, where the seals come ashore on the rocks…and where ships go aground on dark nights."

"Wreckers?"

"Oh Roger, it could be. They said something else, as they passed: something about Jake and the watch."

"Do'ee know a Jake?"

"One of Tranthem's men be a Jake Whitehead."

"Where would he be watching?"

She frowned again. "The Watch. THE WATCH. The Pendeen Watch It's a beacon on the cliff."

"Yes. Yes, I know."

"It's lighted on moonless nights; ships seeing it, turn to seaward and give Gurnards a wide berth. Oh God, if they put it out…"

"The Vaylors may know of a ship due in tonight, making for Hayle."

Rona shuddered; "I remember a wreck on our bit o' coast, one winter's night; the rain blotted out the beacon. After that, Father kept dry firing on the cliff to light up our own beacon for a warning. Roger, that's what we can do first—we can go and get Bugel to get our own light going. Come on."

She kicked the horse into a canter and went bounding up the hill. Roger was hot on her heels, thankful that he had a guide across the baneful moor. Once more she used the wind—this time on her cheek—to guide her to the top. Once there, she knew every stick and stone of the way home.

As he rode, he examined her theory from every angle. It fitted. The Vaylors were determined to have an alibi at the old folks: seen by Matthew, remembered by Matthew, noted by the Miller. The fellow Jake; the Pendeen Watch; the Carracks—he knew those rocks well; then the map on the sand seemed to put the stamp on it. Wreckers. The very thought was repulsive to him.

As a true born Cornishman, he had enjoyed his fair share of wreckage—the flotsam and jetsam of accident; there was scarce a house or cottage along the coast that was not furnished with timber from wrecks.

Handles, hatches, halyards for clothes lines and sailcloth for stack covers; there was no end of uses for the bits and pieces washed up on the shore, or cast upon the rocks; with luck, even a coin or a plate. But actually to bring ships deliberately to ruin appalled him. His father had been drowned as master of a sailing barge; his brother followed the sea, disappearing for months at a time; he could not remember when his mother was not made afraid by a storm, rumoured or real. To fear the elements was a part of life; to supplement the dangers by treachery was an evil intolerable to him. "From ghoulies and ghosties and rocks beneath the waves, good Lord deliver us." He crossed himself and spurred his horse.

As they left the spine of the moor behind them, Rona was convinced too. Though the day had been overlong, she fought the overwhelming need for rest, helped by three things: one, the thought of some ship creeping trustingly along the coast, looking for the light; second, the excitement of seeing her home again; and then something odd—something unaccountable— the need to shine in Roger Vanner's eyes. It was a strange feeling, one she had not felt before—almost akin to fear.

Farm lads and tinkers' boys were the only young males of her childhood acquaintance. Until she fell in with Matthew, she had known no young man. Often she had begged her father to let her go to the fairs, but he would not. Now she recalled with loathing the touch of the thieves as they jostled her in Marazion and she shrank in memory from the boisterous, noisy, throng of rogues, lechers, jesters and cutpurses that bedevilled the safety of sober citizen and honest traders. She hoped that Potter Jane arrived safe home. She thanked God for him with his steady eyes and fine white beard. That he should turn out to be a relative...why, it was a miracle. And he had vouched for Roger; she remembered her intense relief at the assurance: a Constable on her side, on the side of justice, this was blessing indeed. What then was this pang she felt in his presence? Surely not still a pang of fear?—she shook her head.

"Something amiss?" Roger rode up beside her.

"A-amiss? Why, no, Master Constable."

"I thought 'ee called me Roger, back there."

"I beg your pardon, Sir; I was thinking of the Potter: he called thee Roger. Have 'ee known him for a long time?"

"As long as I can remember. A good man. A good potter too."

"It seems his wife was cousin to my mother—we are related."

"Then we are friends all; and 'ee shall call me Roger. Are we not partners in this venture?"

"Y-yes. But I think I shall not, by your leave. It would be..."

"It would be what, little one? 'Twould be no disrespect."

"I don't know," she said truly. Such familiarity seemed, in some way, to commit her to an intimacy beyond recall. It seemed to jump several fences all at once and all too soon.

"One day," she mumbled, "perhaps." She rode on, hoping for a change of subject.

One minute she wanted to please him, the next to back away. It was verily a mystery.

There was another, more urgent mystery: she did not know where they were. The horses had left the track that they had been following and were stumbling about in tangled heather. She strained her eyes to no avail. She could see the north star and knew the heading was right; but that was all. She was so tired that she understood why people could sleep in the saddle. She started to sway.

As for Roger: he was puzzled, but for a different reason. Here was a beauty—and he had acquaintance with many beauties—all had welcomed his attentions, some had run after him. But this one, alone in the world and in sore need of a protector, was not turning to him in thankfulness, grasping at the prospect of calling him Roger; she was aloof.

Aloof and reserved; and she was brave: no doubt of it. In his experience, courage did not go hand with a retiring nature. Her independence quickened his desire for her. But he would not hurry—there would be danger enough in this night's errand that might throw her into his arms. "Careful now," he thought. "Ye could do worse than the Laity heiress…"

"Do 'ee know where we be?" he asked.

"The heading's right; I expected to find the Maidens hereabouts; but the moor seems empty." She was worried.

They went on a little way, furze and heather fretting the horses; then Rona's mare tripped and went down on her knees; and she went over its head in a curve that felt far from graceful. She landed in springy heather that was better than the hard ground, but she was scratched and shaken and near to tears.

Roger reined in sharply and leapt down. "Rona. Rona, are you hurt?"

"Nay, not hurt; just…" She rubbed her neck and elbows. "Just shook…and angry."

"Come, let me raise thee up." He put his arms round her shoulders.

She lifted her head; one instinct tempting her to lean against him; another telling her to beware. She saw his dark form bending over her and the starlit sky beyond. He did not raise her; he held her where she

112

lay; silent unmoving, intense. She heard him breathing almost as if he had been running.

"Roger?" she quavered; "Roger?"

"Hush. Oh hush." He leaned closer.

A practised young man, he wondered which way she would go. Would her surprise and shock slowly, deliciously, leave her; so that he would feel the weight on his arm relax in trust and surrender? Would she suddenly strain towards him, meeting his kiss halfway? It would depend upon how often it had happened before. He was master of the waiting game, letting a situation build itself; letting the excitement mount. It was working on him too: his first light wish to kiss was now imperative. Rona gasped. She was neither trusting nor experienced; she was in the grip of something she did not understand. Ever since she had first seen Roger—as she peeped over the coverlet in Elizabeth's bed—she had felt an urgent excitement. Somewhere, deep in her being, the chemistry of her body had been focusing on just such a moment as this. She was seventeen and a desire for this bold young man had been waiting. Hoping? But hoping for—what?

Now his arms around her made a haven—or prison. Her powerlessness and the isolation of the place were like a catalyst; in a position akin to surrender, Roger's proximity unleashed lightning. She gasped again, half expectant, half fearful, and unable to escape the whirlwind of feelings that beset her.

He judged the moment well—and swooped into a kiss.

Roger Vanner was good at kissing. He never made the mistake of too much, too soon and too hard; crushing willing lips against resistant teeth was not his way; the resultant squeak of pain that always resulted from that mistake, killed all hope of romantic progress.

113

He took Rona into his arms, gently, feeling with the tip of his tongue for the tip of hers, fanning the flame. On and on, until in a mixture of astonishment and embarrassment, she felt her whole body moving under his as if engaged in some primal dance of its own. Confidently, he unlaced her bodice and felt for her breast. At once, her senses were on the alert, and when his hand strayed to undo William's trousers, modesty was outraged and she rolled away. The heather was suddenly painful, the night air chill and the urgencies and compulsions that had engulfed her were gone, blown away like a summer squall. Turning her head away and craning up, she saw her rescuers: "Roger. Roger. Look!"

From her position, low on the ground, she saw the black shapes of the Nine Maidens, stark against the lesser dark of the sky.

"The Maidens. The Maidens; they have found me again."

Up in the saddle, she led the way with confidence. She skirted the Galvers and headed straight for the coast—and home.

CHAPTER XVII

Clem Bugel was in the deepest sleep when the knocking came. "Tonight we can sleep sound," he had said to his daughter. "The two beauties Tranthem put into the house, 'ave rode off." For as long as they were in residence, he felt obliged to sleep with one eye open. Dorothy was a likesome girl and unwed.

"They be up to something; depend on't. An' it's bound to keep 'em away all night; there's nought they can do nearby." He bolted his door, as usual, but with a lighter heart. He mistrusted Tranthem's men; they left him to do the work of the farm unmolested, but hung about with knowing sneers, and the airs of conspirators. As Clem shambled around, playing the dolt, he puzzled his brains to discover Tranthem's next move. Did the men know something? No: surely Tranthem would not take his rank and file into his confidence. He thought the Constable a fool for putting in strangers: local lads would have known that Bugel was no simpleton. Yet shrewd though he might be, there was nothing he could do except tend to his young Mistress's beasts; and to try and survive until a Laity came to claim the property: house, and land, and stock.

The knocking bored into his dreams and he was up and peering through the shutters before he was fully awake.

"What is't lad? Be 'ee benighted?"

"Clem, come 'ee down, Clem."

"Clem is it? Who be callin' me Clem?"

"Unlock the door and you shall see."

Bugel blundered down the ladder stair, answering Dorothy's frightened whisper with a curt "Quiet, girl."

The fire was blanketed with peat and the cottage pitch black. He felt the bar that lay across the door and hesitated. The lad might be a decoy, a forerunner, but of what?

"Clem, let me in—please Clem. Be quick."

The voice was louder and Clem halted. What game was this? "Dorothy come down, my ears are playing tricks. What voice is it?"

"Mon Dieu, for the love of God, open up. Wake Dorothy, she will open to me."

"'Tis Rona. Quick, father. She be out in the cold." They wrenched the bar out of its slot and threw open the door. The young figure in breeches was indistinct in the square of starlight, but unmistakable.

"Mistress. What in the name o'...Alone? Fetch a candle, Dolly, stir the fire, come in, shut the door. Why...?"

"Clem," laughed Rona. "Be still: nay, leave the door; Master Vanner is here."

She seized the cowman's rough hand in both of hers: "Oh, Clem, Clem. 'Tis good to be back; to come home; to see 'ee again. But we are in great haste: we must light the beacon—our beacon. Constable Vanner—'ee remember him—we think there is a plot afoot to put out the Pendeen Watch. Know 'ee some man called Jake?"

"There be a Jake in charge o' us here, Mistress. But tonight he rode off wi' th'other one; aye and to the west."

"Well, Master Bugel—not so soft tonight, eh?" Vanner stood in the doorway.

"'Tis all right, Clem; the Constable knows the truth now and is on the side of justice. But first, there is this matter; we overheard a plan to catch a ship on the head or on the Carracks. Is there plenty of furze in the cave? Dorothy, my friend, put a candle in the lantern and a shawl round your shoulders. Is Eddie here still?"

"Aye, it takes more'n Tranthem to oust out ole Eddie. I'll rouse him as we pass the barn. He shall bring dry straw."

"Come on, Master Constable," cried Rona almost merrily. "Oh smell the air." She sniffed, turning her head this way and that. "The wind is from the west—the rocks are a lee shore; we must be quick."

She led the way across the yard, through the gate and onto the cliff. "In these breeches I can climb down; hold my hand and let go when I say." She clambered over the edge at the point where, with her feet, she could just reach the beacon ledge.

Within ten minutes, they built a beacon the height of a man. Bugel showed Roger the cave, and in the dim light of the lantern, they shifted furze, stacking it

116

to windward, ready to feed the fire. "Enough. It is enough. Set a flame to't."

Vanner reached for the lantern. But Clem was quicker: "Nay, Master Vanner, think on. The instant it is lighted, the wreckers will see it and ride against it to put it out. Sir, I beg of 'ee, take Mistress Rona and my Dorothy straightly into safety. I will fire the beacon and keep it going."

"Good Clem, I will take your daughter with us, certain; but there will be time to build several fires before they can reach us from the watch or Gurnards. Set the flame to it."

"Wait, before us dazzle our eyes." Bugel stared to seawards. They could smell the sea and feel the draught of it; faint surges could be heard against the cliffs, but in the starless dark there was nothing—not the faintest glimmer,

"Would we see a ship's light?" asked Roger.

"Mebbe. Mebbe not. Ahoy!" he yelled. "Ahoy, ship ahoy." He shook his head.

"We're looking too far out, look nearer," said Rona.

"My God—a ship. Set the candle to the beacon."

CHAPTER XVIII

It blazed. The flames threaded through the crackling twigs—the scents of old autumns blew in the summer wind and a red radiance lit up the old farmhouse. The small night wind and the updraught at the cliff top carried the sparks higher and higher.

"Quick, Dorothy, while there is light: come into the house with me. I want clothes and my treasures and Mother's Missal. Master Vanner, I be for the house with Dorothy. Where are the horses? I mean to turn mine into a pack animal."

"I mus' put on clothes myself," said Dorothy, who was still in her shift.

It was a strange homecoming—with a flickering firelight that cast shadows where there never were shadows before, dancing shadows that turned each room into squares of uncertain shape.

Rona's inrush was halted. This was her home—yet it was not her home. It smelled wrong. The long awaited return blew back at her with strange odours: sweat and smoke, tallow and gun oil, rank food and stale beer. The old fragrances of baking were gone; even the old farm smells of hay and fresh mown grass, milk and cheese—all were missing. Rona flinched and hurried to the stairway to reach her own dear room. Please God that no trooper had desecrated it.

She found there no evidence of disarray. The coverlet was still on her bed and she proceeded to load her possessions onto it. Her limbs ached, she longed to lie down; but she knew that Roger would not have time to wait upon her frailty. She walked round, touching her things; remembering. Then she dragged her coffer into the light and opened the heavy lid; her clothes lay undisturbed. One after another, she lifted garments onto the counterpane, and the sweetness of lavender filled the room. She tucked a few trinkets into the pile and turned to go into her mother's room.

A sudden dimming of the bonfire put the landing into darkness and Rona was afraid. As if a cold hand touched her in warning, she went back to her own chamber and to the window. The fire was burning steadily again and she saw the figure of Roger on the cliff top, black against the blaze. His sword was sheathed and he was leaning on a pitchfork. Her heart pounded when she saw him, with the same unfamiliar mixture of excitement, need, anxiety and fear. Why fear? It was not the straightforward dread she had felt when he arrived in the Vaylors' cottage—the dread she felt for Tranthem—no, not that; it had subtly changed to a sharper more personal alarm; almost as if she were afraid of herself. She dragged her thoughts from the confusion of spirit and wondered if there would ever be time enough and peace enough to sort it out. And to sort out that rush of wild excitement she had felt on the moor, when he...when he...She wanted to lie down—here in her own place; to sleep, to remember, to find out who this Rona was; who this Roger.

The ship. She must think of the ship. Had they been in time? Had some unknown man at the helm seen their beacon before it was too late? Or, if it were too early, could they keep the fire going for long enough? As Clem had said, the wreckers would be furious and ride like hell's devils to quench the light. On an impulse, she opened a window. She could not hear the crackle of the fire, though she could smell the smoke. Then her ears picked up another sound, more a vibration: horses galloping. She turned her head this way and that; from the west from Pendeen.

"Roger—Clem." The figures did not pause. "Roger," she screamed, pitching her voice high.

"What is't?" Dorothy came from the cottage.

"Horses. Horses. Go and tell them quickly."

She gathered up the four corners of the bedcover and knotted them together. Then she dragged the bundle across the floor. It was heavy, but even the boots of alien men had not destroyed the polish of centuries. She gave the room a lingering look, vowing to put it to rights one day. Then she heaved her burden to the stairhead and tipped it down. She would get it to the front door, then Dorothy would have to help.

The front door was not commonly used and the bolts were stiff. Rona went to the kitchen for a candle and a hammer. At the back of the house she heard the yelling. Dorothy shouted to the men.

She knocked the bolts and the door creaked open, but flagstones were more resistant than polished floorboards and she could not move the bundle. She went upstairs to see if she could see Dorothy.

She was shocked by the sight that met her eyes: the beacon was in ruins. She saw Roger and Clem fending off three men with sword and pitchfork. She saw Clem nip smartly over the edge and disappear and she saw the sturdy figure of Dorothy hastening back, and panting "Out, Mistress. Out."

"Front door," she called; and dashed back to the landing. "Oh God. Sacré Coeur de Dieu. Lend strength to his arm."

Between them, she and Dorothy dragged and half carried the bundle down the short path that led to the lane. "Can we not leave it?"

"No," Rona answered sharply. "It's all I have. I've lived these three months with nothing but one tattered gown. 'Ee do not know how lost I feel with nought of my own."

"Then let us hide it—behind a rock—a bush..." They found a break in the retaining wall on the moor side of the lane. The long grass was wet but the two girls sank down, collapsing over their task.

"Mother's Missal. I must have Mother's Missal."

"No—no Rona, be still, God knows what they will do next."

"They'll tip the fire over the cliff and stamp it out. With luck, Clem will catch some of it and fire the cave. Stay here."

She ran back into the farmhouse. There was less light filtering through the windows, but the kitchen candle was still in the hall. She snatched it and ran upstairs—the flame nearly horizontal. Two at a time she went, thankful for the freedom of breeches.

Her parents' bedroom was a sorry sight. She held the candle high and steeled her heart against despair. Where, in all this disarray, was the precious Missal? At the Prie Dieu? No. Thrown aside? She looked probing every shadowed corner. These Godless men would have no use for it; her father would have been the last to handle it…where…where? She fell onto her knees beside the great bed, in silent prayer. Under the bed? He might have put it down and, later, some foot might have kicked it underneath. She tore aside the bedclothes so that the candle could not fire them, and there, amongst a selection of boots, fluff and feathers, lay the book—dusty but undamaged.

"Maman, oh Maman; I have this much of you at least."

Always Marie Laity had taught her daughter to counter tears with gratitude. "Always there is something to be grateful for, ma petite." Now Rona forced her mind to gladness for this joy in the face of so much loss.

A raucous voice, very close, forced her off her knees and to the window. The yard was full of movement; at least half a dozen men with torches were approaching the house. To loot? To eat? The beacon was flattened to a mere heap of smoking embers. She could not tell if Roger were there, wounded or prisoner, or lying dead at the foot of the cliff. She shrank from the window and pinched out the candle. Whatever had befallen her allies, she knew she must get out of the house, sharp and quick. She buttoned the holy book into her shirt and felt her way across the landing and down the stairs. Half way down, her senses were assailed by a fearful din: yells and curses and vows of revenge. Then smoke filled her nostrils. The fools! They were bringing the torches into the house.

A figure kicked the door between the kitchen and the hall: it flew open with a crash and through it came a lighted brand. Rona watched fascinated as the blazing stick sputtered and flared on the flagged floor beneath. On the stone, trodden smooth by centuries of busy footsteps, it burned harmlessly, lighting her way to the door: but before she could gather her wits together, a further hubbub was building to a crescendo.

"Ye'll not set fire to flags." Philip Vaylor's voice was unmistakable. He stormed through the door and flung the brand on to the bottom stair. The glare of the flames as they hit the step, sent up a sheet of dazzling sparks and scorching heat so that he did not see the slight figure crouching higher up.

"He did not see me—I mun jump over it—and fly. Mercy!"

"'Ere, gi'me another for the parler."

"Oh no, no, no," moaned Rona.

"And the upstairs—make a proper job." Vaylor laughed harshly.

Rona fled. She leaped over the blazing branch and shot out of the door to join Dorothy. "Come on," she gasped, seizing the bundle. "Out of here they're firing the house."

"But that…"

"That will be the biggest beacon of the century; a beacon that will burn until next week."

"Father has pails…"

"Pails? It will need a river of water to put it out. Pray they do not bother with the cottage."

"Be they drunk?"

"Drunk with fury. Maybe we have foiled their plan. Maybe…they mean to kill us." The Vaylor twins. What was she to tell William and Elizabeth? She shook her head back and forth as if madness had gripped her and hysteria was near.

122

"Rona," whispered Dorothy, "come away. Father will see to the Constable. Father knows the ways down the cliff or into the tunnel."

"The Constable: Roger. I had forgot. We must go back. Back to the fire. He may be wounded, dying."

"And he may be waiting for us by the horses. We'll go to them. Where be they?"

"In among the rocks, round the corner."

"Come then."

Rona was already on her way.

"What about your clothes?"

"Leave them—we'll be back. The horses first."

They were standing quiet, patient, recovering from their trip across the moor. And they were alone.

"We must take one of them to pick him up…"

"Both, one will wander."

"Then we will take none. If he comes back and finds them gone, he will not know where we are or what we are about."

"What say we go on foot, keeping to the lee of the barn and the byre? It be a short run to the edge; in your breeches 'ee could crawl it."

"Aye, and 'ee could wait half way to go back for a mount if needs be."

Young and brave, they set out, keeping well to windward past the blazing building; out of the danger of sparks and heat, they crept closer and hugged the side of the barn. Rona went on alone, leaving Dorothy at the corner, where barn and byre made a right angle. Down on her hands and knees, she wriggled towards the dying beacon and leaned over the edge. "Roger," she called softly. Why softly?—there were no villains to be seen. "Roger:" this time she called more loudly.

The silence under the fading night was oppressive after so much din. Where were the fire-raisers? Not at the house; the heat there was too intense. Had their leader called them off; to the west to Pendeen; or to the east, to the rocky headland, where they had hoped to leap upon a wrecked ship? Or were they answerable to Tranthem, and gone there to report? "Roger," Rona screamed into the darkness. There was a grunt from somewhere below.

"Who's there? Roger…Clem…Oh God I can't get down by myself."

Behind her the flames from her burning home leapt into the sky. She could not bear to look. The light from the fire threw the overhang into even blacker shade. She could see nothing and knew that her legs were not long enough to reach down to the ledge—not without a hand. Dorothy, she would have to get Dorothy.

Running back and calling, calling, she persuaded her friend to return with her to the cliff.

"Oh Rona, be they gone?" she asked terrified.

"Gone: and God knows who with them. But below is someone who lives enough to grunt. Take off your skirt."

"My skirt?"

"We need a rope. You hang on to one end and let me down."

"Oh Rona…"

"Mon Dieu, Dolly, get on wi' it."

Dangling over the cliff, clinging to Dorothy's skirt and feeling with her feet for the flat ledge. Rona encountered something soft.

"Down a little more—more—It's a body—must be." It occupied the whole width of the rock. "Up! I've got to find another place."

They struggled and strained until Rona could lever herself over on to the grass. Puffed and aching, she lay on her back; knowing she must do it again. Seeing her stricken face, Dorothy said, "Shall I go? It might be father." Rona had no strength to argue.

"Further along, then." She hung on to one end of Dorothy's cotton gown, and Dorothy hung on to the other. The girl reached the ledge and let her feet feel their way along along it. There she found the prostrate form and tried to recognise it. "Not father. Thanks be. He be in some sort of tunic."

"Roger. It mus' be he. Be it a leather tunic?"

"No."

A sharp explosion coming from the direction of the house made her spin round. It sounded like her father's arquebus; perhaps it had blown up in the heat. Another shot, closer, sent her into a dive to lie flat on the ground.

A gruff voice demanded: "Who's there? Stay where 'ee are. This be loaded."

"Father?"

"Clem." The two girls spoke together.

"Ye young fools—what be 'ee doing here? Why bain't 'ee on the road to New Mill?"

"We came to see if 'ee and the Constable were in trouble."

"Where's Dolly?"

"Down below—wi' Roger."

"That bain't Roger—that be ole Eddie. I pulled 'im down out of the way; 'e banged 'is 'ead, th'ole fule."

"But..." Rona was bewildered. "Where is the Constable? What happened to him?"

"Last I saw, 'e was chasing three of the fire-raisers, Oh Mistress, it be terrible—the house—it be near 'nuff gone."

"Which way did he go?"

"Who?"

"The Constable."

"Towards Tranthem's land. That way. He ran one through and nicked another in the knee—one of the Vaylors. 'e'll not be doing much running for a while. Come on, 'elp me get up ole Eddie."

125

CHAPTER XIX

A band of leaden light was dawning in the eastern sky by the time they had Eddie snug in the barn.

"I'd be best off to the meeting place. Do'ee come wi' me, Dorothy?"

"Us'll both come. I'll not lose the sight o' 'ee again."

He collected Rona's bundle and laid it across one of the horses, while she leaned against the rock and stared at the smoking, flaring, ruin. She had no words—not even for her own thoughts. Perhaps Roger would have something to say of comfort—of hope. She saw him as her only hope.

But Roger's greeting, when he came up with them was like a cold slap. He was furious.

"Where the devil have ye been? Twice I came here and twice I had to go searching for 'ee. I am delayed—the law is delayed. I tell 'ee to stay wi' the horses, but when I come 'ee are gone. In God's name, where were 'ee?"

Rona saw his cold angry face. "My home was afire," she said in a small very weary voice. "I knew not if ye were o'erwhelmed, wounded, burned—in need. We sought 'ee to bring a horse for your comfort—in case..."

"Give it here; I'll not stay listening to anymore. I mus' get to the Vaylors before the sons can get back and say they have been there all night."

"Nay, Sir," broke in Clem. "One lies dead in the yard with a ball in his belly; th'other was the one 'e got in the knee, wi' thy sword."

"I heard an explosion. That was thee?"

"'Twere the li'l ole arquebus. I took un into my keeping when the Master died. I taught me to use it and kep' it by me o'nights."

"Good work. Then they be done for. But there be

126

others. I'll leave the girls wi' thee—God help 'ee—bring 'em after me in the morning."

He sprang into the saddle, turned his horse's head and was away, in a single flowing action. He rode into the early light of dawn, making for Tranthem's land, without a backward glance.

Rona felt faint and sick. Dorothy caught her by the arm: "'Tis to my bed 'ee mus' go. Look father, she cannot stand nor bear anymore. Gi' her a leg up an' I will walk the mare home."

With all her worldly possessions behind her on the horse's rump, Rona rode to the farm cottage and fell exhausted onto Dorothy's bed.

The sun was high before she woke, but sleep had done little to restore her strength. Was it only twenty four hours since she had ridden so blithely to market? Puzzled, she found she was wearing torn breeches. Her hand flew to her throat—the Cross. It was not there; but in her bosom was her mother's Missal. Memory crept back piecemeal; she remembered that Elizabeth had made her leave the cross. "In a safe place," she had said, knowing the rogues in the market. Elizabeth. How could she find words with which to meet Elizabeth. Now that...now that...

She lurched to the door and threw it open. The scene of wreckage spread in front of her: a wretched scene of ruin and desolation: blackened roofless walls: gaping smoking windows: the stink of death and destruction: a trail of blood leading to the spectacle of two bodies, dragged by Bugel to lie by the wall—one of them Elizabeth's son. She switched her gaze to the blackened window of her bedroom; the window from which she had watched the passing seasons, hailed her mother in the yard, and from which she had finally escaped to freedom. Her bedroom, now burnt out, was gone. And she had no other...She sank onto the doorstep, covering her face with her hands.

"Oh my dear soul." Dorothy came hurrying from the barn with eggs in a basket. "Back to bed wi'ee. Back to bed." She coaxed Rona into the cottage and found a clean shift for her.

"Put it on while I warm some gruel. Refresh yourself. Tomorrow be time 'nuff to look at they. 'Tis certain the problems won't go away. Take 'ee rest meanwhile. Father says 'e will fix up a place for 'imself in the barn, so we can be here to usselves."

Rona lay down obediently: her body reflecting the sorry state of her home. She ached sorely in all her bones and her ankles were scorched from leaping over the flames on the stairs. She felt racked in mind and limb. "Think not on't," crooned Dorothy. "Sleep. Sleep."

But sleep—deep sleep—evaded her. For three days she dwelt in a sort of dappled limbo, criss-crossed with day dreams and nightmares. She saw the Potter, not on the beach, but turning at his wheel: turning not bowls but figures. Figures formed under his fingers: Matthew crouching like a dog in a dark mill: Elizabeth's kind, bewildered face: Philip against a background of fire, like a demon in hell. She felt herself balancing on the brink of a black pit of unknowing and woke, again and again, clutching the blanket to save herself from falling. And weaving in and out of her dreams, she saw Roger Vanner; beckoning, repulsing, smiling, frozen, angry, lusting.

On each occasion that she had roused herself to go out to the privy, she had seen the ruins of her home. Gradually the reality of it took hold of her mind. Facts. Even if justice were done and Tranthem charged with murder and destruction, her estate was still irrevocably changed. Now only the Bugels and the Vaylors stood behind her. The Bugels' tiny cottage could not house her for long; and God only knew how she would stand with the Vaylors when they learned that it was their sons had brought her to homelessness. She prayed fiercely that Roger would not tell them. A fruitless prayer.

Roger; she forced herself to think of the strange and disconcerting interlude on the moor. Sometimes he seemed her main hope and infinitely desirable; but then she had to admit that there was none of the sweet serenity and trust that she believed to be the natural accompaniments of love. She loved God with a great gladness; God was an unshakeable rock, as firm and bright as her native granite. She had loved her parents and Uncle Jacques with unquestioning faith in their goodwill. Loving had been a source of delight. "Tu aime ceux que tu aime." You love the things you like; you like the things you love; you have joy in those whom you love: enjoy the things you like. This concept of loving, liking and enjoying had been learned from her mother and had been the key that opened her heart to the wonders of living. Now, suddenly, it had become a yardstick—a measure demanding excellence. Marie had said: "Do not be stingy, my child; do not be grudging with your love. There are folks that go through life with no more than a guarded liking for a few things: never marvelling: never grateful: never loving. Love only the eternal changeless things of God; then, if you lose your heart—in some trouble perhaps—you will be sure to find it again."

Now she seemed to have lost everything and her heart too. Perhaps the "heart"—the courage—would be renewed; but she thought it without much hope; it was difficult to be brave about nothing.

Her heart—that part of her that needed to love—was trembling violently and heading off in a way that

129

was deeply alarming to her. She knew nothing of the body's chemistry and its native treachery; treachery that made her think of Roger as a prince… when she was not thinking of him as an ogre.

Meanwhile, what was it all for? Bitterly she regretted bringing him to her house; interpreting the map; lighting the beacon. It had destroyed her home as surely as if she had lit the torch herself. And for what? A ship? What ship?

CHAPTER XX

Roger—Prince or Ogre—was far away; and as far again in mind and thought. Rona had not crossed his mind since he had flung off in a fury. He had ridden in ever widening circles to find the surviving Vaylor and the rest of the firebrands. "Wreckers! Cut-throats!" He spat out the words with a sort of relish. Catch these devils and it would be a whole handful of feathers for his cap.

There had been none suspect in the Vaylors' cottage when he stormed into the yard and thundered at their door. In his disappointment, he had not spared the old folks' feelings. "Not here, eh? Well, Mistress, you are surely one son the less this day." Elizabeth's cry choked in her throat as he continued: "One, at least, I reckoned with: a ball in his belly and…"

"He died—quick?"

"He died quick enough. The other's wounded—gone to ground. But I'll catch un." He glared at them without pity.

"The one that was wounded," William said quietly, "was it mortal?"

"He fell. I did not stop to pick up and feel his pulse. They'd fired Laity's farm; so your lodger will have scant love for Vaylors and no wealth to recompense your kindness."

"Rose?" Elizabeth sat down shakily.

"Rose—Rona—what matter? Her house is burnt down utterly."

"Christ in heaven...and she...where is she?"

He shrugged: "Safe 'nuff. I reckon; if she bain't running crazy. All I know is that I mus' chase Tranthem's gang afore they all go to ground." He turned to go, shouting back over his shoulder: "An' if t'other one limps home, tell 'im I'll be back."

William and Elizabeth sat silent, bowed. Then Will rose and put his arm round the old woman. "Don'ee distress 'eeself, my lover. We don' know if one is dead—or which one; not for sure. An' if one is— dead—then 'e be out of the war."

"What war?"

"The war 'gainst folks—'gainst us two—'gainst hisself..."

Ash shifted in the fire and a bee cruised round the room seeking something sweet. Two gulls, arguing over a scrap, and the softer notes of the turtle dove were old familiar sounds. And Elizabeth seemed to hear the cries of two boys calling through the orchard in summers long gone.

"And Rona? Oh Will, the poor child; and none to comfort her. Can she forgive?"

His face grey, his brows drawn together, his eyes unbearably sad, he shook his head. But after another silence, he said, "Aye." But Elizabeth believed it was only to comfort her that he said it.

Roger had ridden hard; looking for trails, raking through barns, prying into ditches, questioning. What little rest he had, had been taken under hedges and stacks: catnaps to give his horse a chance. By midday of the third day, he was silly with sleep and near to dropping out of the saddle. He found a sheltered place in the lee of a low wall: a stone wall warmed by the sun and with good grass nearby. He lay down and was asleep before he had tethered his horse or taken his saddle bag for a pillow. The beast was too tired to wander. His obsession with the hunt had blotted out everything; but as his exhaustion eased, he began to dream.

It was of Rona. Visions of her pale face swam up through the tired mists of his mind—black hair, richly waving; the creamy oval of her face; blue eyes and a mouth both gentle and merry that smiled at him. In his dream he resolved to be the possessor of this woman with such a face.

He slept until the heat went out of the sun, and awoke stiff and cramped, chilled through by lying on the ground. But despite the aches and the pressures of the chase, rags of his dream clung to him. Waking, he perceived Rona as being infinitely desirable, for all her loss of fortune. The land was still hers together with the hidden minerals that Tranthem thought worth killing for. It would be a decided asset to an impecunious Officer of the law. Landless, he had chosen his career because of the authority it carried. There was little hope of authority as a tenant farmer, a fisherman or a tinner; but with Rona's inheritance he would be well placed for swift promotion. He had had many opportunities to observe that money made money. He smiled slightly as he imagined her obvious feelings of relief at the prospect of having him as her protector. He was certain he had not mistaken her admiration and the beginnings of passion. He longed to go quickly to the north, to consolidate her feelings for him; but duty was too strong and, peevishly, he rode south: sure that Tranthem would refuse shelter to cut-throats, and would not risk involvement with the night's disgraceful events. But, even as he rode, he knew that the foxes would have split and gone to earth by separate ways. He stifled the thought that it was Rona who had delayed him at the start of the chase; remembering that it was truly her concern for him that had delayed her in the first place.

For all his handsome aspect, Roger Vanner was a very ordinary young man.

CHAPTER XXI

Dorothy was preparing a "mix 'm, gathr'm" for their evening meal; scrambling together eggs, milk, cheeses and herbs; when a sudden shudder made her spine crawl. She took the skillet from the heat and ran outside. She saw Rona at the very edge of the cliff and she was rocking on her feet. "Rona," she shrieked, "Rona, Rona." She raced across the space between them and dragged her friend from the brink.

After that, as Clem Bugel went about his business he stayed close to the cottage and was ever watchful. He prayed that Tranthem had received no word of the girl's presence; for there she must stay until Nathaniel or Vanner came to escort her safe away. He could be nearly sure that the Squire would not know; for one thing he thought her dead; and for another, all that anyone could have seen was a lad in breeches and a flat cap. Best put them on again. "Dorothy, tell your Mistress to put on the breeches again—jus' in case us gets any nosy visitors."

News of the fire must have gone along the coast; who knows if the Squire would send a spy to see the remains? Aye, and what pleasure it would bring to him…Clem was a realist: he saw no hope of the farm ever being restituted but he must do as well as he might until Nathaniel came and it was in Nathaniel that his own best hope lay. Maybe there would be work in Helford for himself and Dorothy. Since her own mother's death, Rona's mother had taken the child to her bosom. Now the savageries of fate had fallen on both of them; there was no bosom for Dorothy now, nor yet for the daughter of the house.

Bugel did not sigh or even feel surprised at his own sudden lack of security; rather he had been surprised at the former good fortune of having so honourable a master. The lot of serf and servant did not usually permit of a known future. He faced the unknown with no expectations of so much good fortune again. Meanwhile, their positions reversed, it was his bosom that must cherish Rona. "Get she back into trousers, an' keep 'er out o' sight."

It was on the third day when the mists departed Rona's mind and the shackles of exhaustion left her limbs. The sun blazed but a sea wind whispered across the cliffs, cooling the remains of the house and blowing fragments of singed grass and charred wood into little heaps against the boundary walls. On the night before, rain had washed through the house and the mixed smells of fire and water lay unpleasantly upon the air.

Rona and Dorothy were in the cottage and Clem was turning hay when they heard the approach of horsemen. Instantly on guard, Clem saw them while they were still far off. Strangers, they sat their mounts awkwardly, and as they drew near, he saw that they were seamen. The elder one wore the soft flat cap of the times but the other had a coloured bandanna round his head, and golden earrings glittered through his straggling curls. Both of them wore sea boots, and though only the senior man wore a sword, it would have been foolhardy to challenge such a pair.

Clem, being no fool, hid within the barn until they should pass. He was thankful that the lower half of the cottage door was closed: the girls were out of sight. He waited impatiently. To his annoyance, the horse stopped; doubtless their riders were curious and looking at the ruin of the farm.

He heard voices but not words and peered round the barn door the better to see what they were about; he saw them striding to the cliff and stirring up the cinders of the beacon. He saw them gesticulating towards the house and heard one call, "Ahoy there! Ahoy!", then shake his head and turn to stare at the sea.

Bugel advanced, pitchfork in hand; "Good morrow, Masters. Do you seek your way, perchance?"

"We have found what we seek—whose land is this? Whose house?"

"'Tis Laity's land—Laity's farm. And you, Sir?" He looked them over, his blue eyes shrewd.

"I am called O'Sullivan, Captain of the St Finbarr. This is Connor Branagan my mate." Branagan grinned a gapped-toothed grin. "Sure and we are here for a dozen Captains, whose ships were saved from running aground by this—beacon fire—three nights since. Glory be to God."

"A dozen? Twelve ships? Holy Mother…" Bugel crossed himself and then looked up guiltily. But Captain O'Sullivan saw no cause for disapproval in this sign of the old faith.

"Aye, twelve good ships—and all loaded to the gunnels wi' gold for—on England's business."

"So!" Bugel nodded. "That's the way o' it. No wonder Tranthem joined wi' common wreckers. Gold!"

"Wreckers? What is't you're saying man?"

"Aye Cap'n, wreckers. Why, think 'ee the Pendeen watch was not alight that night? It was not, I b'lieve."

"You're telling me…the what are 'ee telling me?"

"I mean that but for my Mistress your twelve good

ships would have piled onto the rocks at Gurnard's Head where there was a wreckers' welcome waiting…waiting for thee and thy gold."

It was the Captain's turn to cross himself. After a moment he frowned. "Your Mistress? Where be your Master?"

"Dead—and by the same hand as would have had your life."

"And your Mistress?"

"About her business," Bugel said curtly.

"I'm sent by my Commodore, wi' a purse—payment for the rick. Sure, we thought it were a rick. We saw the beacon and then a second fire. Th'Admiral thought sparks had blown and fired it. Now, God help ye, we see it was no rick." He gestured at the ruined house helplessly.

"Aye, and it were no spark as fired it. The wreckers were so angered by our signal, they torched the house."

"The devil take 'em."

Captain O'Sullivan brought a stocking purse of gold pieces from within his doublet. He shook his head. "It be poor recompense for a farmstead. My Master will do more, no doubt, no doubt of it, at all, at all. Bid your Master come to Hayle…Master Laity had a son?"

"No son, Sir."

"Your Mistress then; where is your Mistress?"

"Within my cottage, Captain." Bugel made up his mind to trust the Irishman. "Within the cottage with the other servants."

"Bid her have no fear. This money is hers."

"Dorothy," called Clem, "bid your Mistress to come and greet guests. And bring some cider—two pots."

"Rona, quick…put on a gown and come outside. Father says we have guests."

136

"Roger...it must be Roger." She sprang up, she had known he would come. Now she would show him how she could look. She burrowed into the bundle of clothes and shook out her best gown.

"Presently, presently," she called.

Dorothy emerged with two pots of cider, dishevelled in her cotton gown, the apron smeared with grey ash. The men took the cider and wandered back to the edge of the cliff. They looked down at the sullen sea. Its blue innocent face did not deceive them. Looking eastwards toward Gurnard's Head, they saw the rocks, the uncaring relentless rocks, onto which so many ships had been driven by storm and gale or the unforgiving dark. The two men were silent; but in their heads they heard the rasping, grasping, ripping, tearing grip of those rocks on the timbers of their ships: and the screams of drowning men who died unshriven in the crashing rigging. There was no need for words. Only to their Saints—St. Patrick, St Bridget and St. Finbarr—did they mutter thanks. To them and Mistress Laity.

Rona stepped into the sunshine. She wore her gown of primrose yellow silk, the dress made from the length of cloth given to her on that birthday that belonged to another life. It was low cut, and under it was a tucked bodice, high to her throat and hiding the Cross. She had swept up the Cross when she changed into William's breeches on that terrible night and had lodged it in her pocket. She could not leave it for the twins to find. She wore it now and on her head she wore a small cap made from the same yellow silk as her dress. She used Dorothy's comb.

Holding her head high, she left the cottage and rustled down the path.

Captain O'Sullivan and Branagan goggled at her. They were expecting an aged sorrowing widow, crumpled by life and by weather. They saw a breathtakingly lovely young woman. But Rona, searching the road for Roger, saw nothing.

Whirling round in disappointment that was fast turning into anger, she saw the two strangers.

"Why...who are you?" They smiled at her discomfiture. "Oh, I pray you excuse me...I was...I thought..."

"Sure, lady, 'tis a terrible shame that I'm not a handsome young rogue come for you on a dashing white horse—aye, and that with wings." He swept her a low bow. "Allow me to present myself, Captain Dermot O'Sullivan, and Connor Branagan, both of the St Finbarr; now safely anchored in the haven of Hayle—thanks be to God."

She listened to his strange voice in some amazement and looked from one to the other and back to Bugel, her face full of questioning.

"There was twelve ships, Mistress Rona; twelve, mind ye, twelve saved from the rocks by your fire."

"Twelve ships?" She shook her curls in bewilderment. "And ye, Sir, were with them? Out there?"

Captain O'Sullivan bowed and stood over her, very tall. There was some grey in his beard but his hair was as black as her own, his eyes grey-green like the sea; he made Roger seem like a callow youth. She dipped into a belated curtsey and he raised her up, dropping the purse that had been in his hand. "Faith, let it lie," he said. "'Tis the best place for so scant a reward."

"What is it?" Curiosity overcame her shyness.

"Gold—a little gold—enough to pay for a rick or a stack. This was the way of it: we saw the light and stood out into the deeper water. Looking back, we saw the second fire start. The Captains and the Lord Admiral, we all thought that so bold a signal must be recompensed." Then he turned to look at the house; "Alas, no amount of gold can resurrect a homestead."

"It can go a long way to helping," murmured Clem.

"Hush Clem. Good sirs, you have come from Hayle with this? It is kind. We had no idea of a reward. We did not know if there was a ship there at all."

"Why then…?"

"I heard some snatches of talk in the market. Some known rogues drew a map on the sand—I knew it, at once, as this coast. I—it is a long story—let us sit in the sun—and take some refreshment—oh, but we have no chairs."

"We have no meat neither," whispered Dorothy, "only cheese and eggs, and a mite more cider."

"Let Connor help, Mistress." He muttered something to his mate, who followed Dorothy into the cottage.

Dermot O'Sullivan rubbed his hands together in anticipation; "I think you must tell me the long story. There's more to this than meets the eye—and God knows that is enough."

They sat on the grass; Rona with her back to the sorry ruins of her home.

"Now," he said, "tell me how it was that you came to rescue the Queen's Navy."

"The Queen's Navy? Come Captain, we did nothing like that.

Twelve ships? Twelve big ships?"

"Big enough. It is what they were carrying…by my Faith, they carried enough to furbish twenty more— aye and man them too."

Rona felt elated and very uneasy, by turns. How had Tranthem and the Vaylor twins got wind of such a treasure fleet? Was it because O'Sullivan, or some other Captain, had been free with information at the port of embarkation. She looked at him curiously, then asked, "Where is Connor?"

"I gave him a coin and sent him back to the farm we passed on the road. He will get some meat."

"No. NO!" cried Rona. "That is the place where the wreckers made their plans. Pray heaven he says nothing about this—about me being here and alive. And they'll have his blood if they think he can lead them to this gold you speak of. You should not have spoken of it. It is unwise. Quick, go after him and bring him safe back—meat or no. Make haste. Go GO!"

O'Sullivan caught the urgency in her voice and rose reluctantly.

"Oh get up! Move! And make no mention of me, I beseech it. I am supposed to be dead—which is how they want it. Ye can be sure they will question you to death if you can tell them where the treasure is. Where is it anyway?" Rona asked innocently.

Faced with a direct question, O'Sullivan's guard went up. "Safe 'nuff. I'll be off."

"Head off your friend. Prevent him."

He swung round his horse's head and spurred him to gallop.

Rona ran back to the barn and the cottage, looking for Clem. She told him what the Captain had done and what he had said.

"The man's a great lummock, talking so free. Even without Tranthem and his mob, there are thieves enough to track it down once it's known."

"Wait," said Rona desperately, trying to crystallise her fears. "Tranthem does know—I do not believe this was a chance wrecking—and he will not have let that fleet out of his sight. They will have followed it along the coast, watching all the time. And if they have sailed into Hayle river, it will not have been too difficult. They'd better have gone further north, out of sight of land: out of Tranthem's country."

"They know nought of Tranthem; nought of

wreckers. They may be unloading already, in sweet ignorance."

"And with Tranthem making an ambush."

"Where will they be taking it—the gold?" Clem bit his thumb.

"Furbishing ships is what he said. Falmouth Haven is my guess. A cut across the moor."

Clem ground his teeth: "They mun be stopped. They'll be easy targets once on land."

"Then we must turn these fellows round at once— send them back to Hayle afore it is too late. Clem, saddle the horse—the one I took from the Vaylors. I'll go after them, turn them round; then they can tell their Master to take the stuff further afield."

"I cannot 'low 'ee ride alone."

"Clem, Clem, 'ee can't stop me. Quick, to the stable!"

She gathered up her silken skirts to cross the yard and fetched the saddle and bridle. "Help me, Clem. I will be back directly. I'll meet them on the way and bid them back to Hayle fast as they can."

"But…"

"Ye look after Dolly and the farm. Who knows who else may come?"

She took the hem of her dress between her teeth and mounted to ride astride. "I'll be back soon," she called over her shoulder, kicking the horse into a canter and then a gallop. It needed no encouragement; after three days of inactivity, the horse was fresh and went like a mad thing. Rona clung on, the wind in her face and her hair streaming back; riding on the horse's neck, urging it on, they went with a flurry of hooves.

A mile on, she saw a small cloud of dust that resolved itself into the figures of O'Sullivan and Connor. Thanks be to God, they were not prisoners and under Tranthem's lash. She reined her horse with difficulty and shouted to them to turn back for Hayle.

"You? What's up."

"Who was at the farm?"

"No-one, but an old dame who sold us cheese. There was no flesh, she said. But," Connor chuckled, "an old hen jumped into my saddlebag—just for the ride."

"That means they are all in Hayle. Don't you see, Captain? Someone knew about the cargo, and when they missed it at the Headland, they will have followed along the coast to see where it was bound for. They'll be gathering at the harbour, ready to pounce. Hurry. Hurry. Warn the Master you speak of."

"Raleigh will never believe it."

"Raleigh? The great Sir Walter Raleigh?"

"The same. Lord Lieutenant of Ireland. And hasn't he collected it up—this bounty—to be bringing it to the use of Her Majesty Queen Elizabeth?"

"Collected it? From the Irish? What? Digging it up?"

"Devil a bit! Didn't we sail out of Cobh to intercept the Spaniards? And weren't they bringing it to the Low Countries for to pay for their armies there? Out we went, fair weather and foul, and now we mean to use their own gold against 'em."

"Well you won't have any gold if you don't go straight to land it somewhere safe from Tranthem."

"Faith, 'tis safe enough—it's in wine casks and the mules will be waiting ready. Even the guides will not know what they're carrying—the guides across the moor to Falmouth."

"But Tranthem knows," she shouted. "Else why so angry? Why did they fire my house? Why are they not at home? Where do you suppose they are? For the love o'God get moving, Sir."

"Raleigh will ne'er believe it."

"Then I must come wi' thee and make him believe. I have the whole story."

She dug her little heels into the horse's flank and continued along the coastal path. She dared to pass through Tranthem's land, knowing that the lord of it was absent. "Make haste," she called over her shoulder. "They will already be watching your wine casks."

But Captain O'Sullivan still hesitated; he was not used to receiving orders from a woman—and a young woman at that.

And he didn't fancy his chances with the Admiral if he had to tell him to abort the plan. Rona, turning, saw that they had not moved. She went back, wrenching round the horse's head.

"Sacré Coeur, can you not move yourselves? Can you not see that every minute gives the thieves a better start? Can you not see...?" She saw them staring— seeing something quite else.

Embarrassed, she looked down and saw that her bodice was torn. The Amethyst Cross on its golden chain glowed in the sunlight.

"Holy Mother of God—be that the cross of the Brothers? The one Brother Jacques told us of?"

"Brother Jacques? Ye know him?"

"Did I not take him safe to Ireland in my own ship? Back in the Spring gales? He told me to seek out his niece and tell her he was safe delivered."

"Then he is safe...Thanks be to God—and to you, Sir. It is good news indeed. I am that niece; we will talk about that later. Now, by the Cross I wear, swear ye will tell no man of its whereabouts, on pain of hell fire."

They swore, crossing themselves; their eyes never leaving it. She drew the bodice across. "The man who chased Brother Jacques is the same that we chase now. He killed my father, he burned my home, he is after your gold. Come now, no more delay, my Masters; let us go and God prosper our going. Jesu," she muttered, "will they never get a move on?"

They galloped towards the east, striking sparks off the embedded granite, until the horses were sweating and panting. They paused, briefly by a trough, and then went on like bats out of hell, to warn the great Sir Walter Raleigh.

After five miles, Rona lost one slipper, after six, the other.

Outside St. Ives, the shadow on the sundial, on the side of a church, fell across the face of it at two o'clock. They had made good time and rested before the last lap of the hectic journey. There would be no ambush until dark and it was but seven more miles to Hayle. A mile on, and her horse lost a shoe. O'Sullivan hauled her up behind him and she hung on with closed eyes and gritted teeth. The Captain smelled none too sweet, but she clung close, her fingers knotted into cloth stiff with salt and sweat and small beer.

In mid-afternoon, they thundered onto the quay at Hayle and slithered to a stop, on cobbles slippery with slimy weed and fish scales. Rona gratefully slid off and leaned against the horse's steaming flank. Her hair was tousled and her gown—the fine gown of primrose silk—was grey with dust and stained with the horse's lather. She smoothed them down as best she could and, gazing around, urged O'Sullivan to find his Master.

"I sees him, there, at the harbour edge, in the midst o' them boyos."

"Go then. Fetch him out."

"Have 'ee no sense, girl? How do I do that?"

Barefoot, she dragged him towards the group of officers and, as they approached, Sir Walter turned. "What have you been at?" he demanded angrily. "All the forenoon and most of the afternoon—what dost thou mean by't? Ho! I see. A wench."

"No, Sir." It was Rona's turn to be outraged.

His lip curled. "Go to your work; and you, baggage, be off. Go to your work, hear me? Get down to the Jolly boats and load. The job is but half done."

"Thank God for that," Rona said to the Captain. "Go on—tell him. Tell him what we know. What brought us racing across country to warn him. For Christ's sake—tell him." She was shouting.

Raleigh thrust forward furiously but O'Sullivan stood his ground. "Sor, we found the place of the beacon, Sor, it was lit by this lady for our protection. She is no wench, but the owner of the land, your honour. After the beacon was alight a gang of ruffians come to stamp it out. Wreckers, they were, and waiting on the rocks of the headland. When the beacon foiled them, they fired her house, in vengeance. It were no rick, Sor."

"What's this? This fairytale? Tell me later—if you must. Now, get to work."

"Oh, don't be so silly," cried Rona, exasperated, exhausted and impatient.

Walter Raleigh stiffened, he had not been called silly since he was a stripling at his tutor's knee. "Silly?" he thundered. "Ye dare—a fool of a girl—a country chit—"

"I dare anything after that ride. Do you think I come here, my best gown ruined, barefoot and near jolted to death, to be refused a hearing? Mon Dieu, les hommes en colère sont rien que les garçons mèchants." Her mother used to address her brothers so, the men on the farm, and even her own dear husband. Rona went on: "Unpick you ears, Sir Walter, be the great man you are supposed to be."

The "great man" was shocked into silence. And in that silence, she went closer and told him the whole tale of woe—of the market and Roger Vanner, and their dash across the moor to light the beacon; of the wreckers deprived of their prey, running rampant over her land. "The Constable will be chasing them still—maybe to the south—maybe he is near here."

"I see. I owe thee thanks then."

"I don't think you do see, begging your pardon: understand, the wreckers, led on by Tranthem, knew the fleet was coming—someone must have talked in Ireland—think you that they will stop now?" She went closer still and spoke softly; "You may be sure they are here and watching; watching your every move. Where is the—the cargo?"

"In that warehouse and under guard."

"It will not be under guard on the road to Falmouth. This is their country—they know the trails."

"Wine is such a good snatch?"

"Wine? Come, Sir, no amount of wine needs an escort of twelve ships. It is not wine we are talking about. And if a foolish girl can guess at gold, how much better can an informed gang of thieves? They've guessed all right; and guessed at Hayle too. Pity you chose such a well-known haven; there are a hundred coves better hid."

There was another silence when the Admiral drew his sword. Rona wondered if he was going to strike off her head.

"Look around," she said desperately, "look at these loafers watching, waiting. They mean to get at it. If you leave it in the warehouse, they will burn it down—they are good at burning down."

Raleigh looked around and saw that there were, indeed loafers. He took them for fishermen waiting for the tide; then he saw they smoked clay pipes. Only men with money in their pockets could lay hands on tobacco. Even the sweepings and wastage and broken leaf were expensive—he should know, who had first brought it into the country.

146

"Half the cargo is ashore," he muttered to himself.

"Then it must go back aboard; and the ships must stand off."

"You don't know what you say. If you be right then think you they will stand by and see it reloaded?"

"I have an idea: empty the casks in the store and load them empty into the carts. Send them out on their way. That will thin the forces against ye."

"And the cargo proper—have you a master plan for that, pray?"

"Nay, Sir, I am just a fool of a girl. But I can see that things are going inboard; hogsheads full of food and water…there could be anything under yon salt pork…"

He rallied his Officers and strode into the warehouse; and Rona was left standing.

CHAPTER XXII

She was tired out and wanted nothing but to sink down on the nearest barrel or wall or coil of rope. But, true child of the farm, she saw that the horses were even more in need. They drooped, blear-eyed and shivering. Gently she led them away from the harbour and asked someone the way to an ostler. He was not hard to find and Rona decided to play the humble servant.

"My Maaster do say 'ee will pay 'ee 'andsome if 'ee do tend 'is 'orses."

The man eyed her; "'N when do I see the colour o' is money?"

"I do carry none, fule. 'Ee do 'ave the animals for surety. They need rubbin' an' restin' an' warm bran. An' they do need it now—not the day aafter tomorrow. Th'Admiral 'imself'll pay 'ee. Double, if 'ee do't well nuff."

"'Ere then, take the tokens—gie 'em to the Lord High 'n' mighty; tell un there be no better ostler in Kernow."

Nearly asleep on her feet, Rona made a wrong turn out of the stables and found herself in a dark alley. The golden light of late afternoon was lost in shadow and the stench of refuse filled her nostrils. She did not know if she should head out of town and start off home; and even if she did, she had no idea of the way. Pausing to consider, she noticed an old dame sitting in a doorway. She was toothless and leering and smelled horribly of fish and old age. Harmless enough, thought Rona, but the old hag heaved herself up and grasped at her dress, fingering the silk with her filthy hands. Rona resolutely kept her own hands from protecting her neck, and the Cross, but the only thing to do, to free herself from the clutches of the harridan, was to strike at her face. She thus broke free and a torrent of obscene oaths followed her down the lane, past dreadful dwellings where shadows lurked and followed her. She turned right and right until, at last, she caught the tang of the sea and the quay on the air: fish and pitch and weed drying above the tide-line.

She had ridden hard and with no thought of how she might get back, so that only now did she realise that she had lost her horse, had no money, no shelter and no friends in this hostile place. Her thoughts strayed to Roger Vanner. How could he have left her unprotected, with the sparks of her home fanned by the breeze and nothing but the cold moor behind her? In her fatigue, she forgot the Bugels and thought only, to her surprise, of Matthew. "Matthew, oh, Matthew," she sobbed, as she leaned against a wall, "ye would not have left me thus."

Perhaps Captain O'Sullivan would lend her a shilling—on the strength of her uncle and his reverence for him. She sidled onto the quay to watch out for him. The cobbles were wet and struck cold to her feet and the chill of evening was in the air. Wherever the setting sun cast a shadow, it was cold; only in the fairway did the sea have colour—there it was opalescent and the tips of the wavelets were pink. The crowd had thickened; she was sure that there were more onlookers than before, but they were strangely silent: watching, assessing, waiting. Seamen plied their oars as ships' boats fetched and carried goods and supplies. She noticed that none of the ships was still moored alongside, though the tide was rising and almost at the flood. The slipway was under water and boats were being launched onto it directly from the store. Had the Admiral taken her message to heart?

There were old sails draped round the warehouse doors and the canvas was guarded by ferocious seamen armed with bludgeons. As she watched, she saw them launching a boat onto the slip with O'Sullivan at the oars and a large hogshead dripping in the stern. He rowed with short chopping stokes, watching the water spilling from under the lid of his burden. There was something odd about the boat: it should have been stern heavy, Rona guessed that an equal weight—of gold?—was stowed under the Captain's feet, under the sacking that all could see. As soon as he was safely offshore, she ran to the edge and hailed him: "Captain, Captain, is the wine all ashore?"

"Nearly all, lass."

And she heard a murmuring and grumbling all around her; men muttering to each other: "Do they think us fules? Wine? We'll see what sort of wine."

And one said, "What's it to 'ee?"

"Bain't nothing, save when he's done, he be coming to supper."

She tried to be casual and idly watched the boat drawing away. Some way between the Quay and the ships, he met with a boat coming the other way; an altogether smarter craft, for in the sternsheets sat Sir

149

Walter himself. O'Sullivan drew alongside and told his Master that the girl was still on the Quay—and alone.

The great man sat with his seacloak flowing around him, half cursing the interference of the girl and half, uneasily, grateful to her; uncertain whether she and O'Sullivan were sane; uncertain that he had not made a fool of himself in changing the well-prepared plans. Suppose someone had talked in Ireland—someone with ready contacts in Kernow; it would be absurd to take it for granted that they had not been watched and followed. And now, but for the smart action of this Laity girl…now he obviously had some responsibility for her safety: the safety she had sacrificed for the safety of the fleet. No maid should stand alone on a quay swarming with foul-mouthed longshoremen. It would look ill if she were molested. And, besides, she might still be able to help him—in the choice of some other landing ground; she had hinted at hundreds of hidden coves. He leaned forward and gave instructions to the oarsman. Instead of heading for the slip, they made for the steps. Raleigh mounted thoughtfully.

Rona's heart beat faster; she feared his anger and knew that she looked bedraggled and dirty. She knew by instinct that he would seek her out, and smoothed her dress, knowing that it would make no difference. He greeted her deep curtsey with a short bow.

"Come aside, if you please," he said; then, "I am by no means certain that we do the right thing, Mistress."

"Ye shall be, sir, when the mule train is beset. Already, they are muttering about it.

"We shall see."

"Aye, we shall see; I cannot wish your men to be attacked, but…"

"But if they are not, then ye will have fouled up well laid plans."

150

"Yes Sir."

"And I do not forget that ye presumed to call me silly."

She coloured and hung her head; "Can 'ee not think that I warned against it? Do not be silly?"

"People have lost their heads for less."

"Take it," she said sadly. "It is all I have to lose; it would save a deal of trouble, for I know not what to do."

"And I know not what to do with thee."

"Lend me a horse, Sir, and I will go back. I will see that it be returned…"

"The horses…where are they?"

"I took them to a stables. The were all done. Here are the tokens."

"I'll say this, ye are a practical girl; I wish I could say the same of…well no matter. My thanks for taking care of them." He thought: "Perhaps she is not an hysteric, after all."

She walked away from him towards the ostler's stables.

"Come back, I have not dismissed 'ee."

But she stood still and flicking her eyes at the listening crowd, she said: "Sir, whatever ye have to say were better said over here." She held fast her gaze upon his face and again darted a look at the men, now silent, attentive.

He joined her and they walked out of earshot.

"Sir, when I saw the Captain just now, I called out to him; I called: 'Is the wine all ashore?' And these men, all around, they sneered and mocked: 'Wine?' they said. 'Wine? Do they think us fules. We will see the colour of their wine when it is spilt on the moor…D'ye hear the pack mules stamping within the store? They'll not be stamping much longer.' They were laughing."

"Do'ee know any of them?"

"No. God help me if I be recognised."

He walked on, fingering the tokens and looking at the sky. "Ye cannot ride so far this night. Ye had best come with me. Ye can tell me more of the coastline. Eat and rest."

He turned abruptly and led her back to the steps and into his barge.

"Drop me off at the slip and take the lady to the Faerie Queen."

The sailor's eyes opened wide and he looked shocked and sly by turns.

"Take that idiot grin off your face. If I find that one finger has been laid upon this lady, that man will swing—and ye with him. I do know your name, indeed."

"With thee?" Rona faltered. "Would that be proper?"

"Propriety or safety, ye may choose. Nay, i'faith, I will choose—safety." He handed her down to a seat in the stern and glaring at the boatman, said: "Show her to my cabin; and thou, Mistress, do ye bolt the door and wait for me."

The man at the oars looked over his shoulder to get the line of travel and to hide his chagrin, and they traversed the short distance to the slipway where Sir Walter sprang ashore without a backward look.

Rona shivered. The evening breeze was chill and she had nought on to warm her. The sailor looked her up and down and decided to play safe. "Will 'ee be wanting a lend of my jerkin at all?"

"Nay—thank'ee. I—I would like to take an oar and warm up that way."

"An oar? A lady friend of..."

"I be a country girl born by the sea. Give I un. I'll show 'ee." She eased herself onto the thwart beside him and leaned on the oar until he surrendered it.

"There. See? I pull as well as 'ee."

"Begod, an' so 'ee can. Keep time wi' me then; in, out, in, out."

"What be 'ee called?"

"Jonah, Miss."

"That's funny—I be Rona. Jonah and Rona, side by side."

They rowed comfortably until their small craft was overshadowed by the bulk of the Faerie Queen.

"What be 'ee to Sor himself?"

"Nothing, Jonah; I be in fear of him. Will 'ee take care o' I? Be a friend?"

"Sartin I will, Maidy. An' I'll tell me mates that 'ee ain't no grand lady, wi' all airs 'n graces."

"Bain't I grand 'nuff to go up by 'is Lordship's ladder?"

Jonah grinned and pushed the barge round to the Admiral's gangway. He led her through the ship, possessive and important, showing off the best points of the Faerie Queen. She was, he said, Sir Walter's own flagship, named for the Queen of England. "'Ee do say it be a name thought up by a Master Marlow."

"Who be 'ee, then?"

"A ship builder, I b'lieve."

CHAPTER XXIII

The ship was about one hundred and fifty feet long and half as wide, so it took no great time to walk around her. They ended the tour, presently, before an ornate door carved with dolphins. It was at the stern and opened onto the Captain's Quarters in the poop. There were twisted brass handles, exquisitely wrought, and a large keyhole. Jonah brought the key, big enough for a church, from his blouse, and unlocked the door.

The Admiral's cabin filled the entire width of the

ship and had wide windows that overlooked the sea. The windows slanted outwards from window seats to deckhead and, outside, a balcony overhung the water. Centrally, and bolted to the floor was a heavy table; it served as a chart table as well as for dinner. Benches ranged round the bulkheads and underneath them were sea chests, all different. To starboard was a small curtained area. "'Tis 'is cot," said Jonah.

"What be that to I? Why be I here?" A thread of panic ran through Rona's thoughts.

"Sure and it's for safety, Mavoureen; the Admiral said for 'ee to wait for 'is Lordship. See, Jonah'll make 'ee a bed."

He opened one of the sea chests and dragged out blankets and a cushion; he arranged them on the window seat. "Get thy feet up, I should."

"I should like something to eat: 'tis a long time since breakfast."

"Breakfast, is it? Leave it to me." He hurried out and she heard the key turn in the lock.

If she had not been so bone tired, she would have been very frightened. She knew she would sleep if she lay down and she knew, too, that she must think. She roamed round the spacious cabin and, behind the curtain found a scrap of mirror and a jug of water in a bowl. Her face shocked her. Streaked with dust and sweat, hollowed-eyed and pale, she did not recognise herself. Pouring out some water, she tried to salvage some of her respectability. What to do with the dirty water? Was there a chamber pot? Desperation took hold of her as she tried to open one of the windows.

Jonah entered triumphantly with soup and a lump of bread. "Jonah, what will I do with the washing water?"

"Over the side." He cocked his head on one side; "Sure an' ye have a pretty face under all the muck!"

"And what—what will I do for a—necessary pot?"

154

Jonah coloured and went beneath the Admiral's bunk to find his Master's. "And that goes over the side, your ladyship. This be the winder that opens best. Now, draw up and fall to; I'll be back for the dishes when himself gets back to the ship."

"Thank 'ee Jonah. And, Jonah, keep—keep the key safe. Let no-one in.

"Devil a one, little Missy; trust in Jonah. Don't 'ee put me in mind of my own little sister, Bridie?"

He left her and she set about eating the food; then, lying down, she let go. Tears, weary tears, flowed down her cheeks, but not for long. Soon, her eyes closed and she fell asleep.

Raleigh returned to his flagship as the first stars showed in the east. He was tired and irritable, but, under it all, he felt a boyish excitement. There was much to be sorted out in his mind; he wished that there had been time to weigh up the girl's preposterous warnings; it was O'Sullivan's conviction that their plan was discovered that made him take action. Different action—to disrupt the established plan. God, what ignominy would have followed if the gold had been surprised on the moor. The mule train and carts had been sent off along the trail, carrying casks full of sea water; and, with a lot of clinking and whispering, the drovers had armed themselves underneath the hessian smocks and sackcloth capes that they wore to give the appearance of peasant labourers. Small swords and daggers abounded beneath their innocent exteriors; and a dozen outriders, mounted on fresh horses, rode, some ahead and some behind, carrying muskets. Though the "treasure" was worthless, nevertheless the escort meant to capture the rogues, for questioning and punishment.

One of the outriders was to return to the coast, once the outcome of an encounter was determined. He was to light a beacon on that spit of land that stuck out—almost an island—to the west of the harbour of St. Ives. He pictured the mule train straggling through the dark and the robbers crouching on the wild moor and wondered where they planned to strike—if strike they would—and where they intended to hide the prize. What if the child were wrong? And O'Sullivan wrong? He had bidden the captain to sail with him in the Faerie Queen and the man had looked scared to death.

"We'll see...we'll see...meanwhile there is time to rest." Raleigh left off gazing at the stars and assessing the strength of wind and tide, and took himself to his cabin. Jonah sat outside the door. "Brandy and a light—look to't," and Jonah scurried off. He sat heavily in his chair—the Captain's chair, carved and cushioned—and dragged off his boots. Easing his toes, he carefully considered whether to remove his stockings—he was too tired to think of anything more important than his feet. There had been too much of plotting and planning and fearing.

He had given up, long ago, wondering if the ends were worth the candles.

To serve Queen Elizabeth was always a matter of life and death; yet, without the risk there was no hope of advancement. There was no point in wondering what would have happened to him if the gold had been lost. The Navy would have been poorer, his lands, titles and estates would have been forfeit—even his head. Had she wished it, the Great Gloriana could ruin all of it with one prod of her knuckly finger. She could destroy him; and no number of cloaks flung into the mud, would save him, if her face were turned against him. His breath escaped in a sharp sigh; it was his own ambition that had hoisted him up so high that he could crash so hard. He broke into a sweat at the thought of what might have been, but for that girl and her blessed beacon.

As it was, the Queen need never know. Hawkins would know. Hawkins, the Controller of the Queen's Navy, would know because it was with him that the plans had been laid. They thought that they had covered all the flaws and contingencies, dangers and delays. Well, Hawkins would never tell; it was his scheme as much as Raleigh's. Neither of them could afford to play ducks and drakes with such a fortune. Drake. Yes, he thought, there was always Drake. The thought of Sir Francis' dry humour restored his spirits; if there was anything in the law of averages—the laws of the Medes and Persians—Francis should have lost his head in a hundred ways afore now. He had tempted Providence, and Her Majesty, for fifteen years; longer than Raleigh…He felt a tremor under his feet as the ship snubbed the anchor chain. The ebb. What was O'Sullivan at? They must be off on the ebb.

He levered himself up and went to the window; and, even, as he looked, he heard his Captains' shouts and saw sails sprouting from the yards as the little fleet weighed anchor to leave the haven and set a course for Bristol.

"Light ship," he yelled at the door. "I want all to see that we set a course for the north."

Jonah appeared at the cabin door, lantern and brandy in hand.

"Jonah," he bawled, "what kept 'ee?"

"Bos'n denied me the spirits, Sor. S'long as we be in port. I tole 'im 'twas for 'ee."

"The Bos'n was carrying out my orders. Give it here; and now go and see that the Captain has all the lanterns

alight. Tell him that I will be on the bridge presently."
But not yet, he thought; an easement, a drink, his feet
on the table for a moment, these first.

"Aye aye, Sor, Yerronour."

He went back to the window to scan the anchorage,
but the lantern had spoiled his night vision. Instead of
seeing into the dark, he saw his cabin; and, in
particular, he saw Rona.

"God's wounds..." He held the lantern high and
stared at her. He had forgotten her.

What next? Whatever next? He could not have a
woman in his cabin—not he. He would have to be on
the bridge, and fast. But stay—if O'Sullivan came down
there could be no scandal, and he did need to know all
he could of the secret coves and unsuspected landing
places.. He went to the door and yelled again: "Jonah."

Rona stirred. She opened her eyes and saw the silver
ripples dancing on the deckhead; she smelled the
unfamiliar smells of a great ship, and lamp-oil, brandy
and tobacco, and man. Then she saw Raleigh.

"Well? What are we to do with thee?"

The ship heeled over and she nearly fell off the
window seat. "What—what was that?"

"We are at sea, Mistress."

"Sacré Coeur. How long have I been asleep?"

"Not long enough, from the looks of 'ee." Her face
was cleaner, but he could see the shadowed hollows
beneath her eyes. He saw something else too: he saw
a glimpse of gold—something on a chain around her
neck. Gold. So she was not a mere farm wench. He set
down the lamp and put a finger under the chain to
bring out the ornament.

"Holy God," he exclaimed, "what have we here?"

"'Tis not mine—just in my care. One of the Brothers
from the Mount charged me with the care of it. He
was—was being chased by..."

"By the Queen's men? I know. I met such a one in Ireland—a good man and brave. Brother Jacques, if I remember…"

"Aye, Brother Jacques. He be my uncle. I carry this for him, until I can get it into the right hands."

"Ye gallop round the countryside with a treasure round your neck? Be ye mad? Here, give it into my keeping; I have locks and keys."

"Thine are not the right hands. Ye are not of the Old Faith." She paused, scared by her own temerity. "Sir, ye are high in the Queen's esteem; she would have your head if…"

He gave her a bitter laugh and a backward nod. "Aye. That's good reasoning. But, child, in a shipload of rogues, how can ye hope to save such a fortune? Let me see…"

When he came near to handling it, she bit his hand. "Christ!"

"Aye, Christ." Then she looked mightily afraid; "I be sorry. I beg your pardon…Sir?"

He looked at her again; "Thou must be hungry if thou wouldst eat the Lord Lieutenant of Cornwall, Lord of the Stanneries and Admiral of the Fleet."

"Oh, Sir…"

"Meantime, be ye right about the thieves on the moor? What sort of a fool have 'ee made of me?" He sat again in his chair, and brooded on the dilemma of the gold.

He supposed that some Irishman, some rebel resentful of an English Overlord, might have watched; could have passed the word; might even be in one of the ships under his command. He wished he had never been given lands in Ireland: reward for his part in quelling the rebels. He wished he and Hawkins had never got drunk on the Barbican and dreamed up this idea of by-passing the Queen's purse. Brandied claret, that's what had landed him in this mess.

The navy needed new ships; the shipyards new money. The Queen was so busy making royal Progresses from one end of the country to the other that they could not catch up with her, with the inventories of shortages and pleas for funding.

"Then we must get our own gold," he had said, as if it were the easiest thing in the world. Hawkins had scratched his nose.

"How?" Hawkins had reached for the brandy.

"Ha. I have it. Brandy." He poured it out. "Tell me, Walter, how does the brandy come in?"

"The Trade?"

"How else? Let us take a leaf out of their book—a rowlock out of their boat—and bring gold in the dead of night." They had roared with laughter. It was the wittiest of witty jokes.

"And...ho ho...where does it come from? Who's the alchemist?"

"Why, Philip, of course!" John Hawkins had chuckled and belched. "Spanish gold to fight Spanish ships. That pleases me."

All night, they had formulated the hilarious idea until they slept where they sat. But, strangely, in the morning, it seemed an even better idea.

Two or three ships, armed and ready could lurk in some Irish harbour and await the lumbering Spanish cargo ships, en route for the Low Countries.

"The Queen will have to know; without her licence it would be piracy; we must be privateers."

"A quibble. But go if you will."

"It will have to be thee, the great Sir Walter. Ye the favourite; it was a good move to call that new colony Virginia. There's nought she will not give thee; her Captain of the Guard."

160

"She can keep her Guard...Yes, I will have to put it to her if only to get time off. But she must keep the secret; will she, think 'ee?"

"I believe she may. But give her no detail: no names or places."

"Easy, we have no detail to tell."

How long ago? Was it a year? Nearer two since the night on the Barbican. Plymouth's Barbican, where the River Plym flowed into the Sound. Later, in the pearly light of dawn, they had sat on the rough grass of the Hoe, and watched fishing boats beating against wind and tide to reach the haven where the greater rivers, Tamar and Tavy met together to make one of the grandest harbours in the known world. The island, that was later to be called after their friend Drake, loomed out of the mist. "Such an isle would be a good hiding place. I must scour the coasts of Kerry and Cork for one where the currents are right and where there are not too many wagging tongues."

He had worked hard and sailed hard; hidden his captives and stashed his gold; and, now, here it was, unloaded and reloaded, lying higgledy piggledy in sacks and sailcloths and barrels of salt pork; in an operation that should have been secret. This Squire—this Tranthem—who could have passed him the word?—that is, if the girl were right. By God, if the girl were wrong...mad or vindictive...pawn to his enemies...He smacked the arms of his chair and rose to go on deck before temptation to shake the truth out of her overwhelmed him. She could be a spy, a traitor, a witch.

"Sir," a small voice whispered from the window-seat; "Sir, I mun find the—privy."

"Eh? The what?"

"Oh sir...the privy...if you please."

161

"Oho." Raleigh's bad dreams and tensions were exploded. "My little witch is human. Here, Madam." He extended his hand to her; "Behold my own illustrious bucket." He bowed, with a flourish: "It stands at they service, obedient to thy will." He picked up the lamp and hung it on a hook above his head. He bowed again, still laughing. "Forgive me child; I do not mock your need, but it brings me as much relief as you to see that you are no bogey." He backed out of the cabin and closing the door, stamped noisily away.

"Captain," he bawled, "is't not time to wear ship? Set her head to the South West: surely the ebb is still in our favour?"

"Sure, Sir. But we have been on that tack these two hours."

"Two hours? Faith, I must have slept in my chair. It was dreams then, dreams of betrayal." He looked at the lantern by the helm and saw that the marked candle burned steadily and made the time near midnight.

"Time to turn again and edge in, landwards."

"Aye, aye, Sir."

"Then we shall see. Then we shall see."

"What's that, Sir? What shall us see?"

"A beacon, I hope. A beacon to tell us that we do right to quit Hayle and make a new landing. A beacon at St Ives."

Captain O'Sullivan joined them for the change of tack. He took the helm and checked a new star into the rigging.

"There's your heading, Helmsman."

Admiral and Captain paced the deck. "Think 'ee we shall see it? The beacon? What if the messenger is slain?" O'Sullivan was anxious.

"Then we shall know that all has not been plain sailing. No beacon is as much a message as no light will be. As long as we are looking in the right place."

"Aye there's the rub." He scanned the dark. "It will not be the brightness of the burning farm."

"Ye believe the girl...? She could be working a trick—or mistook."

"Didn't I see her home blowin' in ashes? It were her enemies did that wickedness. I'll swear on the Holy Book she's no liar. No maid wearin' the Holy Cross..." O'Sullivan spat to cover his slip, and muttered, "No liar."

"What did 'ee say? The Cross?" What did the rough Captain know about that?

"She has a wee bitty cross about her neck. It will lead us into safety. Let your Honour believe it."

"Ye talk in riddles. I'm famished. 'Tis hours since I dined..."

"'Tis days since the maid dined—shouldn't wonder."

"Jonah," he shouted; and his servant bobbed up beside him;

"Jonah, dinner for three, in my cabin."

"Dinner, Sir? But 'tis the middle of the night."

"Dinner—and fast if ye value your neck. O'Sullivan, ye will join us. Give the helm to the Cox'n and post a look-out at the foretop to watch for the light."

Over dinner, which Rona devoured with a desperation that caused Sir Walter some alarm, she answered his questions. Between mouthfuls of cold chicken and fish pie, her story took shape. Her father's death, the Vaylors, their sons, Constable Vanner, Clem Bugel, Matthew: he noticed that Matthew and Roger Vanner featured strongly in her tale: all took their place.

"Who else? What kin have 'ee?"

She told him of Uncle Nathaniel in Helford: "A goodly man—I s'pose—but so dull. Father said it was his wife made him dull. 'If ye marry a woman call Prudence, you go mad or become prudent yourself,' Father said."

"And Nathaniel?"

"Oh, he took the prudent path; it leads nowhere."

Raleigh laughed. "So, we have a prudent shipbuilder. He has a place by the water?"

"Aye, Sir, between Helford and a tiny place—I forget the name."

"And which God does this Nathaniel worship? The Queen's God or the Pope's?"

"Whichever Aunt tells him to—and she is a plain woman."

"Then he will be safe in the Queen's business."

"Why, Sir, he lifts his eyes no higher than the high tide line; what can he know of the Queen's business?"

"Nothing, I trust; and that is how I mean it to be. We could use this Nathaniel. He is ideally placed and ideally wed."

Rona frowned: it was all a great mystery.

The night was very dark. A young moon had gone to an early rest and little starlight reflected from the popple on the surface of the sea. Now and again, a glimmer of phosphorescence followed in the wake of the ships: a silent magical light, fragile as dewdrops on gossamer. The evening breeze was fresh enough to keep the sails full but they could not see what progress they were making over the land, nor how far off they were. They stood side by side at the stem, Rona in a borrowed cloak; they stood and they watched. The jibsails were not set: the view uninterrupted.

"I believe we should turn a point or two to larboard."

"I'll see to it, Sor." O'Sullivan was glad to get back to his helm. One by one, the other ships turned with them.

"Ye are sure there is no other light hereabouts?"

164

"After the Hayle beacon, there be nothing until the Pendeen Watch. That is why Father kept his own fire ready—for nights that are too dark or too stormy."

They had placed watches along the length of the larboard side and presently a shout from one of them alerted them to a ruffle of water abeam. "Rocks," yelled Raleigh. "Stand off again." He turned to Rona; "Know ye what they might be?"

"How far did we sail to the east, before turning to come back?"

"More to the north; there were too much ebb to make much easting."

"Then that might be Godrevy. We should see the Hayle light by now. I don't know. How is anything seen if it be raining?"

Her companion did not answer. The hazards of the sea were only too well known to him.

"What is that—over there? I see a lot of tiny sparks…"

"Fishing boats. And there, beyond—see, at last—a beacon. It must be Hayle."

"Or St. Ives. There be plenty of fishing out of there."

"Douse the ship's lights—all of them."

They crept across Carbis Bay, watching intently for St. Ives' point. That was the place…that was the site for the signal…Slowly, slowly the fishing fleet was left behind, the little light that marked the entrance to the channel faded to nothing; and to the west—darkness.

Raleigh was profoundly disappointed. Was his outrider prevented? Unhorsed? Lost? It was all very well to say that no news was good news. He tried to imagine the scene on the moor, where, in the same dark, under the same sky, men with mules went step by step, waiting for a sudden deadly attack. He heard, in his head, the clash of swords, the oaths, the panic cries of horses, the shouts...

Someone was shouting. "A light! A light! Nay, two lights!"

It was there, his signal. None but the man who was to light them knew that two lights—a hundred yards apart—were to be the true signal. One for failure. Two for success.

Raleigh clasped Rona to him in a great bear hug. "We beat 'em—thou and I."

"We were right." She meant Clem Bugel and herself.

"Aye, we were."

So. The caravan was attacked and the marauders killed or scattered. Too much to expect all to have been taken, but they would be scurrying, belly down, like rats to their middens. He smacked the ship's rail. "A toast, Captain, a toast. Come down to my cabin; we must decide what next..."

They grouped around the table in his cabin: Raleigh, his own Captain, and O'Sullivan, who had sailed with him because of Rona and his knowledge of the lie of the land.

"And now," said the Admiral, gazing into the candle flame, "I suppose I shall have to sail round, after all."

She looked at him questioningly.

"Did it occur to you to wonder why I came to this coast, in the first place?"

"Aye, Sir. I have wondered at everything."

"I could have left Ireland and sailed south. Then, in due course, turned east and come up Channel to the port of my choice. Hawkins would have had it so. But I—I know those rock infested waters round Land's End: and the Islands that are infested too—with thieves. It would have needed a wide sweep to the west—a long

166

voyage against wind and weather; and then, heavy laden, into the shipping lanes for all to see—and to speculate upon. The short trip across tempted me: the unexpected route…" He laughed, a hollow laugh.

"It was a good plan, Sir."

"Aye, good enough. Had some rogue not been ahead of me with the news."

"And paid well for't, no doubt," said O'Sullivan.

"It is still a good plan, Sir," ventured Rona. "Hayle is not the only good landing ground." Only the most obvious, she thought, but did not say it aloud.

"The rest of the coast is strange to me."

"But not to me, my Lord."

There was a silence that stretched on and on. "I want to go home," she thought; "I do not want a long voyage in this ship. Days and days, nights and nights. Please God let them take me home!"

And Raleigh thought; how can this girl possibly pilot us along this coast, these cliffs? Nay, it was mad. He dragged out a chart and set three candles round the edge. Jabbing it with his finger, he demanded; "Where are we?"

"Here, sor, your Honour." O'Sullivan found the island spit that betokened the west of St. Ives, and let his own finger drift towards the west of it.

"And where's the headland with the beacon—the beacon that was put out?"

"Pendeen. Hereabouts."

"And what's between?" He turned to Rona.

She stared at the map: at the unfamiliar lines and letters. She had never seen a map before. Frowning, she held her tongue; and, suddenly, her eyes caught hold of shapes she understood. She recognised the pattern drawn in the sand by the Vaylors at the market.

"That mun be Gurnards Head—and the Cracks."

"Cracks?"

"Rocks where the seals do come. Some call it Carracks, I b'lieve. Then there be…"

She strained her mind to see the coast as she knew it from landwards.

"Bes' come back'ards from Pendeen…" O'Sullivan had little faith in charts.

"Pendeen…then there's Porteris, fisher folk use that." She tried to trace that with her own smaller finger. "There must be Porthmeor…Yes, there. See, it is marked. And here's our own cove—we call it Porthmarys after my Mother. There's sand there when the water is low. It's all right for boats—we kept our boat in the cave at the foot, before Uncle Jacques took…"

"A cave? How big?"

"How big?"

"Yes. Yes. How big? As a house? A barn? A pig sty? Can you stand upright in it?"

"A man can walk into it about twenty paces."

"Any way out?" Raleigh felt a germ of excitement wriggling in his mind.

"Not by the cave. But there's the path up the cliff. Steep. But not too steep. Then there's the ledge and another cave at the top, where we keep the furze for firing."

"But can you find it?"

"I used to go fishing in the boat—with father….but never in the dark."

"Think, young Mistress, are there rocks in the offing? Sticking up out of the water, or making tidal eddies, bubblings and boilings, out of sight?" O'Sullivan had stubbed his toe on many such rocks in the past.

"There's rocks off Tranthem's," she said slowly. "But, no, not round Porthmarys; we would come straight in—from any angle. But, Sir, ours was but a little boat. Not like this. 'Tis no deep water harbour."

"Let's try it, O'Sullivan. Signal the rest to follow us and to stop when we stop. We alone will get in closer."

"Risk the Faerie Queen?"

"Use the lead, Captain."

They edged towards the west and closer to the land; until Rona, watching from the bows, could be sure she saw Gurnards Head, sticking out like a claw. It looked so different from the sea; foreshortened, unthreatening. No wonder they had beacons. They watched until their eyes ached for tell-tale white water spraying over a rock, submerged or half submerged. For hours they crept, watching, listening. Dawn could not be far off. Light would be a mixed blessing. An early shepherd would be quick to report a strange ship in the vicinity.

Rona's mind was in a spin. Now she wished she had said, "No, I cannot find the place—any place."

Distances were impossible for her to judge from seaward and in the dark. If only there were some clue…something. Perhaps, if they had sailed straight for the Pendeen watch and then backtracked; but the breeze was with them—and not much at that—and had to be used best. It was not like turning a horse's head.

She closed her aching eyes, squeezing them until lights pricked behind the tired lids. Opening them, she resumed her vigil, her search for landmarks.

A spark remained in her vision.

She blinked and rubbed her eyes, wishing she had not closed them so ferociously. She wished she were not so tired. She wished she could sleep. Wearily, she turned her head back to the coastline.

The spark of light remained.

"It is a light," she whispered. But where? Zennor was passed and Gurnard. After that, Porthmeor; then Tranthem's. The Manor was too low, too far low for any light to show. Besides, it was three o'clock in the morning. Then, she thought, there was nothing but their house…and that was gone…gone…gone.

The cliff edge…that was not gone…could it be a little beacon on the edge…? "Clem. Clem Bugel." Sudden tears obscured everything.

"Hey, hey, what's this?" O'Sullivan came to her side.

"I saw a light—a tiny one, like a dying fire. I b'lieve Clem's been lighting me home." She wiped her eyes with her hand. "Look. Look. He'll be watching the lane. Oh, put on some more, Clem; put on some more."

"Where? Where? Holy Mother Mary, I see it. What is it?"

"'Tis Clem, 'tis Clem…lighting me home." She said it again and again; laughing and crying.

O'Sullivan fetched the Admiral. "Be there hills behind your land?"

"The Galvers. I see them. Against the sky."

"Send in a boat—with the girl on board. She'll know if it is the place."

"'Tis Clem," she said as she scrambled into the boat.

CHAPTER XXIV

In fact it was Matthew.

When his young Mistress rode off with the seamen, Bugel was uncertain what he should do. His instinct was to follow. Rona should not be at the mercy of two sailors, whoever they said they were. He still had the Vaylor horse. But he also still had Dorothy; he could neither leave her alone nor take her with him. She was a poor rider and would come off on the first bend. Mistress Miller: she was the nearest woman he could trust. Settling a protesting Dorothy in front of him, he pressed forward, setting a course for New Mill.

"Say nothing to the Millers. Nothing, ye hear me? No word of the fire, or the wrecking."

170

"No, fayther." Dorothy felt sick on a horse.

"And no word of Rona. We have not seen her since the master died."

"But…"

"No buts, girl. She be in danger enough without us bleatin' about it. I'll be back for 'ee tomorrow. Now, mind 'ee, not a breath of it. And be sure, she'll ask. Oh, she'll ask."

Dorothy, white-faced, was deposited at the Mill.

"Mistress," said Clem crisply, "do'ee be so good as to use my darter Dorothy for the rest o' the day—fur to aid 'ee. I do need get to market and she be no good on a horse. Her be a good girl—and willin'—and quiet." He gave Dorothy a look she would not forget.

As he turned the horse, Matthew came running out, to see what business the stranger might have. When he saw Clem Bugel he stopped.

"What's amiss?"

"Nought's amiss," said Clem sturdily, urging his mount.

"Nay, stay, Master Bugel, I must know. Is Rona well? She rode out with the Constable nights ago. It was madness. I would have followed, but Miller—'e locked me up."

The scar, livid upon the boy's cheek, and the anxiety in his eyes halted Clem.

"We could 'ave done wi' 'ee, lad; aye and an army of strong arms; that we could."

"Things have gone ill? There was a rumour of a fire. How is she? Tell I."

Clem looked him over.

"Ye ain't locked in now. Come an' see."

Matthew never hesitated; he leapt up behind Clem and they thundered off to the north.

At the top of a rise, where they could see the sea, they rested the horse and Clem told Matthew everything. He was incredulous.

"Aye, tedden aisy to b'lieve. We'm kicked open a hornets' nest wi' our beacon. An' God knows what the end will be."

"But, dear life, what will become of Rona? Let us begone to Hayle at once. Master Bugel, at once."

"Tedden so simple. We mun set out from Laity land—not cut across. She may be finding her own way back—an' it'll be by that path."

"Aye."

"Then again, there should be someone at the farm; 'case she gets back and finds none there. 'Twere a sin to leave her in that case."

"I'll go to Hayle. Do'ee stay," Matthew said.

Bugle said nothing; he was determined it should be the other way about.

"That wound, on your face—how came 'ee by it?"

"One o' they Vaylors: in the lane."

"It wants for cobwebs. There bain't no cobwebs in t'cottage. Dolly would be arter 'em in a trice. Look in the barn. Look for new ones."

Matthew, used to obedience, did as he was bid. Clem washed the cut and pressing the edges together, held them so with a liberal application of new spun silk.

"No riding for 'ee, lad. Keep the place safe and make a welcome for us when we return."

When Clem had gone. Matthew busied himself as best he could.

But there was little he could do. It was summer and the animals were grazing. Dorothy had left the cottage clean as a scrubbed plate. To make a start on the burnt house was more than he could do. He made his way to the cliff and sat on the rock seat. "This is where she has sat. This is her view—her air." He breathed it in, enjoying the silence. No grain dust up his nose, no grating millstones to assault his ears, no Miller to curse and drive him from one heavy task to another.

He had felt dizzy and light-headed since the Vaylor twins had accosted him and laid open his cheek. But nothing was ever allowed to delay the Miller; Matthew had been made to work harder than ever to make up for the lost purse. He could have found it, had he been allowed; but the Miller enjoyed a grudge; a bitter savage man, he ground himself and all around him, as he ground the grist.

Matthew thought, with a strange cool detachment; "I have left the Mill. I shall never go back. It has just happened. No need, after all, to plot and plan. How I have dreamed of this day, planned how I might seek my fortune. There's no fortune here. But there is need—need for me. When she was rich, well found, I could not look at her; bring her anything. Now she can have the work of my hands and my back. I will build her house again.

"God," he said, "keep her safe in Hayle. Safe! Safe!"

He stretched himself out on the warm turf and let the sun heal him of a hundred ills—in unaccustomed idleness.

He was wakened by a nudge and a shake, and saw a dishevelled girl standing over him.

"Be ye Matthew?" He jumped up, startled.

"Aye," he said cautiously.

"I be Dorothy. Fayther dropped me at the Mill when he rode off wi' ye. I—ran off; soon as Mistress Miller looked the other way. Oh Matthew…what a monster is the Miller. He'll have your head, he were that mad. And the poor lady—she dint know what to do wi' I. So I came home. Is Fayther back?"

"N-no. I don't know. I went to sleep."

"From the looks o' thee, sleep is the best thing. Thy monster works 'ee too much like a carthorse. Rest. I will do the milking."

"Mistress Dorothy, I know how to milk a cow."

"Mistress? Me?" She smiled at him. "Dorothy will do 'andsome."

They went together to the cottage for a long drink of the morning's milk. "Can 'ee catch me an ole hen? I mun get a meal for them when they get back." She stirred up the fire and added dry wood; found the pot and set it to heat with some water and herbs, and awaited the chicken.

Matthew caught a fowl. "Can 'ee kill it and pluck it?" she asked.

"I'd sooner get the cows in."

She laughed and then wrung the neck of the bird expertly. "Go, get 'em in—they're waiting for 'ee, see?" The cows were indeed moving towards the field gate, nudging and barging. They knew the time. The bees were homing and a few scraps of white cloud were turning golden. It was time to look to the lane. But there was no sight nor sign of the two travellers: no dust drifting in the wind.

"I should be there. I should not be here, looking to cows."

The thought of Rona's home destroyed was as nothing to the thought that she might be in danger or abused in a strange town. What had possessed her to follow the two strangers? It was all the fault of that damned Constable: flaunting his authority, showing off before a trusting young woman. Matthew was angry, really angry, and asked himself why; why should it matter so much? Oh God; gentle, kind, lovely Rona was in peril.

Lovely—yes—lovely, lovely, lovely. He had not thought of that before. Now, with a lurch, he knew that she was lovely and in danger. In fact, that very loveliness would increase her danger. He wished she were plain; and safe; and in his care.

The cows milked and the pails set in the cool of the barn, they went in search of eggs and more sticks for the fire. It was then that he had the idea of a bonfire—a beacon fire—in case the wanderers were still out after dark. Dorothy showed him the ledge and the store of furze in the cave. It was nearly used up so he went to look on the moor for anything dry.

As hour followed hour, their anxiety increased. Matthew walked a mile along the lane, just to be doing something. He found he was gazing at the sea—a different sea from the shallow and calmer sea of Mount's Bay. There it crept in and out. There was no creeping below the cliffs of Porthmarys; the Atlantic swell heaved and surged and sucked and swirled, even on a quiet day. On the horizon, he saw ships with sails set, all keeping well out of the way of the rocky coast.

He saw Tranthem's Manor set back from the cliff top and surrounded by a stout stone wall. Dogs barked at his approach so he turned and retraced his steps, with many a backward glance. The place seemed deserted; no man appeared. Nevertheless he had no wish to stay anywhere near to that habitation.

Sea and sky went from blue to opal to grey; and at dusk he made ready his fire. Dorothy joined him on the cliff and bid him in to eat some of the chicken.

"There be plenty. No cause for us to go hungry." She too needed company to put a stop to wild imaginings.

"Think 'ee that the fire be in the best place?"

"'Tis seen further off from there; 'tis where Fayther would expect to find it."

They ate, anxiety robbing the meal of any relish.

"Be it time? Dark enough?"

175

"Dark enough to need a candle within doors, but there's light enough outside for them to see the way."

"Put on a coat—of Fayther's—and we will go and sit on the wall and wait. Oh I be glad ye are here; I would be mortal afeared else."

Matthew was mortal afeared.

They sat on the wall and watched the lane. They heard the small unrecorded sounds of nightfall: rustles and scuffles, crickets contemplating life with their back legs, an owl, a vixen...

"That's it. If it be dark enough for the vixen to be calling, then it be dark enough to light the fire."

They got it going—just a small fire, not to be confused with the Pendeen Watch—not to guide whole navies nor even one fishing boat—just a small fire, a spark of light to prick the darkness and guide the weary travellers home.

Dorothy watched with him for a while, but presently, her head nodded and her body sagged; the events of the day and her long walk over the moor caught up with her. She fell asleep and would have taken cold if Matthew had not noticed. He could have picked her up and carried her into the cottage but he decided that such an action would be treating her like a child. Besides, the comfort of his arms was reserved for Rona.

"Wake up Mistress; wake and we will tuck you safe in bed; your day is done. I had a sleep in the afternoon; I will watch here."

He took a burning brand to light her to the cottage and to light a candle. "I will wake you the moment I see them—I promise."

Back beside the fire, he did not feel lonely. He felt—elemental.

They had no clock but it must be past midnight. He did not live by the sea and could not guess at the state

176

of the tide. Watching the ruffles of water round rock below, he thought that it might be slack water, that the ebb had stopped running. He turned his attention to the fire. Staring into flames was an unknown pleasure. The shapes, the sparks, the unpredictable movement of incandescent sticks, all held a fascination for the boy who had never been allowed to sit by the hearth.

His thoughts wandered, and, as ever, revolved around the mystery of his origins. His date of birth, and the place, his mother's name, his father's, were all unknown. He wondered if he would feel any different if he did know. He would not be different; he would still love Rona: the thought hit him with another shock of delight. To love was a novel idea; he had had no-one to love and had not realised that the enjoyment of sun and wind, spring and summer, was a sort of loving.

"What am I? What am I like?" For the first time, it was important. He transferred his gaze to his hands and studied them. Strong and well made, scarred here and there, and carrying fine fair hairs.

"Too fair for a Cornishman," Mistress Miller said.

"So, I am tall, fair and strong. I can do most things a man can do—shift great stones and carry sacks of grain; drive a horse and cart and thatch a roof. I can count and put it down, but yet I cannot read and write; I can milk a cow but not swim; and to ride a horse would not be so ill if I had a horse to become acquainted with. I do not know if I could be an husband; I do not know what it is to be an husband. If it be to care for, then I can…and, oh, I would!"

He closed his eyes against the dazzle of small flames and turned his head away to look at the stars. He wanted so much to understand about the stars. "Had my father any learning?" he asked the heavenly bodies that moved about the sky, yet kept their station. The Miller never wanted to know anything; not even where the grain came from. It came in sacks; went out, as flour, in sacks. But Matthew wondered; he even wondered about the sacks.

Watching the stars and waiting for the first hint of dawn, he recognised another new sensation: "I am afraid". He had been scared, on and off, all his life—mostly of the Miller. But when the Miller went off, out of sight, and the stones stopped grinding, his fear went away. It was sharply painful in the face of danger, but once it was gone, that was an end of it. It was like that for the dog, he supposed. Perhaps he was very like the dog. And, like the dog, he could enjoy a moment of freedom with an awareness that was not strangled by fears past or to come. If only he had known it, this was his greatest strength and had mended the holes made by his harsh master. His life was full of holes, empty places where there should have been understanding.

This new fear, under the stars, was the sick unease for someone else. Much more difficult; much more urgent. He would not be able to rest until Rona was safe. It seemed as if in her lay the security of all things beautiful, fragile and gentle; she was their essence and harbinger. If she were to be lost…he paced the clifftop, furious with his own ignorance and powerlessness. "I have nothing. Nothing…but hands…bare hands."

CHAPTER XXV

A faint sound, which a man of the sea would have recognised as the shipping of oars from the rowlocks, sounded from far below. He dismissed it, prodding the fire with a stick. Then a crunch on stony sand and a muted cry had him hanging over the cliff, his ears straining. The swish and swell of a lethargic tide joining the rustles of the moor, and the crackle of the fire, were the only sounds he could hear. Yet there was an urgency in the air..."'Tis but a rabbit. It takes but a rabbit to set my heart thumping. I do not need a rabbit—I can do it for myself." Listening fearfully for a minute, he got up from lying prone on his stomach, chiding himself for a big fool. Then a clatter of small stones had him down again in a flash.

More stones chattered below and he caught the unmistakable sound of gasping breath. Matthew's heart stopped beating.

Someone was scaling the cliff. Perhaps it was as well that Rona was not at home. She had had her fill of marauders; but who, in God's Creation, was mounting the cliff at this time of night?

Dorothy had said there was a pitchfork. He could not see it. He had only fire to arm himself. The pitchfork was on the ledge but Matthew did not know about the ledge. He did that most difficult thing—he waited.

The heavy crunch of sea boots, accompanied by grunts and oaths, came nearer as a man heaved himself up the steep path that was not a path; in the dark it was a matter of by guess and by God to find the way round craggy outcrops. "Even so, this man is uncommon slow," thought Matthew. The man, carrying a heavy coil of rope, heaved himself onto the ledge and sat, beneath the overhang, and rested, panting. Then Matthew heard a lighter tread as yet but half way up. He crept nearer and leaning over saw the man was securing a rope. Impossible to see what anchorage he had found, but Matthew saw the free end thrown over the edge to help up someone else. He also saw the ledge. He lay as flat as he could watching the rim.

His eyes, probing the scene, suddenly met with

179

another pair of eyes. They stared at each other in total astonishment.

"Rona!"

Struggling to his feet and jumping down, he clasped her hand and dragged her into him arms.

"Rona…Rona…" He thrust her against the cliff wall away from the dreadful drop to the sea. "Oh Rona. Be it true? How be ye come out of the sea?" He had forgotten the seaman.

"Arl well, Lassie?" asked a strange voice.

"Oh…seemingly it be very well!" It was Connor. He watched the two youngsters: "Sure, 'tis better than a dream o' glory. But there's work to be done."

"Pull me up, Matthew; and Connor too. Let us see the fire that brought us in. The blessed fire." She looked about her:"Where be Clem?"

"In Hayle—looking for thee. He fetched me here to take care o'…Dorothy is abed."

"Why the fire, lad?" asked Connor.

"To light the lady home."

"Aye. And so it did…so it did."

"Oh Matthew, 'tis a tale too long to tell. I do come by sea to show the way. There's to be a landing."

"The trade? What are 'ee about?"

"Not the Trade—the Queen's business."

"I'm away down again to fetch more ropes." Connor took a firm grip and a pull to test his rope. "Fetch some firelight to the ledge. The Queen's business must see where it be going."

"Who comes? Why do they not land in a port? Answer me…why not Hayle?"

"Later. Come to the ledge again and hand down a torch; I can find the lanterns. 'Tis better than a fire. Then come wi' me into the cave and I will tell 'ee all."

Jonah was the next one up. "Top o' the mornin' to 'ee," he said, grinning. "Fix that. I'm for going back to tell 'Is 'Ighness what's afoot. I be parched arter that climb." He peered at them hopefully.

"Jonah, I'll have ale in plenty for your next trip. For the moment, I must find it and my friend."

"Ye seem to have found your friend," said he, winking. "Now here's me for finding the pot o' gold." Over he went.

"Who's he?"

"Jonah, servant to the Admiral, to Sir Walter Raleigh."

Matthew shook his head; it was all a dream.

"Raleigh is here. He carries a treasure in gold for the Queen's Navy, but Hayle is bursting full of robbers. It is to be hidden here."

"Here?" Matthew foresaw more trouble.

"Not in piles round the house, silly. It will be in the caves: here and under the house."

"Then we must clear it out and get all the light we can.

Dorothy must bring candles."

Rona looked at him admiringly: "Why, dear life, aren't ye the masterful one?"

Amazingly, Matthew felt a great anger. Relief let it out. His joy at seeing her blazed; then blazed with anger when she called him silly. If this uncertainty was love, he were better without it. Furiously he forked out all the remaining litter of bracken and furze. If it hit someone coming up...he hoped it would. Rona found the first lantern and saw that the candle was new. Good old Clem. The next one would be along the passage; she disappeared and Matthew was again distraught.

"Where be 'ee now?"

She reappeared. "Don'ee spend all your energy sweeping; there's a day's work in front of we."

Was she concerned for him or mocking?

"Let us wake Dorothy," he said sulkily.

181

"Matthew, I do b'lieve 'ee be cross wi' I."

"Cross? I be more'n cross. I be distracted." 'Distracted' was one of Mistress Miller's favourite words.

"Bain't 'ee glad I be back?"

"Glad? I be filled wi' joy. Joy is more. But for the love o' God, rest 'e'self. And," he added stubbornly, "don' mock I."

The cave was full of twinkling light. In the flicker of the candles on crystals of quartz and tin she came close to him and said softly, "Never. I will never mock thee, dearest Matthew. I did not dare to hope 'ee might be here. I am a little drunk, I think—with excitement—with thankfulness." She took his hand. "Come, my dress is ruined, I am barefoot and I'm sure I smell like a dead gull. To the cottage, before they're back."

Dorothy woke at a touch. "Where be ole William's breeches?"

"Rona!" she gasped. "How be ye? And Fayther?" Rona told Dolly all she could—but nothing of Clem's doings or whereabouts. "Clem will be all right. Clem will know what to do. We mun think now 'what would Clem do?' an' we'll do it and get it right."

Rona stripped off the remains of her primrose silk and climbed into William's breeches and one of Clem's shifts.

"It kept 'ee safe: the Cross."

Matthew took a brand from the fire and found ale in the barn, and bread in a crock, and put the chicken back onto the heat.

Then they went back to the cliff, to find more ropes fixed and men swarming up them. They had brought more ship's lights and were lodging kegs of gold in the cave. It looked and sounded like some hellish forge;

and it was to this scene that Clem Bugel returned. It was lucky for all that he had no fowling piece.

They could not see who commanded the landings, down below, but it was Bugel who took charge of the clifftop. Tired as he was, he took on new strength when he saw his young Mistress was safe arrived. Quickly he saw what was afoot and looked first at the sky. "Not much time," he muttered.

He selected Matthew and Connor as his aides, putting Connor on the ledge and taking Matthew into the depths of the cave.

"See yur, lad, the passage be too narrow for they chests. Come 'long o' I and see if we can get in through th'ole burnt kitchen."

They squeezed through and they made their way from below to the stone that marked the middle of the kitchen floor; putting their shoulders to it they heaved with might and main. It shifted. "I reckon the table will have held off the beams, if the beams came down. 'Twere strong built; the fire burned very bright but not for long; and the floor beams were whole trees. Heave again." Something blocked their way. "Come wi' I to clear the way on top."

Each armed with a shovel they cleared a way through cinders, broken windows, charred furniture and sad unidentifiable things, once objects of affection; until they had a path to the kitchen table. One of its legs had succumbed to the fire enough to break and the heavy wooden top was cocked drunkenly over the stone. They dragged it out of the way and found the ring under a welter of ash.

"Here, let me." Matthew, the larger of the two, took it in his hands. "I have been hauling at millstones all my life; and with no rings set in them to help."

He managed to make it move and Clem put his spade into the gap.

"There's an iron bar in the stable; I can find it in the dark. Do ye move what obstacles atween here and the yard. The bigger sea chests will have an easier ride than squeezing underground."

Clouds of rancid, acrid dust rose as Matthew shoved away the remains of the back door. It was so much charcoal. It occurred to him to use the cinders to build a fire in the yard to light them. There was plenty of kindling and the stairs, what was left of them, would make a blaze.

"Good man. Let's get the stone away and lamps below."

They startled Connor by arriving from behind him.

"Direct the big packets to the fire in the yard; there's another cave beneath the house."

The gold came up the cliff and down into the cave in every sort of container: chests and kegs, canvas bags, hammocks, buckets, even trousers knotted at the knee. The climbers left them on the ledge where Connor and Matthew saw to their disposal.

Raleigh, at the edge of the tide, waited for the word that the top cave was full; for then he would have to stow the remainder in the bottom tidal cave: not something he wanted to do. Chance fishermen, nosy children, excise men, all could stumble upon it…what a haul…what a temptation. His men he was taking straight to sea, as far from the hiding place as possible, and as fast. Before they could put about any word, the goods would be removed by another gang, another team of trusted servants.

All would be rewarded; aye, and these Laitys must be rewarded richly.

The word he waited never came, and, thankfully, Raleigh went up with the final consignment, glad of the guiding rope.

If he expected to see his treasure in a litter of

184

bundles on the cliff top, he was mightily surprised: there was no sign of it. As he climbed, unmistakable in his ruff and cloak, Clem Bugel emerged from the cave mouth. He called for another brand to light the High Admiral's way and beckoned the great man to follow him.

They stooped low and proceeded into the cliff. After half a dozen paces the cave narrowed to a passageway— a wide flaw in the rock—and they had to pass through singly until the crack opened out. There, Matthew, sweating and exhausted, stacked the smaller containers. With the skills and strength learned at the mill, he toiled to line the walls of the cave. With an intelligence unexpected in a labourer, he used all the available space.

Raleigh watched him in silence. In the flickering shadows Matthew did not notice him.

"How many more, Clem?"

"They be all."

"So we seal it off and put more furze on the ledge." He straightened up and wiped his brow with his forearm. "Then it's the big stuff; it is all in?"

"Nearly all—Connor's in the kitchen."

"Well done." Matthew had unconsciously taken command. "Who be this?" He caught sight of Raleigh, "Come 'ee here."

"Matthew. 'Tis himself. Have a care…"

"Peace. He is taking care enough. Great care. I must thank thee, young man. Ye are the Miller's boy?"

"I be no one's boy." Matthew flashed.

"Thy pardon, Sir. Mistress Rona did not overestimate thee."

"Over—?"

"Estimate. I mean she could not rate 'ee too high when she spoke of thee".

"She did—speak o' I?"

"And praised. As I shall. I am obliged to all of ye."

Matthew looked around. "Then let us get to the rest. Can 'ee get 'eeself through this yur? If not, it's overland."

Matthew headed for another, almost concealed, crack and squeezed his body into it.

"Nay, Sir, 'twill ruin thy finery. Follow me." Clem led the way out. He hauled the Admiral over the overhang and set off towards the house.

"What's this? Where—? Sweet Lord, what ruin is here…"

"There be another cave beneath the house. The sea chests would not go through the passage. Aye, my Mistress has no home now."

Matthew was already there, heaving and straining at the heavy barrels and at crates built for cannon balls.

"Lend a shoulder…push…'tis like lead."

Raleigh smiled: it was years since he had been ordered to lend a shoulder. He became a part of the gigantic effort. Stripping off his cloak, he worked alongside Matthew and Bugel, until his face, too, was streaked and grimy. As he worked, he planned his next move.

The ships must go immediately to Ireland but I—I must not waste thus much time. "Have ye a horse, Clem?"

"Aye, Sir, the Master's; and another, borrowed from Vaylors."

He had redeemed Rona's mount from an ostler at St Ives.

"I have a monstrous great problem. Mistress Rona says she has a relation in Helford—a boat builder. Know ye him?"

"A good man. Nathaniel Laity."

"A good anchorage?"

"I know not the depth and tides."

"I must go and see for myself. It needs water enough for a barge—a seagoing barge."

"Is it your plan to get this cargo to Helford and then by water to—?" Matthew thought there might be a job in it for him.

"To Portsmouth. Yes. The danger points are on the road to Helford. Think 'ee that a local Constable can find an escort?"

"No." Matthew was unequivocal.

"No?"

"Master Vanner has been used by Tranthem. Who knows where his loyalties lie. It's my b'lief that Master Vanner has but one interest, and that rests in hisself." He looked at Raleigh and bit his lip. "I be well known as Master Miller's driver. Get me a cart to match the miller's cart and a horse to match his horse; then I can take it over—a load at a time.

Raleigh shook his head. "Alone? All the way?" He shook his head again.

"To Marazion then; under sacks of flour. After that, get a troop to take it on. There's plenty of work for Constables at the market. 'Twill rouse up no 'tention."

"'Tis a thought. I like it well. First I must see this Nathaniel."

"Sir, this matter has lost me my work. The Miller will have no truck wi' me now. I lef' without asking."

"Why?"

"Master Bugel said I wur needed—to care for Mistress Rona's home…the cows…food…the beacon light."

"Ah yes…the beacon light. The guiding beacon. Don't 'ee worry, boy—your pardon, what be thy name?"

"Madron, Sir."

"Good Master Madron, I have plenty of work for the likes of thee. I take it the Miller is not greatly loved? I can make it right with him; if it suit thee."

187

"Never."

"Throw in your lot with me for a while. Who knows where it may lead?"

There was no activity on the cliff. O'Sullivan had drawn off the men and Connor was sitting on the ledge watching the boats pulling for the fleet. He sprang up. "Jonah is below wi' thy boat, Sir."

"Let him take thee. There's work to be done on land. O'Sullivan will set the course for Cobh. I will follow when this cargo is out of here."

"I'm with'ee, Sor; and no word o' this will pass my lips, so help me."

Rona, changed, clean and combed, stood in the dawn wind trying to see the ships as they disappeared northwards. Raleigh partook of the chicken, refused Rona's bed and lay on a bed of last year's straw, in the barn. He lay between Bugel and Matthew, on his back, snoring, his mouth open. They slept until well after sunrise and were wakened by the animals, unused to being kept waiting. Then it was bran mash for the horses, and porridge for their lords, and the cows in for milking, and grain for the fowls. The day began. The first of six anxious weeks.

CHAPTER XXVI

It was six weeks, and more, of work and worry, before all of the gold was transferred to Abraham's Bosom. With the whole Navy to choose from, Raleigh selected a patrol of trusted men to stand guard at the farm; and, while they were about it, to make a start at clearing out the burnt remains. Mutinous at first, they all fell under Rona's spell and would do anything for the pretty lady.

Tranthem and his son had disappeared on the night

of the raid on the moor. Raleigh appointed Vanner to find them, and the ambitious Constable criss-crossed the country in pursuit of Raleigh's enemy. He smelled promotion and put it before all else.

Raleigh left Bugel, Matthew and Rona to see to the dispatch of each consignment; and as Warden of the Stanneries, he was able to raise an escort of countrymen who did not stand out, as sailors did by their gait and clothes and manners, but blended into the background surrounding Matthew's cart. At a place beyond the market, they handed over to other carriers who proceeded to the Helford river and Nathaniel's boatyard. Matthew appeared to be carrying flour; the others appeared to be carrying fish.

There were two kitbags and a sea chest left in the cellar when the Vice Admiral rode back to the farmhouse. Each was full of gold pieces. He bowed to Rona.

"I owe it to thee—all three—to thank ye for the success of our venture. Without thy wits and work and discretion, all would have been lost. And I have something else to tell thee: Your enemy is captured; Squire Tranthem is caught."

Rona paled at the sound of his name.

"Safe in Bodmin Jail, I assure thee. And there's few come out of there alive; one way or another."

"Is he tried yet?" asked the girl. "What will it be for?"

"For murder, my dear, your father's murder. There are witnesses enough, it will not fail. I would save thee the pain and charge him with designs upon the Queen's property, but murder is a capital offence and the quickest way to be rid of vermin." He took her hand. "Fear not, little one, Clem Bugel will testify and most of Tranthem's troop if they think it will save their necks. No need to fret and fray yourself more. I have it in mind to demand that his lands be made over to thee as retribution; then whatever lies herein that he coveted, will all be thine. Shall ye rebuild the house at once?"

The question, put so straight, shocked her. She had been turning away from the need to answer it ever since the fire. The recollection of that night, of the terrible scenes of blood and fire cast obscene shadows across her mind and across the once beloved setting of her home.

"I cannot say, my Lord. I cannot say. I have not the price."

"Where then? Helford, to your kinsfolk?" She shook her head.

"I should be swallowed up by them: married off to my cousin and lost to all I care for."

He took her aside. "Why not make a fresh start? But since this is your land, put Bugel into Tranthem's place. Give it him with a parcel of land and make him Agent for thee here. It will insure him a good son-in-law. Make no decisions too quickly. Go to the south. Remember ye are a possessed of good friends. And I think," he said gently, "ye should go to those who rescued thee before: old William and Elizabeth. I know, I know, ye think they will be too shamed to see thee again. But, consider, do 'ee blame them for their sons? They have lost everything. Tell them they have not lost thee. And what of the Potter? Did ye not tell me of a potter?"

"Potter Jane. Yes, Potter Jane and Mistress Jane who was my mother's friend. I shall ask Matthew to take me. Matthew," she called. "Matthew, ye will take me to find the old Potter—at Marazion."

"Do not lose that young man. Do not undervalue him. Ask, do not command."

She looked at him with sudden understanding and ran to Matthew. "Please, Matthew, will ye take me to the Market? I would see Master Potter. Perhaps he has news of William and Elizabeth."

It chanced to be market day on the morrow.

"I will ride with you thus far," said Raleigh. "Then it be Plymouth for me, and London after that. Now let us go for one last look at the cellar."

Matthew heaved up the stone and handed them a candle lantern. It was the first time that Raleigh had been down since the landing and, holding the light high, he examined the walls; they were veined with black and reddish streaks and pitted with twinkling crystals.

"Tin," he muttered, "and where there is tin, who knows what else may be there. This is what Tranthem was after."

At last his gaze fell upon an ironbound chest. "There by Her Majesty's command lies the price of rebuilding thy house. And there," he gestured towards the two sailcloth sacks, "is personal reward for your help."

Rona was dumb.

"What? Be ye not pleased? Say that ye are pleased, child."

"I—I know nothing of money. It is…" She shook her head helplessly. "It is shapeless."

He took her hand. "My dear, it is your life that is shapeless, is it not? The old shape is gone—the new is not yet known." He sat on the chest. "When I was young as thee, my life was shapeless too. But I was young and my fortune lay in what strength and wit I might have. A man must shape his own life. Ye have wit, and will too; and with this wealth ye will do very well and shape a life of your own choosing. It will need courage—but thou hast plenty of that."

"But Sir, this fortune, as soon as it becomes common

191

knowledge, I will be relieved of it as sure as apples fall to the ground. The only men I can trust are Clem and Matthew, and for that alone, I would give it to them—give it all to them. I am afraid of it for myself."

"Give them some of it."

"Aye, that I will. No...I will not—do thou give it them 'at the Queen's Command'."

"I see ye have wisdom, Mistress. Aye, men must have their pride—not be beholden to a woman." "Though God knows, I am," he thought, "never certain of his Monarch, like all the rest—a Queen capricious in her choice of favourites."

"How's this?" he continued. "I, in the Queen's name, give to Bugel and his girl the ownership of Tranthem's Manor, with land enough to keep it going. The rest of Tranthem's land, that adjoins to thine, becomes part of Laity's estate; provided that he, Bugel, is agent to Laity and gives thee a home until ye have another."

"Yes. Oh yes."

"That should insure a good husband for Dorothy— Matthew perhaps. We could do with a line of honest folk to carry on for the good of the County."

Stabbed with a nameless fear, Rona felt lost, her excitement deflated.

Raleigh poked at the sacks. "Give the boy something of his own; aye, from the Queen in recognition of his help; how about one of these?"

She nodded, doubtful if it were enough.

"Too much? I think ye can spare it m'dear. Why, what is't?"

She had turned her face away, giving her head a small shuddering shake to dismiss this new fear that knifed her to the heart: Matthew and Dorothy?

"Come, the major part is thine."

"I want none of it."

192

"Then be it loneliness ye see ahead? Never fear, a lovely wench with property will not be alone for long."

His joviality made her want to scream and she headed for the kitchen and the sane light of day. Raleigh, not entirely insensitive, knew it was not the sunlight that set her eyes blinking. "A good girl," he thought, "and needing a good woman."

"Please me," he said, "by going to see Mistress Vaylor and putting her mind at rest. Tomorrow, in the market, we shall buy a horse, and ye shall return the Vaylor nag and pay any debt ye have to them. Keep your tears for them. Matthew, I leave ye guardian of the stone. Guard it well. Hide it well. For below is Mistress Rona's fortune."

He strode off to the cliff and stared out to the horizon—homesick for the sea.

"Come, we have time now to explore the villain Tranthem's fields."

"Not I, Sir, not I."

CHAPTER XXVII

Marazion was sparkling and alive with traders as soon as the sun was up. The lanes, the Folly and the beach were thronged; and all the more thickly as the tide was high. Mares' tails streaked the sky and, on the surface of the bay, a lighter wind raised a popple that dazzled the eye and set a brisk pace to the day's business. The little group from Porthmarys reined their mounts as much apart as possible and Raleigh sent Matthew to find what horse traders might be there. He bade his servant tend the horses and took Rona aside. She had ridden in behind Matthew, her arms around his waist and unaware of the effect her nearness had on him. His adoration was doubly hopeless now that her fortunes were restored. Her need of him was gone and all he could hope for was to serve and live from smile to smile, dreading her displeasure for fear she would send him away. He loathed his bastardy and would choose to go away from this place where it was known. Yet he could not. He could not leave Rona.

She, for her part, had been longing to ask him, all along the way, if he knew of his reward. But she had held her tongue; and so had he. She thought that Sir Walter had not told him yet. "Well, has he spoken of it?" Raleigh asked.

"No, Sir, Have ye?"

"Oh yes; and he was struck dumb. He could not have been more silent. He is a deep one, that young man. A pity he is…"

"A pity he is—what?" Rona asked sharply.

"Nothing. A nothing."

"He is Matthew."

"He can look no higher than being a good servant."

"Cannot a good servant raise himself?"

"Blood will out," was his reply. "Aye," he thought, "blood will out—and there's good blood in thee, my girl—better than a small farmer's." He wondered about her mother and the uncle and the treasure she carried round her neck.

"Thy Mother? She was Cornish?" The question surprised her.

"A little. More French. My grandfather was a French Captain who sailed between the two countries and married a girl from Falmouth."

"And this Grandmother—is her family still in Falmouth? Could ye not seek them out?"

She laughed. "Nay. They were grand folk—not noblemen but grand. They did not hold with Grandmère running off with a French sailor."

"I see. Families can be very foolish and don't know what they have lost. Why not seek out the latest generation? Who knows, they could be friends."

"No." She pressed her hand against the Cross until

the stones pricked her skin. "Maman said they hated all things French, all things Popish. It would be useless."

"A pity—I should like to see you with kinsfolk."

She gazed at the bay and at the Mount. She wondered what tormented ghosts had haunted it since the massacre. Would the monks ever get back? Would Cornwall ever have another religious holy place—safe from the whims of monarchs—where the Cross would find a fitting resting place?

Far across Mount's Bay, toy-like ships made their careful way round the Lizard promontory—the southernmost tip of all England. Briefly Rona was curious to see the other side of it; and Helford.

"'Twere a long road to Helford," she said. "Where be the cargo now, think 'ee?"

"At sea. And I must be there to greet its landfall. I must be off this day."

They saw a stall laden with brightly coloured cloth. "See, they have primrose yellow; I shall buy thee some for a new gown."

"I should like the green—oh—but I have no money."

"Here," he said, handling her a gold piece, "this is for the yellow; that first. Nay, take it, the Queen is generous to her courtiers." When they do her will, he thought. "And next time, raid the cellar."

"Thankee, Sir," she curtsied prettily. "I wonder: will 'ee see it made? Will thy business ever bring 'ee back to us?"

"We were going to find the Potter," said he.

She switched her gaze to the stalls. "There he is, on the edge of the grass. Come, come and meet him."

Raleigh said quickly, "There is no need for any here to know my name. I want no petitions."

Rona halted, suddenly mindful of his importance.

She was amazed to be walking with him, her condition so changed since that last market day.

"Thy pardon, my Lord. I forget. I pay thee scant respect. I mean no impoliteness." She looked up shyly; she who had once told him not to be silly. "Perhaps 'tis ever so when—when—fondness enters in…"

"Aye, there's a paradox. And I will opt for the 'fondness' and leave titles be. Call me Captain Wat—and add another secret to the collection."

They reached the Potter's stall.

"Master Jane—good morrow—remember me?" Rona bounced up to him.

The old man shaded his eyes. "Sam'l Laity's girl. The girl of the blue pot. Ye have it still? Why so long, child?"

"I have had—this is Captain Wat, he has been a guest at my house." A guest? Sleeping in the straw?

"I did hear a rumour of trouble and a fire. Squire has been much in the news." He looked at her quizzically: "Then I thought you might be carried off by that young scamp of a Constable. But first he was arter an heiress of Helford, then chasing the Squire. I never did hear if he caught him. So ye be home again."

"They got him," said Captain Wat. "He is charged with Master Laity's murder. Ye were his friend?"

"Sam'l's friend; no friend o' Tranthem."

"Well, Tranthem is gone but Mistress Rona is not exactly home. Rumour of a fire was right; her house is destroyed. It has been my concern to see her safe delivered. So, Master Potter, I want to see her ensconced somewhere where a wise and watchful eye can guide her step. She tells me ye knew her parents."

"'Tis so. 'Tis so. Would I were ten years younger and my Bess still 'live. But stay," he wrinkled his brow, "were ye not with Will and Elizabeth? Howbeit…" He stopped in mid-breath and, going pale, stared along the beach. "Richard Veale," he whispered.

The intensity of his voice and manner made Rona spin round to see who came.

But there was none save Matthew who approached carrying a bundle and leading a riding horse, the trader beside him

"Richard Veale," the old man repeated, still staring as if the saw a ghost.

Unsteadily, he rose and advanced with outstretched hands—to Matthew. Then he swayed and stumbled and all three, Rona, Raleigh and Matthew ran to support him. It broke his trance and he shook his grey locks in disbelief.

"It cannot be." He put his wrinkled hand to touch Matthew's cheek. "It cannot be. Dick Veale would have a beard—white as my own." He peered close. "Who are ye, boy? Where do ye come from?"

"I be Matthew M…"

"Aah—Matthew. O'course. Matthew. From what place?"

"From New Mill."

Potter Jane frowned.

"First from Madron," said Matthew.

"Aah, Madron. And whose son be ye?"

There was a silence, full of pain. The Matthew struck up his chin.

"I know not."

"Richard Veale." The Potter was swaying on his feet.

"Come to your seat, old man; take my arm. Tell us what you see?" Raleigh steered him back to his stall. "Come now," he said quietly, "What is it you see"?

"I see the son of Dick—my friend—Priest of Madron Parish."

BOOK II

CHAPTER I

The Potter took to staring again, though now with a gleam, of intelligent reasoning.

"Come 'ee here, lad; the sun is in my eyes. Ah, 'tis Dick, sure 'nough."

"Matthew."

"How many years have 'ee, Matthew?"

"Mistress Miller says I be seventeen."

Potter Jane started to count on his fingers. "Eighteen," he said. "Born just before Catholic Mary died and Elizabeth came to rule. Born on St. Matthew's Day."

Matthew, excitedly, "Aye, eighteen nex' month."

"You'm been known as Miller's boy?"

"I were found," he said hesitantly; "in a fish basket, in Madron Church. There was but one word wi' I—'Matthew'" Jose Jane nodded and nodded.

Mistress Miller says I were 'bout six months old. She did but guess at St. Matthew's Day."

"She was right. Child, child, was she good to 'ee?"

"She took me in," he said simply. "But when I was big 'nough, I worked in the Mill." Doom-laden words that hung in the air.

The horse trader started to shuffle his feet; "'Ere, this 'ere 'orse…Do 'ee want it or no?"

Captain Wat left the Potter's side to run his hand over a good-looking mare. He examined its eye and teeth. "Gi' me a hand up." The animal was calm and stood well. "Have 'ee another—the same?"

"Mebbe."

"Go and get it. I have the price. And," he added, "I know what the price should be." They watched him go; then Wat said, "Let us sit on the sand and hear about thy friend Veale."

One by one, they sat down, their gaze upon the old man. He looked into some far distance—distance in time and place.

Rona saw Raleigh watching intently and she saw on Matthew's face a naked, urgent hope of recognition. The strange tension, the breathless waiting, fixed the moment for her in time: so that, years hence, whenever she felt seagrass between her toes, or saw two gulls wheeling down close to the water, or fingered the pale pink shells and tiny yellow ones that sprinkled the shore, she was back in that moment—the Mount serenely rising out of the sea, the scurrying market, early shadows still long upon the ground and the Potter's shadow and Matthew's shadow, and the sudden desperate mystery that stretched like a spring between them.

"Friends we were—Dick 'n I. Played on the sand, we did; wrestled and ran; till I got the sickness that put me on my back. Infant's paralysis, they called it. Dick it was got me to my feet, lame tho' I be. Then the priest at Gulval taught me to read and Dick, he joined in the lessons. He were ever more clever'n I. Then there were no end to our learnin': mos'ly Bible learnin', 'course."

Jose Jane paused, remembering. "There bain't never better friends. But, one day, 'e comes and says, 'Jo, there be a halo round the Mount. It says that is where I must be.' And at next low tide he walks over and gives himself to God. He be 'bout your age. Had 'bout three, four, years there and then they sent him to France, to the Brother house. He were safe away when the ole King cleared the Mount o' monks; then we heard no more of him."

"He must have known Jacques—my Uncle Jacques," gasped Rona.

"We heard no more till one day he turned up. Homesick, 'e was. The halo was here."

"This halo?" questioned Raleigh. "What did he mean?"

"He said it were a light that lights up where God wants us to be. 'Where be thy halo, Jo?' he asked me. 'Reckon it mun be here, says I, everywhere else is in the dark.' 'Then here it be,' says Dick. Dick said everyone can see his halo if he looks. Well, his brought him back home. An' it weren't easy; no monks was allowed. He had to grow his hair and wear common clothes, but he was God's priest and the Church was short of Priests. Madron Parish took him and glad of it. Vows or no vows; Reformation or no Reformation. Dick was happy serving his flock. 'Ye be one o' my flock now, Jo, y'old tup.' I teached 'im to make pots for the poor 'n needy and 'e teached me to pray—an' not to the Pope in Rome and not to any Bishop."

"What about Saints?" asked Raleigh.

"What 'bout 'em? Dick said they were good Christians and the better they were, the less they would've looked for clouds of glory." Old Jose grinned in recollection.

'They'll not find a lost sixpence, if that's what 'ee mean."

"What did they call him, in the Parish?"

"Them o' the Old Faith called him Father. Them, more careful, called him plain Master Veale. But he was uneasy; if the King's men came sniffing round for priests of Rome, what would befall? He cared not for Church Politics; his allegiance was not to Rome nor to King Henry—it was to God. He was afeared that he might be prevented, so he went to London to get a Dispensation. I know not what that means, but it seems he could dispense with Rome and embrace the new Church of England. It took six weeks—Madron had him in his grave—a week to get there, riding hard; a week back; and a whole month sitting in line waiting for Thomas Cromwell's scribes to scratch out one name and put in another. There was no argument, just a lot of others wi' the same idea. The more the merrier—it confirmed the King's claims to head a valid Church. He cared nothing for Henry, nothing for Cromwell; he wanted to do his work without fear of being chased out. O'course, no-one knew that Mary and Philip would put matters in reverse. He crossed his fingers and sat that one out; the Parish loved him and protected him—and it is a long ride to Madron.

"He had Annie Trevant to keep house but she was lame, lame as a hobbled goat. The hill got too steep. Jus' 'bout then, when it got to be too much for Annie, there came a fever and our neighbours—Trevose—sickened and died—both on 'em—an' it lef' Rose Mary all 'lone. My Bess sent Rose up to Annie Trevant to learn the ways of a housekeeper. Rose, she had her letters and her mother had teached her how to cook, so Annie knows a good thing when she sees it and takes to her bed—and stays there, issuing orders, mind, and ruling the Minister wi' a rod of iron. Rose loved her Master from the first—nigh on worshipped 'im—told my Bess so. And 'twas our b'lief that Dick loved her. But he dint know it, what with his flock bleatin' and baa-in' every end and turn. He'd put aside any marriage notions, o'course—Monks an' their vows an' all.

"But poor little Rose Mary, she got she couldn't bear it—being so close. She tole Bess an' Bess said, 'Come 'long o' us, stay wi' Bess a while—get over it. There's a score o' Parish women longin' to cook 'is pasties—you'll see—'e won't go hungry. Let ole Annie get back on 'er trotters. Tell un Bess is sick of a fever an' ye need a coupla weeks.' Oho, I'll ne'er forget the two on 'em whisperin' an' laughin' over't. It took a bit o' doin' but Bess winkled 'er out of Parsonage. All she wanted was to go back. And before the week was out,

202

Dick comes down the hill, all out o' joint, wantin' 'er back too. But Rose held out; we near had to lock 'er up but she had to find out if it be just 'er cooking. They both found out. Found they coont do wi' out each other."

"And?"

"They were married, sweet and happy. Maytime wi' the gorse still ablaze and the bluebells ringing out to the sky."

Rona listened to the Potter with her whole body and all her senses; tense and anxious for the conclusion that would bring the story back to Matthew. She listened with an uneasy thread of fear, knowing that her hope of offering him a home was a danger. She never thought that the offer might have been a humiliation; for her it would have been more a plea. But now, with money and—if Jose Jane were right—a name, Matthew would be free.

The Potter went on with his story: "There was never a couple more happy than Dick and Rose. She was so quiet and kind that none of the Parish murmured against the Priest taking a wife. Their only sorrow was that they had no child. Four, five, years passed; month by month Rose hoped and sorrowed; keeping her disappointment a secret. Bess knew, she told my Bess. Bess said, 'I b'lieve Dick cares as deep—ye should share the sadness.' 'No, Bess, I chose him for himself. He must not ever wonder if it were just for his babes. I shall not have one, I know it, so I shall take Jenny Fisher's child. She has come to me, frighted of her father.' 'Jenny? She never…who is the father? When is it due?' 'Not yet, seven or eight months. I cannot say who —' 'Cannot or will not?' And Rose smiled.

"Arter that, it seemed as if deciding, putting it out of her mind, gave Rose a new spring in her step. She went about again like a bride, pretty and fleet of foot.

Ye can imagine our maze when Rose comes in, white and puking, before the month was out."

Jose looked round triumphantly as if it were his own tidings. "Yes, ye've guessed it. She was with child herself. She remembered her promise to Jenny and brought her to the Parsonage. The two helped each other. Jenny gave birth to a fine girl in July and Rose's child was due in the middle of November. Three weeks before, on St. Matthew's Eve, Rose comes to visit. Everything is right as rain. She come in the pony trap. 'It will be the last trip afore I be delivered of this blessed burden. I'll bide at home from now on.'

"While they were together, a sou'westerly blew up: one o' they sudden storms that come wi' the equinox. It swep' in from the sea, the wind slamming the rain onto the houses, rattling the window. It got dark and they sat in the gloaming listening to the thudding wind roaring in the chimney. Bess lights a lamp and sees Rose, pale as a ghost and gripping the table, her knuckles gleaming white. 'Oh Bess,' says she, 'it's my time, come early. I want to go home.' 'Not in this. Ye stay here wi' Bess. The storm will pass. There be plenty o time: first babbies are in no hurry.' By and by, the wind slackened and the rain took off. She wanted to go. 'Sit 'ee tight, my lovely, we will send someone for to fetch Dick.' And Bess, she went into the village to find a youth to go for Richard. When she came back, Rose had gone. She had taken the trap and was clean out of sight. The road to Madron was rough and rutted, full of holes and the holes full of water. Bess prayed she would not hurry and jerk and jolt the baby. The boy was already ahead, on foot, fetching Dick. No-one saw the accident. It remained for Dick to find the gig tipped over and the pony still trying to drag it along. Rose was in the ditch groaning and frightened. Dick got her home as the pains came thick and fast.

"Between them, Rose took Dick's hand and whispered, 'I cannot do it, love. You'll have to fetch Mistress Wallis.' The midwife. So Dick leaves her with Jenny and goes out again. The storm broke as he set out and twilight turned to dark. He went to the midwife's cottage to find only her aged husband. 'She be out—shelterin'—I b'lieve the Hendra girl was ready. Ye'd best shelter here, Reverence.'

"He were the last person ever to see Dick. He set out into the howling dark and he and his horse disappeared. The gusts were coming in from the sea savagely. I tried to get out myself and was driven back. I'll never forget that night. It was like the world fell to pieces." He was quiet and near to tears.

"What—what was the end of it?" Raleigh asked quietly.

"The end. Aye, the end—it were and end—verily." He pulled himself into the present. "Dick were lost. God only knows what happened. Did he lose his way and fall into some pit—or a mine? The Parish searched for him in the lanes and byways and on the moor; never found a hair of his head. 'Tis my b'lief 'e was set upon by thieves; there were plenty would knock a man off 'is horse and throw him down a shaft. Never a hair…never a hair…"

"And the baby?" asked Rona.

"Ah, the baby. Jenny and Annie Trevant did their best. Annie had had ten babies in her time; she got herself out o' bed and charged Jenny to pull. It were feet first, see? Rose coont do it and was getting weaker all the time. He came, at last. A boy." The Potter's gaze went back into the distance and the tears trickled down his wrinkled cheeks.

"A boy. Jenny wrapped him up and put him into Rose's arms and she smiled. 'We'll call him Matthew,' she said and fell asleep, content.

"She never knew that Dick was lost. Between two breaths her soul fled away. They, neither o' them, knew the other was gone."

"And the baby?" Rona asked again.

"Jenny. Jenny stayed and fed the baby with her own. We wrote to ask the Bishop to appoint a single Parson, one who would be glad of the girl to look after him."

"And did he?"

"Might've."

"What do that mean?"

"It means there never was no need. Jenny took up wi' 'er young man and they ran away. Oh, she didn't stop nursing Matthew—he went too. We never knew where. Some said it were P'zance and some said Mullion and some said Falmouth. The lad were a fisherman. All we could do was to pray. Pray that Rose's child would thrive and lead a good life."

"Ye did not go back to Madron—later?"

"It were an end, see? My end. The doings of that night—they left Bess—touched. She were never the same. Blamed hersel' and all the saints and angels. Blamed God above. She were never the same. If she had not gone for to find a boy to fetch Dick—never left Rose 'lone it would not have fallen out that way. She hardly spoke again and pretty soon she paled away."

"Poor lady—poor Master Jane."

The gulls cried and the wind sighed and the tide crept out, and the little groups at the edge of the grass were silent as empty sea-shells.

"So ye never heard of the baby found in Madron Church come Easter?" said Raleigh at last.

"Never heard o' him. Jenny must've weaned 'im and brought 'im back. Matthew. It were Rose as named 'im and Jenny remembered."

His voice trailed off. He stared at his hands as if he

did not remember them, and picked clay from under his fingernails.

At last, Matthew got up and stood in front of him.

"And you think that I look like Richard Veale?"

"Think? I know. I usta wonder if we would recognise him, if he ever came back; by a look, a mannerism, a voice. But thee, thou art the very image. And everything is right; the time is right, the name and the place." He struggled up to embrace him. "Oh Matthew, my boy, my boy, my heart is full. And bids 'ee welcome."

They clasped each other for a long minute. Then Raleigh said: "Did anyone think to register the boy's birth?"

I'll go and see," exploded Matthew. "To know I be born, at last. It is like a great gift. Do ye go with me, Sir?"

"I have tarried too long," said Raleigh, "but maybe a little longer will not signify. I will come and act midwife to the signature."

"And Rona, ye will come? And Master Potter?"

"Let us get this matter of horses settled and then we will all go."

Raleigh could ill afford the time, but he knew that curiosity and a sense of ill-grace would ride with him all the way to Portsmouth and beyond, if he did not.

There it was: "Birth of a son, Matthew, to Parson Richard Veale and the late Rose Mary Veale, on the twenty third day of September, in the year of Our Lord 1558."

1558. When Mary Tudor lay upon her death bed; when Calais was lost to the French; when she, at last, nominated her hated sister Elizabeth as her successor; when there remained but two months before Elizabeth was proclaimed Queen: Matthew Veale was born and registered in Madron Church.

No more fear of Inquisitors knocking on the door in the middle of the night to discover them, but for Richard and Rose Mary, too late.

"I suppose they thought my f-father would be found. Oh would that he had."

"If he had—been found—he would have turned ye into a scholar by now," said Raleigh slowly. "Would ye have liked that? I knew a youth once, who left the west country, bare arsed and rustic as thou, to seek his fortune. He did tolerably well." He laughed. "Come with me and I will put your feet into the same footprints. I'll show ye the ropes, get ye a doublet and a measure of learning."

"Learning? Learning? How the stars keep their stations and to read God's Work in the Latin tongue? Could I?"

"There seems to be no doubt of this man's Priestly progenitor. Aye learning, boy. The young man, of whom I spoke, had no horse and no coin in his pocket; and he managed. If he could, so could ye."

"Oh, I will come, Sir, that I will." He turned to Rona, "And I will come back too; come back worth something to ye. And, before I go, see what I have for ye."

Rona's little world was rocking round her and her brain was whirling. In a daze she watched Matthew turn to his horse and collect his bundle. Inside a plain wrapping was a length of green silk.

"I bought this for 'ee wi' my first money. It be a pledge—a green promise, like Spring, that I will be back to see 'ee wearing it. Here."

"He held it out and, slowly, her eyes brimming, she received her gift. "Thank 'ee Matthew," she whispered; "I be right glad for thee. I always knew ye were someone special. I..." She looked resolutely at the green silk, determined not to cry nor make her love and her dismay show to them all.

"I bought it to make 'ee my Sweetheart," he said.

"Oh Matthew, don'ee go away. I'll be thy Sweetheart—I am—I already am."

"Ye are?" He held her at arms' length, disbelieving, amazed. "Then indeed I must go; nought but a fine husband will do for my Sweetheart."

His hands on her shoulders, he stood memorising her face. Next he went to the Potter. "Take care o' her—as ye took care of my mother. My mother..." he repeated the word with reverence and wonder. Then he went to stand by Raleigh.

"I am not one for long farewells," said the great man. "Ye have my thanks and good wishes. God be with thee." And he saluted, turned and rode away; Matthew, on his new horse, following at a trot.

CHAPTER II

Potter Jane and Rona stood watching until they were out of sight and the dust settled. Slowly he limped to her and put an arm around her shoulders. "Come, little one, thou and I have much to think about—much to do—if we are to be a credit to that one. He will do handsomely, I know't, he is his father's son. We will make the trip to the Vaylors now; it be Elizabeth ye need until your lover comes home again."

She went without a word, back to the market, to load his stock and take it back to Gulval. For the first time she went into his cottage and was appalled by the chaotic muddle within doors. Bowls, pots, jugs were stacked upon the floor. The floor was nearly invisible under splashes of clay and slip. The wheel stood half blocking the doorway and a table nigh on filled the whole of the room behind. A fat cat slept on the window sill and flies buzzed lazily round crocks smeared by the remains of meals long gone.

"I will stay and help ye," she said dully, starting to put things into some sort of order.

"Nay, I'll do well 'nough. My neighbours take a pot or two in exchange for a meal a day. What more do I want? Do'ee come and see me, now and then. Aye, that's what I'd like. But I be used to my own company—old ways and memories—they are like old friends."

Rona looked across the dark room to where the door framed a view of sky and sea. A brilliant square of light fell over the potter's wheel; no wonder he chose blue for his special glaze.

"How do ye glaze these?" she asked feeling the bowls, some smooth and some rough under her fingers.

"Master Mellin, he does a firing once in a while, down in Lyn. He was a miller turned baker, when he grew old and slow. Close now, we mun be going if I be to get home by dark."

But Rona wanted to put off the visit to the Vaylors; the more she thought of it, the more sure she was that they would turn away from her.

"Do he fire the pots in the baking oven—'long o' the bread?"

"Be off wi' thee—the bread would burnt to a cinder in that heat. No, he makes a very special fire that day. Well I be goin', whatever ye may have in mind."

He mounted the donkey and she rode the mare chosen by Raleigh, walking the Vaylor horse beside. Together they proceeded through the village and turned right up the hill; then, right again into the lane to New Mill. Between the high banked hedgerows, all a-flower with scabious, honeysuckle and brambles Rona savoured the scent and colours of late summer and was suddenly sorry for all the old people whose senses were muted and who had but a few summers left to them.

Jose Jane, William and Elizabeth, all old. Her mother had died savouring everything; and her father too, for even his sadness had been tinged with gratitude— gratitude for his Marie and his joy in her. They died with the scents of Autumn and of Spring, of wood smoke and of soft rain, all still a pleasure to them. But even as she thought of the passing seasons, Rona was faced with—how many of them? And all alone...For, now, now that she had discovered Matthew, life without him was all alone.

Soon it would be winter again; what would she do with a whole dark winter, and him away?

Slowly, keeping to the donkey's gait, they wended along the lane, seeing through gaps in the hedge the stream in the valley that ran into the sea at Chyandour, into the bay that circled the Holy Mount. At the twist in the lane where the Vaylors' cottage came into view, her heart also gave a twist; the sweet familiarity of the ancient homestead with its backing of noble trees and magical view, wiped away, for a minute, the uncertainty as to the seemliness of her coming. A plume of smoke from the chimney seemed like a beckoning finger and she forgot the report that William and Elizabeth were too ashamed to look her in the eye.

She kicked the horse's flank and broke into a trot. And Potter Jane smiled with relief, holding back his humble mount so that the girl should arrive alone and of her own volition.

So Rona Laity came back to the Vaylors. Not broken and dispossessed as she had been the first time, but restored to her lands and recompensed—and beloved of a good man.

Yet she was still in need of a home.

She could not banish Clem Bugel to the barn to use his bed in the cottage; and it would be many months before Tranthem was tried and his Manor made available to Laity ownership; many more before her home could be rebuilt. She looked up at the Vaylor cottage, so dear to her, and to the upper window and the sill she had leaned upon when she first saw Matthew in the lane. Turning in the saddle, she looked back at the view, the changeless yet ever changing view. It shimmered in the evening light and seemed to smile.

The yard before the door was empty but the spinning wheel with chair beside stood waiting for the expert hand of its mistress. The cat warmed itself with one eye on the scratching chickens. The smell of cows and the coo-ing of doves reached out to her senses. Slowly she dismounted and quietly, fearing to disturb a sweet dream yet wanting to enter into it. Noiselessly she opened the gate; just as Mistress Vaylor came through the door.

"Elizabeth. Elizabeth. Oh, I be right glad to see thee."

The old woman stood stock still, the sun in her eyes.

"'Tis I. Rona. Oh, it's been so long."

She ran across the yard to envelope her old friend in a joyous hug. But Elizabeth, with a sudden horrified look, held her off.

"Hush. Be quiet. What do 'ee want? Whatever it be, 'twere better 'ee were off."

"Elizabeth? What…is something amiss? Where be William?"

"A-milking." Her voice was flat, her face expressionless, only her hands, clenching and unclenching betrayed fear and alarm.

"I do believe I cannot wait for him. I have such news."

"Tell I what ye want and I'll tell William."

The coldness of her voice dismayed the girl.

"I want to tell ye of my good fortune...I hoped I might stay for..." Her own voice trailed away.

Only then did Elizabeth steal a frightened glance at the upper window; and, only then did Potter Jane come through the gate and into view.

"Good day to 'ee, Elizabeth."

The old woman turned quickly as if to fend off another blow and Rona saw, for the first time, how ill she looked, grey and bent and fearful.

"Elizabeth—what is the matter? Are 'ee ailing?"

"Not ailing. Leave me alone." She cast another look at the window, her face dark with apprehension.

Joseph Jane said: "So. It's true then—what they say—ye do have Philip here."

Elizabeth gasped.

"Philip?"

"Philip?" Rona whispered.

"There bain't nothing else would make my friend Elizabeth so unwelcoming."

Rona saw again the firelit demon face of Philip Vaylor as he threw the blazing brand into the hall of her house. She shrank back, astonished at the Potter's coolness.

"Well, the Constable told me he was missing— vanished and wounded. A wounded man cannot easily vanish—into thin air."

Elizabeth's stricken face was his answer.

"He threatens 'ee even from his bed, eh? Oh, Elizabeth, why did 'ee not seek help from friends?"

"Use your mind, Joseph Jane," came the sharp retort. "Which friend would not throw him to the wolves? God knows what he'll do if he hears us now."

"He cannot blame thee for my guessing."

"He can—he can do anything. And he knows that I

213

will not send for the Constable—send him to the hangman. He is still my son—my child—yet I am treated like an enemy—his mother. Oh God in Heaven…" She sank into the chair, sobbing bitterly.

Rona went quietly over to put her arms about her. "Hush, my lover, he shall not hurt ye anymore. See, I be strong now; I will help 'ee—and I will not tell, I will keep silence."

"Help? How? How can anyone help us?"

"Well, let us see…" Potter Jane passed into the cottage and a quick look told him that Philip was not in the living room. He stumped across to the foot of the ladder. "Here, child, help me up a step or two. Hold the weak foot to the rung."

He hauled himself onto the bottom step with his good leg and Rona lifted the other to join it. Twice more, and he could raise the trap an inch or two. The first intimation of the occupant of the upper chamber was the stench of sickness.

"A man in that stage of disease is not going to hit me over the head—one more step."

The man looked like a trapped animal. His eyes, red with fever, glared with hatred out of a draggled mop of hair and beard. He growled in his throat and reached for a stick that lay to hand on the floor.

"Ye can save your oaths for someone else, Philip Vaylor. Ye need all your breath for living." He surveyed the wreck that lay on a foul straw mattress, his leg, huge and bandaged, stuck out in front of him.

"I heard 'ee was struck in the leg. Perhaps John was the lucky one—he took the ball in the chest."

"'E be dead?"

"Aye, and 'ee look nigh to follow him—straight to hell, shoont wonder. No cause to look at I like that—Jose is friend to William and Elizabeth and will not bring more trouble upon them. I bring a maid to help—

er—Rose Jane, my brother's child. If 'ee lay finger on her—or curses, or any such misuse, I will call in the Constable. Behave, and we may defeat the gallows. Get me down, girl."

Struggling to a chair he jerked his head upwards; "Elizabeth can't tend that. Ye want to aid her?" She nodded. "Then put a kerchief over your nose and take a look."

Vaylor was a shadow of the man Rona had seen at the farm, ravaged by the poisons in his wound, fevered and racked with the pain of it, there seemed no doubt that John had had the better part. "Well, can 'ee bear't, think 'ee? Wi' William's help the room can be cleaned. Have 'ee a clean bandage? And vinegar? Don 'ee go up alone." He prodded the trap with a broomstick and called through the gap; "I be off to get physick. Mark my words—no harm to Rose or ye'll be finished."

They went in search of William while Elizabeth crouched at the foot of the ladder, amazed that Philip had not hurled his stick at Joseph, or his drinking bowl, or chamber pot. Perhaps some of the fire had gone out of him—some of the life...

"Will, my old friend, us will clean the room and look to the leg." He turned to Rona. "Can 'ee bear it? 'Tis not a pleasant sight and a worse thing to change the bandage; it smells of corruption but it must be done." He returned to the donkey. "I have some of the poppy physick. Wait till I be back; 'twill be better if all of us work at once."

"What did bring 'ee back, Rona lass? Not this trouble?"

"I have news for thee—such news. Let me fetch Elizabeth here to the byre, then I will tell 'ee both together."

While they waited for Jose Jane to come back with his simples and nostrums, Rona told them of her ventures

215

and adventures; of beacons and ships; of Raleigh, the great Vice-Admiral of England: of treasure safe delivered and of her reward. And she ended up with the best news—that of her promise to Matthew, and his to her.

"But I have nowhere to stay for the present. I—hoped—that I might throw myself upon your mercy—again. And, perhaps, to help with the work..."

"Sorry work—and not for a fine lady."

"Oh William...did 'ee not nurse my leg? Aye, and in your own bed too?"

It was dark with a rising moon before they heard the patter of the donkeys' hooves returning; they mixed the potion by candlelight and William took it to the upper room. "This will take thy pain away and tomorrow us'll set 'ee straight. Jose will keep his tongue still for Mother's sake."

That first change of bandage was something that Rona strove to forget. Three times she had to run to the window to heave and retch, and three times forced herself to return and kneel again beside the hideous man with the more than hideous wound. She marvelled at the Potter's calm and deftness of touch; it was her first encounter with rotten flesh.

"I would cut if off if I knew how," he said grimly; and Philip Vaylor bit upon his stick as the old man prodded and pressed in an effort to expel the putrefaction.

"There's many a man suffers thus after a battle or down a mine; innocents who did no man any wrong. This—this is punishment. Take heed and mend thy ways. I remember thee as a good lad with clear eyes. Whatever happened to they clear eyes?"

He was finished, at last, and climbed painfully down the ladder to wash himself in water poured from a bucket by William.

Before Rona followed, she paused to stare at the wretch on the floor. White-faced, she regarded him, remembering many things: so much braggart sin come to sickly death; and, to her own surprise, she felt a pang of pity. Pity for waste and for Elizabeth's forgotten hopes for her children. She knew she would nurse him for as long as he needed it, for his mother's sake.

"Let Rona fetch and carry for 'ee—she needs 'ee as much as you Vaylors need her." And to Rona he said, "We may cheat the gallows, child, but not hell, I think. He has not long. Let God do the judging. Do 'ee and William protect Elizabeth from the worst of it."

She watched him ride away. All the time people seemed to be riding away. Where were Matthew and Sir Walter now? When they went she had felt lost. At least, now, she had a task; and for all the evil in that upper room, she felt safe—and at home.

They arranged themselves for the night; Rona, once more, sharing the wall bed and William taking a quilt to the barn. A tiny oil lamp, no more than a scrap of wick in some fat, stood by the stair in case Philip cried out in the night.

He did cry out; and through the next day, constantly. It took all Rona's fortitude to tend him. Once, as she bent to give him water, the kerchief slipped from her face and he recognised her. "The Laity girl!" Then he swore a terrible oath, cursing her and the Constable for bringing him to this pass; and when she backed off to descend the ladder, he threw his chamber pot and struck her in the chest.

On the second day, the Potter came back, carrying a small phial "I had this from an apothecary in Helston. Hemlock. Ye may give it him a drop at a time. Three drops today, four tomorrow, then five. Five at most." He dripped one drop into a swallow of water and handed the cup up to her. Philip spat it out. The second drop, introduced into a spoonful of honey, calmed him. The Potter came everyday bringing more honey and more hemlock.

In a week, Philip Vaylor was dead.

CHAPTER III

There began, from that day, a new era in the life of the Vaylors. William had not realised, nor cared to know, how much he had feared his sons. His greatest fear was of his own death which would have put Elizabeth at their mercy. Mercy...No longer did he flinch at the sound of an approaching horseman, nor dread having the cottage burned about his ears.

"It were nought that us did, wife; 'twere bad blood, maybe from someone in the past: my gypsy Grandam, like 'nuff. I be sorry...but let it lie...'tis finished."

"And God—He has sent us another charge..."

"She will go, one day; we mun never b'lieve she be ours."

Elizabeth rejoiced in the new spring in his step and the whistle on his lips. It was over—the fear. The descent of the Constable with some unimaginably bad news upon them was a thing of the past. And there was some future for them: the gentle pretty Rona to console—at least for a while. Elizabeth sighed; if only she would stay. Then she thought of banishing William to the barn, night after night, and shook her grey head: it would not do; and there was never any question of using the upper room for sleep—not yet.

Of course, everything was burned and scrubbed and aired; but memories cannot be exorcised with soap and water. If only Rona could live nearer...nearer than the farm on the cliffs. There was no farmhouse on the cliffs, she knew that, but she supposed the building would start soon...but must...it start there? Excitedly, she went in search of Will. The spark of her idea shocked William. Then it began to burn with a small flame and, bye and bye, he began to question Rona.

"Be 'ee thinking of the building of thy house, my lovely?" It cost him an effort to ask; it cost him an effort to sound casual. She must never think they wished her on her way.

"I s'pose so." She shook her head in bewilderment. "Truth to tell, I am afeared—of starting again; all 'lone with the sea and the wind...It's so different here, so pretty and warm. The north is full of ghosts..." Pictures of death and of the house's destruction haunted her. Her dreams were all fire and blood and black cold. She could imagine, all too well, waking in the night with a northern gale howling down the chimney and tearing at the window panes; even with Matthew at her side, she would fear her fears. And there was no knowing that Matthew would be at her side. She shuddered and with a deeply troubled heart gazed hungrily at the serene bay and its holy Mount.

"I wish..." she began,

"What do 'ee wish, child?"

"Oh, it is nought." She looked at the cottage and barn, at the rising land behind with its garment of sheltering trees and, with half closed eyes, pictured a fine house there, with big windows to catch the sunshine and the magic of the view. No scatter of outbuildings to distract the eye, no midden, no pigsty, just green grass and a hedge of sweetbriar. Then she opened her eyes and saw the familiar group of poor little buildings. She heard William's voice but vaguely:

"I were thinking..." he said, "I were wishin'...for something...Ye wouldn't think of settling hereabouts, would 'ee? Using the money for a new house in a new place?"

She stared at him, wondering if she had been thinking aloud.

219

"Oh, I know it be a liberty I be taking…"

"A liberty? Why William, it be what I would like the best. But where? This valley is owned already. Besides, it slopes so. This land of thine is the only flat piece for miles."

"T'ain't mine, lass. 'Tis Crown Land, I pay my rent to the Agent. Happen, Queen might sell it. The Millers bought their plot years back—from the old King. But 'course, I never asked."

"Sell it?" Rona repeated softly. Oh, she must not let her dreams run away with her. She did not know the extent of her fortune, had never counted the reward hidden below Laity farm. She must go to Joseph Jane and talk to him.

"Certain ye must have a freehold before you build on any land; but how to do it? That is the question," said Joseph.

"I wish I knew who to ask."

"Ye know Captain Wat," said the old man with a twinkle.

"Sir W…"

"Sir Walter Raleigh."

"Ye knew? Ye knew it were him?"

"He told me. That is why I let Matthew go so sudden. Think 'ee I would have parted wi' him on the instant, if it were not for so great an opportunity? Why, I'd only just found the lad. But the great Sir Walter has a finger in every pie—even a Royal pie. A man like that can help our boy to catch up on lost time, show him the way of things—be a friend at Court. A friend at Court is what 'ee need now and Captain Wat is surely the one. Come, let us compose a letter to him. Between us, we should do very well."

"Who shall take it?"

"Let us write it first."

They cleared a place on the table and sharpened a quill.

To Sir Walter Raleigh.

Good my Lord,

Master Jane says I may write to thee in favour of thy counsel; on the cause of building myself a house. I fear to build again in the north: I would as lief live in a graveyard.

Think Ye that I can use some of my reward to buy a parcel of land in Gulval Parish? Master Vaylor says it do belong to the Queen. Master Potter says I must hold freely any piece where I would build. So, therefore, I must needs buy from the Crown, or do without. What say thee?

I prithee commend me to Matthew if he be with thee. I miss him. As I do miss my dear Captain Wat. Marry, we did have some good times all together, when we was moving the stuff.

With all due respect from thine obedient and faithfulle servant,

Rona Layty

Joseph hunted about in an old chest and found a roll of parchment and after much scratching and restarting and re-sharpening of the plume, Rona produced a fair copy.

"'Twill suffice. It must be sealed somehow; perchance there is wax at the Parsonage. Come."

"But how shall we send it? Who shall take it?"

"I know a sea captain who sails to London from Newlyn. He lives in Marazion. We will seek him out and pay him a little to deliver the letter—and maybe to bring back an answer. If we be lucky, we will hear by Christmas."

"Christmas? Why, that is months…"

"If we be lucky."

By good fortune they did not have to wait so long. The morrow was market day and together, they went down to Marazion with the cart of crocks and the Potter's stall. They found that the tide was out and coming across the causeway from the Mount was a procession. Horsemen, carts, pack animals and a litter came slowly towards them over the sands.

"Ha. And if I'm not mistook, that be a progress to Court. Wait, I will speak to the Chaplain. Give me the scroll."

The Potter limped to the edge of the causeway and anxiously scanned the faces as they passed. Servants, some of them armed, rode by with haughty looks. There followed members of the household—installed by King Henry when the monks were dispossessed— family and friends, riding in the wagons; and, in the centre, riding a high horse, richly caparisoned, rode the Lord of the Mount. He saw the old man, his arms upraised to stop one of the company. "Who is that old man? Bid him make way."

"Ye wish to ride to London?" a courtier mocked.

"Tell your Lord I be entrusted with a letter for the Lord Lieutenant of the County and would importune his Chaplain to carry it for me."

"A likely story…to Sir Walter?" He extended his leg. "Come, pull the other one."

"Gilbert, send him about his business; I want no delay."

"Show him," commanded Master Jane, thrusting his scroll into Gilbert's hand. "It is a message and Sir Walter waits for it. He will want to know why it is not come."

Gilbert swung his horse to ride beside his master.

He leaned over and Rona, watching from a little distance, thought what a splendid picture they made. The men decked in fine cloth, the servants in livery, the curtains of the litter gleaming richly in the sunlight. And, above all, His Lordship in a huge snowy ruff and a satin cloak, fur-trimmed, that shone like cloth of gold. He gave the old Potter a brief nod.

"Come to my stirrup, Sirrah; where got ye this document?"

"Sir Walter commanded me to report on a matter close to his heart, m'Lord. I wonder he did not tell 'ee of it. He will welcome your arrival wi' it."

"Ye speak well. What is the matter of the letter— the subject of his concern?"

Master Jane's eyes twinkled; "It concerns Crown Lands, m'Lord."

The great man nodded sagely. "Very well." It would suit him to get close to the Lieutenant, he thought. "I will see to't myself." And he spurred his horse and called his retinue to follow.

The Potter was shaking with laughter when he rejoined Rona. "How the Popinjay loves to shake his feathers. 'Tis well we managed to seal it...Crown Lands...Crown Lands..."

They stood together and watched the procession leave the sand, and stream up the road to the east. As it wound up the hill, preceded by a trumpeter, they saw flashes of colour showing in the gaps between the cottages.

"How grand they go," said Rona with envy in her heart.

"They'll cover up quick enough as soon as there be no-one to see. Dun coloured riding cloaks is the order of the day for men upon the open road."

"How do'ee know so much? So much..."

"I be an old man, little one, and an old soul. All my

223

life I have had an enquiring mind and it has taken me into many curious places. I would have liked a son to send along the same roads. Now there is more to be found; always more…"

"That's what 'ee hope for Matthew?"

"Matthew must choose for himself, but he has a great curiosity and is inquisitive."

"Aye, it is always questions: why some stones glitter and why some are dull and if there is a wind among the stars."

"Ah."

"Can he find the answers by book-learning?"

"Happen." He watched her face as he asked;" How long will 'ee wait for him?"

"Why…if I knew, for sure, that he would be coming back, I will wait for as long as it takes…It's not knowing…"

"Ye do know. Think on't; ye do know. And remember this, Matthew has never known any other love. The wind that blows among the stars will soon feel cold. A man needs to belong. He needs a home from which to wander; a home to return to. Make that home, Rona child, and he will come hurrying back."

Looking back across the years to that moment, she saw the letter as the first stone, the foundation of her house; the house in which she was to live and love and bear her children. But, when she got back to the Vaylors' cottage, she was silent, uncertain; and the wait for Raleigh's answer was as tiring as a heavy task. It was easy enough for Jose to say "make a home", but where to make it, and how, were two different matters.

Christmas he had said; Christmas. That was weeks and weeks away. And Raleigh might not have any advice to offer—might not reply at all. She began to realise the huge distance between Cornwall and

London. Damn London: why should everyone want to be centred there? It might as well be a foreign land; France was nearer.

CHAPTER IV

The berries ripened in the hedges and the bees, frantic to replace the honey robbed by men, hummed all day in the heather. Corn fields, gold by day, were silver under the harvest moon. Rona had helped Bugel with the harvest at Porthmarys and Bugel had ridden over to give a hand to William. That year there was an Indian Summer and the tall trees that cast long shadows across the yard were still in leaf.

But gradually the lingering scents of summer mingled with autumn and gave way to the smells of leaf-fall and woodsmoke. On such a day a dusty messenger trotted up the lane. Rona had long since given up listening for any arrivals and was inside the cottage cutting bread. The messenger paused; he could not believe that his Master had any dealings with such a poor homestead; indeed, if his throat had not been dry, he would not have stopped at all; as it was very dry, he hollered: "Anybody there?"

A dark haired girl emerged, tall and graceful, and looked at him questioningly. It was no-one she had ever seen before.

"Good morrow, have 'ee pity enough for a parched traveller to spare a pipkin of water?"

"We can do better'n that: we have brewed and we have milked. Take your pick—milk or beer?"

"Ah. Beer, so please 'ee. Alcazar will take the water." He patted his horse's neck.

"The trough's over there; I'll open the gate."

As he passed through, Elizabeth came out to see what strange voice was there. The man gave her a courtly bow and Rona saw that under the dust of travel there hid a well-found young man, with manners not learned in the country ways of Penwith.

"Whence came ye, Sir?" she asked curiously. Would Matthew come back with such courtly bows?

"From London." Rona's heart gave a great bound. "I have been these three weeks on the road."

"May I ask your purpose?"

"I deliver messages along the way. Instructions, bills and dues from my Master. I am charged with one for somewhere near here."

The two women waited, not daring to ask the all important question.

"I have ne'er been so far to the west. Am I at the Land's End? I would like to see it, having come so far."

"Eight miles or so—depending on the road. Aye, 'tis a fine sight—so long as ye can stand on the edge wi'out falling over."

"They say the cliffs are like stone walls, and the rocks to westwards like long ships."

"They say right." She took a deep breath: "Tell I— who...?"

"I have one more mission: to find one Mistress Laity: then I shall go to the end of the road."

"I—'tis I—I be Rona Laity. Ye be from Sir Walter? Here, give me his message. I burst for news."

"My. My. Me thought my Lord had trouble enough at Court with females—without coming so far afield."

"Sir, you are mistook. I long for news of my Sweetheart who is in his service; and of my property; and of my fortune. Oh, give me the letter or ye shall never see Land's End nor any other end save thine own."

"You can read it? Without help? I can help with that."

"I can manage very well." She broke the seal. "Elizabeth, give him a crust to stay his tongue. What does Sir Walter say..."

She went, with a little run, to the well, and sat on the low wall that encircled it. She heard the tiny splash of a pebble knocked into the water, and the clucking of a hen and the whine of a late mosquito as, with shaking hands, she unrolled the parchment.

Oh Lord, it was difficult; she stared with dismay at the spidery script. What did he say? She sought out the signature to learn how he made his letters: his 'a's' and 'ee's', his 'W' and 'T' and 'L'; and gradually the words became clear. MATTHEW sprang out of the script.

"'Matthew. He is well,'" she read, "'and will put his name to this.' And he has, so he has." She folded it to her heart.

"I will just put it safe," she said hurrying into the cottage.

"Later," she muttered to herself, "later, I shall take it to Master Jane. Oh, I wish the messenger would go away."

But the young man was in no hurry. It would only be civil for them to offer him lodging for the night. Though, on the other hand, the comforts of so humble a dwelling would be scant indeed.

Divining his thoughts, Elizabeth said: "We have little to offer a traveller, but ye are welcome to rest here. There is room in the barn with Master Vaylor."

"Thankee. But, I pray thee, make no special preparations. I will press on and, if there be time enough, I will return this way—to collect your answer."

"My answer?"

"To my Lord—there will be an answer surely?"

"Ah. Yes. I will pen him a line. So, if ye think thy horse has another twenty miles in him…best be on thy way."

"Twenty?"

"Ten there and ten back. Why not tarry and proceed

tomorrow? Ye can tell us of Sir Walter and of London, aye, and of the Queen." Whatever the young man decided, Rona meant to go to Gulval immediately to fetch the Potter.

The traveller wavered. He was weary and even a bed of straw was better than many a night spent on the road. "Very well." Then remembering his manners, he added, "My thanks, Mistress."

"May I ask Master Jane to supper? I will go and ask him presently." And she ran into the stable to saddle the black mare.

Master Fairfax, for such was the messenger's name, was astonished to see her clatter out of the yard on a fine bred horse and riding astride, her skirts hitched to her knees. The letter in her bosom, she kicked the horse with her hard bare heels and sped down the lane.

Joseph Jane sat outside his cottage enjoying the last of the sun's warmth. Soon it would sink into the mist and treetops and he would have to find something to eat for his supper. He was delighted to see Rona and surprised as she was herself at the speed of Sir Walter's reply.

"Come child, we will spread it out flat and read it word for word."

"Good Mistress Laytey,

Thy letter, come to my hand, was a great surprise; and no less astonishment was in the contents therein. Upon reflection, I see much to commend thy thought. Better a cockleshell of quiet in a sheltered place than a mansion exposed to wind and tide. Tranthem's place could be turned into a mansion, no doubt of it; but I think ye do not want a mansion. Touching upon the matter of land; I am presently much praised for the safe delivery of the gold and the Queen knows all. She is much pleased and bids me say that ye may choose whatever parcel of land in Gulval Parish that may suit thy purpose. Choose well. Send me word of it. Matthew is well, and does well. He will put his name to this when Will Fairfax passes by Eton, where is the King's Grammar School, a place of learning, where he lodges. He lives monkish, working all God's hours of the day and night. But he is homesicke and will not linger long enough, methinks, to become the Astronomer Royal. He sends his devotions and commends himself to his friends. Write to him—such a letter as another could read the difficult words.

I entrust this to Will Fairfax: an honest youth with much to learn. Give him thy message, spoken or wrote.

Captain Wat bids me send Rona his love.

Thy friend, W.R."

Potter Jane began to chuckle, then threw back his head and laughed aloud. Rona too, though she knew not why—exactly.

"Oh, Master Jane, 'tis great news. But what is so funny?"

The old man wiped his eyes: "'Much to learn'! He makes sure that Master Fairfax is put in his place if he dares to spy on his Master's business. And 'Astronomer Royal'! Oho, that tickles my ribs."

"What is a grammar school?"

"A place wherein to learn grammar—letters and Latin and Greek."

"What for, think'ee?"

"To go on to something else; law, perhaps."

"Why the law?"

"The Law is a mixture—Latin, English, History and Government—a good base to start from."

"And, think 'ee that Matthew will be a lawyer?"

"Nay. I think he could become an Agent of the Queen. Old Trewern, he who takes my rent, and all the rents hereabouts, is growing old; if Matthew learns well, who knows—he might be chosen."

"I don't see him sitting on a stool all day, counting up rents and debts and scratching with goose feathers—not Matthew."

"Well, my lover, we shall...we shall see. Now, get'ee back in daylight and take my greeting to Will and Elizabeth, I'll not be coming wi'thee. Tell me the news from London tomorrow."

She rode back slowly, elated—half elated. Raleigh's news gave her freedom to leave Bosigran and the old Laity land and choose elsewhere; but there was only one place she wanted and that was impossible.

As she rode she studied the now familiar terrain. Behind her it sloped to the seashore and turning in her saddle, she watched the changing scene, moving, as her perspective changed, and always beautiful. In front lay the bleak moor, out of sight by about three miles; and, in between, the woods and pastures made possible by the stream that tumbled from the moor, past New Mill, and down to the sea at Chyandour. Water and shelter in a land where the granite lay close to the surface were treasures indeed. To be able to make a garden and have tall trees and little lambs on rich pasturage there had to be a valley. She examined the land to the east of the lane; it sloped both ways, dropping down to the stream on her right and then climbing to a ridge of trees. To build on rising ground would be difficult. The land to her left rose more gently and there was only one plateau: Vaylor's plateau.

Beyond them it became steep again, the wooded hill sheltering the cottage and the meadow. Vaylor's meadow.

She sighed. It was no great wonder that the Vaylors' homestead was the only one on these sloping fields. There were other valleys; one ran down into Newlyn: the Coombe, they called it: a leafy place and very pretty until the smell of fish blew up to remind you of the nearness of the fishing quay. Helford, they said, was verdant and prosperous, but Rona did not want to be too close to Uncle Nathaniel and his kill-joy wife. No. She had grown to love this valley above all else; she wanted nothing better than to make this lane her own homeward way; but, of all the people in the world to whom she owed the most, after the Bugels, came the Vaylors. To dispossess them was unthinkable.

She rode in slowly, sick-sad that the one piece of land in the whole county was the one she could not have. At the gate, she turned to look back across the bay; to see the distant Lizard picked out pink in the rays of the setting sun, and the Mount rising from an opal sea. And she signed again—and again.

"A nice one, ye be, to ride off and leave I with Master Fairfax and he a visitor from London, the first ever."

"Where be he?"

"Gone. Wi'out thy charms to tempt him, he took his leave."

"Good. I've no wish to be a temptation to Master Fairfax. Ye be glad he's gone, bain't ye?"

"Very." said Elizabeth, with a grin. "I bad him try 'The First and Last'. There be a fine buxom maid there and hot food for travellers. He wanted to see the land's end, he said; I did not hold him back."

Rona was relieved. She was tired. The anxieties with

which she had awaited Raleigh's reply were gone; but new worries supplanted the old ones: now the field was too narrow—or too wide. She sat disconsolately on the doorstep.

"What is't, my lover? Is something amiss? What says the letter? Tell Elizabeth."

"There be nought amiss. I jus' be ready to drop…" Her voice trailed off.

"Here's William. We'll sup directly. Rest 'ee and then tell us the news together."

They ate their supper in the gathering shadows; the old couple manfully containing their curiosity.

"Well then—how be Matthew? Do'ee have news of he?"

"Oh—yes. Yes I do. He be well. Already he writes his name. He resides in a place called Eton, by a school. He is missing us—Raleigh says."

"And what else do His Lordship say? Does he approve the plan to leave the farm? What…?"

"He approves."

"He does? Why that be good news—he will help'ee to start afresh." William and Elizabeth exchanged happy glances. "What more?"

Rona hesitated: "He commends himself to ye and to Master Jane."

"That's nice. Very nice. So his mightiness sends a messenger a few hundred miles just to tell 'ee that 'ee may do as 'ee please? Child, I be a poor man, I have no letter, no learning; but I know men: I've wrestled wi' em and I've worked wi'em and I b'lieve that no man, who has reached up to be Lord Admiral and Captain o' the Guard, will write a letter without telling o' his mind and a'giving of advice. 'Tent nature. What do 'ee say 'ee should do?"

"He says—he says I should get me some land hereabouts and build fresh. He says the Queen would let me buy the land. But..." She faltered and the old people sat silent, anxious; "But 'ee have no cause to fret—I shall not intrude on thee—thy piece...I shall look around about and—and see what there be..."

"There bain't nowhere else flat 'nuff," said William firmly. And still they sat unmoving with puckered brows.

"Don'ee look like that. William, Elizabeth, I would not get in thy way for all the world."

"Humph," grunted William, and Elizabeth rose and puffed and gathered up the pots. The old man flashed a sideways glance.

"We did hope 'ee might choose this land."

"What?"

"This 'ere. 'Tis the best. 'Twas well chosen. Sheltered at the back and flatter than most roun' 'bout." He looked hurt.

"But...'Tis thine...thy land."

"Tent. 'Tis the Queen's Majestie's. Very soon I won't have the strength to work it; then it'll go—go to strangers; and all I've put into't will be lost. If ye has it, 'twont be lost."

The girl leaned on the table and stared at them wide-eyed; "But, I don't understand...It is the one place, above all, that I would like—for Matthew and me. But ye bain't finished wi' it, not yet, not for a long while, and truly there bain't room for us all."

"There's plenty—if us builds big 'nuff. Ye be going to build a house somewheres—build it here. Buy the land an' I'll pay my rent to 'ee. I'll build the house."

"Oh, William, William, where? In your best field?"

"Right 'ere. I've had a mind to burn this lot down ever since—since Philip died."

"No. No. Not this cottage.."

"The yard then."

"What? Right in front of the windows? What an idea! 'Twould block off the view."

"What view?"

"Wha—I don't understand." She rose to pace up and down.

"Bless me, lass, I ain't seen no view for many a long year. I can see 'bout as far as the privy. The rest is grey or blue, 'cording to the weather."

"Elizabeth?"

"That's right. 'Tis all of a blur. Build 'ee in the yard; it'ud keep off the wind."

CHAPTER V

Rona sat again. She could not believe what she heard. After so many disasters, she could not—dared not—believe in a dream coming true. But there they were, sitting solidly at the kitchen table, calmly putting their precious plot at her disposal; and looking at her out of their short-sighted old eyes, anxious lest she should go away.

Suddenly she saw their lives and the uncertainties of their future. She saw how they could get too old to work the land and pay the rent. She saw them dispossessed, unable even to die in the home they made. She saw how she could give them security. She could buy the land, William could pay her the rent and she could see to it that he had enough to do so. He could lay out a garden and till the rest for the good of them all.

It seemed as if all three were holding their breath. Time itself stood still, thoughts suspended…dreams running on. And dreams take no account of time. The little room became full of dreams.

The dreams sorted themselves into plans; the old heads started nodding and Rona began to smile.

As soon as the Queen's grant of Freehold came to Rona Laity, the footings were hewn out of the bedrock of the yard. In the year of our Lord 1579, on September the twenty-first—St Matthew's Day and Matthew's birthday—the first foundation stone was laid; and Rona wept that he was not there.

The weather held fair that year. And well before Christmas, the first few courses of the outside walls were bravely rising from their granite footholds. They surrounded the well, with doors to the fore and behind. Then, at the turn of the year, Atlantic gales took charge, driving rain before them: lashing rain that briefly turned to snow and slush, making the lane impassable to the stone wagons that plied between them and the quarries at Mousehole. But, even then, William hung on to the masons and carpenters, housing them in the barn with threats and promises and praise if only they would continue to work at dressing stone, hewing floorboards and making doors and sills and panels.

Rona and Elizabeth fed the work gangs, struggling with huge pots and cauldrons of hot stews and groats.

"Jus'ee look at my 'Lizabeth, why she be a new wumman wi' thee for a daughter; an' both o' ye so 'andsome."

And Rona, excited by the progress, by the planning and designing, rejoiced with William and Elizabeth and tried to resign herself to the long wait before she should have a roof and hope of seeing Matthew.

She lay awake at night as the wind rattled the shutters, wondering how he was, what he did. Their sudden recognition of their mutual love had been so brief, so rudely interrupted that sometimes she wondered if she had dreamed it. Then she remembered his steady faithful ways. Here was no light-o'-love, no fortune hunter; knowing of her crock of gold, he had, nevertheless, taken his leave to make his own fortune: "To make me worthy of ye, Sweetheart." He was faithful unto himself and that was good. She fell asleep enumerating the small proofs of his virtue and his love; searching her memory from the very first moment when she had cradled his head to her bosom in the lane outside and first seen the delight in his eyes at his first sight of her.

Twice, during the winter, she rode over to Tranthem's where Clem and Dorothy lived in unaccustomed comfort. She stayed with them and listened hungrily to Dorothy's praise of Matthew and her certainty of his devotion. "Why, Rona, the times I've seen him gazing arter ye, wi' a sick hopeless longing; the times 'ee's 'id 'isself to see 'ee pass by…"

"'Tis true? I can truly b'lieve it?"

"Would I deceive ye, my lovely? Aye, 'tis true—true as the sun in the sky." And Dorothy would sigh and wish it were she who had such a lover.

Sometimes she went to Madron Church. And, lingering, one day, she knocked on the vestry door. "May I see the Parish Register?" She wanted to see Matthew's registration again.

"Register? What do ye want with such a thing?"

"I want to see—to look up a birthday if you please."

She thought the shabby, crabby old man was the Sacristan and might not be able to read. "I can manage for myself if ye will just show me the book."

"I shall do the looking," he said. "What year, young Miss?" "September 1558. Let me see. Let me see. Who is't? The name?"

"Veale. Veale is the name. Let me look, prithee, I can read."

"Veale ye say? A man called Veale was my predecessor here."

"Ye be the Rector? Pray what year did ye come?"

"In 1559—I think. 'Tis so long ago and I was old then…"

"Then that is the year I want—the year the Richard Veale dis—went away. The time of the storm when his son was born. It is Matthew Veale I seek."

"Saint Matthew's Eve…September twenty—twenty-first…" He put his eye close to the script. "I be too old to read writing nowadays. I have to rely on my memory for Collects and Gospels. Look 'ee for me." He pointed with a bony finger and Rona scanned the crinkly parchment. The ink was fading and the paper yellowing with age.

"I see nothing on this page," she said. "May I turn over?"

The pages were wider than they were long, and heavy in the hand. They had been pressed together for twenty years and were hard to separate, but she slid her hand underneath the page and lifted it over. The writing was scholarly and regular, all written by the same hand. Names, dates, places: parents and infants and trades and addresses—none hinted at a Matthew Veale. She lifted another page—and here was a difference, a change in the script. Halfway down the page was a new hand's work. She peered. The writing was not so good. But what it said made her heart leap with renewed love: "Birth of a son, Matthew, to Parson Richard Veale and the late Rose Mary Veale, on the Twenty-Third day of September at two of the clock."

"Yes. Yes. This is it. Who wrote it?"

"Let me see, girl. There is a mark, and writen beneath it the word 'Sexton.'"

"Of course. Poor Richard could never have written the entry himself. I wonder who did. The Sexton must have asked someone to write the words in for him." Seeing the entry again comforted her.

She thanked the old man. "When ye came to the Parish, what did ye find at the house?"

237

"An old crone who stayed to take care of me; with tales of a dead girl, a lost priest and a fostered babby. 'Tis long ago and I was aged then. I forget the names."

"Who looks after ye now?"

"The Parish hacks—in turn: they keep body and soul together, more's the pity: I would feign join my forebears: enough is enough…"

"Let us pray for the souls of Richard and Rose," she said. "Let us pray for the soul of thy servant," said he.

They went into the church, he limping and she following. Quietly she closed the door to the vestry behind them.

CHAPTER VI

As a country girl, born and bred, she savoured the seasons as they came and went. She noted the imperceptible slide from Winter into Spring and Spring into Summer; noting them with a greater intensity as love added its new dimension to everything. The colours seemed brighter, the air softer and cornflowers and fruit, more mysterious and more a part of herself then ever before.

At harvest time, she went to Clem and Dorothy to help them with the Harvest Feast and the Crying-of-the-Neck. Was it only two years since she had heard her father perform the ceremony? She remembered him holding aloft the final swathe of wheat and crying: "I have it to the North. I have it to the South—and to the East and the West."—A gift to the four winds—a placatory prayer to the Seasons' Gods.

"Do 'ee do't, Mistress," said Clem.

"Nay Master Bugel, this is thine own harvest." And Clem, straightening up to his fullest height, cried the Neck with tears of pride.

But every hour of every day, she missed Matthew. On his birthday she went back to Madron Church. It was empty and she opened the gate of one of the few pews and sat trying to feel a contact with him and with his mother who might have sat there herself. To make sure of this, she sat in each of the pews in turn, willing Rose to look after her child in the wildness of the world, to plead with God for his safety—and for his return. She remembered her father and mother—Protestant and Catholic—saying; "God is no Papist, no Lutheran nor Henry's man. God is God. You may ally with Him, but do not expect Him to make you a special favourite."

"Tell me. Tell me," she begged, "how to be that ally. And how to make this house we build into our home, where Ye may be."

The Parson found her clinging to a Cross she wore and gazing, with tears upon her cheek, at the east window, as if, by wishing, she could see through it into the future.

"Ye are troubled my daughter? Can an old man help?"

She started; "I did not hear thee."

"Is't the young lady who sought the name in the Parish Rolls?"

She nodded.

"What frights 'ee?"

"I am not afeared for myself—for someone else."

"That is the most difficult. But we are all God's children. All in His hand. Have faith."

"Faith in what? What is Faith?"

Now he was startled. He looked at her in astonishment. "Faith. Ye know what Faith is."

"No, I don't. I know what The Faith is. But The Faith did not save my mother nor stand in the way of my father's murderer."

"Murdered?"

"Aye, and before my own eyes. And Faith did not protect my Uncle who is a Priest of the Faith. Why should I believe that the Faith will take care of Matthew?"

"Place him in God's hand…"

"Oh, I have, I have. But it seems God's hands are full; I do not blame Him if…"

"Blame? Blame God? Ye do blaspheme, daughter."

"I said I do not blame. Nor do I expect any special interest."

"Have faith," said the old man miserably, knowing that it was all he had.

"That sort of faith is just shuttering the mind against seeing the dangers," Rona persisted.

"Not so. It is a certainty that, in spite of the dangers, those souls who belong to God are safe." Lonely, he thought, but safe.

"In this life? Or the next?"

"In Eternity."

"Eternity? That is too far away."

"Eternity is now, Mistress. 'Tis not somewhere after death. It is here and there and everywhere. Ye can belong to the things of eternity or to the things temporal. Choose."

"Eternity is not heaven, then?"

"I did not say that. 'Tis better to say that heaven is here."

"I—I see." She did not see, but with a strange sense of illumination, she believed that she would see—sometime; that here lay the answer to her deepest uncertainties. Such a timeless and universal concept unnerved her. It discarded the cosy security of Church as an irrelevance; God was not someone you prayed to, but someone you joined. She wanted to talk to Matthew about it—to link hands with him in this eternity.

"Well.. I have the whole winter to think about it," she said and could not see why the Rector laughed. It had taken him eighty years.

CHAPTER VII

She saw the months stretching ahead. Another winter. It was two years since she had waved goodbye to the little group bound for London. Now she was faced with more months of wind and rain and darkness. Work would again be stopped on the house and there was, as yet, no part complete enough for her to move in. No, there was not—but it gave her an idea.

"It is but September," she said to the Master Builder, "and we may get another Indian Summer. Please make one room secure, with door and ceiling and window glass, before the days close in. I wish to live in my house. See to it if you please."

"Wur…I dunno…Master Vaylor, he wants the larders finished for to store the winter meat."

"I do b'lieve the owner comes before the meat— but let us do both—and quickly, while the weather lasts."

"Master Vaylor says…"

"Master Vaylor…Master Vaylor…'Tis my house ye are building."

"They do call it Trevaylor's in the village."

'Trevaylor.' She had not thought what to call it. 'Trevaylor's' sounded good—sounded right.

"So be it," she said; "but does Master William find the gold for thy wages?"

She got her room; and William got his larders. The first frosts saw them full of salted meat and fish dried in the sun and the wind.

All his life, William had driven his beasts to the Autumn market; where they were bought for

241

slaughter, salted and resold at a handsome profit. Cottages had no space for a full season's supply and meat was a luxury unknown in January, February and March. This year William pondered: "Shall us salt down two beasts or three?"

"Why not four? As much as we can store. We can store it and feed the masons. I b'lieve they will stay and work for meat."

The masons did stay and worked well enough. But as the time went by the enthusiasm cooled; the ginger went out of the bread; the work slowed down. They blamed the weather that crept down their necks, and the mud in the lane, and the shortening hours; they never blamed the masons. Rona, who tried to keep their spirits up, found it hard to keep up her own. She became despondent and restless.

William went to see the Potter.

Several days later, Joseph Jane's donkey picked its way up the lane. A light rain had bedewed its mane and the old man's beard. Elizabeth hurried him to the fire: "Dry y'self, Joseph. Drink some soup. Are ye warm? What brings 'ee here?" She fussed and bustled and called to Rona for help.

Their old friend grunted and groaned; "Ah, my dear life, my joints will hardly move." He wrapped his fingers round the bowl of broth, then flexed them stiffly. "I need a 'prentice."

"Get 'ee one then, Joseph."

"Bain't no lad wants to know—not in Gulval."

"Why, Master Jane, surely there be many a boy wants to learn a skill like thine," cried Rona, indignant at the folly of all boys.

"Nay. Like as not 'twill die wi' me."

"No. No. 'Tis shame to say it."

"Rona, child," began Elizabeth, as if fingering a vague idea; "ye'll need a whole houseful o' pots soon

242

'nuff. What if Master Jane was to teach thee? Take thee for his 'prentice. And while ye learn there will be pieces made for thine own kitchen—thine own new kitchen."

"Nay, Elizabeth, whoever heard of a woman potter? I doubt a girl could do't."

"Why not?" flashed Rona. "What be so special 'bout potting? Or so unspecial 'bout girls?"

"Well," said Joseph, "'tis a matter of patience—"

"Patience? 'Tis well known that females are more patient than any man. Why, men have to be patient wi' life and women have to be patient wi' life and wi' men too."

"The ye'll do it? Ye'll be my 'prentice?"

"Yes, I will. I will, till'ee find a boy. And ye shall see how patient we are."

"Are ye sure, my love? I doubt..." began Elizabeth, with a wink at William behind Rona's back.

"Course I'm sure. Have I said so? When can I start, Master Jane? And may I really make cups and bowls for my own house? After thy work is done, o'course."

"Certain sure—and very handsome they will be."

From that day forward, Rona hurried though her chores and rode to Gulval to the Potter's cottage; while William and Elizabeth shook each other by the hand.

There she watched him at his trade; learned how to thump the clay, how to throw it and centre it and work the treadle. She learned about pressures and slip and soon, she turned a pretty presentable bowl—fit for the fire.

"I will give it to Elizabeth for Christmas—shall we be able to get it fired by then?"

"If we work hard enough to make a full load. To work..."

Rona went every day. She walked; because there was nowhere there for the horse. She watched the hedgerows turn to bronze, then to yellow, draped with bryony and the wild clematis, and then to shed it all, except for a few stubborn berries that eluded the birds. The weeks passed quickly and, returning in the dusk, she hardly noticed the delays and frustrations in the building of her house. With tremendous pride, she brought back the first basket of crocks, neatly packed in straw, to be stored in her new completed kitchen.

Christmas was coming. Christmas would bring more keenly to the heart the absence of Matthew. She would go to Madron, to the church where he had lain in a basket of straw, like the Christ-child, and she would pretend that she was not afraid. Afraid for his safety; afraid that he had forgotten her. Her work at the wheel was punctuated by sudden tears and smothered sighs; and Potter Jane, seeing all, said nothing but shared her fears and felt for her young sorrows.

He had never been to London, but he had knowledge enough of the world to know what excitement and new discoveries could do to old loyalties.

One day the light began to fade early. They could not see to work any longer and the old man went to the door just as a wave of rain swept in from the Atlantic. It came in swathes and curtains, dropping from low cloud heavy with more and more water— tons of water. "Lucky it comes in drops," he said, "or we'd be flattened." He stuck his head out to see if there were any break, any sign of a lightening of sky. Solid rain blotted out the view. "Hard to b'lieve it be still there. Well, ye must stay here till it clears. Come to the fire and we will toast that bit of bread."

"We bain't done much today."

"Nemmine, there be plenty of other days."

"Oh aye, plenty. Too many days. Too much plenty.

Master Jane," she burst out, "how do'ee get through so many days?"

"One at a time. They come...they go...each one gone is one less."

"Less?"—she faltered.

"Less—to your heart's desire—less to live. 'Tis true, whatever age ye be. 'Tis the end getting nearer. And when ye be old, every day is dear."

He threw wood onto the fire. The rain-wet surface fizzed and steamed, then the sparks caught and blossomed round the edges.

"See. 'Tis pretty—and warm. Could be worse."

"Ye are so calm, Master Jane. I wish I could be."

"Are ye not? Ye do not seem rough to me."

"Ye jest...t'ain't fair to jest...I am so much afraid...so much, it makes me feel sick and empty. And my thoughts go round and round."

He looked across at her, seeing youth and beauty, health and wealth; and behind her a house a-growing—such promise. He shook his head and smiled. "And heartsick withal. Well, well, let us face these fears, one by one."

"I hardly know what they are," she whispered, ashamed when put to the task of speaking them out loud.

"Ye fear that, perhaps, ye do not love Matthew after all?

That ye have committed thyself unwisely? That is easily undone."

"No. Never." Her astonishment made his smile even broader. "Oh no—I love him—so much—that I know not how to bear it."

"Ye want to wed with him? Then ye want to know his heart—whether he wants to wed wi' thee."

Her silence was his answer. "Face up to it, my dear. If Matthew do not want ye—then ye must stop worrying and enjoy the freedom of a whole heart. But,

245

think ye, consider, is not Matthew not the more frightened? Lest he should lose thee?"

"Lose me?"

"Aye, truly. How does he see thee—from afar? A beauty. An heiress. One who reads and writes and has the Queen's favour. How many young women can claim so much? Does he not see some knight errant coming into thy ken? And how does he set himself against such a one? He sees himself as a poor miller's boy wi' nothing of his own—nothing but his own wit and a strong arm. He has courage: courage to leave thee at the moment of discovery, so that he shall be worthy of thee—so that ye shall not scorn him."

Rona hung her head; her heart and mind reaching out to tell him she should never scorn him. She was ashamed—she had never thought of his fears—there, all alone in a strange place.

"I wish I could go to London. I would tell him—show him…"

"To London? That would get thee nowhere—save an early grave and all lost. No woman can travel without a strong guard and, like as not, he would rob her himself and leave her in a ditch. 'Tis a sorry thing, but true; and much good it would do Matthew."

"Then I must write to him—say that there is no man else."

"Best just to say I love thee—do not frighten him wi' dragons."

"A la folie."

"French, eh? Aye ye remind me much of your mother. I well remember her waving her pretty hands and sprinkling her speech with French excitements."

"Did my mother know Matthew's mother?"

"I never saw them together—but 'tis very like. Bess and Rose were friends and Bess and Marie. Aye, surely they would have met."

"I hope so. I hope so. I pray they may be our guardian angels."

Joseph nodded to himself and looked across the hearth to the place where Bess used to sit. He nodded, and smiled.

The girl rose and reached for her cloak. "It is getting dark now; I must go, rain or no rain; Mistress Vaylor will fret. See, it is not so heavy; I'll begone. I will see thee tomorrow, Master Jane." She looked back, hesitating; "Thank'ee for talking to me. I am sorry to be so foolish—so impatient." She ran back to hug him, then turned to the door and slipped out into the twilight.

On just such a night, Rose had slipped out into her twilight.

CHAPTER VIII

The rain was little more than a mist but the roads ran with water. Within minutes her hems were soaking and her skirts clinging to her legs, dragged at her steps. She jumped the ruts and puddles but when she came to cross the stream that ran through Gulval, she found it in spate and lapping over the low wooden bridge. She lifted her skirts as her shoes filled and squelched, and skidded on the wet planks. Once on the other side, she hurried to keep warm.

The clouds were heavy and colourless, and the water, lying in great pools, reflected steely grey. There seemed to be more light on the ground than in the sky. And it was cold with a whining wind that sought out all the damp patches of her clothes—the sodden shoulders, the soaking petticoats. The brief uplift to her spirits in the warmth of Jose's cottage seemed removed from reality; a tale told by the fire. Her doubts returned and as she stumbled along the darkening lane, dull with winter's death, this felt like the only reality in which dreams had no place.

Depressed by her thoughts and the need to pick her path, she did not at once hear the sound of a horse's footfalls. They were some distance behind her—by the bridge, perhaps. When she did notice them, all she thought was that the horse was tired—as tired as she was—and hoped its stable was in Gulval. But, gradually, horse and rider gained on her and she realised that they had turned into the same lane. All that the Potter had said about the dangers of the road came into her head and a thread of fear sent her feet hurrying through the mud.

The horse came on. Who could it be? Someone hoping to get to New Mill before dark? Or to Ninnis Farm? Or—she looked behind her. She could see nothing. Storm-blown clouds obliterated the view; the hedges, dark and whispering, obscured the outline of the stranger. She thought quickly, "If I cannot see him, then he cannot see me; I'll let him pass." She drew the cloak and hood tightly around her and shrank into the hedge, turning the pale oval of her face into the bare twigs and brambles. The indistinct pattern of the footfalls told her that the man was leading the horse; she hoped he was walking on the side away from her.

They drew close; abreast of her; passed. She relaxed her tense muscles and took breath again. She heard the man encouraging the horse. "A little way, only a little way."

She froze, every sense alert, and moved her head, free from the folds of her hood until she could see the pair ahead. Even in the thick gloaming, there was no mistake. No mistaking the tall figure, the square shoulders and the bright chestnut curls; no mistaking—"Matthew," she whispered. Was this a figment of her imagination? Had she gone mad? Was she conjuring up a dream figure?

"Matthew!" she shrieked, as if in pain; "Matthew! Matthew! Matthew!" She threw herself from the ditch in such a frenzy of energy that her cloak was left behind. Her slight form hurtled into the road, determined to prove her wild hope—or to banish the ghost.

He whipped round, believing that his thoughts had suddenly taken form. Believing—disbelieving—he ran back; then stopped.

"Rona?" he said uncertainly.

"Matthew—'tis thee? Really? In very truth?"

"Oh, 'tis I, Sweetheart. But what—what be ye doing here? Come. Oh come to me."

She ran into his open arms and they clung together: two wet and trembling creatures, holding on for dear life. His arms enclosed her small shaking body and, not only held her—close, but held her up. And she, gazing at his face, strained against him in a sort of panic lest this was too good to be true, and that he would vanish as quickly as he had come, and be back in London, hundreds of miles away.

She was like a frightened bird, he thought. "My dove," he murmured, "easy...easy." He tried to soothe her and to control his own mounting excitement. The desperate need that had driven him to undertake the monstrous journey from one side of the country to the other: the fear that, by his absence, he should lose her: the call of Christmas which he dreaded alone or among strangers, all this had sustained him through the weary miles, the frugal meals and makeshift lodgings. In fits of self-doubt, he had imagined this meeting and dreaded that she would be indifferent, distant, mistaking his sudden departure for personal ambition only.

As he had drawn nearer and into recognisable territory, his hopes and longings and despair had intensified. He still had nothing to offer her. Once or twice, he had turned his horse's head to return to London and his studies, resolving not to come without some degree of scholarship; better not to know that he was spurned until he had something else to fall back upon; but the tug of the country—his own country—beckoned him on. This was where he belonged—for better or worse.

And here she was, risen like a sprite out of the very land itself. Not distant...not calculating...but in his arms...so close, so close that their hearts were beating together with only a few wet clothes to separate them; and nothing to separate their souls.

He suddenly felt his manhood and a superb sense of pride and of responsibility to protect this, his chosen woman.

Trembling, her breath coming in little whimpers of excitement and relief, she devoured the security of his arms, the warmth of his body and the love in his eyes. She parted her lips to say something but the word was never said; instead his mouth sought hers and they kissed. They kissed, standing alone in the cold, wet, winter's night, dwelling in a private world of stars and cosmic fire. At first, her lips were all he could have dreamed, but soon it was not enough; his questing tongue joined hers in a wordless conversation of love that was to them the beginning of an intimacy and belonging unknown, undreamed of, full of eternity, awe and delight.

"Oh, my love," she whispered at last. "Come home."

The tiny light of Elizabeth's candle twinkled down the lane to greet them; darkness softened the raw outlines of the new building; and, as they approached, hand in hand, they felt that, indeed, they were coming home.

Such a fuss and bustle: Elizabeth squawked with astonishment and pleasure when they crossed the threshold.

"See who I found in the lane," the young ones said together, then laughed.

"Oh ye are wet—wet—my children. Take off those things, Hurry, before ye catch 'ee deaths."

"I mun see to the horse."

"William will do that. William…" she shouted through the door. William, just on the other side, scraping the mud from his boots, recoiled before the assault of her voice.

"What? Is't the end o' the world? Lordy. So it is. 'Tis Matthew come back. Welcome boy."

"Master Vaylor. Oh, 'tis good to see thee. My horse is dead beat. He has carried me many miles through many days—I forget how many—he deserves hot oats and a warm stable; may I ask it of thee?"

"Come, we will do it both together."

The men gone out, Rona turned impulsively to Elizabeth: "I be so happy. He has come to me. To me! And, oh, Elizabeth, he do want to marry wi' me. I was afraid, so afraid…"

"I know my lovely; ye was sore afraid. I am happy for 'ee." She helped the girl off with her soaking gown and warmed a wrap before the fire to put around her. She saw the naked beauty of Rona's body, young and lovely; and, curiously, she remembered her own and William's pride in her all those years ago. They must not waste time, a-wondering, she thought.

"When shall ye wed?"

"Tomorrow."

"Tomorrow? What about the Banns?"

"Oh Lord—the Banns. How long…? 'Tis three

weeks…I cannot wait three weeks. They will be long as a lifetime."

"Wi' Matthew here, they will fly. Talk to him, child."

Elizabeth knew very well the contrary ways of men in matters of love. How they would run careless into romances that did not touch their hearts—wooing, pleading, seducing; here today, urgent, urgent; and gone tomorrow. But where the heart and soul were involved, they would handle the precious object of their desire with such care and wonder, that the woman, who had given her own heart, was impatient; confusing his wish for perfection with doubts, his circumspection with coolness. She believed that Matthew would want all things to be proper for his bride.

She was right; but they were spared any argument by Matthew's patent exhaustion. Even Rona, blind and dazed with love and surprise, could not fail to see it. While they supped, he could scarce keep his eyes open, and, with William to help him, he stumbled up the ladder to lie in the upper chamber. Rona returned to the wall bed; sleeping on the outside, the better to rise first and blow up the fire and set the kettle to boil.

On the morrow, she woke and sleepily regarded the shutters. They were rattling and a blinding shaft of sunlight came glittering across the floor, and across William's body curled up on the hearth rug. Sunbeams danced in the light and a skinny fragment of blue showed through the cracks. Yesterday's rain had blown away with one of the sudden changes common to Cornish weather. Yesterday, thick and grey and—she sat up suddenly, her eyes wide, remembering…remembering…Matthew.

She leapt out of bed and ran to the ladder; then frowned. Had she dreamed it? Was this abrupt transition into bliss a wild fancy? She looked down at William and up at her gown hanging to dry beside the

252

mantel; and at Matthew's cloak hanging on a hook and his boots on the hearth; and fully awake, she knew it was no dream.

"Oh, Matthew. Matthew. Wed wi' me, my love." And remembering that kiss, she blushed and wondered if that were, indeed, a marriage already.

She opened the shutters and the bright morning sun streamed in. Nothing was stirring outside and long shadows from the new buildings crossed the yard and blocked the view. She crept out to the well and pump, now sheltered within the house, and washed her face. Then she went to the byre to milk Bloody Mary, pressing her head against the warm flank and talking to her. "Three weeks...'tis too long...'tis not long enough...so much to do. The ground floor is complete but I have not a stick of furniture nor rushes for the floor; the lower windows are glazed but the panelling not done; the men are still asleep in the barn...and will soon be over, hammering and swearing; I must show Matthew before the place is a hive of two-legged bees. What to wear to my wedding? Oh glory..." She wished fiercely for her mother and wished, too, that she had paid more attention to her own sewing.

Milk in hand, she went back to the cottage. Again she looked at the ladder; and, this time, she cautiously went up it. He looked so young, so beautiful, so untroubled. She wanted to lie beside him and hold him close. One day—one day soon—she would. She crept away and went to milk the other cows.

CHAPTER IX

At last a shaft of sunlight found the upper window and woke Matthew. He looked across the tiny room, remembering where he was and thanked God for his safe arrival. He thanked Him for William and Elizabeth's kindly welcome, for the dear familiarity of his childhood countryside, and, above all, for Rona, her beauty…and, amazingly, her love. The memory of the passion in her greeting was still startling.

All along the way, for every mile of the journey across from east to west, he had felt a person of less and less consequence. He had learned prodigiously—only to be aware of the fathomless well of knowledge as yet untapped. He knew now that he must not only learn but also teach; particularly he must teach boys, who, like himself, were separated from the springs of knowledge. He must, like his father, bridge the gap between Creator and Creation: God and man. He had spoken to his teacher and asked what he must do to become ordained; and the man had laughed; "Well you have made a beginning—you have your alphabet—but the end is far over the horizon."

"I do not want to be the Archbishop," he had said hotly.

"I'm sure his Grace will be mightily relieved."

Rona would understand—wouldn't she? She would not laugh at his dreams. He must go and tell her—if she still cared to hear him. He must test his new experiences against the matrix of the old. His travels were so confusing; they were sweeping him along too fast. Was he really for ordination or was his dream of Cornish Parish really a reaching out for his father? He must find out.

Meanwhile, he knew he had nothing to offer her and his portion of the reward was nearly spent. But drawn by the magnet of her beauty, by his love and by homesickness, he had come, mile upon mile, through all the weather that winter could send to stop him, resolutely telling himself that it was "only for Christmas". He knew that he was still of little worth and had no expectations. Just to see her—just to be at home again; one day, he might come back with scholarship and a chance to earn his living: and take her to wife.

Rona's welcome on the road, so unexpected, threw him out of kilter. Its rapture was all he might have dreamed of—had he dared—but it made things more, not less, complex. He knew now that he could woo her and win her; but where lay wisdom when such commitment of heart could only lead to inequalities, patronage and parting? He would have to tell her of his determination to follow his father's example; of his wish to become ordained; and then of the necessity to go where the Church might send him. Then, if she would follow him...if she would come to him wherever it might be...then...He rose softly and went to the window. Carefully, quietly, he opened the shutters and, leaning out, secured them.

And, for the first time he saw it—the house—and it was like a blow between his eyes.

"Great God...what's this?"

William stood watching from below. "Ah, 'tis great, sure 'nuff. 'Tis Rona's surprise for thee. 'Tis all for thee."

Matthew groaned. Sweet Jesus...Help me out of this.

He had guessed that she might turn away from the Laity land, with its memories and sorrows; but this...He had not seen his Patron, Raleigh, for months and knew nothing of the plan to build here. He had hoped that indecision would have delayed any building and that Rona would be free to follow his calling. Now this— her surprise for him—this was a trap.

"Ye say nothing, lad, what is't?"

"What can I say?" he mumbled. "Except that I have not finished and must go back to London presently."

"Go back? To London? Do she know?" Matthew shook his head. "Last night, we met so sudden; I was tired. I did not know if she would be glad to see me. There seemed no hurry to talk of going before I had proper arrived."

"Poor little girl. Poor little—hush, I hear her."

Rona came from the barn with the milk pail. She hummed a little tune as she set it on the step. "Elizabeth, may I save some whole milk for Matthew before I put it in the churn?" She disappeared into the cottage and came out with a jug to dip into the new milk. "Let us not wake him; he should sleep his tiredness out of him. Such a journey—it will take a long sleep." She picked up the pail and went into the new house by the back door.

Never had Matthew known that kind of tenderness. The Miller had kicked him awake for as long as he could remember; his months on the road and in Eton had been months of long, lonely, self discipline. He watched her recross the yard and enter the shining new building and longed to run after her and lavish the same care on her as she had given him. Perhaps it was just as well he had on only his shirt.

"Oh Master Vaylor, what a problem is here? How did such a house come to be built? Is it not your land?"

"Mine? Marry, I be but a tenant. His Lordship writ to say the land do b'long to the Queen and that she would sell it to Mistress Laity. I will be her tenant when the Deed comes through. And serve her gladly. And thee, young Sir."

"And this is your work? Rona could not have ordered masons and carpenters…"

"Only until thy return; I will step back now."

"Nay. It is I must step back, Master Vaylor. William," he burst out impulsively," do ye come up here. I must talk wi' thee." He paced the floor, turning and turning.

"What am I to do? Tell me. I have found myself: found my true work. I have been a servant—less than a servant—all my life, with never a thought to be a free man. If I come here, what am I? Rona's Bondman; no more than an Agent; dependent; he who has been a nameless slave so long. I cannot put a house before my vocation; yet how can I throw it back in her face?"

He stared out of window; it was going to be a beautiful house. The granite was plain and solid but full of colour; after the rains, it shone and twinkled; it was better than all the bricks in the world. He had seen plenty of brick and timber and wattle and daub; this was durable, desirable.

"An Agent—aye—and it is God's Agent I would be. His man. To serve Him who made us both; and to earn her respect, and keep her as my father kept my mother. This fortune—'tis too easy. One day we would disappoint each other."

William was dumbfounded; but, as a man who had always followed his own star, he knew the boy was right. He would not have let a pile of stones stand in his way. But what of Rona? She loved the lad. If she followed him…if…what would become of the plan? Of Elizabeth? He closed his eyes and forced himself to face again the uncertainties of frail old age.

"Go," he muttered; "go onto the moor and think it out. There is ancient wisdom on the moor. It will tell ye the most important way."

Matthew pulled on his hose and quickly descended the ladder. "Good morrow to 'ee, Mistress," he greeted Elizabeth; "I would fain go to my father's Church. May I take a crust—and do ye tell Rona."

"Will 'ee not take her wi' thee?" quavered the old lady. But he was gone. "Will? What's to do, old man?"

"Dear knows…He saw the house."

"'Course he saw it: it stands there, don't it?"

"It—it has no place in his plans. He is not here to stay, seemingly."

"Not to stay?" Elizabeth was horrified.

"He has not finished his learning. He says he wants to be a clerk—a priest—and, who knows where that will take him?" He sat down dispirited and reached for her hand.

"And Rona do love him. Shall we lose the both of them? And, oh William, what about…"

"Hush, my lover, hush; whate'er come to us, we must not stand in their way."

Rona's voice, calling as she ran across from the butter churn, interrupted them: "Matthew, time to wake. 'Tis a fine day, and so much to tell." She laughed as she entered. "Is he down?"

"He be gone."

"Gone?"

"Gone out."

She halted looking with bewilderment from one to the other.

"Where's he gone?"

They shook their heads.

"Ye don't know? Why not? What's afoot? Why did he not take me with him? What did he say?"

"He saw the house."

"The house? Yes, I s'pose so. And I hoped to share that first seeing. Was he surprised? Did he say it was lovely?"

"It were a shock."

"A shock?" The girl looked at the old couple, their distress penetrating her own shock.

"Something be wrong—what is't?"

"He don't know what to do 'bout…"

"'Bout what, Elizabeth?"

"'Bout thee."

"He knows well 'nuff what to do 'bout me—aren't we to be wed and—and live happy ever after? He came back, didn't he? All that way."

"He came on a visit. For Christmas. To see thee."

"A visit? He came here to live—in the house."

"No—not—not yet."

She leaned against the table.

"Sit, girl, sit 'ee down; I will tell'ee what Matthew said to I. Matthew loves thee; he couldn't stay away any longer wi' out a sight o' thee. But he still has work to do—learning work he has plans to tell; he has hopes for the future."

"But he need not work."

"All men must work."

"I mean in London—or anywhere far away. I mean, he can work—we can work—here. The Laity land and this land." She was near to tears.

"William..." Elizabeth jerked her head at William, who quietly left the cottage. "Rona, child, listen. A man is a funny creature. He wants to serve the woman he loves; at the same time, he has to choose the way of it. Because, he has to be his own master—if he is to be a proper man."

"I don't understand—he can be Master."

"But child, it is not the same for ye to make him Master. He must put himself up: for his wife to respect."

"I respect him. I love him. He can't go back. What shall I do if he goes away again? I cannot bear it. I shall not."

She bowed her head onto her arms, seeing another weary stretch of months, empty of youth and purpose and love. Vaguely, she had thought, watching the house going up stone by stone, that it would ensure her desirability—be, in itself, irresistible; now, mysteriously, the house was a stumbling block. He had seen it—and fled.

"No—no—No..." she cried, rising hysterically, and knocking a trencher to fly across the room. "It be all a mistake. I don't b'lieve thee. What have 'ee said to

Matthew? What has William said? What...?" She stopped abruptly as she saw Elizabeth advancing with her hand upraised. The old woman crossed the room and administered a stinging slap across the girl's face.

"Sit down—and take heed. If ye love Matthew, then think on him. All his life he has been nothing—a servant—a slave to that miller and his primping wife. Now he has a name and a chance to make himself something—maybe a leader. If ye love him then ye mun help him. Wait until he is ready. Wait or stay or go. He mun set the pace. Better leave they house than let it stand in his way. Better to pull it down."

"Pull it down?" she whispered incredulously.

"Better a pile of stones than a trap. Think on't. Give him his freedom—his own soul. He will love thee the better."

She went out, biting her lip; afraid to say more; afraid that Rona still mistook. "Dear soul...Poor child...Poor children."

She found William in the front, staring up at the house that the workmen had already called Trevaylor.

CHAPTER X

Matthew, for his part, galloped up the lane to the freedom of the moor. He paused, as he passed New Mill, to look long and hard at the place of his servitude. He could be a miller, he thought with surprise, he knew all the facets of the trade; from dressing the stones, with thrift and bill, to selling the meal, by pound or hundredweight. Perhaps he should save all he could and buy out the miller of New Mill—that would be a lark—then shuddering, he spurred his horse and made for the deep lanes and rutted tracks that led to nowhere. In the bright cold air, silent save for the wind and a blown gull, he tried to marshal his thoughts; to put into perspective this new development of Rona's house. Damnation to the house. He could never compete with such a place for her to live; no teacher, priest, could hope to make so fine a home for her. To hell with the Queen and her bounty. He sat on a stony outcrop and beat the ground with his fists. Little men inhabited the moor, so they said, in huts of stone and turf, and made do, and worshipped their idea of God; they built Him alters and lived nearer to His creation than any modern man. No houses of dressed stone and glazed windows for them, no fancy chimneys and panelled doors. He ground his teeth—and in so doing, restored his humour; they probably had not any teeth either, gnawing at bones and cob-nuts.

His mind advanced and recoiled; heart and body reaching out to Rona; heart and head reaching out to scholarship and worship. The house, which he saw as her commitment to Cornwall, divided these two great desires; and his heart involved in both, was torn. However, Matthew was unaccustomed to considering his own feelings, and, unloved for so long, expected no consideration from anyone else. Loneliness and day-to-day survival were his familiars and it was this spiritual hardiness that had carried him through thus far.

How they had jeered at the country clod as he had tried to make a place for himself among the youths already blessed with some education. But, used to blows, hard words were nothing to him and soon the lads stopped mocking his country speech, respecting his good temper and enormous strength. Oh, he had so much to tell. All along the way, he had assembled in his mind the dozens of impressions, the scores of marvels to recount to them—to Rona, if she was of a mind to hear. If he could fire her with some of his own enthusiasm, would she join him in his pursuit of learning? Learning and teaching. Would she?

He looked, unseeing, at the winter scene and struggled to re-order his thoughts. How, in God's name, could he turn away from her? And from all the hard work done in the hope of his return? From the house, built for him; where he would never be more than a lodger. Time was, when to lodge in such a place would have been like heaven; but now, his very identity seemed to get in the way. He could not separate himself from himself.

A freckling of gorse scattered gold on the bleak moor. He smiled wryly; he knew the old saying: "When the gorse is in bloom, 'tis kissing time." The gorse is always blooming in some corner or other but Matthew dared not think of kissing.

How the boys in Eton prated of their kissing; boasting and crowing like roosters in a barnyard; and caring as little for their conquests as the cock for his fowls: fluttering on and off, and on to the next one.

Matthew had eyed the young women on his visits to the market for Master Miller; eyed them shyly, if he thought them pretty; anxiously if the roles were reversed, and they were after him. But the solitary boy had no-one with whom to discuss this phenomenon and so the natural instincts of modesty and self-protection weighed against puberty to make a proper balance. He found the Easterners' promiscuity contrived and uneasy; hectic and meaningless. Anyway, he had not courage enough to accost the pert flighties of the town; and now, in the clean air of the moor, he was glad of it. If this was being a prig—then he was glad of that too. Nevertheless, he was very sure that the Roger Vanners of this world had less scruple. As he had drawn nearer and nearer to 'home', he found himself thinking more of Roger Vanner—and the possibility of other dashing young constables coming in the hopes of easy pickings. For, with her inheritance translated into gold, Rona was a prize. Damn the gold.

Perhaps he could persuade her to leave it, safe hidden in the cellar, and come with him into the brave new England of Elizabeth. Only if he failed her could she return to Laity's farm and security.

Now, he thought dismally, there will be no more gold in the cellar; all turned into blocks of glittering granite and piled one upon the other: a temptation to everyone save himself.

This was getting him nowhere. What would his father have done? He turned his horse toward Madron.

The little church, grey and squat and already old, filled him with yearning; for Richard and Rose; for what might have been his childhood joy; for guidance and wisdom. Perhaps, he thought, I am destined to be alone. Lifting the latch, he went in.

It was dark inside and rather cold. The small warmth of the winter sunshine had not penetrated the church, so Matthew left the heavy door open to let in the warmer air.

"Who is this? What is that light? Shut the door, whoever it is." The querulous voice came out of the shadows.

"Oh," said Matthew, startled, "I beg your pardon, Sir; it is so dark within and I want to see the church, if you please."

"I do not please. I have said my Office and now I want to break my fast. Come back another time. I want to lock the door now."

"Let me stay. I will lock the door—if it must be so—and bring thee the key."

"What? Have ye never seen a church before? 'Tis like all the rest. Humph, ye be not country bred. I see; that coat…there will be finer churches where ye come from, what want ye with this?"

"None finer, Sir. And I do come from here. My father was priest before thee—Richard Veale."

The old man frowned; "He disappeared. And he had no son—that I ever heard of. Though there was a young woman who came lately to find—something...I forget."

"He had—and I am he. And I want to follow in his footsteps if I can."

"More fool, thee. There's poor recompense in this place. Better marry the young women and till the soil."

"What young woman?"

"The one that came—seeking some name—I forget. It was Veale, I think; and she had the same garble as thee. She told me she was building a house for the pair of ye. Best go and live in it, I'd say."

"Would ye, Father? Would ye? Is't not better to improve oneself, with prayer and praise, to the glory of God, and..."

"Be humble. 'Tis ever the best. Take up what's to hand, be it shovel or hoe, and work as a servant of the Lord—if ye must."

Matthew was silent. His long apprenticeship to servitude had taught him that there was little glory there. Such talk was a sop to the poor, the idle; a sop, maybe, to himself. "'Tis all very well to say that to a man who has neither wit nor will—who can do nothing else."

"Oho, so ye think y'self a cut above the common run...'Be ye humble,' Saint Paul says."

"Saint Paul says many things: 'I am nothing,' he says; but all the time he was a free man and would have been at pains to better himself—for the better preaching of the glory."

"And who do ye expect to preach to, young man? Ye'll do the duties, say the Offices and grow old. And any who comes to church only do so because of the Act and the fines."

"Teaching then. I would have welcomed some teaching, Sir."

"'Tis not part of thy duty—"

"Duty? Duty is not all. 'Though I speak with the tongues of men and of angels…it must be love.' To teach the ways of the stars in the sky or the fish in the sea, the flowers in the hedge and the birds in the air—these are all part of God's Creation and lead to Him."

"Better go fishing and do thy duty by thy woman. Make children and harvest—leave the shadows to the old." The priest grunted and grumbled and edged towards the door.

"Ye did not, Father," said Matthew, standing in the way.

"I had no choice; a younger son, ye understand; with neither the taste not the means to marry. Ye have both, I think, and nought but spiritual pride to prevent ye. Make thyself as nothing and be grateful."

"Nothing. Nothing…Does God want a world full of toadies? This self-denial is sickly, lazy, a sort of trance. Our Father must surely value a man higher who aims himself high and gives it all back to Him. What of the talents? Our Lord had little time for the servant who hid his away. 'Blessed are they who hunger and thirst'—but not if they sit and do nothing but say 'I hunger, I thirst'. Righteousness must be the best sort of righteousness—not just a failure to sin."

"Thou are all words, boy. I want my breakfast. Widow Bennett will eat my portion at this rate."

He climbed the steps to the door, his knees clicking. "Come, make haste." He heaved the door shut and turned the huge key in the lock.

Matthew, dismissed, went crossly down the road. Presently his disappointment and frustration turned into real anger. He was disgusted by the priest's excuses. It was no wonder that the people only came when they must: to be married and buried, according to the Act: when all he had to give them was a lot of "duty" and self-negation. He was more than ever sure that too much so-called humility was the bushel that hid the light. Oh God, would no-one advise him? "Richard Veale, my father, what am I to do?"

He was not even buried here, Matthew thought bleakly. But Rose was—Mother was—but where?

There was an aged man sitting on the wall beside the gate who had not been there before.

"Know ye the Churchyard?"

"Should do—I be Sexton, bain't I?"

"Do'ee remember the lady, Rose Veale, wife of the Priest here, who died nigh on twenty years since?"

"The one that died wi' the babby? The night the good man went astray? Aye, I remember. 'Twas I who made a sign in the church book."

"Where be the grave?"

"What's it to thee?"

"I be the babby."

The old eyes peered at him. "Dieu, 'tis the Master returned...Master Veale, yer Reverence...Where'm ye been all these years?" The Sexton levered himself off the wall and made to embrace him.

"I favour him?" Matthew was excited; here was another who knew his father and saw the likeness.

"Bain't'ee Master Veale?"

"I b'lieve so—but young Master Veale—the babby."

"I allus thought the Master would come back. It were the storm see. There bain't such a storm as that since."

"Where is the grave?"

"Give me my stick and I'll take 'ee there."

It was against the wall in the Priest's Plot; and it was tidy and well trimmed.

"Who do I thank for keeping it neat?"

"I done it; she were a sweet lady; and the Potter give me money for the stone."

ROSE
BELOVED WIFE OF RICHARD VEALE
PRIEST OF THIS PARISH
DIED SEPTEMBER TWENTY THIRD
1558

AND IN MEMORY
OF THE SAME RICHARD VEALE

place of death unknown.

"When—when was my father's name added? Do'ee remember?"

The Sexton shook his head; "We didn't give him up for a long while."

"Thank ye, Sir, I would to be alone now, if you please."

Matthew knelt on the grass and stared at the grave. "I belong here," he thought. "I do not belong to London nor any of the places I have seen. Mother, I want to be God's man—Oh but I want to be here, especially now I have found thee. What must I do?"

Perhaps the answer came from her or perhaps it came on the wind; it told him to go to the Potter: to his father's friend, Jose Jane.

CHAPTER XI

Rona had got there first. She had run, her cheek stinging and her ears ringing with Elizabeth's admonitions. She was shaken and full of misery. Her world was topsy turvy, an incomprehensible place, where long established values were suddenly changed. She did not understand; she did not want to understand. She had waited so long for Matthew, building, planning And now, after a welcome beyond her wildest dreams, he had run off, after a few words with William and the merest glimpse of the house. There was no-one in the world so disappointed and bewildered. Perhaps Potter Jane would help, would understand.

The bright morning lifted her spirits a little. The distant sea was blue and urgent with white waves raised by yesterday's wind. They lashed against the rocks in the bay with a fine explosion of spray. Her cheeks were pink when she reached the cottage and he saw nothing amiss.

"Come in. Come on in, ye be late. 'Tis time to make a start." Her silence was unusual.

"Why Miss, is something wrong?"

"Everything!" she burst out. "He's gone."

"Who's gone?"

"Matthew. He be back...and gone again."

"Gone where?"

"I know not where. We met in the lane last night; and, Master Jane, he was right glad to see me. 'Twas like a miracle. But he was wet and tired and said but little. 'Tomorrow,' he said, 'tomorrow; there is so much to tell.' Then he wakes up and—says Elizabeth—he saw the house and went off in a hurry. I don't understand."

"Has he come back to stay? Is he returned for good keeping?"

"William says not. They had some small talk when he saddled his horse, and I were milking, and Matthew said he was but on a visit. Oh, he can't go back...don't let him go back..."

"Child, child—Aye 'tis upsetting—but we can't hold him back if his work is unfinished. Enough that he be come for Christmas. Why, we never even hoped for that much."

"Elizabeth says the house frightened him; she says I must give it up if it don't please him..."

"Give it up? But, surely, it will please him greatly. It would please any man."

"Not if he wanted to live in London—or somewhere different."

"I see, I see." He could not believe that Matthew would want anything of the sort. But then he remembered Dick: and Dick's joyous acceptance of whatsoever the Lord might send. "I see," he said again, and added slowly; "then maybe you will have to do the choosing."

"What choosing?"

"Well, between Matthew and the house. There is no choice, really, is there? Ye would not put the place before the man? Perhaps he rushed off because he feared that ye would."

"Would what?"

"Put Trevaylor first?" She stared at him, uncomprehending.

"Trevaylor?"

"The house. Know ye not that they call it Trevaylor for its name? It being Vaylor's land all these years and William directing the builders. Did ye not know?"

"Yes, I had heard it," she said slowly. "But I did not mind. 'Tis a good name—and a right one." Perhaps it was an omen, she thought; an omen that it would not be hers after all. Just a house for William and Elizabeth, and, maybe, for her in old age when all else was gone...Tears welled up and fell down her cheeks and the Potter rose and went to the window, to give her time to recover herself. "Perhaps it will be mine—if Matthew does not want me," she mused to herself. And then she knew, without doubt, that the house, without him would be an empty shell.

"Rona, he comes. I see him. Wipe them eyes. Oh, he looks well."

He opened the door and called out: "Matthew.

269

Matthew. Come in, my handsome. And see, Rona be here, looking for 'ee. Come in, boy."

Matthew hesitated; how could he discuss his problem with Rona there? Then he saw her coming shyly out of the shadows, so sweet, so beautiful that his heart seemed to stop beating.

"Good day to thee, Matthew. Did 'ee sleep well? I had to come to Master Jane for I be his apprentice. And...I thought ye might come...to see him."

"Rona. I be sorry I went riding off. I thought to find the Priest at Madron for—advice."

"Did ye find him?"

"I did—but his thoughts were on his breakfast. But, Master Jane, the Sexton thought I was my father. 'Tis not only ye who sees the likeness." He looked excited. "And Master Jane, I found my mother's grave—the grave of Rose Veale."

"That is good. Very good."

"It was very good of thee to tend to the matter. I thank 'ee."

"Breakfast...Let us see what we can find for thy stomach. We must not think of graves on an empty stomach."

They crammed into the tiny room, the Potter clearing one end of the table while Rona busied herself with cutting bread, and finding cheese, and stirring the fire. Matthew stared around with the eyes of one who has come home after a long voyage. His gaze rested upon Rona with such yearning that she turned and blushed—blushed to a bright pink.

There was a silence, uninterrupted, save by the small sound of domesticity. The old man, looking from one to the other, thought it time to voice the question that hung between them.

"Thou must have seen Trevaylor."

"Trevaylor?"

"The house. The one that William and Rona have been so busy a-building."

"Trevaylor," he repeated. The place of the Vaylors. It had a ring about it, as if it had been there since time out of mind.

"It is for William and Elizabeth," said Rona desperately.

"They had only a tenancy, but now the land is safe. They were mighty glad and…I can be there too, if there be nought else. I could not bear to go back to Porthmarys and Bosigran…not without seeing the fire in my mind."

A wild hope possessed Matthew. He took several deep breaths. "Could ye a-bear to leave this place altogether? I mean…if I was to go to some other …somewhere else…and if we were…?"

Rona stood like a statue, all time suspended.

"If ye were to…marry with I?"

She smiled. "Ah, Matthew, Ye know I will go wi' thee, wherever it might be."

"Oh Rona…Oh sweetheart…"

"Oh ye two, all they 'Oh's' and 'Ah's!' Come, set to, drink some ale, then tell us, boy, of the adventures, the places, the plans ye have made."

And so he did. He told them eagerly, excitedly; in his relief at her answer, the words came tumbling like a moorland stream.

CHAPTER XII

"We went to Helford River, first, to Uncle Nathaniel." Matthew chuckled; "Captain Wat told 'em ye were bespoke: 'To a man of learning and good fortune'…Well, he said to I when we were gone, 'Ye are learning and ye have the good fortune of Mistress Rona's affection.' He looked sideways at her shyly and she nodded, dimpling.

271

"We joined a Pilgrimage after Plymouth—Oh ye should see Plymouth, such ships and harbours. The Barbican was crammed wi' sailors: some serving the Queen, some serving theirselves. Captain Wat seemed to know them all. He sought a man named Hawkins, while Crispin and I wandered 'bout, marvelling."

"Crispin?"

"The servant—Captain's bodyguard—ye should see him at the Palace in the Admiral's livery. In the country, he goes about plain-dressed."

"What was the Pilgrimage?"

"To Exeter Cathedral. 'Bout fifty of us gathered together on the greensward above the bay: the Hoe 'tis called. 'There's safety in numbers,' says Sir Walter; 'and mind ye call me Cap'n Wat. I want no petitioners; no pleas for the Queen's ear; nor no daggers in my back. None must recognise me.'

"After Exeter, we took up with another Pilgrimage; a mixed lot: some leaving Exeter, some meaning to go to Canterbury: some just needing the safety of a big company. But it were slow—too slow for Sir Walter. Once we were into open country we rode fast. Always eastwards, with the sun in our eyes in the morning and our shadows before us after noon. It was a long succession of days. We slept in taverns by night, in villages along the way, like beads on a string they were, all 'bout the same distance apart—as far as a man can walk to tend his fields in the morning and back at night. Wat slept within doors, Crispin and I in the stables.

"Sometimes it were wet with the rain in our faces and everything wet. At Salisbury, we had to buy new blankets and bags to keep them dry. Captain Wat took our clothes into the inn to dry before his fire, while we wrapped ourselves in the dry covers. One night, he came into the stable to change places with me. 'Sleep in my bed and leave the candle alight. I believe

I be recognised; let them find their mistake.' I did as I was bid and lay watching the door. Sure enough, the latch lifted. A great bearded man came in; 'Cap'n,' he whispered. 'Tis Ben Drake, I have news for ye o' Francis.' 'Cap'n?' says I, 'I be no Cap'n—jus' a traveller between Salisbury and London.'

"'God's death,' he says, 'must've been the rum. I was sure I saw me own Cap'n Wat.'

"'Sit by the fire, warm thyself,' I said; 'So ye think I be like this Cap'n?'

"'Same height—no more—but I could've sworn.'

"'What would ye, wi' this Captain?'

"'Ain't I sailed wi' 'im? None like 'im. An' I seeks to sail again. More'n that—I've news. News wot I seen wi' my own eyes off of the coast of Spain.'

"'Ye've been sailing there lately?'

"'More lately than 'isself.'

"'And what would a sea Cap'n be doing up country?'

"'Dint I 'ear 'e was in Plymuff and bound for Lunnun; thought I caught 'im up.'

"I thinks for a bit; 'Sleep by the fire,' I said; 'and look to my pockets first, to see I be not worth robbing.' When he was snoring, I stole out to the stables and told Cap'n Wat. We changed places again. By morning Ben Drake was gone. 'Ye did well,' says Wat. 'That were an old friend and the news was good.'

"We found a Roman road, straight as an arrow, to Andover; and another, the Portway, mile upon mile, to Silchester. It must've been a known road to London for there were two villages called Little London on the way. The Romans made more roads than ye could imagine; at Silchester no less than five came together. We took the one to the east as far as Caesar's Camp and a great forest. Sir Walter was making for Windsor and found a forester who guided us north through the forest—full of deer it was—to Windsor and the River

273

Thames. 'I shall go by water from now on,' he said. 'But first, I have business here, and a place to find for ye.' That was me.

"We lodged in the Castle. There is no Castle like it. The kitchen was like a Cathedral. And the smoke from so many fires—ye would not believe it—and the heat; our clothes were soon dry as a bone. And there was a choice of meat; a choice, mind ye. Crispin and I we stayed in the garrison; I know not where Sir Walter went. Then the next day a man came to the garrison calling out 'Matthew Veale...Matthew Veale.' It sounded right strange to be called out. I did not jump up upon the instant; Crispin nudged me and we followed the man. He took us to a tailor in the town where I was to be fitted with new clothes. There was a street called Peascod Street; it went past the Castle wall to the river where there were fields and fields of peas. The Castle is a huge place, and full of souls—all eating pease pudding.

"There was an old man in the tailor's, name of Thomas Fozard. 'I be appointed to teach you,' he said, 'and to see you dressed fit and proper.' He had been a teacher at the new school in Eton, across the water; but was a little deaf and had lost his position. Captain Wat gave me into his care to learn my letters and to read in English and Latin and Greek. He had money to do it and would take none of mine. 'When you be proficient—perhaps. Meantime ye are paid for.'

"'Pro...what?' I said.

"'Proficient—able to do it—you are to be secretary to Sir Walter,' he said. 'We had better make a start.' He took me with him across, on the ferry, to Eton Wick, to his cottage; and Crispin went on to London with our Master.

"'Get under the pump, boy,' he says to me every day, 'before putting on thy pupil's gown.' I saw other

274

boys wandering around in pupil's gowns—but they were at the Grammar School: King's Scholars, they were called.

"I lived with Master Fozard right through that winter. Christmas came and went, and ice and snow; 'tis much colder than hereabouts. There weren't a lot to eat and Master Fozard was thin as a railing; till, one day, a stray dog came to the door. Ole Fozzy quite took to't and gave it a bone. That dog taught me rabbiting and our fortunes changed. 'Oryctolagus cuniculus'—a rabbit. That dog was a genius.

"An old dame used to cook for us, and for a rabbit or two, she took more interest and tried to please us; and that were a change, I can tell ye. She'd bring in new bread and sometimes a bit o' butter. Her son worked up at the Castle and brought peas and green stuff for his Ma, so we would get a share of that too. Even old Fozard fattened up a bit.

"And, all the time, I was at my slate, writing and doing figures. Ten new words every day; ten new sums. There was never a boy who wanted to learn as I did, he told me. At school there'd been boys, but all they wanted to do was to fish and swim in the river. 'But I be no boy,' I told him; 'I be a man.'

"'You are a boy to me, and will stay a boy until you say "you" and "are" and "aren't"; not "be" and "bain't".'

"We enjoyed those months. It was like a game, a race, to see how much I could master and how quickly. I miss him and the tiny cottage on the edge of the Brocas."

"The Brocas?"

"A water meadow beside the river, lying between the King's School and the Thames. There were geese there and haymaking and the Chapel of St. John facing east across the grass.

"One day, I was sitting on the river bank, reading my Lexicon, when a lad ran up; 'Where's old Spindleshanks?' he asks; 'The Senior Tutor wants him; there's a teacher ill with fever, he wants Spindleshanks.'

"'Master Fozard,' I says, laughing, 'is in Windsor.'

"'S' death—that's torn it—we'll get the Head. I hate the Head.' He ran back and I watched him running between the geese, grazing. Then, suddenly, he turned back and shouted: 'Why don't you come?'

"Imagine, he asked me to go, not as a scholar, but to teach...

"'I'll come. I'll come. If the Tutor will let me. Will he?' 'Sure to. Lazy muffin. He'll not want a class twice the size.'

"I found myself following him across the grass and the street and through the arch to a great courtyard. I'd looked through it before but never thought to walk into it. There was a statue of the Founder, Edward the Sixth, in the centre with cobbles and flags underfoot. The wall were brick and the panels oak—it was built to last—but it was cold. I went up a wooden stair into a room full of desks and, oh, it was dark and cold and the boys looked half perished. They looked at me, some curious and some indifferent.

"'Well,' I said, not knowing what I was meant to do; 'What is it to be today?'

"'Latin—what else?'

"Master Fozard had told me to write an essay about my life and I had written about the mill. It was all I knew anything about. So I had the words for Miller—molinum—and grindstone—mola—and molere, to grind. First I told them all about it in English; how it worked, the stones and the grist and the meal at the end; then we tried to put it into Latin. We couldn't find the words for the bill and the thrift—the tools for dressing the stones. 'I will have to ask Master Fozard.'

"'And who, pray, are you?' A man's voice came from the back of the classroom.

"'Master Veale—Sir.' I had never said it before: it sounded right funny—Master Veale.

"'I thought Fozard had shed some years and put on some flesh. Where is he?'

"'He was in Windsor, when the boy called. I am his pupil.'

"'And what makes you such an expert on the milling of corn?'

"'Eighteen years in a mill—before I took to my books.'

"'Go on then—carry on. I know nought about milling.'

"So I told them. All the way though from making the furrows and the lines and the stitching on the stones, to collecting the meal at the end of the day.

"'What of the sails?'

"'Paddles, Sir; ours was a water mill.'

"'There's a windmill up the hill behind the Castle.'

"'I should like to see it. It must be much the same; wheels and cogs to turn the thrust from vertical to horizontal.'

"'Put that into Latin, Master Veale.'

"'I have not the words. I shall have them by tomorrow; if I am to come again.'

"'Do you want to hear from Master Veale again boys?'

"'Yes. Yes, Sir, please Sir.'

"'Back to the Latin tongue again, if you please. You may return to the subject of the mill tomorrow—with the words.'

"What to teach them? I had no idea. Then I thought, the boys like to run races. So I made them put that into Latin—'The boys raced to the river and there sat down to fish. When the boys were hungry, they went to the baker; the baker went to the miller; the miller went to the farmer for corn.' And so on.

"'Where are the Roman legions?' asked the boys.

"'They're dead, I think.' They thought that very funny. One wrote, 'Why do the boys run races?'

"'To catch the girls,' I said. The laugh—I shall never forget that laughter; it told me I could teach and they would listen. Another teased me about my speech—it was still very Cornish.

"'Where do you come from?'

"'Cornwall at the land's end.' And I told them about the journey. They crept up close, quiet as mice, and I was telling them 'bout life in Cornwall: the wind and the rocks and the ships on the rocks. I was telling them of the night of the beacon, when I saw a beard on a face at the back. It was the Head Master. 'Quick,' says. 'Put that into Latin: The fire burnt bright to warn the Queen's fleet of the danger.'

"I thought I would be sent packing; but the Head Master gave me a silver piece and told me to come back on the morrow. He'd not heard the boys so quiet, he said.

"Master Fozard, he was right glad. He said I would learn better by teaching and he would find the words that were not in the school books. He said, 'Now you can say you have been to school at Eton.'

"I taught until the turn of the year and Springtime came to the countryside. I was homesick for the Cornish lanes, I can tell you. Homesick and restless and tired of the boys' pranks. I think old Fozard knew; it made me feel ungrateful; but we were both glad when a man from Sir Walter—Fairfax, he was called—"

"I know Master Fairfax, he came here, with a letter, in the Fall."

"He be—is—Sir Walter's messenger. He brought a summons from London; I was to go back with him."

He paused, remembering his excitement, his apprehension—and Fairfax' scorn.

"He took me for a country bumpkin, though, by then, I had more learning than he. 'Can you sit a horse?' he asked. My horse—you know, the horse we picked out at the market on the day I left—it had been lodged and exercised at the garrison, paying for its hay by working. It was in good trim and Master Will was put out of countenance when I told him it were mine.

"We went by way of Richmond, straight across country, through orchards and farms that supplied Londoners. The nearer we got to London, the closer together were the villages; we could see the smoke from the next village chimneys before we had left the one where we stood. At Richmond, we followed the river and saw famous palaces along the way. You never could believe such places as we saw. Wolsey's Hampton Court—'tis no wonder Henry coveted it for himself. At Richmond, there were deer under the trees and geese on the common tended by a little child. It was there that the Queen heard...but I talk too much. Your pardon."

"Oh no," cried Rona, "go on, so please you, or else to please me, go on."

"Master Jane will be weary of my voice."

"Master Jane is eager to hear all." He was thinking how like Dick he was; the words used to pour out of him, too, after his travels. "Tell us, now, about London."

"I must think clearly...how to begin...what lingers most strongly? The smell, I think. Phew! In every weather, the smell is over all. The houses are so close; there is no privy to each house, no middens set apart: the streets are the middens. Rubbish and filth are thrown into the gutters. I can still hear the buzzing of the flies. For all it's cold and wet in winter, yet there is more sickness in hot weather—sickness unto death.

279

Nay, I should not care to live my life out in London; though Londoners scorn anywhere else: it is the centre of the world, they say. The streets are narrow, crowded and dirty so we took to the river to reach our destination. I must agree, there are grand sights from the river: the Savoy Palace, all towers and pennons: great private houses and Religious Houses, each with its own stairs into the water. The Temple Stairs led to my new place of residence: the Middle Temple, where lawyers ply their trade…Sir Walter wanted me to learn something of the Law—to be of use to him perhaps: as Bailiff or an Agent. I was loath to go but our Captain Wat had arranged it. I would lief have studied Astronomy or the sciences of Philosophy and Health. It came to me quite sudden that it was our Creation I wanted to know about, in all its ways; not dusty law and pages of numbers. Master Jane, did my father come to God by way of His Creation?"

"I believe it was the other way round for Dick. He had a sense of holiness—'the magic' he called it; 'the halo': some things, some places had the halo, some hadn't. So he said."

"The halo is not a dream then? The fancy of an artist? Nor yet the lure of something that you want to do?"

"Never discount the halo: never try to explain it: never doubt it. It is the mystery that runs side by side with knowledge."

Matthew was silent. His eyes strayed to the Mount in the Bay. There was a halo there; and his father had seen it.

"How now? What next?" asked the old man, after a pause.

"I b'lieve it is real enough—not a Will o' the Wisp, I follow, not achasing of rainbows," said Matthew slowly.

"What, my son?"

"Why, my wish to teach—and to preach, if God wills it. If I dare."

"Dare?"

"I think one must dare much to teach about the Lord God."

CHAPTER XIII

Rona was to remember that scene through all her years to come. Matthew's far horizons and enthusiasms, his dreams and vocations: they carried her along as on the crest of some wave. She realised, and it came to her like a body blow, that here were things about Matthew that she did not understand. This compulsion to find God, to teach God, even to a parcel of schoolboys, was beyond her comprehension. Then she realised that there were things about her that he did not understand. There would always be something to learn. The thing that mattered was trust—and she trusted Matthew without doubt.

She stopped fearing the reasons for this morning's flight and dared to ask: "Why did ye leave so early?"

"I am sorry, my dear love; I saw the house and the trouble you have taken. It—confused me."

"A la folie," she said, hoping that she sounded carefree.

"'Tis just a house; 'twill do for William and Elizabeth, if it don't suit we. And," she added, "'twill be there for our old age."

She looked at Joseph for approval and he nodded and twinkled at her.

Matthew crossed the tiny room and, taking her hands, looked long and searchingly into her eyes. "You mean that?" he said at last: "Then I know we are together." Unaccountably she wanted to cry.

Master Jane suddenly remembered something that he needed from outside and eased himself out of the door. The two lovers looked at each other wonderingly and she moved into his arms, knowing the timelessness of eternity.

Rona made her gown out of the green silk stuff that was his first present; and they were married at Gulval Church on the fifth day of Christmas.

Dorothy was her Bridesmaid, and Bugel, who had known her father, gave her away, in his name. Such goings on, and Christmas too. Joseph Jane stood up beside Matthew, seeing in memory, his friend Dick. Matthew surprised them: he went, cap in hand, to the Mill, bearing a Wedding invitation to the Miller and his lady; and they surprised him, by accepting and bringing gifts, of flour and lace—enough for a veil.

Rona dug into her dwindling store to buy meats in the market and Elizabeth exceeded her own best expectations in producing a feast. They wished Captain Wat could have been there. Matthew was nervous, when he thought of it, of what Captain Wat would say to him—the student: wedded before he was finished with his studies. It crossed his mind but fleetingly.

For one week they lived at Trevaylor, with furniture for one room. Together they stood at the window and watched the sunrise and the moonrise.

The Cornish sun had the warmth of summer: the Cornish wind had the wrath of tempests: the Cornish mid-winter nights were crisp and shining: that week held all the seasons; and Rona held Matthew's head against her breast as she had on the day of their first meeting. Then he had thought he had died; now he died a thousand deaths wondering how to consummate their marriage—how to dare.

"I asked Master Fozard…"

"Yes?"

"But he was never married."

"Oh."

"I wanted to know how it was to be wed."

"And?"

"He did not know."

"I be glad."

"Glad?"

"I do not need Master Fozard at my wedding."

"But I do need to know how—how to please thee."

"And I thee."

"Always, always you please me. But don't you see,
I know nothing of—the ways of loving."

"What better? Is it not best to find out together."

"Oh, my Love, let us now find out together."

"Rona, wife, will you come to London with me? London
and then, perhaps to Oxford?"

"Would you have me stay behind?"

"You cannot ride so far; we must go to Falmouth
and thence by sea."

"I know not how I shall sail—perhaps I shall
disgrace you."

"Nay, Love, we shall spew together: so long as it be
to leeward."

"Matthew, husband, look over yonder; there is a ship
like the Faerie Queen—the one I was aboard with
Captain Wat. And there's another."

"I heard that Hawkins is training seamen, in and
out of Port o' Devon. 'Tis said some do not trust the
Dons."

"Dons?"

"Philip's proud Admirals."

"There'll be no war, Love—will there?"

"There's a war already. In London, they talk of nothing else."

"What? Nothing?"

"That and the Queen's newest ruff."

"Matthew, the water smells different: looks different."

"'Tis London River, come out to meet us. See the gulls following? They are scavenging the rubbish. Londoners throw all their rubbish into the nearest stream. They all flow into the Thames, and the Thames out into the sea—and all are foul."

"All the time?"

"Aye, Sweetheart, all the time. 'Tis the price of gathering so many people together—all eating and voiding. 'Tis nature, I s'pose."

"The great city is like an open drain, then?"

"You'll see presently."

"What do they do, Matthew? Without fields to plough and beast to tend?"

"They serve each other: depend upon each other. A crowd depends upon a crowd. The builder builds for the crowd; the baker bakes; the shoemaker makes shoes; the potter pots—just like at home—but it is all turned in upon itself. And, in the end, they all depend on the country. So there are many, many carters, all bringing in produce; flour for the baker, leather for the shoes. To be a farmer on the edge of a town is to be rich. Money is all: to be without money, in the town, is to die."

Rona wondered if they had money enough. She asked him.

"Not enough. That is why I must work while I still learn." Secretly he worried on the question of how they would manage. He could not take a wife into the precincts of the Temple: but he wanted to be done with that—he was no lawyer and the law held no magnetism for him. Nor did Theology, for that matter. But it would have to be the next hurdle, like it or not. It would be a severe test of his intentions. People—living people—were his passion. He had known so few; the Miller and the market folk. As soon as he began to meet men of importance, men of different trades, men of wealth and of poverty, he had discovered within himself a capacity to meet each one eye to eye and heart to heart. And they forgot his funny ways and country speech to share with him the living experiences of their existence. Even his teachers questioned him. They were, on the whole, a dull lot. He liked old Spindleshanks; hard times had preserved in him a sense of humanity; the men in the Middle Temple, from whom he was supposed to learn, were second-hand men—all books and no heart; and second-hand books at that. Everyone said he must go to Oxford. He hoped it would smell sweeter and that there would be good lodgings for Rona.

They went first to the Temple, Matthew sought the gatekeeper, Ezra Judd, but he was not there. Another man, a stranger, Ted Crutchman, told him of a place where he might stay with Rona for the time being. He sent them along the river bank to Upper Thames Street. The address was set back from the river and the row of dank cottages they found did not bode well.

"Well? What is it?" a sharp-faced woman asked. She spoke through a hole cut in the door. She had black teeth and only a few of them.

285

"I came to ask for lodgings. Master Crutchman sent us. He said you took clerks and the like."

"Who's she? I'll have no fancy woman."

"This is Mistress Veale. This is my wife."

"Hm…Proof?"

Rona held up her finger.

"Yer lines—anybody can get a ring."

"I have them, but they are in my baggage."

"Are yer with child? I'll 'ave no squawking brats…"

"Let's away. She is a fearful woman," Matthew whispered.

"We must find lodgings for tonight. 'Tis getting late."

"Make up yer minds—are you or aren't yer wi' child?"

"No, Ma'am, but I be right tired. If ye will not open the door, we will try another. Come Husband."

The door opened. Dark smells tumbled out and dominated the air around them, even overcoming the rank odours that rose from the river.

"No. Come away. If I were with child—which Heaven forbid—this is no place for it."

"Heaven forbid? Do ye not want a child?"

"Not now. Not here on the road—like Mary."

She picked up her bundle and led the way back to the river and towards the bridge.

It was the most extraordinary bridge imaginable. Quite overgrown with houses, it spanned the Thames between the City Strands and Southwark. How it did not fall into the river was a mystery and a miracle. Water gushed in fierce streams between the piers, smoke poured from a thousand chimneys, washing and bedding hung from windows like tattered banners, and slops hurtled through the air as folk upended pails to empty into the water below. Houses seemed to be built one on top of another, and all upon the Bridge— London Bridge.

"There must be a room somewhere among all that."
They found one under the sign of the White Swan.

"Matthew I can feel the bridge moving."
"Nay, Love, it be the memory of the ship."
"'Tis the bridge."
"Come, I will hold you safe." Matthew hoped he was right; he too could feel the bridge moving, indeed what was there to stop it? It creaked and groaned, and the thought of all that water swirling around the piles determined him not to spend another night in such a place.

"Why, Master Veale, yer back. We fort the Wolves 'ad gotcha." It was Ezra.
"Good morrow Gatekeeper. Not wolves—a wife."
"But Master, there's no wimmin 'llowed in 'ere."
"I know. I know. And I seek a lodging. You know mos' things. Where can she stay? Ted Crutchman was no help."
"Oh, 'im. Upper Thames Street? Oh Lor'. Yer should 'ear wot my Missus 'as to say 'bout that. My Missus might…"
"Might take me?"
"Lor' no. Not wi' ten nippers at 'er skirts…lemme see. Tried the bridge, 'ave yer? The Bridge is stacked full o' inns and the air is sweeter-like."
"We like terra firma—dry land—better."
"I'll 'ave a think. Um. Hey, now I gets ter thinkin', there's a message for yer somewheres. Arf a mo."
He shuffled into his lodge and emerged with a piece of parchment. On one side was written "Matthew Veale"; on the other, "Come to my rooms on your return. A letter awaits you." It was signed by the senior clerk, his mentor.

287

The letter was from his Patron.

"Greetings Matthew Veale,

So ye are wed, I hear. Master Jane writes me the news and I be well pleased; although it is soon enough, in all conscience. But youth will out and the maid was fretting, no doubt.

He tells me ye are wishful to follow your father's steps, to profess the Lord. Better a Bailiff of souls than of fields, eh?

Go ye, therefore, to Oxford, to Balliol, where I was. I will write to them of your coming. And give your Theology as much diligence as ye give your wife.

If ye reach London before Saint Valentine's Day, send word to me at the Court. Mistress Veale—by which I mean my little Rona—will without doubt wish to see the inside of the Palace.

Your friend and Patron,
W.R.

"What day is't, husband?"
    "The tenth day of February."
    "And what day is Saint Valentine's feast?"
    "I forget—if ever I knew."
    "Find out, my dear one, find out."

"Shall we see the Queen?"
    "The Queen is on a Progress. 'Tis on the Broadsheets."
    "Oh."
    "Are you sorry?"

"I think I be glad. I think I would be too afeared. But I long to see Captain Wat. Do ye not long to see him too?"

"I would as lief have waited until I had something to show him—some achievement."

"Oh dearest, how could I have married such a fool?"

Raleigh sent a message for them to meet him in Covent Garden. It was a great open space, beautifully tended, belonging to one of the Queen's favourites, where there once had been a convent.

"What is a Progress?" they asked.

"'Tis when the Monarch goes out to see her people. Much of the Court goes with her—like it or not. Their official functions come into play; often they forget why they're here. They sit about preening themselves for most of the year, then Masters of Horse and Wardrobe Mistresses have to stir themselves; Ladies in Waiting, Pages, Farriers, all take to the road. It is always wet or dusty and either way it is uncomfortable... They say a cloud of dust hangs about for days, or else a sea of mud, in their wake."

"Where do they lie?"

"First in one Manor, then in the next. They send word ahead; a word much dreaded by the Lords of the manors. He must make ready to be host to a plague of locusts. They swarm through their storerooms; and woe betide the Landlord or Squire who has not enough."

"Squires be not poor." Rona thought of Tranthem.

"They are after a Progress." He laughed. "I was let off this time to reorganise the Palace Guard. Thank God, I am excused."

"So we shall not see Elizabeth."

"No, only the cobweb—the cob is away."

"Cob? Oh, Sir, how can you say so?"

"'Tis said she eats her victims," Matthew dared to tease.

"Certain, she eats them out of house and home."

He gave Matthew a Palace Pass and bade them come tomorrow.

"Do I look well enough? The Court ladies will be fine and grand."

"Give me the glass—now look for yourself. Believe your own eyes, my love."

Rona stared at the mirror: she saw a young woman with a sea-bronzed face and sparkling eyes. Her black curly hair, shining and luxuriant, escaped down her back from the pretty halo cap that framed her face. Her gown was the green silk, now her wedding dress, low-cut with a cream underbodice and wide sleeves of pleated mousseline. She wore no jewels except that round her neck could be seen the flash of a hidden golden chain.

"If it were summer, ye should have a deep red rose for your bosom."

"Piff, I look a country bumpkin as it is. Worse, a sea bumpkin with my dark leather face."

"Dark? Leather?"

"Well, 'tis not the fine white stuff court ladies are made of. I saw one looking out of her litter; she did not see me; she would not have seen me if we had been but an inch away."

"None seeks to see the one who makes him jealous—or her—least of all 'her'. I know that all the men in London are envious of me, with such a Bride on my arm." He swung her off the ground in a swirling hug.

290

CHAPTER XIV

"Come, wife, we are here. Come."

"Look at the Guard, how still they stand; even their staves do not waver. They will never let us pass."

"I have the paper. 'For the Captain of the Guard,'" he said to the soldier.

The man could not read but recognised well the Raleigh Seal. He turned on his heel and banged on the portal with his halberd. An officer took the parchment, looked them over and led them through the arched gate to a covered courtyard.

They were passed from hand to hand, and court to court, Rona's eyes growing wider as they passed through ever finer halls.

The polished floors gleamed like wet satin and the walls flashed with lights reflected from swords and shields. What sort of servitude was this, she wondered, that set servants to polish all through the night—for there were none in sight. There were no looking glasses: the Queen had banished all mirrors, large and small.

People, in grand attire and uniforms, strolled about without hurry; a few pausing to stare at the strangers. None stopped them and presently they felt sufficiently at ease to go more slowly and examine the rooms with curiosity and attention. Rona wanted to remember all and everything about it, for the rest of her life. What a thing to be able to tell her children!

Their guide left them in an anteroom and they sat gratefully on a cushioned settle. Flames licked and crackled round sweet applewood logs, sparks leaped up the huge chimney and were echoed in a myriad of bright surfaces—sparks of broken light dancing on escutcheons and polished wood.

"Will ye look at that window?" Rona had never seen

such a window: high and wide, stone mullioned and with a hundred panes. She rose to touch the delicate tracery of the leading, remembering, with a pang, the windows at Trevaylor, so far away, which she had thought the finest in the world. She and William had insisted that they be bigger than any the builder had made. "To let in the view."

"Our view is best," she said over her shoulder. She had not heard the door open that admitted Sir Walter to the chamber.

"And what view is that?" He opened his arms to them. "Matthew. Rona, my dearest child—nay, I must remember, Mistress Veale." He bowed with ceremony and lifted her up from her curtsey. "My Cornish primrose. Do you recall that it was in primrose silk that I met thee first? How do'ee find the court of Saint James?"

"In need of a nosegay," she said teasing.

"Aye that's good. I must tell that to the Queen. Have you no nosegay, Madam? Come, I will find a pomander."

"I jested, Sir Walter," said Rona, embarrassed, "'tis London Town that needs the nosegay. 'Tis all sweet here."

"Aye, the Court's away."

"One more soppet, Matthew." Raleigh handed Matthew the trencher and the young man took a small square of bread to mop up the last of his gravy.

They had eaten well: a soup made from fish, a pie, which the cook claimed was of swan, but, with the Court away, was more likely pigeon, Raleigh said. Swan or pigeon, it was delicious and full of subtle flavours—of wine and herbs.

"I'll take no dessert: just a glass of Malmsey. But

292

what have we for our guests? Marzipan fruits? For you, my dear?"

Rona whispered to Matthew, a look of extreme anxiety on her face. Matthew rose and circled the table and bent to his host's ear. Sir Walter nodded and rang a handbell: "Send in a serving maid to take Mistress Veale to the tiring chamber."

A girl came in, shy and silent, scared of the Captain of the Guard.

"Mistress Veale wishes to retire, take her, my girl."

The girls gone, he said: "Our turn I believe, follow me."He led him to a small room with a huge round saucer in the centre of the floor. There was a hole in the middle and a number of men were ranged round the rim, aiming, as their age permitted, at the hole.

Back again, Matthew waited for the older man to speak.

"Is something discomfiting you?" asked Raleigh.

"I—I hoped to provide you with proof of some success, Sir, before coming before you; but…"

"There has scarcely been time," Raleigh responded pleasantly.

"And I hope that—as my Patron—you have no objection to my marriage. I had no intention when I took myself home for Christmas…"

"No objection in the world; think not that I have forgot what a lusty youth is."

"Nay, Sir, my own feelings were of the least importance. But Rona—she was so lonely. And so lovely too; Master Jane was worried for her. He said I must set her heart at rest—as she did mine."

"Ah, yes, Master Jane. He wrote me." Raleigh regarded Matthew shrewdly; "I wonder if you know what you are about?"

"In what way, Sir?"

"This notion of becoming God's man. I fear you

know little of what it means. The Queen—may God give her a long life—is a Protestant: but who knows how long that will last? Her cousin Mary is hot for Rome: also she has good claim to the throne if ought befalls Elizabeth. And you are now married, Matthew. Have you thought what might follow if Priests are again required to be celibate?"

"I confess—no, I did not think on it when we were wed; but now, now I have thought. With your permission, I would like to take the Cloth; and trust in…"

"In luck?"

"If my Church be taken from me, then I can teach in school; or even start one. I want to do that, anyway, if I can; and in that, a wife can help me."

"Especially a wife with a house, eh?"

"The house may be in the wrong place."

"Well I see you have thought on it."

"There was time in plenty as we journeyed to London. Sir Walter, it was thee I feared, more than the future."

"Me? Why, what have you done?"

"I am sensible of my debt to you, Sir. Without you, I should be but an unlearned miller's boy. The Queen's bounty and your guidance have set me here."

"And your own hard work."

"I should have told you of my hopes before I rode to Cornwall. But there seemed time enough. I meant to finish at the Temple, then talk it out with my teachers. And with you, Sir, if you would hear me. Now, it seems you know of my dreams from Potter Jane, and news of my marriage went before me. I could wish that the old man…anyway, I meant no disrespect."

"Matthew, Matthew, you speak like a servant. You are your own man. Believe that always. It pleases me to set talented young men on their way; fortune has favoured me. Life is a pilgrimage—it ill befits us to withhold the helping hand. We may be in need of it, each one of us, in the unknown future. And, as for you, you have borne the costs of it yourself: out of what you call the Queen's Bounty. It was not bounty: it was reward for hard labour—a just reward. But, I fancy, you will be in need of real 'Queen's Bounty' before you are done. Leave it to me. A married priest needs more than a Church and a cell. Have you thought of that? A Living in the gift of the Queen might carry pittance enough, but there must be a house." He fell silent. "You want my advice? Move on to Oxford: to the College of the Scotsman Balliol. Study your Theology, if you must, but do so without the distractions of Housekeeping." He looked up sharply, "Is Rona with child?"

Matthew flushed: "I think not, Sir."

"Good, then send her home before she is. There is no need to compound the problem with mewing babes."

"Send her home?" Matthew was aghast.

"Take her home, then; it will be but two months lost: one to Cornwall and one back. If you work at your Gospels as you have at your Lexicon, it should not take long to get a Degree."

"And what shall Rona do, pray? What think? Her lot will be no better than before: alone with old folks— old and frail."

"Hm. Hm. Well, well: perhaps there is a case for a child, after all. That should keep her busy." He laughed. "'Tis your affair; but, as I see it, we are talking of a year—maybe two—out of a lifetime. Don't spoil the lifetime for the passing pleasures of a long honeymoon."

295

"What be it like to live in a palace?" Rona asked the maid.

The girl jumped. "Ye speak to me?" she asked, amazed.

"Well, there's none else that I can see," Rona smiled. "What an empty place this be."

"Oh my—when the Queen's 'ere, 'tis so full and so busy, we 'ave to get the work done by night."

"Work?"

"Polishin' an' that; cookin' an' all."

"By night? And what by day?"

"Runnun' arter the gentry, 'course. Emptyin' the slops an' that."

"What be thy name?"

"Jill."

"Tell me Jill, what do the gentry do?"

"Why, Mistress, I 'ardly knows... 'Tain't my place. They eats and drinks—they does a lot o' that—an' pees of course. Then they dresses an' undresses: a lot o' that too. Then they jostles to get near the Queen—or near to those what are near to 'er. The men chases arter the Queen—for favours—when they ain't chasing deer and hawks and such like. And the ladies—they chases arter the men."

"No making butter, nor gleaning, nor cooking, nor mending," muttered Rona. She had never been a servant as this girl, but neither had she been a lady. She had not thought of it before. What did they do, these "ladies"? How did they spend their days? Living for the nights? And how did they make out in the matter of love-making?

She was not at all sure how she was making out. Yes, they had found how to do it—by the light of the moon; but even without candles, she had been glad of her shift. They had found the way, but it was best over and done with. She found herself wondering at the thought that her father had had it this way with her mother and whether her mother had been as puzzled as she. She was right glad that Matthew seemed to find satisfaction; that he found her pleasing. Yes, she was glad of that; but—but it was a funny sort of thing to have to do in order to be married. Oh, she understood about having to sow seed for the making of a child. She had not known that it took many such sowings before the child responded.

"Do ye have a husband, Jill?"

"Me? Lor' no. A lad from the stables calls on me when he can."

"So ye don't know about—lying together."

"I din't say that, Ma'am; arter all, it's onny natrul; a good fuck's the onny fun of an evening."

Rona shook her head: she did not understand. "Do'ee like it here, Jill?"

"Lor', Ma'am, no. 'Oo does? But father's in the mews and mother's in the washhouse; I dunno nowt else."

"Well, thank ye for helping me, Jill."

"'S'all right—we all 'as ter piss. I never spoke to a gentry afore. Can I ask yer something?"

Rona nodded.

"Where does yer get yer brown skin an' funny clo'es. Where does yer come from?"

"Funny?"

"Plain like: no fur, no Jools nor nuffink."

"I come from Cornwall: from the Land's End: from as far as ye can go. My clothes are not funny in Cornwall."

"Maybe 'funny' ain't right," said the girl consolingly, "but—well—they covers yer up more'n most."

At that moment another woman came into the closet. Rona stared. Her white painted face and reddened lips startled her. The gown she wore was stiff and crusted with beads and bows. There were yards and yards of rich stuff, falling from a hooped and padded hipline; but what was excessive below the waist was lacking above it. The bodice, scanty and tight, pushed up the woman's breasts, in pulpy lumps, so that they came perilously close to breaking free from their uncomfortable prison. There were red chafe marks where the damask cut into the skin, and powder to hide the chafe.

"God's wounds, don't stand there gaping," hissed the newcomer to Rona. "Help me hitch up this damned skirt before it's too late."

Rona obediently lifted the skirt; the weight of it astonished her. The commode was free-standing and the two girls held the skirt clear and then dropped it, like a tent, while the woman sat. Then Rona, in a fit of devilment, seized Jill's hand and dragged her from the room.

"Hay, come back, damn you. I'm not done. I'll have your heads....the Queen shall hear..."

Jill was shocked but Rona bubbled with laughter.

"She will have our heads."

"She'll have to get off that thing first."

"It will tip over."

"She should have said 'Please'," chortled Rona. "Never fear, Sir Walter will protect our heads. Nay, do not look so fright. I will come back and let her out of prison."

The woman beat her knees with clenched fists—furious. Rona danced in front of her. "What an ado...what a paddy we are in. Say 'please' and I will help you off that thing—the great leveller."

"Who, in hell, are you? No servant."

"No servant.,.I be a favourite..." She was going to say "of Sir Walter".

"A favourite? Oh do not tell HER I pray thee."

"I shall tell her that her Court should treat her servants with more courtesy. ("Ho. Ho. How pompous I am!") Imagine working in here. It is disgusting."

CHAPTER XV

"Rona, some more wine? A comfit? Come, sit by the fire. Matthew is gone to inspect the Guard."

"Dear Captain Wat: it is good to see ye. When shall ye come to Cornwall? Thy County misses thee."

"When I can.. when I can...the Queen keeps me here at Court."

"Why do you not make this Progress with her?"

"I've had my share of Progresses. With half the Guard with her, I said I must stay to defend the Palace. You look well—but not so well as at home. My primrose needs a green frame."

"To tell the truth, I do feel homesick, Sir."

"To business: Master Jane tells me you have a house."

"Aye, and 'tis near finished. And, Captain Wat, it is beautiful. Do ye remember the Vaylors? William and Elizabeth? Their land was the best in all that part. But it was Queen's land and they were afraid to lose it to another tenant. When Master Fairfax came with the letter that said I could choose, they wanted me to take theirs—cottage and all—it safeguarded their old age. The masons call it Trevaylor; Matthew and I like the name, for it gives honour and thanks to Will for his work."

"Master Jane says it is a goodly house."

Rona nodded, staring into the fire.

"So, what will you do with it, now you are wed to Matthew?"

She shook her head.

"You are content to leave it?"

"Not content—but not content, neither, to deny Matthew his wife or his soul."

"You will follow him?"

"I will."

"A poor parson has little to offer."

"I shall not ask him to change his mind," she answered stoutly. "Because of God's Glory?"

She was silent, knowing it was more a fear of losing him.

Raleigh lit a pipe of tobacco. "You look pale."

"Oh, my Lord, everyone here thinks me nut brown."

"Not so nut brown as I remember. Was the journey bad?"

"Bad 'Bad 'nough. The sea was winterly."

"You were sick?"

"Mightily sick."

"And it was the sea?"

She looked at him, and then quickly away. "I b'lieve so."

He sighed and she frowned. "What a pity." He puffed more smoke. "You see, my dear, if you were with child, I would know how to advise."

"And if—that were so, what would ye advise?"

"That you go back to Trevaylor, to look after yourself and the child—and pray."

"Pray? What prayer?" she whispered.

"Pray. And I, for my part, will pray too. You pray to the Lord God and I to the Queen."

"The Queen? Ye have her ear so close?"

"For the nonce, I have, but one never knows with Queens. At present, she loves her Captain of the Guard. These days, favours are all by word of mouth—or lips to ear."

The fire crackled and the draught tugged at the blue smoke that drifted in rings round Raleigh's head. It was cosy and she was safe in the custody of the Queen's own guard, but Rona shivered. The open-ended possibilities of life stretched before her, cold and featureless: homeless and drifting in Matthew's wake.

"What will ye whisper into her ear—when ye pray?"

"Silly goose! Oh no, I will not say that to Elizabeth

Regina. You are the goose: a brown goose in her first feathers." He chuckled, then leaned forward to stir the ash below the fire. "I shall suggest to Her Majesty that she be fortunate to have an up-and-coming young priest in her loyal Duchy. I am the Lord Lieutenant, remember—and that there are one or two Livings in her Gift in that neck of the woods." He tapped at his pipe. "Also that she could save herself the cost of a Parsonage by appointing this same priestling to a certain Church at—Gulval is't? Aye, Gulval. The other, Madron is not in her gift."

"Captain Wat. Oh, ye be a genius." She rose and knelt at his feet in one swift movement. "Can it be done?"

"The Queen is unpredictable. It will take time. She must believe that she thought of it herself. The man there at present…is he old enough to retire or young enough to start anew?"

"Young—enough."

"Then somewhere must be found for him. Be he a Cornishman?"

"I think not."

"I wonder…Do I need a Chaplain, think ye? Come, speak! Should I do better with a Chaplain? To guard me as you guard that cross about your neck?"

Her hand flew to the gold chain. "How…when…?"

"How do I know? You forget that you slept in my cabin aboard The Faerie Queen. 'Tis very fine…very like another such cross. But that belongs to the Church of God—and to Cornwall." He watched her face. "It is the same—is it not?"

He colour drained away, then flushed, as she struggled with the secret and the relief of a confidant. "It is the same. It belonged to the monks of Saint Michael. My Uncle Jacques had charge of it—to take to the Benedictines in France, until it could come back safe. He was fleeing for his life—and near 'nough lost it. He hid in our cellars—ye know the ones—and gave the Cross into my care until he should come again. But he may be gone—for ever; and I know not what to do."

"You could put it into Matthew's care now. Why don't you?" A thought struck him. "The Custodian of the Cross of Cornwall has a mighty ring to it. What better man for the Parish that watches the Mount?" He smiled. "Your secret is safe with me, but with such a treasure round your neck you stand in danger. Give it to Matthew, or to me to lodge in some safe place— in Matthew's name."

"Thy name would be a stronger safety."

"Oh no, little one; men at the top can be toppled to the bottom—and beyond. I have enemies. Matthew has none. Besides, your Uncle Jacques would not take it amiss if the Cross were to work a miracle for you."

"She is miracle enough," said Matthew, entering the room.

They told Matthew of the plan and Matthew's eyes were alight.

"It may come to nothing. It most surely will come to nothing if it is noised abroad. The Queen mislikes nothing more than to be taken for granted."

"I will deserve it, my Lord, I will indeed. Whatever the cost."

"The cost is high. You must go to Oxford and work. You must go straightly and not have your wife idling in lodgings, fretting and alone. Near to you but out of sight and sound. Give her a babe to nourish and send her home."

"Send…"

"Take her home. Remember sailors are husbands— don't I know it?—but have to sail away. Think of yourself as a sailor, searching the oceans of Holy Writ. And when you have captured your prize, bring it to lay at your wife's feet." He looked at the young man with something like envy. "Now, can you make a sketch? I want a fair representation of the Cross to show Her Majesty."

And, before they could argue or even think, they were sitting side by side, copying the Cross in all its detail, size for size, fit to set before a Queen. "Does the Queen paint her face?"

"Hush, that is a question never to be asked."

"I should not wish the Cross to worn beneath paint."

Raleigh watched them, thinking. And after a moment, he left the room.

CHAPTER XVI

"I have commanded that the guest room be made ready. I wish you to stay the night here. You would like to lie in a Palace, once in you life?"

"Oh!" squeaked Rona. "But, Sir, I have no shift."

"What need of a shift in your honeymoon?"

"Oh, Sir…"

"No shift. Rather a fire and as many candles as may be lit. Hide not that light under a bushel. No shift."

When she had gone, led to the chamber by a maid and a footman, Raleigh turned to the young husband.

"Know ye how to pleasure her?"

"I—I have found the way," stammered Matthew.

"Ah, the way. The way to the gate? The gate of heaven? But have you dallied along the way? Found new paths, searched out the light and shade, the little hills and valleys? To make them dance? Have you kissed the hollows and tasted the nectar of her breasts? Do

303

so before your son grabs them for his own. And linger over't—a woman is in no hurry and likes to be tantalised. Gaze upon her, in all her glory; and let her see you in all yours. These are the gifts of the Gods—the gifts to youth. See that thou dost not waste them."

"I—should be shy."

"So much the better: tentative and shy will make it last the longer. It is a dance, Matthew. All life is a dance, and love is the best dance of all."

Rona had been shaken by the notion of nakedness. And, to make matters worse, the back of the footman had stirred a memory. It was an arrogant back; it reminded her of Constable Vanner, who had tripped her on the moor, under the stars, and sent her heart into a spin and lighted a fire in her loins. "Mon Dieu," she thought, "he was after my maidenhead." She had suppressed that fire and made fair to forget it. But now, she had given her maidenhead to Matthew—gentle Matthew—and there was no need to suppress it. Would he—would he—be shocked to feel a response—the writhing response—that had so frightened her in the heather? She felt it again.

"No. No," she cried, dismissing the doubt. "It is the cry of life to life—a sort of—dance."

Their coupling that night, in firelight and candlelight, was tempestuous, unforgettable—and blessed.

CHAPTER XVII

It took two weeks for Matthew to extricate himself from the Temple, where they had found him very useful as a junior clerk. And it took a month more to get to Oxford and establish himself at the College of

John Balliol: none could gainsay the Lord High Admiral. They had a final dinner with him.

"Why Balliol?" Rona had asked him.

"Nothing but the best for Walter Raleigh. It is one of the oldest colleges, founded in about 1260—some say '63. John was a Scottish Landowner and was married to Dervorguilla, a granddaughter of the Scottish King. It was her Foundation as much as his. You must do her honour, Matthew; it was for your like that she made provision for learning."

In Oxford, they wandered through the ancient buildings, marvelled at the broad streets—so different from London and Penzance. The stones were golden and the air sweet. And, on a fine spring day, shortly before she was to leave for Cornwall, Matthew took her on the river—the same river that was to flow through London. It was a still day and full of promise.

"The river is like sword blade reflecting the sky; see the ripples behind us, spreading like the wake behind a duck."

"We shall leave a wake behind us," she said, mysteriously. "Can the oarsman hear us?"

"I think not."

"Ye must not be anxious for me. I shall miss my love but I shall not be too lonely. And it will not be so indifferent or dull for me as 'twill be for you: poring over dusty books at all hours. It will not be dull for me, Matthew."

"It is unfair for me to seek my own benefits and leave you to the milking of cows."

"Sir Walter was right: we must both look to the future. We must put aside our present pleasures for the good of—of—God and the child."

"The child?'"

"I b'lieve so," she nodded happily.

"Does Sir Walter know?" He felt a terrible jealousy.

"Only thou, my love. Only thou and I."

"Rona. Rona. What can I say? When will it be?"

"Before Christmas comes."

The ferryman, sculling over the stern, smiled.

Spring came and went: Cornish hedges bloomed with primroses, bluebells and wild garlic. Apple trees blossomed and set in the orchards, with new generations of piglets to frolic in the grass. The corn grew green, then gold, and Rona waxed large and bonny. The harvest of 1582 was rich and abundant and Rona fought Elizabeth to be allowed to go and help to bring in the Laity crops.

"Sit'ee down, my lover, give the little one a rest, do."

The house was slowly finished, shuttered and panelled. Logs and rushes were stored against the winter; shelves and dressers were furnished with pots and crocks. Feathers were washed and bagged for beds and pillows. And Jose Jane turned his clever hands to fashioning a cradle.

One day, as the leaves began to fall, he rode up the dusty lane on his donkey.

"A letter. A letter," he cried. It was from Captain Wat.

They never knew how it was done.

Did Raleigh, as Lord Lieutenant, claim a right to choose his parsons?

Did he tell the Queen of the dispossessed farmer's girl with the courage of a lion, who lit a beacon to save the Queen's treasure fleet; only to have her own house put to the torch?

Did he plead the case of the foundling boy whose curiosity and determination took him to teach in her Royal Brother's Grammar School on the banks of the Thames by Windsor; and thence to Oxford and the Church?

Or did the Cross of Cornwall work a miracle?

Matthew and Rona were never to know. Only that Her Brittanic Majesty, Queen Elizabeth, Patron of the Church of Saint Gulval, in the Penwith Hundred, in the County of Cornwall, gave the care of her church, and its souls, into the hands of Matthew Veale—called Richard Matthew Veale—in the year of our Lord 1585, together with her lands and manor known as Trevaylor in the same Parish.

"But it be yours already, Rona," said Matthew.

"Nay, the Queen is wiser than that—it be yours. Besides, I have never settled the Bill for the land…it be yours."

"Yours or mine, 'tis no matter. One day it will be the boy's."

The boy, Richard Samuel Joseph William Veale, yawned mightily and gripped in this tiny hand the sweet air of his inheritance.

"Open the window, Matthew. The sun is shining from behind the Mount. There is a halo around it."

THE END

AFTERWORD

Trevaylor is a house. It is a real house, in the Parish of Gulval. It has been enlarged over the centuries but the Elizabethan kitchens and the well are still to be seen.

The old Manor and the lands were granted to one Richard Veale, by Elizabeth, the Queen, and he was the Vicar of Gulval from 1585.

There is no record that Sir Walter Raleigh promoted the scholarship of this particular young man; but there are many instances of his patronage, both of the arts and of youth.

And there are many records of his accrual of treasure for the royal coffers. During the 1580s, he was very much a Favourite of the Queen's; he remained so until, in 1592, she learned of his secret marriage to Bess Throckmorton, a Lady in Waiting. She then committed him to the Tower.